P.R.I.S.M.

PRISONER RELOCATION INTERNMENT SECURITY MANAGEMENT

FAE ROWEN

FAE ROWEN LLC

Copyright © by Fae Rowen LLC

ISBN 978-0-9977706-0-5

Printed in the United States of America

Cover by Deranged Doctor Design

ACKNOWLEDGMENTS

This book would never have made its way into the world without *my team*.

First, I must thank Laura Drake, critique partner extraordinaire, whose prodding and cheerleading kept me on task when I wanted to do anything but work on my computer at *the hard stuff*. Jenny Hansen and Greg Henry gave valuable feedback in the early stages. Margie Lawson, my awesome writing teacher, helped me bring *fresh* and visceral to the pages. Tiffany Yates Martin (bless her patience and wisdom) applied her editing skills to make me put my heart and personal experiences into the *inner lives* of my characters. And finally, thank you to my English teacher friend, Sheila Silver, who volunteered to be the last eyes on P.R.I.S.M. She took a real chance reading an entire novel written by a math teacher and kept me from some embarrassing grammatical mistakes. Thank you all for breathing life into P.R.I.S.M.

To my friends, thank you:

Anne, for listening to my complaints and for making sure we walked our miles.

Ann, for checking on my sanity and well-being when I crawled into my cave.

Dona, for your teachings.

Marcia, for helping me stay on the path.

Rosemary, for your guidance and healing hands.

Aleida, for being the voice of reason when I became irrational.

Tracy, for playing *Dutch uncle* when I neglected my health to meet deadlines.

Dr. Julie, for helping me learn to *eat clean* and pass blood tests!

Greg, for your acupuncture needles, carefully placed to fix all my complaints.

Darcia, for your lessons to help connect my body to my brain.

Angel, for listening to scenes and dialogue while you trained me.

Renee, for taking care of my neglected skin and making me feel relaxed.

Mary Ann, for the stress-relieving massages.

For my mother and father.

And for Gary.

Ever and always.

Official Montgomery Corporate Earth News, Twenty-five Years Ago

The World Board showed mercy and fairness at the sentencing last month of the eight hundred political and military leaders of the world governments, whose lives were spared. Today they began the journey via the new Montgomery Conglomerate cryoship to Prism, an uninhabited Class M planet, where they will build their own society in exile.

Journal of Perseus Montgomery/RETINAL SCAN REQUIRED:

I would have preferred to put a pistol to the skull of every one of those sniveling politicians and their bastard military leaders. But I'm getting a free cryogenic colonization ship for turning over that worthless dirtball to the World Board to use as its prison world. Everyone thinks I named the planet Prism because it's covered with crystals, but PRISM is short for Prisoner Relocation Internment Security Management. The bribe I gave the captain to destroy their supplies should guarantee the deaths of the prisoners before the next supply ship, then the World Board will have to return the planet to me. I'll have my cryoship and my crystal-

covered planet. One of the best deals I've ever concocted. Still, it would have been satisfying to see Liam Neill's brain splattered across the World Boardroom's walls. /PM

Prism, Present day

O'NEILL NEVER EXPECTED a glorious red and purple Prism sunset to be her enemy.

But running endless grid patterns on the Great Plain all day, every day, had revealed no sign of her missing father save his mangled, empty single-seat skimmer. He'd apparently survived the crash, only to wander into the crystal field. And after two weeks of searching, her father would be declared KIA tonight. The letters couldn't be more painful if they'd been branded on her heart. She glared at the setting sun.

Jocko Neill had been Prism's best pilot. After sunset, she would be.

A klaxon sounded. The official thirteen-day search ended with the last shriek of the blatting buzz. She clapped her hands over her ears and screamed. Not because the electronic clanging hurt her eardrum. Her breath quickened, without getting more oxygen to her lungs. The ground spun and she fell to her knees. Her heart raced, as if it could find her father before sunset. Solo sat next to her, providing support, and she reached for his fur. When he'd arrived as a cub seven years ago, with her father's help, she'd trained the tiger to be her constant companion—her personal bodyguard.

Patrick Reagan pulled her to her feet as if she were still a little girl. "I'm sorry, O. Go ahead and let it out." He opened his arms for refuge.

She stood stiff and removed, shaking her head. If she started, she'd never stop. For the past thirteen days she'd refused to believe that her father would not be found. Alive.

"We can hope that one day soon, he'll walk into town." The sadness and sympathy in Jocko Neill's best friend's eyes clashed against his words.

How could the man give up?

In uncommon cooperation, first- and second-gen convicts, soldiers, and politicos had waited every day at the spaceport, swapping stories about her father helping them in the early years and beyond. They'd jockeyed for one of the twenty-four seats on the search shuttle. Those turned away had arrived earlier the next morning.

Tonight, the would-be rescuers rested arms across shoulders and around waists, supporting one another in a dejected shuffle toward the shuttle. They'd set aside differences and long-standing feuds. Given their precious free time to search together for Prism's best explorer, whose discovery of translithium had improved every Prismer's chance at survival by guaranteeing the twice-yearly return of the supply ship and providing an income by mining and selling the rare fuel to Earth.

"My father saved your life." She hated the tremor in her voice. "Several times." Widening her stance, she stood straight, to look strong. "Dad's your best friend, even if you are a politico."

Reagan swallowed and stared at the setting sun. "Jocko *was* my best friend, even though he was a soldier."

Amid rainbows of dying, fractured light streaming through towering crystals, O'Neill's hope slipped away on every exhale. The cold beauty of the surrounding multi-sided, colorful prisms growing from the soil stood uncaring. None pointed where to find her father. The ground swam in long, dark shadows.

The last sliver of the sun slipped behind the distant hills.

She wanted to squeeze her eyes shut, to dam the tears. She wanted to feel her father's arms holding her against his beating heart. She wanted to ram her fist into the nearby pillar of purple crystal. "I know Dad's still alive. I'll wait for him at home."

"You know the law." Cal's father's tone had never been so harsh.

"It's a stupid law."

"That everyone obeys." He inhaled a long breath. Took more time on the exhale. "Your father would want you safe."

The Neill temper churned, coursing hot through every cell of her body. By the time she was old enough to remember, her father had stopped using his fists to settle disagreements. But she'd heard stories. Lots of stories.

Punishment be damned, she wanted to hit something. Hit someone. "It's been twenty-five years since the landing. Men don't outnumber women five-to-one anymore. Things are different now. There are no gangs of convict psychopaths kidnapping and raping women."

"You're no different from any other female on Prism. You need a male protector."

"I can take care of myself. Besides, the men of the Citadel volunteered to be my protectors."

"Until the day after the Battle. Then you'll have to make your decision. If things go badly…"

"You mean *if* Dad's dead." Her father was not dead. Could not be dead. He'd survived over three hundred flight missions during the Earth war. He had to be alive.

The politico leader shook his head and attempted a smile. But it twisted up then fell at the corners.

If she won the Battle, the annual competition of three military-styled athletic events, no one could force her to give away her freedom. She waved him off. "I'll find him."

She stepped around him and strode to the shuttle. The dusty volunteers waited in line at the base of the short boarding ramp. Every night she'd thanked the exhausted men and women before they went up the ramp. This would be the last time.

She gulped air and, despite the painful lump in her throat, responded to each of the two dozen mumbled apologies and dejected condolences. Solo stood beside her, his lean tiger muscles taut under his fur. The twitch of his whiskers betrayed his agitation at sensing her clenched fists as if she were ready to defend against an attacker. She was.

Her father was too good a pilot to have crashed on the Great Plain. The past week she'd begun to wonder if his skimmer had been sabotaged, but her grandfather' technicians had found no evidence of tampering. No other footsteps had been found on the powdery silt around his craft. If he was dead, where was his body?

Patrick Reagan stood at the end of the line. "If he's truly gone, you know the protection of the Reagan house is yours." Kindness didn't dull the firmness in his tone.

Her throat closed, choking off protest. *It might come to that.* She nodded, but she didn't agree.

He stepped past her and climbed the narrow ramp.

What could a seventeen-year-old second-gen *girl* do against the First Law of Prism? Hands fisted tight, her close-clipped nails dug into her palms. She swiped a tear with the sleeve of her flight suit before squinting to scan the horizon of the Great Plain one final time.

Losing her home, even if the loneliness there ate her from the inside out, living in the Politico Compound with her mother and stepfather was not a sane option. It would give Ray Reagan, Cal's uncle, the power to dictate her every move, even force her to marry —whomever *he* wanted. He'd marry her off to gain influence and power. And whatever else he could get in the deal. All because of a twenty-five-year-old edict agreed to by the first gens that every female must be protected by at least one man. It was time for that first law on Prism to die.

The shuttle generator engaged. She strode up the gangway, Solo at her heel. Settling into the co-pilot's seat, she buckled the safety harness and put on her headset. Solo squeezed into the space between her chair and the partition separating the cockpit from the main cabin.

The pilot revved the engines. Her earpiece couldn't dampen the thunder of the straining propulsion drives. While they synched, she rubbed her father's salvaged earpiece in her pocket. He'd taken her everywhere, taught her to fly, shared his love of this convict world.

She wasn't afraid of anything. But she didn't know how to be alone. She didn't know how to live in a world without her father's laughter. Without his love.

The pilot gave her a nod. He was another first-generation friend of her father's. But then, who wasn't? The three hundred exiled military leaders had worked together to try to defeat the corporation takeover of Earth, and they either knew, or knew of, one another long before their boots landed on a planet as far away from Earth as a cryoship could travel.

If only she could bury her face in Solo's soft fur and give in to the grief. But that wouldn't fly. Now, less than a month before her eighteenth birthday, she had to be an adult, had to show she could take care of herself. Every day her father remained missing ran down the clock on her freedom.

She pushed the throttle forward.

Engines engaged, the transport lifted, banking hard for the only spaceport on the planet.

———

Three hours later, the last volunteer exited the shuttle. The only reason Prism had shuttles was to ferry miners to the deposits of translithium, which powered everything on Earth and its colonies. The Earth corporations hadn't known the rare energy source existed on the planet when they'd exiled the first gens here. The leaders of Montgomery Conglomerates must have kicked themselves around Earth's equator when they found out they'd given Prism to the exiles for their prison.

O'Neill checked the docking clamps. When Captain Hennessey started connecting the maintenance lines, she volunteered to complete the post-flight routine by herself. She waved the pilot away, saying he'd already missed too much time away from his family.

It wasn't an empty excuse. She needed time to think. Whenever her father went on one of his exploration trips, she was so busy covering his piloting responsibilities shuttling miners to the mines, that she didn't have time to worry about his absence. Sometimes she'd even fallen asleep listening to his recorded nightly story about his day. He'd started the bedtime tales after her mother left the two of them for politico Ray Reagan. Her father had never missed a single night—until two weeks ago—when his skimmer crashed.

There would be no more messages. Her stomach rolled. No more surprises from Jocko Neill's explorations of the planet, planned with her grandfather and carried out with the Warden's blessing. No more shared holo games, her one Earth vice. She bit her lip. Solo trotting behind her, she almost tripped on a docking clamp. She slapped the hull and a hollow ring echoed her frustration.

At least she had a short reprieve, thanks to her neighbors. They'd been part of her father's squadron during the Earth War between the world governments and the megacorporations. The giant corporations had only been interested in selling unhealthy, overpriced food and products to Earth's billions while raping the planet for profit.

When her father went missing, her neighbors had volunteered to be her joint protectors long enough for her to compete in the Battle. If she won the military-based skills competition, she could name a boon. She'd demand freedom from the First Law. Like most second gens, she could defend herself. She didn't need a male to protect her or tell her what she couldn't do.

By the time the post-flight check was complete, Prism's giant moon added its glow through the open spaceport roof. O walked past the row of vacant, unlit docking stations. Disconnected maintenance lines snaked everywhere, waiting for the next morning's crews to restore order. The supply shuttles, loaded with Prism's precious translithium crystals, had already returned to their berths aboard the corporation cargo vessel high above the surface of her world. Even with sublight and FTL drives, the ship would take three months to return to Earth.

She pulled in a deep breath. The stench of daytime dock-workers unloading protein canisters and other requisitioned goods from the twice-yearly supply ship had dissipated to a nose-wrin-kling whiff. Solo stayed close, his head almost touching her hip. The nearly deserted spaceport echoed as her boots fell against the plazsteel deck when she rounded the corner.

A lone Earth shuttle sat at the last berth by the long corridor to the spaceport's gated entrance. In the brightness streaming from the ship's open hatch, a silhouetted crewman watched her approach. Hands in his overalls' pockets, he walked down the ramp and blocked her way.

She stiffened, fingering the illegal knife hidden in her sleeve.

"You Jocko Neill's daughter?" The hissed whisper quivered in the air.

Solo growled and stepped between her and the stranger.

Had the Earther recognized the scar on her cheek? She positioned herself at the tiger's flank.

The man stumbled forward a step, forcing her back into the dark shadow of the dock. A nervous flick of his chin toward Solo betrayed his fear.

She didn't give the animal the hand signal to stand down. "What makes you think so?"

"The tiger."

Blood roared in her ears, and her stomach twisted in a mix of hatred and fear. Frag, she hated Earthers.

But if this one knew anything about her father's disappearance, she'd spare time for him. She unclenched her jaw. "What do you want?"

Solo rose, circled the man, sniffing. Only the Earther's eyeballs moved. Circuit complete, Solo stood beside her, his tail twitching against her thigh.

The man drew a sudden breath as if he'd forgotten the need to oxygenate his cells. "I've been waiting for Jocko to show up for the past six days. He has a standing purchase order. A dozen bubble chips. This is the last shuttle up to the cargo hauler. We're lifting in a couple of hours, as soon as the rest of the crew returns from town. Then we head back to Earth." Lips pursed in question, he glanced at the open hatch before his gaze searched for information in her expression. "Did he send you to pick them up?"

No. Fragging. Way. Dad and contraband? No other option, since buying *anything* from an Earther was illegal. And not just drunk-and-disorderly illegal.

Bubble chips... What were they for? Cached information? An electronic sensor? Dad's skimmer? *On his squadron's honor!* Was it for a blaster? *Frag her.* No matter what they were for, they carried a sentence of death. She'd never thought of that when she'd played the Earther holo games with her dad.

Was that the reason her father's skimmer had crashed? Had someone found out he was importing forbidden technology?

Was he in hiding?

She had to think of a way to find out what the chips were for without endangering herself or anyone else.

The crewman shifted from one foot to the other. "I'm putting my butt on the line out here talking to you." The hissed words barely reached her ears.

He peered over his shoulder at the empty hatch before whispering, "They're paid for. Take this. If somebody sees me give it to you, I'm a dead man." He reached out to her. "Shake my hand."

Shoving a small packet into her palm, he pumped her hand once in an Earther farewell and double-timed up the ship's ramp.

Her mind raced as she hurried toward the bend in the corridor, out of sight of the shuttle before stopping to stare at the metallic golden wrapper. The Earther had been genuinely frightened to be caught with it. Her chest tightened. Her mouth was dry, but she tried to swallow. Something fluttered in her stomach.

She turned the packet over, its thin foil blank. She fumbled, and spinning end over end, it arced away. She tried to catch it, but her hand swatted it away toward the neighboring berth with its tangle of cables.

Her heart pounded loud enough that she was surprised the sound didn't echo off the docking bay walls. Her lungs labored as if she'd raced the length of the spaceport instead of five feet.

She had to retrieve the chips before someone saw her, or worse, scooped them up. A soft ping sounded when the packet hit the deck. It tumbled toward the ledge down into the maintenance area. She scooped it up just before it skidded into the pit of tangled cables and machinery. Before her breath steadied she tried to rip the foil open, but it wouldn't tear.

She wanted to scream.

She wanted to see what was inside.

She wanted her father.

What had he been illegally importing for Warden-only-knew how many years? Information? Skimmer parts?

Weapons?

She wouldn't take a chance opening the packet here. Even her grandfather's influence couldn't protect her from the Warden's wrath if these were chips for a weapon.

She stowed it in the pocket of her flight suit. After tugging the zipper closed, she looked toward the exit and froze. A single figure advanced.

Her hand slid to her sleeve for the crystal knife in its wrist sheath, until she recognized Washington's lanky stride and dark skin. Her jaw relaxed.

Wash stepped close. "Easy, O."

She fist-thumped his shoulder. "Geez. Didn't your mama teach you not to scare a girl?"

"Nope. Heard you got zilched today. I don't have words to tell you how sorry I am." Her friend stooped to pat Solo and then one-arm hugged her. "We agreed to meet at the Burnt Engine for dinner. You didn't show. What happened?"

"I needed time alone, so I volunteered to do the shuttle post-flight check myself. Took longer than I thought."

Wash stepped away, nodding toward the sound of approaching voices. "They're here."

Cal, Hoshi, and Novy stepped into the light from a dying glow-crystal set in the wall. Closing the gap in silence, her best friends watched her.

Cal stepped toward her and drew her close. His touch was more comforting than his father's had been outside the shuttle tonight. She rested her head against his shoulder and her body molded to his. His breath brushed across her ear. "I'm so sorry about your dad. But I'll take care of you. Everything will be fine." She knew he believed his words.

Too bad she didn't.

They'd never go back to search those caves for her father. No one would. Except her. First Law be damned; she'd go by herself.

He gave her a quick kiss on the mouth, then pulled back. Eyeing her from her boots up, he shook his head. "I know it's been rough, but damn it, O, you can't afford to lose more weight. The Battle's in eleven days. What you need is good friends and a decent meal. We're your escort."

She pressed her lips together to stop their quivering. "Thanks." She'd never been to the pilot watering hole without her father. And as much as she wanted to crawl into a cave, these were her best friends. She'd gone to school with them, trained with them, been punished for breaking rules with them, learned to hold her own with them. She counted them as family. The only real family she had left, besides her grandfather. When her mother deserted her seven years ago, O stopped considering the woman as family.

Worry lining his forehead under a flop of straight hair, Hoshi gave her a short bow. "Words cannot contain my sorrow."

Novy's sudden bear hug encased her in muscles and musk. His mustache and carefully trimmed golden beard scratched at her cheek. "Tonight is night for serious drinking." He added something in Russian and let her go. The comfort and safety she felt in the circle of his muscled arms evaporated.

Solo at her side, O and her escorts strode abreast out of the building into the circle of light below the watchtower. Hoshi signaled the guard on duty.

The second-gen peered down at them, then saluted. "Sorry about your dad, O'Neill. In the early days, he saved my dad's ass from the crazies."

She returned his salute, unable to get out even a single word. After two weeks of denial, the reality of her father's killed-in-action status walled off her throat. Not only had she lost her dad, she'd lost her life. Or rather, how she would live her life. Her future was no longer in her control—unless she won the Battle. If she didn't win, she'd have to move in with her mother and stepfather or marry Cal. That would be better than living with her mother and stepfather, but she didn't want to get married and let Cal dictate what she could do with her life. Not yet. Maybe not ever.

Single file, they stepped through the narrow gate and threaded the turns of the tall-walled metal labyrinth that protected the entrance to the spaceport. She was the last to emerge into the far edge of Convict Town. Cold, thin fog obscured portions of the night sky and details of the structures ahead.

Glow crystals flickered at the edge of the path leading to the tavern, providing scant light. So many times she'd walked this path with her dad. Pulverized minerals shimmered on the ground, giving what passed for a street the look of a moonlit river. Life might be hard, but Prism's beauty could take her breath away. Her dad had shared his love of his exile world with her, taking her to locations not yet on the maps.

Outside the boundary of Convict Town was no-man's-land, no sanctioned buildings for business or housing. Dumped cargo canisters and a couple of three-sided shacks made of random cast-off materials littered the winding hundred-meter walk to the bar. Encounters with a convict gang were unlikely, and groups of soldiers were rarely bothered, but this late at night, she must always be on guard.

Novy, the oldest and most experienced of them, took point. According to the original settlement document drawn up by the

Earth corporations, all weapons were illegal. But most everyone had a blade for defense, carved from one of Prism's crystals. Wash lived in Convict Town and held a wicked-looking curved knife that he used with great skill to protect himself and his mother. He and Hoshi flanked O. Cal had her six. Always did. Standard-op formation against a grab-and-run attack. Her friends were taking no chances.

Her lips quirked at their concern. Prism was civilized now. They'd never had to fight off a group of attackers. At least, not when she was with them. Maybe no one wanted to mess with Jocko Neill's daughter. The last time someone had, they'd all gone missing. She fingered the scar on her cheek.

Solo paced ahead, sniffing the area in front of the lean-to shacks.

She flexed her fingers. She'd be happy to reach the warmth of the Burnt Engine. The air chilled her exhaled breath, crystallizing it. The cold was enough to warrant an attack for her flight jacket alone. Of course, her female body was worth much more than the jacket.

Solo growled a warning, then crouched and bared his teeth.

Novy stopped, signaling with a closed fist at shoulder level. Everyone froze. Listened.

Hoshi and Wash melted into the shadows while Cal closed the gap between himself and O'Neill and stood in front of her. They were in the open. No shelter. No protection. Fifty feet ahead, cargo canisters could provide cover for Convict Town ambushers looking to steal what they could, as did the three-sided rooms on the other side of the street.

Aware of her increased sensitivity to sound, she slid the knife her father had carved for her from its sheath. She'd excelled in hand-to-hand combat classes at the Soldier Compound, but she'd been in only one real fight, during the kidnapping seven years ago. All she'd done then was run to escape. Was she good enough now? She slowed her out-of-control breathing, adjusted her grip on the knife and waited for Novy's next signal.

From the shelter of the cast-off containers, ten second-gens stepped into the street. A gust of wind blew from behind them, swirling grit past her. Half were armed with sharpened metal grappling rods that were no less deadly for their original intent. The others brandished homemade knives. This was a large gang for Convict Town, especially since reports of random violence and lawlessness had diminished over the last couple of years. Shock rolled into a dense ball in her gut, and alarm bleated a sharp warning in her brain. She resisted the urge to turn and run.

The group's V-formation split. Their leader stepped forward, raising empty hands. "We want only the girl. Give her over and you can have free passage." Head cocked to the side, he smiled.

Her heart tried to pound free of its ribbed prison. Could this have to do with the bubble chips in her pocket? Was her father supposed to deliver the packet to someone in Convict Town?

Cal spat on the ground. "You've got shit for brains, fragger. Do you know who this is?"

"Girl with Kitty. We've been waiting for you." The largest advanced, hand in his pocket. "Word is, your daddy's dead and you got no protector. I will make you purr, little girl."

The leader swore. "Shut up, Bobby."

O'Neill's fury fired.

She acknowledged the flames, remembering her Soldier Compound classes not to fight angry. Skin prickling, she gripped the knife her father had taught her to use. Its serrated crystal blade flashed with inner light. Ten to five weren't good odds, but Solo would help to even them. Thank goodness her father had demanded the tiger as his boon after finding a second translithium mine. "Go back to the cesspool you crawled from. Or I can paint the road with your blood." Her shouted words sounded like an order. "I don't care which."

The thug froze.

She needed to buy time for Wash and Hoshi to get into position. "I'll count for you, dipcod, since you probably don't know how. When I get to three, if you and your buddies aren't off the street, my *kitty* will eat your guts for dinner." Her fingers gripped the fur of Solo's neck. He roared, and the vibrations slammed against her chest.

"I told you not to mess with her, Zak. Her grandpa's army will fillet your ass." The shortest attacker sprinted behind the building.

The man in the middle planted his boots, glancing from Solo to O'Neill. "Her General-of-the-Losers Grandpappy can't piss on a rock. When was the last time you saw that coward in town?"

She pressed her lips together to keep from flinging a few choice words at the prick. The residents of Soldier Compound were not her grandfather's personal army. He'd just been the ranking officer when they were all exiled to Prism.

The leader bounced on the balls of his feet, clenching and unclenching his hands. "Tell me you guys don't want a piece of this." He pointed at her, his circling finger looking like an obscene gesture.

This went beyond a simple grab-and-run kidnapping, but these jerks didn't know about the bubble chips. Her father wouldn't have dealt with anyone who could put her life in danger.

The rest of the convicts hunched but stood firm, muttering warnings at one another.

Frag them all. "One."

The grungiest tapped the leader's elbow, then pointed at Solo. "No credits are worth fighting that." He slipped into the shadows. The others closed ranks around their leader.

"Two."

Solo crouched before her, saliva dripping from his open jaw. She released her hold on his neck fur and touched his flank. Best to get the jump on the jerks. She wanted someone alive to question. "Solo, defend."

The tiger leapt at the closest man.

Novy sprang, reaching the next convict spawn at the same time. He slammed the poorly trained jerk with an arm-breaking chop that sent the guy's improvised spear skittering. Novy kicked it away and turned to meet the next challenger.

Wash and Hoshi jumped from the shadows with war whoops, engaging the closest convicts. Another attacker's boots slammed a retreat on the packed dirt. Those remaining yelled at each other, trying to bolster their courage to attack Solo with their grappling rods.

Her heart squeezed. Solo had never been in a fight like this. But he was doing his job; he was protecting her. If he got hurt, she would have to be restrained or she would do murder.

The tiger snarled. A high-pitched wail shredded the night.

"Stay back, O." Cal sprinted to intercept an attacker running straight for her.

She wanted to yell. She wanted a piece of the fight. She wanted to prove that she could protect herself.

But he was probably right. As always. Levelheaded, calculating Cal always knew how to do the right thing.

Alone, O'Neill crouched low. Cal's knife slashed. Her body leaned to one side, then the other, mirroring the thrusts at Cal. Novy, Hoshi and Wash fought to disarm their opponents. Her fist bunched. If one of the attackers got through, she might get in the fight.

Loud grunts and thuds of the fighting pairs hitting the ground distracted her. The leader and a spear-wielding man advanced on her.

She straightened, widened her stance, and steadied her breath, maintaining a death-grip on the wrapped handle of her knife. After the kidnapping, her father had trained her to stave off as many as five attackers. Though she'd never been in a real fight, she could handle two. She hoped.

They stopped ten feet away. The big man's mouth contorted into a parody of a friendly smile. "I don't want to hurt you, Baby-cakes." The leader spread his arms wide. "Drop your knife and call off the tiger."

In a flash, she cocked her arm, took aim, and threw the knife. She hated to lose her weapon, but taking out the leader was worth the risk. End over end, it whistled through the air. Her target jumped aside. The knife sank deep into the upper thigh of the bodyguard. His homemade spear clattered to the ground. The man toppled, screaming and hugging his injured leg.

The leader launched himself at her, pinning one hand to her side before she could move.

Solo's yowl split the night.

She rammed the heel of her other palm into the man's solar plexus, then raked her boot down his shin and stamped on his instep. A silent wall of pain contorted his face. Her forehead connected with his nose, followed by the hard thrust of her knee to his groin.

He crumpled at her feet.

Her blood raced through her veins, screaming victory. Her lungs struggled to supply extra oxygen to cells vibrating with unreleased tension. She fisted her right hand.

Solo skidded to a stop beside her, locking his teeth around the man's neck. She grabbed a hank of fur. "Stand down. Stand down. Solo, stand down. I want him alive." The tiger finally released his death grip on her attacker.

She stepped past the whimpering bodyguard, ready to help her friends. They didn't need her assistance.

Hoshi's foot was planted on the chest of a pimply kid wheezing for breath. Cal threw a punch, and the man before him fell face-first into the dirt. Wash and Novy double-teamed the last attacker, pummeling him to the ground.

"Move. Give me a reason to kick your face off your skull." Wash had never sounded so furious. The bloody victims sprawled, unmoving.

Cal studied her approach. "You okay?"

She swiped her face with her sleeve and nodded, noting the leader's blood on her flight suit. "Not a scratch. You?"

He flexed his bloody fist and winced. "A-okay." He glanced over his shoulder. "Everybody ambulatory?"

Novy chuckled. "Am fine. Goons not moving." He was the

best of them with a knife. Two wide swaths of blood, not his, swirled across his uniform.

Hoshi shook his foot, then gingerly tested his weight on it. The leg of his pants had been slashed, but the bleeding looked superficial. He waved her away.

Wash swiped at his split cheek and nodded.

Breathing hard, she brushed at the blood and shimmering dirt on her flight suit, leaving light powdery streaks.

"This is why you need a protector."

She whirled in the direction of her father's voice. But he wasn't there. When she glanced at her friends, no one else looked like they'd heard it. She stared at the empty space. "Did you hear that?"

Cal shook his head and moved next to her, scanning the area. "Are you okay?"

"Sure." *Unless I'm going crazy.*

Hoshi motioned for silence.

Footfalls–lots of them–growing closer.

PRISM Administrator Report from Cornelia Schultz to World Board (Present Day) re: Supply Shuttle 51

Attachments: Cargo discrepancies, Administrative requisition, Joint Committee requisition

For the fifth straight Supply Shuttle, the Joint Committee has over delivered on the negotiated number of translithium crystals, activating the bonus section of the contract for additional supplies, including rations, a new mining shuttle, and building supplies.

There is talk among second gens about a twenty-five-year review for colony status. I would be happy to facilitate any reports you may need in this regard. I can guarantee the safety of a small committee of representatives to visit Prism if you wish to compile a detailed study.

Private Journal Notes of Cornelia Schultz: *I met with Liam Neill yesterday. I agree with his ever-present concern about food supplies and lack of sufficient reserves if Earth stops sending supply ships. I've met with some resistance from the World Board bean-counters to the increased rations I've padded into my last three reqs, and questions about additional hydroponic supplies. I* *continue to offer access to Prism to World Board members and the press in an effort to show them the human side of the people here. I believe it is now safer on Prism than on Earth.*

THE POUNDING STEPS GOT NEARER. O's breaths came closer together, in rhythm with the approaching threat.

Frag. Frag. Frag. The Soldier Compound, her second home, was safe. She'd put up with a couple of shouted insults in the Politico Compound but never felt physically threatened. She'd never been attacked in Convict Town. Now twice in one night?

Did whoever was on watch on the roof of the Citadel, her home high on a hill overlooking Convict Town, have her in their sights? Were they running to her rescue now?

Cal bent and picked up his fallen opponent's knife. "We can't make it to the Burnt Engine before the sons-of-whores catch us. If we make a stand, using the canisters as shields, maybe we can scare them off. You live here, what do you think, Wash?"

"Worth a try. No other options, unless I recognize one of them."

She grasped a discarded spear and ducked behind a large canister. Her friends grabbed extra weapons and arranged themselves to take advantage of what little cover there was.

Solo moved to her side, unprotected by the canister she crouched behind, his fur spiked and haunches tight, ready to spring. "Steady," she whispered, more to calm herself than the tiger.

The footfalls slowed and men streamed around both sides of the nearest shack.

She peeked around the canister. Her throat tightened. Ten older men, first-gen convicts, stared at the downed second-gens in front of them.

Wash gave the all-clear signal and stood, hands in the air. Since he was the only one of them who lived in Convict Town, he must trust, or at least know, someone in this group.

Hiding her shaking hand, she tucked her knife up her sleeve and stood.

A man in tattered fatigues stepped forward. "This isn't a place for a female to walk without Convict Town escorts, miss."

She nodded. Even with Solo, she and her friends couldn't have won the fight against the men arrayed before them. Relief washed over her, steadying more than just her shaking hands.

The man nodded. "Headed to the Burnt Engine?"

Cold, damp wind slapped her cheek. "Yep." She rubbed her numb hands together.

The man stood taller. "We'll escort you there and wait to return you to the spaceport."

Cal moved beside her—for protection or possession, she couldn't tell. He glanced at the unmoving bodies on the ground. "Thanks, but you can see we can handle ourselves. It's not much further."

"I'm not here to help you. I'm here to help Jocko Neill's daughter." He met each of their gazes. "I'm Vicar."

The Sheriff of Convict Town. O'Neill remembered first-gen stories about his fearlessness. Stories approaching old Earth Superman status. How, single-handed, he'd fought off a dozen of the psychopaths after the cryoship left. He'd pulled protein canisters from the fires ignited by the rocket blasts.

"I owe my life to your father. He took out someone who had a knife aimed at my back in the early days. It didn't matter to him that I was a convict and not one of the military exiles. I pledge my protection whenever you are within the confines of Town. The guard on the tower will notify me and I'll meet you at the labyrinth entrance."

The way in which he remembered and honored her dad brought tears to her eyes. She'd loved her father, but she hadn't realized what a good man he had been until so many people volunteered to search for him, sharing their stories while walking the grid pattern. Before anyone could see the tears streaking down her checks, she turned away and wiped at her eyes.

The watchtower guard must have already been on call and had gotten word to the Sheriff tonight. She stepped forward, right fist over her heart, the soldier tribute to a trusted comrade. "I'm deeply honored to meet you. I am most grateful for your protection."

His lips thinned but his gaze remained gentle. His men tied the unconscious or groaning attackers. The leader tried crawling away, but received a kick in the ribs before the Sheriff's men tied his ankles together and secured his arms behind his back.

Vicar walked over to the now-trussed criminal and squatted beside him. "Thomas. Who paid you?"

The man sneered at the sheriff. "No one. Who'd want her? She's crazy."

"I don't think so. This is quite the group you put together. They wouldn't have joined you just for a," he looked over his shoulder at O, "little fun. You and I will have a nice conversation when I return. If you can't remember who's paying you, there are specialists in the Soldier Compound who can help you recover that memory. I think they'll be quite motivated, considering your target." Vicar rose, gave orders to some of his men to take the attackers to jail, and returned to O's side.

The rest of the would-be rescuers, those who helped maintain order in Convict Town where the convict exiles had settled together, surrounded them. They all set off at a trot, and soon they arrived at the door of a low, corrugated metal building. Vicar opened the door for her.

She reached for the lone protein bar in her jacket. Her fingers brushed the bulge of her father's packet before wrapping around the bar. She slipped the meal into his hand. "Thank you."

He gave her a salute. "Jocko was good people. Never looked down at the likes of convicts. I lost a friend tonight." Agreements rose from his men.

She scrubbed the back of her hand roughly across her cheek. "Thanks. That means a lot." Her father was merely *lost*. Maybe the chips contained a clue to his location.

She trailed Solo's proud stride into the bar, wishing Jocko Neill were inside regaling the patrons with his latest adventure.

Although it was dim, she took advantage of the brighter light, kneeling to check her tiger, running her hands through his fur, feeling his bones, looking for any hint of blood or flinching reaction to her touch. Relieved, she nuzzled his neck. "You did good tonight, big guy." The tiger relaxed into her. "If I'd had you back then, those Earthers never would been able to kidnap me with that damned wristlock." Her skin prickled.

She rose and ran a visual on the condition of her friends. They didn't look much worse than if they'd been unloading cargo all day. A thick strand of her wavy hair escaped its clip and fell in her eye. She brushed it behind her ear.

Conversation ceased. Patrons craned for a better view of the bloodied group.

Cal cleared his throat to gain everyone's attention. "Be careful on your way home. We were ambushed by ten second-gens with weapons." His politico speech-making tone warned but his smile boasted victory. "We subdued them, with Solo's help. They're in the custody of the sheriff." His oratory timing perfect, he paused then lowered his voice, a look of concern flitting across his features. "You won't have to worry about the fraggers, but there could be others out there."

Excited chatter grew, interspersed with disbelief at the size of the group that had attacked them. Even though he was the son of the politico leader, Cal didn't lie. Every resident of Soldier Compound knew that.

She crossed to the length of polished metal that passed for the bar and addressed the owner. "We didn't find him, Sarge. He's officially KIA." The words carved a gaping hole in her heart, big enough for a mining shuttle to fly through.

"O'Neill. My regrets." The owner brought two fingers to his forehead. He'd flown in the Aussie Brigade alongside her father after the corporations started the war by destroying all the Earth-orbiting satellites and stations so they could attack without warning. He'd known her grandfather long before Liam Neill had been tapped to lead the Global Coalition Armed Forces against the megacorporations. The man nodded to a room filled with mismatched tables made of everything from large cable spools to dented metal crates. A string of small glow crystals hung from the ceiling, separating the bar from the dining area. "We already heard. Word got passed when the search party made the spaceport."

The hard physical activity of running a grid for the day's search, fighting off her attackers, and declaring her father dead for the first time in public made her empty stomach threaten revolt. She should have begged off this excursion. Her leg muscles quivered from too much adrenaline. Fear, anger and grief scoured her veins, straining the eternal leash that tethered her emotions. *I will not cry.*

Cal's arm came around her. Although she was grateful for his support, she didn't think about him every waking moment. She didn't crave his kisses. And she certainly didn't want to go to the Fertile Field to get pregnant with his child. She needed to love the man she would choose as her partner, and as much as she wanted to love Cal in that way, she secretly knew she didn't.

He guided her to a table with a shielded glow crystal, helped her onto the tall barstool, and sat on the empty cable spool to her right. He motioned to the waitress to bring mugs of water to the table. "Warm ones all around."

While her friends debriefed the fight, O stared at the table, letting their conversation flow over her. Numb.

Not caring what she ate, she let Cal order for her while she dodged the sympathetic looks from customers at the other tables. A female dockworker lifted her mug in salute. "To O'Neill," she called. More mugs were raised.

"To Jocko Neill." The deep voice said her father's name with reverence. "His laughter echoed off these walls. He was the best man I've ever known. Duty first!"

Every person in the bar stood, lifted their mugs high, and shouted the battle cry of her father's Earth brigade. O's raised arm shook as much as her voice, and she had to lean against her stool for support.

After what seemed like forever, the patrons settled in their seats and their muted conversations resumed. She blinked back her tears. One overflowed, and she used her sleeve to scrub it away and sat.

When their drinks arrived, Cal pressed a mug into her hand. She wrapped chilled fingers around its warmth.

Wash raised his tankard. "To O winning the Battle."

The Battle. If she won, she would ask for a prize that could not be purchased for any amount of credits—the right to ignore the First Law on Prism. If she didn't win...well, maybe she should start thinking about what she'd do next.

Nine months ago when her father had suggested she compete in the contest, she'd been unenthusiastic. But her father convinced her into signing up for the Battle by suggesting she request her own skimmer for her prize, and he'd offered to train her. He'd won the Battle himself twice, and he'd reminded her that a skimmer of her own would allow her more freedom.

Cal planned to participate next year, since he didn't want to compete against her. He'd volunteered to train with her and had a list of building supplies he wanted her to request for their house if she won. Everyone expected them to get married...someday.

Wash's mother, a gifted psychic, had predicted that O would marry Patrick Reagan's oldest son before O was even born. And Madame Esmeralda was never wrong. She'd met O at the space-port one morning during the search and told her, "Your father is not dead." The woman had refused to say more. O held on to her belief that Wash's mother had never been wrong.

Her grandfather had suggested the Battle to the first warden, who'd arrived shortly after Jocko Neill discovered the first translithium mine, as a way to encourage focus for the soldiers and an opportunity for convicts and politicos to compete for goods that were otherwise unavailable on Prism. As part of the shipping contract with the World Board, the winner could request either a full crate of supplies from Earth or a boon, like a year free from service in the mines while still receiving all the benefits given to miners.

Now, more than ever, O *needed* to win and to demand her independence, freedom from the First Law, as her prize. She didn't know if her request would be granted, but winning the Battle was her only chance.

She'd be competing against older entrants who'd battled before. This year the Joint Committee had approved applications from ten soldiers, one convict and two politicos. O had trained hard. She stood a solid chance of winning the piloting event. If she did well in the other two, winning the entire Battle was possible.

She clinked her cup with her friends' and took a deep pull of the spiced spirits—for luck. She'd need a lot more than they'd had tonight. A chill raced across her skin.

Cal raised his drink again. "To Prism's reclassification and colony status!"

Damn political dreams. She couldn't face the interminable second-gen politico debate about fighting the twenty-five-year-old Earth edict that had exiled their parents to Prism. Not tonight. Who cared about fighting for planetary rights when her father was missing and a mandatory protection order hung over her neck like a laser ax?

She slammed her metal mug on the table. "Throttle back, you jerks." She reached past her mug and jabbed Cal's arm.

"I don't know why your aft-burners are lit, O." He patted her hand. "The Joint Committee will push the colony issue with the new shipping contract. Most colonies negotiate independence on their quarter-century anniversary."

O snorted. "The first gens were dumped here with supplies and nothing else. No warden, no guards, no buildings, no rules. Prism isn't a colony. It's a prison world. Two protein bars a day, three with mine service, is the only lifelong guarantee we've got from the Earth corporations and their World Board.

"They gave Prism to the first gens and wrote them off. If it hadn't been for activists on Earth and our translithium, the corporations probably would have stopped sending the supply ships years ago." She snatched her hand away. "If your father wants to help, why doesn't he get the Joint Committee to repeal the archaic protector law? Second-gen females are smart enough to know when we need an escort. None of us want to give our freedom away to some male dictator."

Cal's mouth opened, then closed.

Her friends shrugged, shooting each other don't-try-to-reason-with-her looks. They'd been classmates together at the Soldier Compound school. Hoshi and Novy lived there with their first-gen military parents. Wash's father worked for her grandfather repairing electronics, earning Wash an education that wasn't offered in Convict Town. Cal's father, the leader of the politicos— the exiled government politicians—had worked a deal with her grandfather for Cal to attend the afternoon training classes there, after his morning classes in the Politico Compound. The five of them had trained and stayed friends as a unit.

Hoshi nodded at her. Like them all, he'd searched for her father on his days off. He knew her well enough to recognize she was panicking now—he had four younger sisters.

She glared across the dim glow crystal at Novy. His sculpted face wasn't hard to look at, but when he turned his 'Lady Stare' on her, irritation flared hotter. He wouldn't win her over with the charm that made other girls cuddle up to him or to his co-pilot rank.

On her left, Wash shook with deep, closed-mouthed laughter. He appreciated the rare occasions she stood up to one of them, even when it was him.

And Cal. Her closest friend and supporter since she could remember. Who'd saved her sorry butt more times than she could count. Who'd argued with the warden for what freedom she had following her dad's disappearance so she wouldn't have to move in immediately with her mother and her lying, asshole husband. When her father went missing, Cal had escorted her to the Politico Compound for her weekly dinner with her mother. He'd brought her a share of his rations, fresh produce and extra protein sticks for Solo.

Since she was a little girl, she'd heard the prophecy and had taken for granted that she would marry Patrick Reagan's eldest son. After all, their fathers were best friends. She liked the way Cal cared for her. She liked the appreciation in his eyes when he looked at her, his tender touch when his arms encircled her, the coarseness of his voice when he wanted her. "Cal's easy on the eyes," her father would say.

Used to say.

Cal brushed aside a curly strand of hair that caught in her eyelashes, using the movement as an excuse to kiss her cheek. "Come home with me tonight. You don't have to be alone."

Did he know how she curled up on her bed and cried from loneliness? Cried the same way she had seven years ago when her mother deserted her?

But tonight she wouldn't start sleeping in Cal's bed, no matter how hard it would be to stay in her home. Alone.

She wasn't giving up her independence. Flying was freedom. She wasn't ready to marry, to be owned, to give Cal the legal right to restrict her activities. To guard her from the most dangerous thing for a female on Prism: men.

She fragging well could protect herself. With Solo at her side, she'd held her own tonight. Her father had seen to that. He knew she needed freedom. Teaching her to fly had given her responsibility along with independence. And he'd transferred his love of piloting, and his skills, to her during her lessons. She was the youngest full pilot on Prism.

Her chest tightened.

Cal shook his head. "It's not like you have a lot of options, O."

He was right.

But she wouldn't trust anyone, not even Cal, with her independence. Since her father's disappearance, a possessive authority had crept into his treatment of her, and she didn't like it. He'd promised they wouldn't go to the Fertile Field until she was ready, but the truth was, as a man he could, over her objections, take her there on their wedding night. She sat up straighter. For the past year she'd flown a mining shuttle, and she was good at it. But flying wasn't just a job. Flying was her life. No man, not even Cal, was going to ground her.

She had a plan. Cal wasn't going to like it. He might hate her if the plan worked, but she'd take that risk.

Working a knotted muscle in her forearm, she inhaled the pungent smells of fermented protein ale, cooked vegetables and a room full of bodies laden with sweat from unloading the semi-annual cargo shuttles from Earth. Solo curled on the dusty stone floor next to her bar stool, grooming his fur.

The bartender brought a bowl of water and placed it on the floor. "For the laddie."

"Thanks, Angus." With her boot, she nudged the metal container toward Solo's head. "Can you send out something from the kitchen for him with our dinner?"

"Aye."

The sheet-metal door shrieked. Like everyone in the place, she turned. The raucous din subsided while the bar patrons scrutinized two newcomers.

Even with the dark night bleeding through the opening, O recognized the nicely pressed, standard-issue light blue supply ship coveralls as offworlder clothing. The older Earther ducked inside. A man who looked young enough for this to be his first shore leave followed. He could pass for a second-gen.

The young one was tall. Maybe taller than Cal. Sure of himself, from the way he walked. Dressed in an unstained jumpsuit that looked like it had been tailored to show off his muscled build. He didn't look like any Earther crewman she'd seen before. He looked too...pretty.

He peered around. His gaze stopped when it met hers.

She held his stare. After a full five seconds, she looked away.

"Residue fallout." Washington kicked his boot against the table leg.

She shook her head. "What in the fragging Corporations' names makes Earther crewmen stupid enough to wander through Convict Town at night?" They'd be lucky to make it back to their ship alive.

Hoshi raised a brow at Novy's puckered lips. "There are few crewwomen on a supply ship."

Cal winked at Wash. "Sarge won't be happy if those Earthers think he runs a brothel."

The younger crewman settled at a table in the corner of the bar, protecting his back and affording him an unobstructed view. He had a little sense after all. The older one sat in a chair near the door, a good exit strategy. Maybe they'd be okay. Not that she cared either way. They weren't her responsibility.

The bar's noise level rose. She returned her attention to her own table to find Cal studying her. He did that often these days. A shiver rippled across her shoulders.

He touched her wrist. "You're off duty."

"I know, but why are Earthers so incredibly arrogant?"

"*Baka*," said Hoshi. "Crazy. O, on the other hand, is merely *aho* for refusing the family of the esteemed Cal-ifornia."

"I'm no fool. And I haven't refused Cal or his family. Heck, my mother is still married to his uncle."

"Join my family, Golubushka." Novy grinned; his brows waggled. "In dark I teach you all Russian words you need to know."

Her face heated. "I'm nobody's sweetheart."

Cal raised an eyebrow.

She twisted on her stool and encountered Washington's smirk. "You have anything to add?"

He raised his hands. "I know better than to blunder into a mine-field." He shot a look over her shoulder at Cal and winked. "Hell, if I could figure out a way to live in his family's compound, I'd grab it."

The others snickered.

She didn't. She hit his shoulder. "Then *you* can marry him." Her words could have been dipped in venom.

Cal's sharp inhale made her pivot to confront him.

"Throttle back, O. You're about to say things you'll be sorry for tomorrow."

His even tone and serious eyes reminded her of how he chided his little brother. She was not going to let him treat her like a child. He had no right to tell her what to do. He wasn't her protector.

Solo raised his head from the floor. She grazed her boot across his flank. "You're right, boy. Dinner isn't worth this conversation."

Cal nudged her stool. His compressed lips spoke volumes. He was readying the first lines of a worn-out speech.

Crap. She couldn't outargue this politico.

Cal made an effort to smile. "Come on, O. You haven't eaten. You've got to be hungry. Keep your strength up for your training. The Battle is only ten days away."

Cal had been nothing but compassionate and supportive. Wash was right: She was being stupid—pulled taut at the finality of her father being declared dead. Cal was her best friend. She'd never thought of spending her life with anyone else. But her mother and father had been very much in love, and that hadn't been enough to keep them together. After twelve years her mother had walked away from her husband and daughter to marry Cal's uncle. O'Neill would never do that to her child. Or the man she loved.

Her father had advised her to "give it time." Maybe that's all she needed–time. There was no law that said she had to get married by a certain age, though most second-gen girls married by their eighteenth birthday.

Her stomach rumbled. One protein bar didn't begin to balance the calories she'd expended in the search today. She hadn't been to the Quartermaster to pick up her weekly rations, so the cupboard at home was bare.

Cal moved his hand atop hers and gave her fingers a quick squeeze. Sometimes the comfort of his touch settled her. Tonight her hand felt caged. She pulled it back to her lap.

The smell of pepper and garlic and other Earth spices teased her nose and throat. She was hungry, hungry enough to swallow her pride.

Angus's wife brought their meals. Tomatoes grown in imported Earth soil in O's rooftop garden were mixed with long beans and fresh herbs supplied by Hoshi's hydroponics. As a child, she'd grown and sold produce to Sarge. Her plate included a very expensive texturized protein patty. Cal must have ordered it for her.

He took a bite of his meal and grinned.

Novy gulped his vegetables. "Frag, I love fresh food."

Wash nodded. "I'm glad we aren't required to sign up for the Battle."

She had to keep exercising to have a shot at winning the Battle. She would train tomorrow while searching the caves in the area her father's skimmer had crashed. Hard physical activity might take her mind off her missing father. And drain her energy so she could fall asleep at night.

Washington rested his long-fingered hand on her shoulder. She closed her eyes, remembering how his fingers could work magic on tight neck and shoulder muscles after hours piloting a shuttle.

Cal brushed Wash's hand off. "Don't."

The word and its tone screamed "mine." Her jaw tightened. He had no reason, no right, to object to anything she wanted to do. He'd never said anything before when Wash massaged one of her knotted muscles.

She slammed her fork down instead of skewering him with it. "Were you talking to Wash or to me?"

The others froze and stared at her.

Cal kept chewing as if nothing were wrong. Except he crushed his food long enough to juice it. Finally he swallowed. "Both."

Frag him. Pushing her plate away, she waved a finger at him. "That's it, you dipcod. You can't tell me what to do." She needed to shake him up, teach him a lesson, so he knew he couldn't order her around like he'd been trying to since her dad had gone missing. "Hoshi, what would it take for you to be my Battle coach?"

Cal coughed.

Let him choke on it.

Hoshi clasped his hands, a clear cease-and-desist signal.

Novy grabbed her wrists, pulling her toward him. "You cannot change coaches! I bet all credits from last duty rooster on you."

Every cell in her body vibrated with remembered terror. His firm grasp around her wrists returned her to the moment of her kidnapping, when the Earther in a dirty blue jumpsuit circled her small wrists in his big hand and clamped on the hand restraints, then dragged her, screaming and kicking, behind him. One hard slap on her cheek had knocked her unconscious.

She jerked her arm, and him, toward her. "Let me go!"

He started to protest; then awareness washed across his face. He released her. "Apologies for wristlock." He sank back on his stool and shrugged. "My bet is that next year you will be pregnant and living in Politico Compound with Cal."

His bold statement of her worst fear made the hairs on her arms and neck rise. Her father gone. *Imprisoned. With no say about my life.* Her heart beat a call to arms. She shot across the table like a missile. Someone was screaming. It sounded like her.

Bar patrons scrambled out of the way. Furniture scraped across the floor. Drunken shouts of encouragement skittered around her.

The table teetered when she leaned across it. Solo leapt up next to her and, together, they rode the metal plank to the floor. She slid toward Novy. Fisting her free hand, she rounded on him. A crunch, and warm, sticky liquid, told her she'd hit her mark, even if she hadn't heard the stream of curses traded by her companions.

Someone yanked her waistband, hauling her back. Her foot lashed out but connected only with air. Wash and Cal anchored her with rough hands.

Hoshi knelt beside Novy, sprawled in a heap on the floor. Solo stood over them. The tiger's sub-vocal rumble threatened bodily damage if they moved. The overturned table rocked to a standstill.

"Call him off, O." Cal's tone could have flayed flesh from bone.

It took a couple of panting breaths before she could muster the command. "Stand down, Solo."

Cal caged her with his arms while his breathing evened out. A vein on his neck pulsed. "Cluster frag. For a smart girl, you can be really stupid!"

He'd never shouted at her. It cut through her righteousness but infuriated her.

Hoshi soothed Novy's whimpers of pain. She tried to think of something to say, but words—any words—eluded her. Blood pounded through the veins in her head, drowning her thoughts.

She closed her eyes, took a deep breath and envisioned Solo purring in the sun. The calming technique her mother had once taught her to deal with the legendary Neill temper worked—but only so far. Fairly certain she wouldn't hit someone else, she opened her eyes.

She peered over his shoulder as Cal surveyed the broken dishes, shattered glow crystal, and precious food scattered across the floor. Some of the patrons were already sorting through the far-flung mess looking for edible bits. "You're paying for this."

She'd expect him to be angry, not cold and logical. Not dictating what she had to do. Not acting like the protector she dreaded. She crossed her arms over her chest, wishing to be anywhere but here.

"You broke my nose." A blood-soaked rag muffled Novy's garbled words. "Again!"

She felt a sting of remorse. He hadn't deserved to be the target of her pent up anger and frustration.

"She didn't mean it the first time." Hoshi offered a clean rag. "You turned into her move during physical training last year."

"I'm sorry, Novy." She tried to slip under Cal's arms.

Cal released her shoulders, but bracketed her knees with his legs to keep her on the stool. His hands curled into tight fists. If she were anyone else, he'd settle it with those fists. "Stay put until we settle this." He stared at her with that familiar look, trying to will her into feeling the way he wanted.

But she wouldn't bend to his will this time. He wasn't her protector. She didn't have to do what he said, as if she were a child. "I need to leave now." She needed to go home, cry, and defuse the Neill temper that had reached megabomb tonnage. Fear, grief, and desolation must have lit the fuse of her anger during the fight with the second gens. She had to escape before she did any more damage that would lead others to insist she needed a fulltime protector right now.

Cal stood firm. "We've worked too hard together for you to go rogue on our Battle partnership." He took her hand. "I'll help pay for the damage."

"Let me go. Unless you want what Novy got." She shook her hand free.

Solo circled, snarling, the ridge of fur along his arched back standing upright.

Cal backed away, both hands in the air, but surrender didn't reach his eyes. "We're not done."

"Maybe we are." She stepped around the stool. Solo padded behind her, tail slashing against chair legs. She strode toward Sarge, who leaned against the end of the bar.

Cal yelled after her. "We're a team, O. I won't let you throw away your chance to win the Battle."

Across the room a man stood. "You're a crazy bitch, O'Neill. You need a protector to knock some sense into your head."

Frag. She wanted to deck the stranger, but stayed on her trajectory.

"Shut up, you asshole." Cal's voice cracked with a rage she'd never heard. "Maybe I should split your skull and let the crap run out."

"Leave the girl alone! Her father's just been declared dead, for God's sake." Sarge's wife stepped between the two men.

At the bar, O pulled crumpled bills from her pocket, grimacing at the smears of food staining her jumpsuit. "Sorry, Sarge. If this doesn't cover it, I'll bring you tomatoes until we're square."

The weary-faced man didn't count the bills. "We're even, lass."

He smiled and scooped up the money. "Just like the old days, with a Neill throwing punches in here. Take care of yourself, little *scodai.*"

Wild one. That was one part of her father's reputation she'd rather not claim.

The middle of her back heated. Sure enough, when she turned, the Earther in the corner was staring at her. *Oh, hell.* At least she could set this one straight.

The Earther stood when she marched to his table. More like towered. She wasn't used to someone her age bending his neck to look at her.

"Seems you could use a friend." He pulled out a chair. "Would you like to join me?"

She raised her chin. "You've been misinformed. Not all Prism women find Earthers irresistible."

"You tell that fragging Earther garbage we don't want his kind here," a high-pitched voice shouted.

When O turned her head to see who had yelled, she heard the man's sharp, indrawn breath.

With the deliberate slowness of a dock crane, her gaze rotated back to the Earther. He stared, slack-jawed, at the jagged scar on her cheek. He cleared his throat, pulling his gaze away and reached for the mug on the table between them.

The movement drew her gaze. He had beautiful hands. Not the scarred hands of a crewman. Clean-shaven, azure eyes and healthy-looking skin. Not the insipid face of a spacer.

She wanted to spit. "I'll give you some free advice. Don't sit down. Don't finish your drink. Take your friend and run. Run back to your ship before you get hurt."

Civic duty done, she steamed for the exit, leaving the stranger in her wake.

With no idea of what she'd do tomorrow.

3

Official Montgomery Corporate Earth News,,
Twenty-three Years Ago
With the discovery of translithium on Prism, the World Board is sending an administrator to the prison planet to oversee the mining effort. The World Board will have to find a way to work around the original land grant, in which Montgomery Conglomerates gave the use of the entire planet in perpetuity to the prisoners to build their own society. What that means to you and me is that the exiles own the translithium. Maybe it's time to raise the price of their food?

Journal of Gatfield Montgomery/RETINAL SCAN REQUIRED: *I warned my father not to deed Prism to those damned exiles, but he said we'd end up with a* better deal *once they were all dead since we'd have the planet* and *a colony ship. When's that going to happen now? We should never have sent that first supply shuttle. At least the food we send them is loaded with anti-birth meds, so we don't have to worry about a second generation. Since mining translithium is so harmful to the body, I should be able to reclaim the planet in ten years. That, and my impending* *wedding to the daughter of the owner of* Thørsongud *Shipping, ought to double our stock price.*

Present Day Prism

Jericho Montgomery had made it back to his ship unbloodied the night before, despite fending off an eager prostitute on the way back to the spaceport. His longtime bodyguard handled the woman with his usual efficiency.

Beaming a genuine smile, he walked across a hand-woven carpet hauled from Earth and greeted the Administrator of Prism. "Good morning, Aunt Cornelia." The last time he'd seen her he'd been only nine. She'd visited his mother before taking the job, succeeding Cornelia's father as Prism's warden when he retired.

"I was your mother's college roommate, not her sister." She walked around her desk with outstretched arms.

He hugged her. "And her best friend for life." He stepped back. Much thinner than a person of her position would be on Earth, she had the same shimmering skin as the Prismers in the bar.

"Please don't take offense, but if this contract is important enough to Montgomery Conglomerates to warrant a six-month round trip, why would they send you rather than their Chief Negotiator?"

"Just another twenty-two-year-old Harvard postgrad looking to land a high-paying job." He chuckled before deflecting a response to his answer with a question of his own. "How do you like life on Prism? Any plans to return to Earth?"

"I've spent the last twenty years here. Life on Prism is uncomplicated. The planet is beautiful. The exiles have developed a society that needs little interference from me. The political exiles debate; the military ones train; and the convicts, well, they probably have a better life here than in prison back home. I'm in no hurry to live on Earth. It changed a lot during the five years after the war. So much poverty. So much fighting and death." She seemed to catch herself. "But tell me about you. The things that don't make the offplanet newsfeed."

"The last batch of releases included a piece on my amazing ability to sign the next music sensation, the top-rated vid series I produced, my new Bortigetti sports car. Oh, and the usual conjectures about wedding plans."

"And those plans?"

He grinned. "Highly overrated."

"The World Board reports I receive don't include much information about the individual corporations. Montgomery Conglomerates still holding on to North America?"

"Absolutely. We provide everything to everyone in our territory, from medical supplies and food to entertainment and clothing. And we have trade agreements with six of the other seven corporations to trade med-tech in exchange for food and technology research."

"So you've got enough supplies for the entire population?"

"Pretty much, but food is tight. There are occasional riots, usually incited by underground rebels that we can't locate. At least there haven't been demonstrations about the supplies sent here."

She nodded. "More than a fair trade for the translithium they receive. Siberia still a nuclear wasteland?"

"Fu-Chin Corp finished cleaning it up three years ago. Built housing and factories for resettled workers. Their profit margins made it into the black last year. They've paid for dropping that nuke."

She gave him a tight smile, but her body language told him she agreed with the majority of Earthers. If they'd had it their way, Fu-Chin would have been chopped into tiny bits and sold off to punish them for the only "tactical" strike of the global war.

He surveyed her unadorned tan shirt and pants that had never been fashionable on Earth and made a mental note to send her selections from the Montgomery Couture Collection when he returned home. Reaching to the inside pocket of his jacket, he plucked a long, velvet-covered box from his pocket and offered it to her.

"You didn't need to bring me anything. But I'm grateful." She winked and opened the lid. "Oh, my goodness. This is beautiful." She removed the necklace and held the amber pendant to the light. "I can see an insect wing."

"Let me help you fasten it." Jericho stepped behind her to secure the clasp at her neck.

"Jewelry from Earth is a real treasure. Thank you." She hugged him, then stepped back to study his face. "I see your mother's eyes and smile. You've grown up." She cleared her throat and pulled him to her again, burying her face in his shoulder. "I was so sorry to hear of her passing."

Jericho wrapped his arms around her shoulders, feeling a surprising closeness to the woman he'd seen only a handful of times in his youth. She didn't seem tough enough to be the leader of any world, let alone a prison planet. He released her and stepped away. "It's been a rough year. Sometimes I forget and touch her number on my comlink."

"Sit down and tell me why you made the long trip out here." She motioned to a leather sofa, obviously imported from Earth, since there were no animals on Prism. Except for that tiger, owned by a very interesting young woman.

The massive wooden desk, a holograph of leafy green trees, and a painted antique ceramic vase made this room a museum of Earth artifacts. He waited for her to settle on the couch before he sat. "I intend to win the shipping contract for the new translithium mine."

"The other two companies in the bidding didn't send representatives. One sent a series of sealed bids; the other will call the Joint Committee via burst laser. No one has ever sent a live negotiator." Her look could have pierced his ship's hull.

A wince threatened to crack his casual façade. He wasn't going to tell her how he'd pleaded with his father, offering way too large a cut of his future profits for the chance to visit Prism and present the shipping proposal in person. Growing up, his mother told him enough stories about the planet that he could close his eyes and picture the Great Plain, site of the two-month failed archaeological dig she'd led in search of an ancient civilization. "This contract opportunity is my graduation present from my father. When I win it, I'm out of the fashion and entertainment divisions. I'll be a VP in charge of planetary negotiations." He smiled and gave her a conspiratorial wink. "It's a sure bet to make my first billion before my next birthday." And to fund Mom's charities and continue her legacy, since his father had cut them off at her death.

"Ah, independence from the golden chains of Gatfield Montgomery." Her tone implied she knew more than she let on.

But he didn't want independence from his father. He craved the hard man's acceptance. Craved the man's love. If adding to the conglomerate's bottom line fulfilled his lifelong hunger for a genuine connection with Gatfield Montgomery, Jericho would produce the biggest damn increase the accountants had ever seen.

His mother had filled him with stories about Prism, its people and its beauty. She'd hoped he would find a way to visit the planet one day. This contract proposal seemed the perfect opportunity. He gave Cornelia his best All-American model smile. "I know my age and lack of experience could work against me. I'll deliver an offer too good to reject. I have no intention of leaving empty-handed."

"I wish I could help, but the Joint Committee has total authority over the shipping contracts. And no, I can't tell you anything about them, other than the convicts choose a representative, as do the politicos and the soldiers. In the early days, because of trust issues, the three groups settled apart. When translithium was discovered, they had to learn to work together. The mines give everyone an opportunity for more, for a better life."

Jericho didn't bring up the health problems related to extended time spent underground in a translithium mine. On Earth and in the corporation colonies, only prisoners sentenced to life—or death—worked full-time in the mines. If they survived for five years, they earned their freedom. No one had yet.

A chime sounded. Cornelia rose and stepped behind her desk to peer at an outdated monitor. "Your pilot has arrived. She's young, but she was trained by the best."

Jericho couldn't help but grin. "I'm sure there are those who say the same about me."

After a single sharp rap and the snick of the door opening, Jericho stood. Before he could turn to face his pilot, a tiger glided up to him, muscles rippling. Lips parted and nostrils flared, it inhaled his scent. He froze. He'd read somewhere that tigers attacked moving prey. He took shallower breaths.

How many damn tigers roam unleashed on this supposedly animal-free planet?

"Good morning, Administrator Schultz," a familiar female voice said behind him. "Solo, stand down."

The big cat blinked once, then sat on it haunches, assessing him. With a forced smile, Jericho turned to greet his pilot.

The girl from the bar last night. Her expression changed from confident to cautious when recognition registered in her eyes. She shot him a *so-you-want-to-make-something-of-it* glare.

The scar that looked as if some insect had burrowed round and round through her cheek was concealed by her profile. Her bare-skin complexion shimmered like a well-painted model. Her tangle of lighter than Norwegian blond, wavy hair couldn't be contained by the military-style cap perched at an angle. *This screaming, nose-breaking girl will guarantee my comfort and safety?* Only if he didn't make her angry.

Efficiency and purpose transformed her features, masking her emotions like a good negotiator. Maybe she'd make a decent pilot after all. She probably needed the work. "We've met."

Standing at military parade rest, she focused her attention on Cornelia, who put her hands on her desk and leaned forward. "Sit, O'Neill. You, too, Jericho. You've already met? When?"

They said in unison, "Last night."

He waited for the girl to sit first, but she ignored him. He sat and she perched on the edge of a chair next to the sofa. The tiger settled on the floor at her feet. A low-pitched vibration in its throat was an unsettling reminder to Jericho of the too-close-for-comfort wild animal.

Cornelia typed a quick series of keystrokes on the pad before her and sat back. "Explain yourself, Lieutenant." Her tone warned of stern consequences if she didn't like the answer.

Her name is Lieutenant? Or was there some kind of military structure to their society? This would be the perfect time to get rid of the hot-headed pilot, but something made Jericho want to bail her out. After all, she had given him good advice last night. "I know it wasn't the best idea, but after three months on my ship I wanted to see a bit of the city when we arrived. My bodyguard went with me and we ended up at a bar near the spaceport."

Eyebrow raised, Cornelia shot a knowing look at the young woman. "The Burnt Engine?"

Impossible, but the girl's back went more rigid. "Yes, ma'am. Begging the Administrator's pardon, last night I simply offered safety advice to someone I believed was an Earther crewman." The pilot turned toward him. "No offense, sir. I apologize."

Not exactly apologetic. But she looked him in the eye. Truthful.

Cornelia scanned her datascreen. "The morning report mentions a scuffle there last night. Know anything about that, O'Neill?"

"Situation normal. No report to file."

The administrator turned to Jericho. "Hmpf. How about you? Did you get to see the floor show?"

Jericho silently thanked his father for the thousands of hours spent at his father's side during meetings, and even more hours of questions and instruction afterward in reading body language. At eight-years-old he hadn't understood the necessity for his silent attendance in his father's office and boardroom, but he'd treasured the time sitting at the table in a suit that looked just like Gatfield Montgomery's. The fights between his mother and father about his "training," well, they'd driven home how to listen in silence and read a different type of body language.

His silence would put this girl in debt to him. "I saw nothing. She was kind enough to inform me of the best way to return to my ship."

The pilot was very good at hiding her feelings, but not good enough to fool him. A slight quiver in her chest betrayed her surprise at his response. Even more interesting was the fractional tilt of her head as she studied him, like a bug splayed and pinned under a dissecting microscope.

He returned her scrutiny in the length of a slow blink.

Cornelia cleared her throat. "Well, if we're all done making nicey-nice, you can get to work, Lieutenant. I have real issues to address."

His pilot jumped from the arm of the chair. "But, Ma'am, the Dockmaster is supposed to post me as off-duty for the next two weeks due to my father and training for the Battle."

What's wrong with her father? And what is this Battle?

"I've read the search team's final report. Your loss is all our loss. I'm sorry, but your father's disappearance screwed pilot schedules, to say nothing of work schedules around the supply ship arrival. I need you to stay in the rotation." She sounded like a judge delivering a death sentence. "If it's possible, you can work your training around, and into, your pilot duties."

His pilot widened her stance. "I'm sure Ensign Novakov would be a better choice for, uh, Mister, uh …"

She pulled her bottom lip between her teeth, and looked at his hands, at his feet, at his hair.

Of course she couldn't recall his name. He'd never given it.

"Montgomery." He stood and offered his hand. "Jericho Montgomery."

The tiger rose and positioned itself between them. It snarled a warning, revealing large, sharp fangs evolved to rip limbs from lesser animals. Jericho didn't move.

"Stand down, Solo." She reached for Jericho's hand, shaking it with a firm grip. He shouldn't have been surprised at her strength, but he was.

The older woman frowned and looked from one to the other. "I thought you two met last night."

"No one introduced us," the young woman said.

"Jericho is the son of Gatfield Montgomery, the richest man on Earth. His mother was my best friend." Cornelia's voice was laced with precision. And nostalgia. "Jericho, if you can overlook O'Neill's stubbornness, she really is the best pilot for your purposes. Besides her mining contacts, she is an expert in navigating the tunnels your mother discovered when she was on-planet for the archaeological dig."

His pilot looked surprised, then blanked her expression. Why didn't she want anyone to know what she was thinking?

Exploring the tunnels where his mother had hoped to find ancient artifacts was one of his personal priorities on Prism. And touring with O'Neill was going to be entertaining. "I trust your instincts, Aunt Cornelia."

"I hope your stay is productive. We'll continue our visit another time." She turned to O'Neill. "I'm sure you'll give Mr. Montgomery the assistance he needs to prepare the shipping contract he's here to negotiate, as well as show him the beauty of Prism. Except for safety and the usual security issues, he's cleared for whatever he wants to see and whomever he wants to meet. Novakov will head the escort team. He's been notified." She looked at her data screen. "I will miss your father, O'Neill. Notify the dock master of your new residence."

Had her father died? When his mother died last year he'd been nonfunctional the first weeks. He'd offer a compassionate shoulder to the proud pilot.

"Yes, ma'am. Thank you, ma'am." She inhaled a long, measured breath. On the exhale, her spine loosened as if her body were a deflating balloon. Mournful yearning peeked out from her unfocused eyes before she pulled her shoulders back and shuttered the look.

She nodded to him. "All right, Mr. Montgomery. We'll collect your survival gear and start your planetary training." She strode to the door. "Come, Solo." The tiger followed her.

If that tiger went everywhere she did, he would have to learn how to keep it happy. Maybe if he thought of Solo as a larger version of his mother's treasured Siamese cat?

Not a chance.

"She won't wait for you." Cornelia chuckled.

Jericho rushed toward the closing door. *Survival gear and training?*

4

Prism, Present Day

MONTHLY JOINT COMMITTEE MEETING, Personal Notes of Patrick Reagan

The convicts (pop. 103) re-elected their leader. I guess graft pays. Of course, Liam remains the choice of the soldiers (pop. 401) and I remain the leader of the politicos (pop. 327). Our communities remain separated by distance and walls (no wall around Convict Town yet) though there is a good deal of interaction, more between the second-gens. The Battle organization falls to Liam. Thirteen competitors have been approved for his annual equivalent of medieval jousting. Anything goes during training, from ordering special foods and supplements from Earth to special clothing, as long as the participant can pay for the requisitions. I think more politicos would sign up if there were rules to his "event," but the Battle is something all Prismers look forward to, so I'll just keep trying to convince him with subtle arguments. He was stoic when I made a special trip to the Soldier Compound to tell him we hadn't found Jocko.

O'NEILL DIDN'T WANT to be impressed by Jericho Montgomery. But after a day of lectures, drills, and physical tests, she couldn't help it.

Filthy rich Earthers were soft. A couple had made the trip to Prism thinking they could bribe their way to the translithium mines, but their bluster and credits couldn't force their way past the rules. Once a year a mine supervisor arrived for safety inspections, but with the blacked-out shuttle ride, the mines didn't give up their secret locations. The Earthers all complained incessantly and cracked under the stress of the orientation survival training and their first day exposed to the subtle vibrations of Prism's crystal fields.

But Montgomery hadn't fallen asleep in the small spaceport classroom. She hadn't had to repeat herself. He'd remembered everything she told him. Identifying dangerous crystal structures that could be unstable or could burn his skin on contact and putting on his life vest underwater hadn't fazed him. He even tested clear on his first attempt for troubleshooting a failed breathing apparatus in case of an emergency water landing. Unlike other Earthers, he never once relied on his bodyguard for help, even during the crash sim.

He and his bodyguard, Yancey, finished the sixteen-hour safety orientation in less than seven hours, a new Prism record.

A trip to Prism was expensive, even for the richest corporations on Earth, so not many made the journey. Montgomery was the youngest passenger she'd ever been assigned. Maybe his age was why he treated her differently. He'd never been rude to his employee, Yancey, even with the stress of the day's training. His behavior was a puzzle.

She'd pushed him hard and he hadn't complained. Not once. She suspected Jericho Montgomery was the fittest, smartest

Earther she'd ever encountered. He definitely was the best-looking one. Even sweaty and exhausted after just finishing the crash landing and escape sims.

Heck, she was sweaty and exhausted. But tired didn't excuse her from duty. She still had two hours of Battle conditioning and three hours of rooftop watch at home before she could roll into her rack. Thank Prism Earthers slept late.

She hoisted her backpack from a chair. "I'll escort you back to your ship. Get a good night's rest. You've earned it." She couldn't help a smirk at his tired smile. "Tomorrow morning your guards will meet you at your ship at oh-nine-hundred."

"Thank-you, Lieutenant O'Neill." Yancey remained as formal with her as he had been to his charge all day. He picked up his jacket and waited for his employer.

"None of the literature said anything about survival training." Montgomery's factual statement carried no complaint. "Or tigers." His tone lifted, like the corners of his mouth. The heir had a humorous streak. Another surprise.

"Most Earthers, the ones from the supply ships, rarely venture beyond Convict Town, so they don't have to demonstrate survival skills. They view us as untamed wild animals, but Prism is a quite effective cage. There are no indigenous animals on Prism. Transporting animals and their food is too expensive."

"Then why do you have Solo?"

She crossed her arms and held on to her elbows before swallowing with a suddenly scratchy throat. "Long story, and I'm tired."

"Okay, we'll save that for another time." He stretched and stood. "You're thorough, O'Neill. I might wish for a little less efficiency in the future."

"You shouldn't. We don't have the medical facilities you have on Earth. Prism is dangerous. If I'm hurt or killed, something I taught you today might save your life. Your guards are trained to protect you from the very real threat of abduction or worse." She slung her backpack over one shoulder and led them through the door into the rabbit-warren corridors of the docking facility.

"Add medical facilities to the list of proposal items." He spoke into the gadget he wore around his wrist.

He'd been doing that all day. A rude word hissed between her teeth. "You don't have a clue how Prism functions or what Prismers think is important."

"And enlargement of the docks." He caught up to her. "Then tell me what you think is important."

When had an Earther, a very attractive one, ever cared what a second-gen female Prismer thought? She wasn't going to fall for him or his pseudo-interest in her opinions. "What I think doesn't matter."

Her tiger walked ahead, winding on the narrow ramp, opening a path through the dockworkers going off-shift. Once the cargo ship's delivery of supplies and empty canisters for the next translithium shipment were stored, most of the dockworkers would return to their jobs at the mines. O'Neill gave a short whistle and the big cat slowed. "Solo and I have to go on our run."

"I could use a good run."

O'Neill shook her head. "Not this one." She raised a hand to stave off his protest. "I'm too tired to protect you while I train." *I'd rather be searching a grid for my father, but I have to babysit you.* "I have to stick to my training schedule."

He looked relieved. "Another time, then."

O escorted them the last hundred feet to their docking station, then stopped dead.

She'd never seen such a huge private yacht. Portholes and an aft rectangular viewing port that was larger than any window on Prism. Retractable wings. It could easily bunk a crew of twenty and just as many passengers. *Two* FTL engines.

Turning to her, Montgomery waved Yancey on. "Want to come aboard for a tour? No safety drills, I promise."

She was tempted. She wanted to see the inside of that yacht and its faster-than-light engines. But she wouldn't visit her passenger aboard his ship. When she got a rare piloting assignment from the Warden, Earthers were her clients. They weren't friends. She didn't fraternize. Corporate and World Board authorities only came to check on the mines and assess the status of the exiles. They stayed on Prism long enough to see what they wanted to see, then returned to Earth. Earthers always left Prism. Always went home. Montgomery was no different.

Why do I wish he were different from the rest?

"Another time, maybe." Solo paced around her. She dug her fingers into the fur of his neck. "It's time for our run."

"Thanks for fast-tracking our orientation so I can get out to the mine tomorrow."

"Uh, okay, then." She wasn't used to receiving thanks from Earthers. They enjoyed reminding her of her status. Hired *prisoner* help.

She watched Montgomery stride up the yacht's spacious gangway and disappear as the hatch hissed shut. She'd missed a full day of training because of him. She had to figure out a way to train daily so she didn't lose her stamina. Otherwise she'd have no choice of living arrangement except Cal or her mother and stepfather. Making that choice would have been so much easier two weeks ago, before her dad disappeared. Before Cal wanted to lead her around by a protector's imaginary, but very real, wristlock.

This next week promised to be interesting. And maybe unsettling, if the fluttery feeling in her empty stomach meant anything. No passenger had ever made her nervous before. She needed a good run. And not just because there were only nine days to the Battle.

———

SOLO DRAPED across the skimmer seat beside her, O'Neill throttled back to land on the dark rooftop of The Citadel. The tallest building on the planet, her home housed the families of all six of her father's Aussie Brigade. They'd been exiled as a group, deemed a rebellion risk for their military expertise and popularity not only in Australia but around the Earth. They'd been the most effective flight squadron in the government forces. There had been too many holograms broadcast of them helping civilians in the war zones for anyone not to recognize their faces and emblem.

Tired and upset last night, she'd forgotten about the foil packet hidden in the pocket of her dirty flight suit. Awakened by pounding on her door at daylight, she'd been afraid someone had found out about it. But it had only been her downstairs neighbor, telling her to report to the Warden's office on the double. She'd done nothing but worry about those chips during her run tonight, cutting her workout to return home.

Now the full moon lit the evening sky, and stars sparkled across the heavens like crystals scattered by a generous hand. She was exhausted after the ninety-minute run along Soldier's Beach, but not so spent that she missed the outline of another skimmer parked on the corner of the roof.

She noted the markings. Which one of her neighbors had a politico friend important enough to have personal access to a skimmer?

Powering down the engine, she popped the canopy. "On me," she told Solo, levering out of the skimmer. The tiger began growling before he landed beside the visitor's flyer. "Grumpy? We've still got three hours of watch before we go downstairs, big guy." She rumpled his fur, but he kept growling. "Maybe nothing will happen down there. Maybe they're all asleep." He padded toward the large cargo canister that held the building's water supply.

A tall figure wearing goggles stood near the opposite edge of the roof, scanning buildings in distant Convict Town. "Welcome home, O. If you need anything…"

"Thanks, Julio. I'll relieve you now."

"No one on the move. No groups of thugs wandering the streets. Cold weather must be keeping them all inside." Her father's communications officer removed the night vision gear and handed it over, along with an electronic pad for making notes that would be shared with one of Granddad's officers tomorrow. Julio gave a jerk of his chin toward the water tank. Under his breath he added, "Careful. You've got a visitor. Reagan."

When Julio disappeared through the trapdoor to the stairwell, she turned to the shadows. Cal had never visited her alone at her home, but why would Julio look worried? Was he acting like he thought he should as her protector?

If this were Cal's idea of a welcome surprise, he'd find out just how unwelcome he was at her home in the middle of the night. "Who's there?"

A short man stepped into the moonlight.

Frag. Not Cal.

Ray Reagan. His uncle. Her lying, asshole stepfather.

Not that she'd ever call the slime sucker anything that had "father" in it.

"What are you doing here?" The chill in the air couldn't make her words any colder.

He advanced. "Nice to see you, too, O." He stopped, a step too close.

Solo, still growling, positioned himself beside her. A shiver skated down her arms under her jacket. "What do you want?"

"Your mother is worried about you. She's taken to badgering me to bring her here to talk sense into that thick skull you inherited from your father." His eyes narrowed. "I'm not bringing her."

"Good. You can leave now."

He chuckled, but there was no lightness in the sound. "In ten days you *will* move to my house. I will tell you what you can and cannot do, and believe me, your life will change." He held up a hand. "Oh, you'll still be able to pilot the mining shuttle to bring in credits. For a few months anyway, while I evaluate offers."

Offers? She exhaled the breath she hadn't known she was holding.

He gave Solo a stabbing glance. "I haven't decided what to do with *that*."

"He's mine. My father gave him to me."

The man's chin lifted, even though they were the same height and he couldn't look down on her. "I have my sons to protect, and no wild animal is going to roam free in my house." One side of his mouth lifted. "But if you're a good girl, I might give you a share of the credits I get from his sale. I wonder what tiger steak will taste like."

Fire flooded her cells. She grabbed his jacket, pulling him off-balance. "I'll kill you." It would be so easy.

He shook free, brought his hand back to slap her, then glared at Solo, who stood ready to attack. He lowered his arm. "You won't have a chance. I've already arranged for your foray to the Fertile Field." He took a step back.

Good thing. She'd kneed a convict twenty-four hours ago in self-defense. Tonight it would be a pleasure to watch this fragger writhe in pain. She had no intention of visiting the Fertile Field with any one, and the sooner he understood that, the better. "You'll be frying in hell before I visit the Fertile Field."

His unhurried visual inspection made her want to scrape off her skin. "It will be interesting to watch you move when your belly is ripe with a bastard."

The only way to get pregnant on Prism was inside the boundary of the crystals that made up what the first-gens named the *Fertile Field*. It had taken them three childless years to discover it, twenty-two years ago. "Frag you to hell." She wanted to rip the smirk off his face and shove it down his throat. "Cal would never …"

He turned and walked toward his skimmer, laughing. "Who said it will be Cal?"

———

THE NEXT MORNING Jericho sat in an ancient flyer, wedged between the center console and the emergency breather apparatus. Something was off with his pilot. Her muscles were tight and there was a distractedness about her, like part of her brain was working on an insurmountable problem.

Behind the partition dividing the cockpit from the passengers, he'd taken the smaller seat. Yancey, legs cramped with knees almost to his chin, looked like he'd have problems standing. The Prismer guards who'd shared her table at the bar sat in the aft section on the floor. Up front with O'Neill, the co-pilot, Ensign Novakov, sported a crooked nose and a black eye from the altercation Jericho had witnessed. His pilot could defend herself.

O'Neill's hair wasn't the blond of his mother's when she was a girl in Norway. It was white. Pure white, like virgin snow in the fjords. The color matched every one of his guards and the co-pilot, but her wavy curls were unique. He didn't know whether white hair was a common characteristic of all the young people born on Prism or particular to those in the protection services. Maybe the trend was to strip out the natural color. He planned to find out.

The skimmer was aptly named. It skimmed mere feet above the ground. Newer, more comfortable models were used by corporation families on Earth. This one had to be the one sent twenty-three years ago for the first mine. Clear of the spaceport, O'Neill, with the tiger curled at her feet, pushed the craft to its shuddering limits.

The terrain of Prism almost made him forget his discomfort. Sunlight reflected in thousands of glittering mini-rainbows from the sheer planes of the multi-faceted crystals below. Several spiked high into the sky, like the tallest trees of Earth. In the distance, tall prisms looked like the skyscrapers at home.

But there were no vast cities on this planet. No forests or vegetation. No birds or annoying insects. Nothing at all reminiscent of Earth—except humans. How did they survive such a simple existence without collectively going insane?

The reports said that the first year, the prisoners had grown their own food in the powdery, shimmering white soil, but when they ate it their cells began to crystalize and they died. Over the years, a hundred cubic meters of Earth soil had been included with the ration shipments. That soil produced edible produce, but not nearly enough to sustain the prisoners. The corporations hadn't invested credits to research the farming problem, or why there were no animals on the planet. He made a note that it might be worth investigating.

"I have to opaque the windows for the rest of the approach to the mine. Committee policy." The archaic com system distorted O'Neill's voice.

The windows grayed and a narrow band of lights he hadn't noticed in the ceiling winked on. On the way back he'd ask her to leave the privacy partition down. He had questions. "It won't be long now, Yancey."

"I'm glad she'll be able to trade up tomorrow for a larger skimmer." His bodyguard tried to straighten his legs. "I'm not sure I can get out of this seat fast enough to save you from anything."

Jericho laughed. "Welcome to Prism luxury." He closed his eyes and mentally reviewed the extensive mine reports he'd read. Today he was Mr. Price, a mining representative from Montgomery Conglomerates. Yancey was his assistant. O'Neill had drilled into him that his true identity must never be revealed, citing threat of kidnapping or revenge murder for his grandfather's atrocities.

Atrocities? What had she been told? Definitely on his list of questions.

His goal on this visit was simple—meet the local manager, view the operation, discover methodology or machinery that would make the translithium mining operation more efficient. That meant more energy for Earth and bonuses for the miners. He reviewed possible proposals like a cardsharp organizes the suits in his hand. His task was to beat out the other two corporations bidding for the shipping contract. He had no qualms about using his advantage of being on-planet. He needed the shipping credits to secure his mother's charitable legacy. Without the huge signing bonus, he couldn't save a piece of her—her goodness, the humaneness she'd tried to spread across his world.

That first contract gave the prisoners the power to decide which corporation would receive the translithium shipping contract for a period of up to three years. The contract was so profitable for the Earth corporation that the prisoners had received many concessions in subsequent contract proposals as long as there was a guaranteed quota of the challenging-to-mine crystals. The contract was more than just a shipping contract. He'd be acting as the prisoners' purchasing, shipping, sales, and distribution agent if he won the contract. And receiving a cut at each step in the process of getting translithium into the hands of people and businesses on Earth.

The World Board was happy it no longer had to bear the expense of sending a supply ship every six months. The corporation cargo vessel brought the prisoner supplies—provided from that corporation's warehouses for even more profit—and returned with the carefully packed crates of translithium crystals, which they controlled and sold at exorbitant rates. The longer the contract, the higher the guaranteed profits. He was determined to sweeten the prisoners' pot enough to guarantee the maximum three-year deal. His mother's legacy would remain intact.

After an hour, he took a long pull from the waterspout attached by a tube to the pack on his back. O'Neill had warned that dehydration was a potential problem in the shuttle and in the extreme dry air in the mine. He couldn't take a chance that anything would dull his observations.

A couple of hours later, she slid back the privacy partition door. "Grab the overhead straps; we're going in."

Jericho glanced at Yancey, who gripped the strap above him with white-knuckled strength. Jericho held the strap the way he'd been shown and waited for the landing bounce they were warned about in their briefing. It never came.

The windows deglazed and he saw a cluster of flimsy tents and a couple of sheet-metal domed huts. The clear canopy over O'Neill slid back. She stood and climbed out of the skimmer using a metal ladder built into the side of the craft, popped open their door from the outside, and pulled out an unrailed, narrow gangway. A good plank of oak would have been sturdier.

"Welcome to Translithium Mine Number Three," she said. "Mind your head when you disembark."

She waited at the base of the short ramp with the tiger, holding two pairs of sunglasses. "Be sure to wear these at all times while outside. The reflection of the sun on the crystals could damage your retinas."

He took the glasses and decided he'd ask her later why she didn't have a pair. Maybe there were only enough for Earthers.

The four young men serving as his guard formed around Yancey and him.

A leathery-skinned man approached. "Welcome to Translithium Number Three, Mr. Price. I'm Robinson, the mine manager." He offered his hand. "Knowing 'Smooth Landing' O'Neill, I trust your ride was uneventful."

She'd put the fear of pestilence and pollution into Yancey yesterday with her talk about "hard landings" being just short of controlled crashes. She'd had some fun with them. What other hazing did she have in store?

Jericho shook the manager's outstretched hand. "Your planet's beauty hasn't been done justice on Earth. I'm looking forward to seeing everything I can and meeting as many Prismers as possible in the next ten days."

"You're onplanet for ten days?" The man looked at O'Neill for confirmation. "I've never heard of any Earther staying that long."

She stood, hands clasped behind her back. Giving nothing away. Jericho's opinion of her rose.

He gave the man a polite smile, but no information. "I'd like to see the mine now."

"You must be tired. Wouldn't you like some refreshments and a brief rest before beginning your tour?" Robinson shuffled his feet and one eye twitched.

Why is he nervous? "I'm fine. Got my water." Jericho tapped the tube on his shoulder. "Let's get on with it."

Before Robinson could react, O'Neill strode toward the mine entrance, feline at her heels. Jericho followed with his guards, leaving Yancey and the manager to catch up. "That tiger is going in the mine with us?"

The one introduced as Cal crowded next to him. "Solo goes everywhere she goes."

She handed Jericho a breather. "The mine air should be safe, but the dust can play havoc with your lungs. Put this on and let me check it."

Jericho placed the apparatus across his nose and mouth and pulled the fasteners. He touched the sunglasses.

O'Neill nodded. "You can leave them off until we're up top again." She handed the second breather to Yancey. "You're next." She watched him adjust the straps. "Not too tight."

She nodded to her friends adjusting their breathers, then pulled on her own before motioning to Robinson. "You lead the way. Solo will follow, then me, then Mr. Price and his guardians. If I see a potential problem, Mr. Yancey exits first, followed by Mr. Price and myself, then the guardians. If you're in violation of any safety codes, you'd better tell me now."

Robinson wouldn't meet her eyes. "There won't be any problems. We're compliant."

Jericho decided he'd keep an eye out anyway. He'd never visited a mine on Earth, but he knew their reputation for danger. Not that he'd know an unsafe situation if he saw it.

Robinson gave them each a pair of goggles from a rack attached to the stone wall. "The translithium veins can be very bright underground, but the tunnels are dark. Best to keep these on to protect your eyes from the extreme UVs." He didn't check their goggles before starting down the mineshaft.

It was dusty and dark. And hot. Uncirculated air held fermenting human sweat and machine oils. They walked down the steeply angled, narrow corridor long enough to make his thighs protest. The goggles amplified the dim illumination from the shimmery powder coating the tunnel. Jericho reached for his water tube and took a long drink, hoping they didn't have much farther to go. Sticky sweat glued his shirt to his back. Around the next corner he pulled up fast to keep from knocking his pilot over.

A wide vein of translithium crystals froze him in his tracks. He stared, transfixed by the beauty of the opalescent rays radiating from the crystals embedded in the rock. Bright light and heat bounced off the walls surrounding them. Young teens shuttled tools and boxes between men perspiring like waterfalls. Miners worked like surgeons with small electronic tools to free the multi-sided prisms from the matrix of stone. The radiant energy created a subsonic pulse that ran across his skin like an army of insects.

Yancey looked as uncomfortable as Jericho felt. Sweat dampened his shirt in several places. Even through the breathers, the odors of the hardworking miners mixed with the dust of disintegrated crystals and a crisp ozone-like scent. Not a healthy atmosphere for a prolonged stay. No wonder translithium miners didn't have a long life expectancy.

The exiled prisoners didn't have to work for their two meals a day. Jericho made a mental note to ask why some volunteered to work in the mine. Those incentives had to be included in his proposal.

O'Neill and her friends didn't appear to notice the discomfort, though her flight suit showed patches of dampness. She scanned the miners, nodding to ones who stopped to look at them.

"How many veins are there like this?" he asked.

"No idea," said Robinson. "When we go deeper we'll find out. From the energy signature, this is the biggest concentration of translithium we've found yet. We'll be working this mine for the rest of my life."

"How deep are we?"

"About fifty feet. Trans Two is at three hundred feet."

"How stable is the ground?"

Robinson tapped the wall beside him. "Standard Prism matrix. Looks like rock but easier to dig. Safer than your Earth mines, I'm told." He pulled out a large cloth and wiped his sweating brow. "Seen enough?"

"For now, yes." He was even more determined to win the shipping contract, after seeing the crystals that powered most of Earth's
transportation and electronics.

His pilot leaned close. "Don't eat or drink anything he offers
you in his office."

He nodded, but he wondered why she gave him the warning.
Another question for the ride back to the spaceport.

5

Handwritten *note on wall in Pilot Locker Room at Spaceport:*
Pilots/CoPilots in Rotation: 6/8
Mining Shuttles: 3
Skimmers (4+ Passenger/2 Passenger): Soldier Compound:4/7
Politico: 2/4 Convict: Ha!
Go Soldiers! Win the Battle!

"CHECK YOUR BELTS, LIFTOFF IMMINENT." O'Neill's voice carried over the rumble of the engine. Privacy screen down, she glanced back at the passengers. They appeared calmer than this morning. She hoped she didn't look as tired as they did. Upset by Ray Reagan's visit and too tired after serving her watch last night to trust herself not to lose one of the tiny chips, she'd bunched up the dirty flight suit with the foil packet unopened in its pocket and put it in the dirty clothes sack. It would be safe there until she returned. No matter how tired she was tonight, she had to examine the contents of that contraband pouch; then she could decide what to do with it.

She sighed. Her father should have been their pilot. She might have been his co-pilot. They'd worked that partnership several times. She glanced at Novy. He was well-trained. But flying with him wasn't the same as flying with her father.

The skimmer rose. A shudder told her the landing gear had retracted and locked. "I'm going to raise the privacy screen and pump extra oxygen into your compartment. You look like you need it."

"Wait," Jericho said. "Is that really necessary?"

"Even though Prism has only eighty-nine percent of Earth-normal gravity, we also have only eighty-nine percent of your oxygen concentration. The Administrator would take a dim view of my letting you pass out. It's like being at high altitude in your mountains, I'm told. You'll acclimate in a couple of days. You can use the com to ask your questions."

She checked Jericho's reflection in the mirrored read-out surface. No Earther had ever asked to leave the privacy screen down.

He glanced at Yancey. "We're in no danger of passing out. Do you have a protocol or safety issue with the screen down?"

"No, sir."

"Then leave it down. Permanently."

He didn't care that his conversations with his bodyguard weren't private? He wanted to be able to talk to her for the entire trip? "Yes, sir. But I'll still need to opaque the windows. Policy."

"Fine. And O'Neill, it's Jericho, not sir."

No Earther had ever asked her to be addressed by their given name. He didn't seem to want to lord his status over her. Were there other Earthers like him? "Yes, sir. I mean, Jericho."

"Why did you warn me not to enjoy Mr. Robinson's hospitality? Would he really have poisoned me with you and my guards there?"

She paused, considering how much to tell him. "While Prism water is safe for locals, it contains minerals that would cause you, uh, digestive concerns. The water in your packs is purified for you."

"And the food?"

He wouldn't let anything pass. He questioned everything, but not in a way that disputed her authority. Jericho confused her. Confused her perspective of Earthers. "I suspect Robinson would prefer the current company retain the shipping contract. He receives good credits from them. It would be easy to taint your food to make you sick enough to neglect your preparations."

"He believes I'll replace him?"

She nodded. "Happens every time a new corporation gets the shipping contract."

"I wouldn't have, as long as everything continued to run smoothly. I will now. I can take suggestions—even dissent—in the spirit of improving a production model, but dishonesty and disloyalty are absolute deal breakers."

Yancey spoke into his wrist device. "Pack toxin kit."

The bodyguard is efficient. Good. "I don't think anyone will try to poison you, but it probably is best that you bring your own food everywhere."

A stomach grumbled behind her.

"I'd hoped to sample some of the local food to help me adjust the rations section of my offer," Jericho said.

"Why? It's only protein bars and powders from Earth, augmented with the few fruits and vegetables we can grow. Did you see what came out of the kitchen at the Burnt Engine? Nothing as fancy as you're used to. The food your cook packed is in the port console. It's a four-hour flight to the spaceport, and the first half is opaqued. You may as well enjoy your lunch now."

She checked her vector and ran a system diagnostic while her passengers pulled food out of the compartment. Wash's enthusiastic, "Okay," signaled that her passenger had offered to share his provisions. "Novy, why don't you go get something to eat. I can handle this segment."

He cocked his head. "Later you eat?"

"Sure thing. Enjoy yourself." She waved him out of his seat.

After a few minutes, Jericho poked his head into the cockpit. "Lieutenant, would you like a sandwich?"

A sand witch? "No, thank you." It was becoming harder to class him as just *Jericho the Earther*, but she didn't have to eat his food.

"You need lunch, too."

"Actually, Prismers eat only twice a day—breakfast and dinner. We receive two proteins per day in our allotment."

"Yes, I know that. I also know you earn extra rations working a job. I've got plenty to share. How about an apple?"

Her face heated. Thank goodness he couldn't see her embarrassment. Since Ray Reagan had credits and influence as the politico supply master, she'd tasted bites of Earth foods at her mother's weekly dinners, but she'd never eaten an apple and had no idea what it was. Besides, she couldn't risk making herself sick when she was on duty. "No, thank you. I've got to be careful about what I eat because of my training."

"What exactly are you training for?"

"The Battle is a physical endurance competition. I can't risk getting sick from strange food so close to the first event."

"Is it like a triathalon? Do you swim and run?"

"Swim. Fly. And fight."

"Fight what?"

Did he never tire of asking questions? "Each other."

"What do you fly?"

"Personal skimmers. If you don't own one, you can borrow one. As long as you're pilot-qualified." He asked too many questions. She knew what the next one would be, so she answered before he asked. "My dad got his skimmer when he discovered Translith One. Cal's dad got one when he won the first Battle."

"Are the rules very strict?"

She almost laughed. *What rules?* "What do you mean?"

"On Earth, athletes have sponsors. There are rules about how the competition is conducted, what the athletes can do, the help they can accept."

"Each Battle participant can *accept* whatever help is offered. There are no rules. In fact, we're encouraged to help our favorites by sharing rations, training tips, special clothing, mechanical help with the skimmers, even giving credits so our friends can purchase goods from Earth."

She hoped he'd start eating, but he said, "I don't think there is anything in the lunch that wouldn't be nutritionally sound for training. Except the brownie. But you know your own body."

Thank goodness he didn't press the issue, because the scents behind her had Solo sitting up and sniffing. She pulled a strip of protein jerky out of her pack and gave it to him. After Reagan's threat, she knew moving in with her mother was a definite *no go.* Solo was no threat to the six-year-old twin boys her mother had with Reagan. Her half-brothers.

They were good boys, and they loved her. And her tiger. Solo let them maul him every Sunday, with nothing more than a lick of his big tongue when he wanted them to stop. He might be her bodyguard, but she wasn't going to let anything happen to the only animal on Prism.

While everyone else ate lunch, her stomach ground in uncharacteristic protest. Eating a bar wasn't an option after refusing Jericho's offer to share. If his food tasted half as good as it smelled, she understood why some Prismers were willing to pay ridiculous amounts for tiny bits of the stuff.

This morning she'd found an old single-serving packet of protein powder, used half for breakfast and saved the other half for dinner. Maybe there would be some ripe tomatoes to harvest on the roof tonight. She really had to get to the quartermaster's tomorrow for her rations.

She let her brain chew on the inconsistencies of Jericho for a bit. But in ten days he would leave, and she would already have competed in the Battle. Her training schedule had to be revamped if she wanted any chance of winning. To say nothing of time to search for her father. Madame Esmeralda had said he was alive. O would find him.

When her father had convinced her to train for the Battle, she hadn't cared so much about winning. But now, in nine days, she'd have to declare a protector and move from her home. Submitting to the will of her mother's husband–she'd never call that man her stepfather–would mean death for Solo. Winning the Battle was the only way to save them both. Unless she could come up with another plan.

———

AFTER LANDING her father's skimmer on the roof, O'Neill gave the food Jericho had pressed on her to Miguel, who was serving her duty today. The injured plane repair chief lived on the roof and in the basement of the Citadel. After a quick hug, she ducked through the rooftop trapdoor to her home on the top floor of the building and descended the stairs after Solo. She gave him his dinner stick.

She opened the door to her father's bedroom and passed through the narrow hall that connected his room, the bathroom and the rest of her home. Scooping the laundry bag up, she sat on the bed and pulled out the suit she'd worn the last night of the search. Bloodier than she remembered, it was going to take work to get the stains out. At least it wasn't her blood, or the blood of her friends.

Touching the tab of the inside pocket, her fingers fished inside for the packet. Pulling it out, she turned the small shiny package over and over, wondering how well she'd really known her father. No matter what he'd done, she couldn't imagine him as a criminal. But maybe what she was holding had gotten him killed.

Maybe he was meeting someone out there on the Great Plain about the chips. Maybe he belonged to a group of … what? Rebels? He'd been exiled as a rebel threat. She sighed. Her father cared more about Prism and Prismers than anyone she knew. He wouldn't do anything to harm anyone. She had to believe that. Or she didn't know him.

She pulled out her knife and cut the seal. The micro-thin foil packaging unrolled to reveal a dozen bubble chips in various shapes. One slipped to the floor.

Retrieving it took two attempts. Resting them all in the palm of her hand, she shook her head. What was she going to do with these?

She recognized one of the shapes. It matched the dozen hidden in her father's closet along with the reader for it. Her birthday present from her father. Her secret vice was playing holographic Earther games with him. He'd gotten her a new one. She set it carefully on his nightstand and fingered the other disks around the palm of her hand.

Fighting an impulse to fling them across the room, she closed her fingers around the bits of Earther tech. Sharp corners bit into her palm. The physical pain couldn't compare to the waves of grief pounding her heart. Jocko left her holding something she knew was important. And dangerous.

Keeping the other chips in her home wasn't smart. Especially since she would probably be moving soon. Her only option was to take them to her grandfather. Wash's dad worked for Granddad. Maybe he could figure out what they were for. The chips would be safe in the Soldier Compound, and she'd be safer with them out of her home. There'd been no word yet about why the second-gens from Convict Town had attacked her, but if the chips were mentioned, someone would come nosing around soon.

She counted the tiny bits of forbidden technology back into the foil wrapper and rolled it tight before taking it to her corner of the living room and stashing it in the inner-zipped pocket of her only clean uniform. Tomorrow morning she'd visit the quartermaster and her grandfather before reporting to the spaceport.

After she secured the packet, she looked at the strip of material that served as a door in front of where her father kept his clothes. The holographic game reader they used was in a box in his closet. She'd never wondered where it came from before. Hadn't considered that the game reader and the chips were contraband, even though they weren't lethal or addictive. Were other smuggled Earth goods hidden in his room?

Certain that he'd return home, she hadn't touched any of his things. Going through his room now would feel like he was really dead. Her fists closed tighter, nails digging into her palm.

After her mother left them, he'd spent extra time with O. He'd introduced her to the Earther hologram games. The only thing better than figuring out how to beat the machine was the time they shared together, laughing, strategizing, and celebrating when they finally completed their quest. The games gradually eased the pain from her mother's abandonment. Instead of crying herself to sleep every night, she planned strategies for the next game. Strategies that would make her father beam with pride. Or with laughter. It didn't matter which.

He'd started taking her everywhere with him, teaching her about what he did and why he loved doing it. A few years ago she realized the games were another way her father taught her to solve problems and think for herself. Amid laughter and tears, she'd learned to try options that seemed hopeless. She'd learned never to give up, even after months of losing.

Her stomach rolled. He'd had so much more to teach her. She had so much more to learn.

Brushing at a tear she hadn't known was skimming her cheek, she stood. She didn't have time to play games tonight. She didn't have time to have her heart ripped from her body. Again.

In the kitchen she removed one of three mugs from a shelf above the sink and pulled a spoon from a drawer. She unscrewed the top of a protein container and shook the rest of the powder into the bottom of the mug. She re-screwed the lid and put the empty canister in her pack. Filling the mug with water, she stirred and stirred, but not all the protein powder dissolved. Wouldn't be the first time she'd had a gritty dinner.

She stood at the sink and drank the half-ration, then washed the dirty dishes. *What would it be like to enjoy fresh food at every meal like Earthers did?*

Earthers? Her own mother prepared and ate food every day from the extensive garden in the Politico Compound. O couldn't understand that need-for-luxury existence. Couldn't understand how her mother would leave her father–and her–for Earth luxuries and food. And another man. Especially, *that* man.

That man who touched and kissed her Mommy. But her mother hadn't acted like she had when O's father had done those same things. Before. Her mother had leaned into Daddy's embrace, reached up to put her arms around his neck and kissed him, giggled when he whispered in her ear. When Ray Reagan did those things, her mother shrank away from him. Hissed at him not to touch her.

Before her mother left, O remembered her mother braiding ribbons into her hair, remembered her mother sewing dresses for her, and the two of them getting *pretty* for Daddy's return from *work*. Her mother used to grind Prism's crystals into powder for paints. The three of them painted the walls of their home, but her mother had painted scenes of Earth that looked like holographs. One, a vine laden with *grapes*, covered the wall above the kitchen sink.

Why her father had made O visit her mother once a week for dinner for the past seven years was a question he'd never answered. In the first year, every time he dressed her up for her visit, O had yelled then cried with misery about having to see her mother with *that* man. Once, her father carried her, kicking and screaming, to his skimmer. He'd looked so sad she'd never made him do that again. As a teenager she'd argued. He'd just shaken his head and handed her a jacket.

They'd flown to the Politico Compound, and he'd walked her to her mother's house from where he had to leave his skimmer. He'd waited outside while O ate. She couldn't remember her parents exchanging a single word at her mother's door. He probably hadn't even eaten a protein bar while she dined on a variety of fresh vegetables from her mother's garden.

She would have enjoyed a roasted tomato for dinner tonight. She sighed. Cal had taken her to her mother's the past two

Sundays. He'd gone in with her, sat next to her at the table, played catch with her half-brothers. Her mother had been happy to see O, even though she'd looked distressed that her ex-husband hadn't been found.

A shower and early turn-in would give her extra time in the morning to pick up her weekly rations from the Quartermaster in the Soldier Compound. She'd be close enough to run by her grand-father's to check whether he'd heard anything from Vicar, the sheriff of Convict Town, about the attackers—and to give him the chips. Granddad had sent her a message yesterday, but she needed to see him. Needed his hug, his comfort. Would his eyes be red from tears like hers were now?

But she didn't shower and hit her rack. She walked back into her father's bedroom, found the reader and sat on the bed. Exchanging the game chips was a simple process. She stored the old one in a container with the others.

She had no idea how long she'd been staring at the unlit unit in her lap when she heard a raspy voice. "Are you going to play or stare it into submission?"

She jumped to her feet. The reader thumped to the floor. Her heart jumped up her throat, blocking off words.

Her father. He was home. Her gaze jerked to the door.

He wasn't there.

"Dad?"

Nothing. But she'd heard his voice. Knew that joking tone.

I'm going crazy. She looked around the empty room, disap-pointment crushing her. Solo walked in and lay at her feet.

"Did you hear him, big guy?"

The tiger tucked his chin on his crossed paws.

Frag. I. Am. Going. Crazy. Her dinner curdled in her stomach. Did she miss her father so much that now she was imagining his voice? "Just frag me." Now she was talking to herself. Great.

Hoping that the translithium crystal that powered the reader still worked, she thumbed the power button. Across the viewscreen trailed *Save the Princess*.

"Really, Dad?" She was talking to no one. Again.

"Most popular game on Earth." His voice was stronger.

Her mouth opened and her hand covered it, without her thinking. She wasn't going crazy; she was already there.

Solo stood, looking at the door like he, too, had heard her father's voice.

She dropped the machine to the bed and strode to the other room. "This isn't funny, Dad."

He wasn't there.

She shook the curtain that was pushed back from her bed, peered under the bed, pulled the chairs out from the table, opened the cupboards under the kitchen counter.

And found no one.

Looking around the room for somewhere else to search, she bit her lip. "Okay, you've had your fun. Come on out." The last words wobbled. What was she thinking? He'd never play such a cruel joke on her. "Come out, Dad." Her voice cracked. "Please." Tears ran down her cheeks and fell off her chin onto her uniform.

After sobbing a few minutes—maybe it was longer—she decided someone was playing a trick on her. Pissed, she stomped into the bedroom, stopping to hold back the curtain in front of her father's clothes. She leaned in and waved her arm in the small space, brushing her fingers against the walls. Nothing.

Whoever was playing this cruel trick must be hiding under his bed. "So help me, I'm going to drag you to the roof and push you over the side, you fragger." Angry as she was, her voice didn't shake now. Ready to pull the culprit out, she dropped to her stomach and looked under the bed.

No one. Not a sound.

She sat cross-legged on the floor and stared at Solo. "I'm insane, big guy. To think that you heard him, too…"

She climbed onto the bed and sat cross-legged, elbows on her knees and forehead resting in her palms. No more tears could be wrung from her devastated heart. To imagine that her father had returned home and then find nothing? Sleep wasn't going to be an option anytime soon.

Maybe the new game would connect her with the good times shared with her father. "I'd be up anyway, Solo, if I were serving night watch. I'll play for a while; then it's laundry and a shower. At least I can be clean, even if I am crazy."

He curled on the floor, nose tucked into his fur, but his eyes were open and riveted on her.

She inserted the chip and activated the holo projection. Nothing happened. Maybe it was defective. She checked the charge indicator, which registered over half-full. She tried again.

A hologram of a beautiful young woman with flowing blond hair stared forlornly at an empty plate on a wooden table. "Feel free to jump in anytime, Dad." The tone of her words was distant, biting. She read the minimal directions to begin the game aloud, like she used to. Did she really expect him to comment on them, like usual?

Much later, she fell asleep remembering the excitement of discovering a strategy with her dad to begin a new game. At least she could dream about a time filled with joy.

6

P ersonal Log of Liam Neill: Exile Year 25, Day 191

The second gen who led the ambush on O wouldn't give up intel, though I know Vicar used extreme physical force. But when my squad arrived this morning to transfer the prisoner to us for further questioning, he was dead. His throat had been slit during the night. Vicar didn't do it; he wants the man behind the attack as much as I do. Which leaves me to wonder who put out the grab-and-run on O. And why.

AT SUNRISE, a tired O'Neill flew her dad's skimmer to the Soldier Compound. Leaving the master sergeant's office, she put both arms through the straps and hoisted her supply pack to her back, grunt-soldier style. Two weeks of rations, forty protein bars and a can of powder, not only filled her pack but weighed it down. "Thanks, Sergeant Robinson."

Cal didn't have to pick up his rations. They were delivered to his family's house. The politicos operated by different rules, but every person on Prism was allotted only two meals per day by the Earth decree that established the planet as a prison world. If you wanted more to eat, you had to work to pay for it or grow it yourself.

O'Neill did both.

She walked beside the long stone wall that enclosed the military compound until she reached the school where she'd learned to read. And fight. And fly. Following Solo, she ducked through the too-short door.

"I could have knocked you on your ass if I'd wanted to, O'Neill."

She faced the gruff-voiced man and bowed. The face of the first-gen soldier bore a white vertical scar from the middle of his right eyebrow to the middle of his cheek. His sewn-closed eyelid covered an empty socket. "And I would have deserved it, Master Chief." She shifted her pack. "My grandfather around?" Solo walked toward the bowl of water that was always left full for him.

The bent old man jerked the long crystal staff he held toward a door. "Ward room."

"Thanks."

"You coming to train?"

"No. I have to pilot an Earther for the next nine days."

A low whistle escaped the man's thin lips. "Long time on-planet. Makes training for the Battle hard, don't it?"

"Yes, but I'm squeezing in my conditioning. Maybe I can swing by tonight for some melee practice." *Seven days to the Battle. Better make time.* She walked toward the wardroom door. Solo caught up with her when she knocked on the metal.

"Enter."

She cracked the door intending to peek in, but Solo nudged the door open and walked through.

No instructors shared the space so early in the morning. Teachers and students would arrive within the hour. Her grandfather rose from a long table strewn with papers. "I've missed you."

She stepped into her his embrace. Within the circle of his strong arms she could relax, knowing he loved her no matter what she did or said. She'd never thought of him as *old* before Jericho's comment yesterday, but there was no denying his age-grayed hair. "I've missed you, too."

O hugged him, smelling the sweet strawberries he'd eaten for breakfast on his breath. "I haven't been around because I've been piloting an Earther."

"I heard."

She didn't tell him about the new holo game—or hearing her father's voice. Twice. She should ask a medic to check her hearing. But she couldn't risk Granddad thinking she was going crazy. It was scary enough for her to think that. Going crazy would make the need for a real protector immediate. She'd overheard first gen stories about *combat exhaustion*. Maybe she could use that as an excuse.

He released her and motioned to the bench on the other side of the table. "Your father used to do that when he wanted to talk about something. Problems with the Earther or at the Citadel? Maybe with your training?" He sat, pushed back from the table and rested his elbow on the back of his chair.

She wished she'd practiced a speech to give him. "Something else. Something bigger."

"Will I need to interrogate you to find out?"

He always knew how to make her grin. "No." *Why am I so hesitant to tell him now?* "I don't want to declare a protector."

"Say again." He pulled his elbow to his side and sat forward.

"I don't want to declare a protector after the Battle. And I want to keep living at the Citadel."

He eyed her as if she were an overheated translith crystal. "First Law of Prism. Can't help you there. Maybe Cal can move in with you, if he'll sign the Citadel agreement. Does he want the soldier life?"

"I'm, uh, not sure I want to marry Cal. Maybe later, but since Dad, uh, crashed, Cal's been acting like he has the right to order me around." She shrugged. "I don't like it."

He started to laugh then stopped. "Cal's just being protective.

He's learning a new skill. Give him time. Meanwhile, you can live with your mother."

"And her jerk of a husband?" The pitch and volume of her voice rose with each word.

"Throttle back, O. We may not be happy at your mother's choice of another man, but he's kept her safe and she's happy."

She stood and slapped the table. "He's a monster. When my mother isn't in the room he says mean, hateful things about Dad. About you. About me. You haven't had to endure a weekly meal with him for almost eight years. Sometimes he frightens me so much that I puke up my dinner when I walk outside to go home with Daddy." Her stomach clenched so hard the sharp pain made her gasp.

Her grandfather gave her a hard look. "Sit down, Lieutenant."

Considering whether to walk out the door or follow his order, she recognized she had no choice. He was a male and, since her father wasn't there, it was Granddad's right to tell her what to do in his home. *Fragging First Law.* How had she never seen it before? *Felt* it before? She plopped back on the bench. "I might kill him if I live there. Can't *you* be my protector?"

"I gave you an order that you fought to obey. You'd have to live here. You'd have a different set of responsibilities, be assigned new duties. Is that what you want?"

She hung her head. "No. I just what everything to stay the same."

"O, I'm old enough to be able to tell you this with more than a general's authority. Everything in life changes. Nothing stays the same. That's what makes life interesting."

"Well, an interesting life is a curse." She lifted her chin.

"Indeed. A very old culture on Earth would curse someone by wishing them a life during interesting times." He scooted forward, put both forearms on the table and winked at her. "You're a smart girl. You'll figure something out. In the meantime, I suggest you talk with Warden Schultz. She may have some ideas for you, being a female herself."

"Granddad." Her exaggerated exhale sounded just like the hundreds she remembered through the years sitting at this table, talking to him about her childhood frustrations.

"Have you neglected your PT?"

"A little. But I've been running after hours, and today I'm swimming at Soldier Beach."

"Get out there now and train with the Chief." He sounded like her father.

The foil packet with the bubble chips was in her pocket. He'd know what to do with it. Since he was alone, she could give it to him without fear that someone would see the contraband. "I have another problem."

"Oh?"

Maybe she shouldn't have said anything. What if her father had been dealing in contraband all these years without her grandfather's knowledge? Besides, giving him the chips would put him at risk. She should have buried the fragging packet on the mountain behind the Citadel.

"That bad?"

She jerked to attention.

"O?" Brows together, he examined her face.

Had her mind wandered that long? "Two days ago, in the spaceport, an Earther from the supply shuttle asked me if I was Jocko Neill's daughter. He said he recognized me because of Solo."

Her grandfather frowned. "Go on."

She reached into her pocket to retrieve the torn packet with the bubble chips inside. "He gave me this." She extended her open palm.

Granddad used his thumb and forefinger to grasp the foil and shook the chips into his other palm. His jaw set in harsh lines. "Have you shown this to anyone else?"

"No."

"Told anyone about it?"

"No."

"Did you put them in that game player of your father's?"

She gulped. He knew about that? "Yes, sir. They were unreadable."

The chips disappeared inside of her grandfather's closed fist. "You never saw these. You never saw the Earther who gave them to you. You will never speak about this to me or anyone else. Do you understand?"

He was serious. Dead. Serious. General. Voice. She'd never been in the same room when she'd overheard that voice. Not once had he used that tone with her. "Yes, sir."

"If someone *ever* asks you about them, come to me on the double."

"Yes, sir."

He didn't seem surprised by the chips, so he probably knew about them. Knew how dangerous it would be for her to be connected to them. But how did he know? How long had her father been receiving contraband tech from Earth? She knew better than to ask what they were for, even though she would have given the rations she'd picked up earlier to find out.

Granddad cleared his throat. He only did that when he didn't want to answer a question. "There's something you need to know. The convict second gens who attacked you had no idea who put the Grab-and-Run on you."

When she opened her mouth to ask how he knew about the attack, he shook his head.

"Vicar told me. He questioned the leader, but before he got any intel, someone slit the fragger's throat. You're smart enough to know this, but do not go anywhere without a couple of soldiers. At night I'd prefer you had a whole squad around you. Be ready for anything, anytime."

Holy global war. "Do you think that attack was to get the chips?" What were her dad and grandfather smuggling?

"I don't think so. As far as my intel goes, no one knew about them. But we don't know what we don't know. Be smart. Be careful." He drew in a long breath. "And don't mention them again."

"I won't." But what were her dad and granddad smuggling—
and why? Those chips were not just spare skimmer parts. She
thought of Wash's dad. Hadn't he been exiled for something to do
with computers? And chips? "Thanks for having my six,
Granddad."

"Always. You're a good girl, O." He took a deep breath and
smiled. "Now get out there and let the Chief kick that too-skinny
butt of yours around."

She knew a dismissal when she heard one. "Yes, sir." After the
workout she'd have to return home for a shower before reporting
to the spaceport to pick up Jericho. "Come, Solo."

"Don't forget your pack."

How did he know she'd seen the Quartermaster before coming
here? Her pack sat on the floor outside what passed for Granddad's
office.

She walked into the drill room and saw a few of her former
female classmates in a corner. "Hi, ladies."

"Hello, O. It's good to see you for morning practice." Hansen
smiled. She'd always been friendly. "I've missed our daily swapping of," she rolled her eyes, "intel."

The four of them had bonded when Hansen first *discovered*
boys. Together they'd wondered about everything from male
anatomy to the nitty-gritty of sex. And when one of them learned
something first-, or second-, or third-hand, a whisper-filled
briefing had been called.

Eva hugged O. She'd used powdered crystals to dye her hair
alternating stripes of green and blue. "I'm so sorry about your dad.
Will you be moving here?"

"No. I'm staying at the Citadel." She hoped. If she convinced
one of her father's squad to be her protector, she could stay there
permanently.

Dona, the only one of them who worked full-time as a miner,
shook her head. "Who's going to be your protector?"

"Nobody." If she had her way.

The girls laughed. Hansen, with a checkerboard pattern of

bright yellow and white hair, shrugged. "First Law. You have to declare a protector. Even if you don't want to."

"Well, I'm not going to. The Joint Committee can throw me in the brig."

"Not likely, since your grandfather is on the committee." Dona smiled. "What about Cal? Are you playing hard to get?"

O wasn't close enough to them to spill her personal business. "No. I'm not going to be forced into declaring for anyone."

Eva nodded. "I wish I had your guts. And fighting skill."

"Hey, I bested half the circle last week at one-on-one practice." Hansen looked thoughtful. "You know, my mom was a fighter pilot during the Earth War. But she's only flown a skimmer here. I wonder if that's because my dad didn't want her flying a mining shuttle."

Dona pointed across the room at the clump of second-gen guys. "Maybe I don't need a protector either. I don't like the idea of one of those jerks telling me what I can and can't do. I'm smarter than any of them."

"Let's talk to the other girls before our duty time today." Eva sounded excited.

The gong rang. They all turned to the raised dais and bowed, ready for the daily workout.

———

ABOARD HIS FATHER'S YACHT, *Freedom,* Jericho sat at his desk, re-arranging notations about the shipping proposal on the holo projection. The smallest compensation necessary to close the deal would give him the greatest profit, but if he bid too low, he'd lose the contract. Concessions and payments to the three-prisoner council who would decide which proposal was accepted would be the tricky part. In what form, and how large, did their bribe need to be?

He was willing to cut his personal profit, but his first major contract had to command his father's respect. He could hear

Gatfield Montgomery's investors-meeting voice. *Give them a taste of what they want most. Then make them give you what you want.*

The com unit chimed, followed by his captain's announcement. "Burst laser connection enabled, sir."

"Thank you." Jericho switched on the vid screen.

His father sat behind a steel and glass desk in the penthouse corporate office, sipping his favorite scotch from a centuries-old crystal highball glass. He raised the glass in salute. "Jericho."

Burst laser communication was expensive, even for Montgomery Conglomerates. Jericho wouldn't win points squandering precious minutes on social niceties. "I went to Translithium Three yesterday."

"Find anything useful?"

"My pilot thinks the manager supports one of our competitors."

"Prismers are fools. What do you think?"

He allowed himself a deep breath to stave off a confrontation. "I think she's right."

"She? Does she have the experience and contacts you need to close the deal?"

"I don't know yet. She's young."

"How young?

"Younger than me."

"Screw her, then get a different pilot."

The muscles in Jericho's throat tightened. He fought for a no-contest expression. "She's a good pilot, Sir."

"You need a man with connections to that Citizen Council or whatever they call it. Fuck her, pay her off, then get rid of her."

Jericho's fingers pressed deep into the padded armrests of his chair. Gatfield Montgomery treated women that way, but his mother had taught him the value of all human beings. She'd scorned the way his father wasted the potential of his female employees by looking at them only as objects to warm his bed. His father's lack of respect for his mother's sensibilities disgusted Jericho. "She knew the mine manager wasn't trustworthy."

"She must be ugly if you don't want to screw her." He swirled the amber liquid in his glass.

His father only cared about his reputation as a man who slept with the most gorgeous women in the world—and the more, the better. Jericho suspected that the stories and risqué pictures in the tabloids were planted by one of Gatfield's PR men. "No, she's rather attractive." *In spite of the scar on her cheek.* He hadn't given a lot of thought to O'Neill's scar. He'd been more attracted by her straight-up answers and honesty. When it came to speaking her mind, his feisty pilot didn't seem to care if he had a bazillion credits. She didn't tailor her response to his bank account. He liked that about her.

His father shifted in his chair, a clear signal his argument would shift as well. "See if you can meet her family. Use their connections. What's her name?"

"O'Neill."

The crystal tumbler thudded to his desk, followed by too long a pause before he responded. "O'Neill, not Neill?"

Strange reaction for a man who didn't bother to find out the name of his current sexual plaything. "Right."

An extended exhale. His father picked up his drink. "If the girl can't get the job done, use that friend of your mother's. What's her name, Schultz? As the administrator, she's plugged into the workings of the damn locals."

"Cornelia picked my pilot. She said O'Neill was the best."

His father's upper lip curled into a leer. "Did she say what your pilot was best at?"

Jericho couldn't control the heat that rose from his neck.

On Jericho's fourteenth birthday, he'd been summoned to his father's suite of rooms on the other end of the enormous estate. A naked woman sprawled across his father's bed. Jericho was told to sit on a chair and watch what his father did to the woman. Afterward, his father sat on the chair and shouted lewd advice as the prostitute deflowered his son. The memory brought stomach acid to his throat.

Gatfield's humorless chuckle prickled the skin on Jericho's arms. "You need to do whatever is necessary to get that shipping contract. That fucker Jocko Neill discovered the first translithium mine, wouldn't tell anyone where it was, then got concessions for additional rations, Earth soil and seedlings, building supplies, and other goods from the money-hungry San Andes Conglomerate in return for a guaranteed quota of translithium crystals. The World Board screwed up when they didn't build a prison with cells and guards rather than an exile society. We have warehouses of expired protein inventory to offload on Prism. I want a monopoly on the next three years of translithium shipments so we have control of the distribution. We're going to reclaim that planet."

Reclaim the planet? Didn't he mean reclaim the shipping contract?

His father made no secret that he hated the very existence of Prism. But without Prism's translithium, there would be far less fuel for global transportation, for industry, for space travel.

That would mean trouble for all the corporations on Earth, because without energy, there were more jobless, starving masses, and unrest. The trouble was, Montgomery Conglomerates couldn't go in and steal it from the Prismers. That would start a war with the other corporations. "Yes, sir. I won't let you down."

Gatfield Montgomery downed the rest of his scotch. "See that you don't. It would be a damn shame to waste your high-priced education on fashion and entertainment for the rest of your life."

The screen went black.

Take care of yourself, son. I love you. Ha. Jericho knew better than to expect words he'd never heard from his father. So why did it still sting?

No wonder his mother had made a separate life for herself, even though she'd lived at the Montgomery estate. Her charity work had been a constant source of irritation to his father. She'd stood up to his rage-filled yelling and curses over it. But he'd never divorced her, even though he made no secret of the women who rotated through his bed. Probably wasn't willing to hand over any portion of his fortune in a settlement. She'd stayed because of Jericho, because Gatfield Montgomery would never have given up his heir, and she wouldn't give up her son.

Jericho rubbed a palm across his face and stood. He enjoyed the entertainment division, but the thought of one more season of models and runway shows made his vision blur. He had to get that shipping contract. He crossed to the connecting door and pressed the keypad. A ball of fluff bounded in and rubbed against his leg.

"Hey, Mitzi. Sorry, but I didn't want the old man to see you." He picked up his mother's cat and petted her. If he'd left the cat behind, his father would have discarded her, just as he'd done to everything of his wife's after she died.

Other than the fact that the animal belonged to his mother, Jericho hadn't cared much for the feline, but he'd grown to enjoy her company on this trip. He paced the cabin with her in his arms, accepting her calming purrs. When she fidgeted, he placed her in her bed and brushed at the cat hair stuck to his clothing.

Sitting at his desk, he activated the holo pad to rework proposal details. First, he needed to learn about the leaders of Convict Town, the Soldier Compound, and the Politico Compound, since they would decide who won the contract. Apparently the exiles had stayed with their own groups after landing on Prism, though he wondered about Convict Town. Only politicians and military leaders had been exiled. Maybe cast-out criminals from the original two groups had built Convict Town. Second, he needed to find out what the miners craved so he could include those items in his proposal. It would take insider help to gather data and set up meetings.

He could demand the information and O'Neill would have to oblige, but he'd rather gain her willing support. But how? From his observations, her well-deserved confidence came from more than just piloting skill. Today he'd find out more about her loyalties, strengths and weaknesses. And this training for the Battle. He was very interested in what she needed.

Her constant companion, the tiger, could provide an opening to discuss life on Prism. How did she come to be in possession of the only animal on the planet? How did she learn to fly?

A single rap at the door surprised him. He waved his hand at the sensor and the door recessed into the wall, revealing Mattie—cook, housekeeper, and wife of the captain of *Freedom*.

"Your pilot has arrived and is waiting on the dock, Mr. Montgomery."

He stood and rounded the desk. "Thank you, Mattie." There was a flutter of something deep inside at the prospect of seeing O'Neill. Probably just excitement at finally putting together the details of his proposal.

The middle-aged woman took a step aside. She held out a light-weight short coat. "Jamie thought you might need this."

He accepted the jacket, draping it over his arm. "Thank him for me. I'm lucky the two of you agreed to accompany me on this long journey."

She harrumphed. "How could we refuse your father?" Then she winked. "Or the bonus he offered? Now, get along with you."

Jericho chuckled. His father's standard negotiating ploy: offer what amounted to pennies to him but a fortune to his help to get what he wanted. It worked.

"We'll be back for dinner. I'm going to invite the pilot, so if you'd make something special?" He didn't wait for her answer before he stepped on the gangway.

O'Neill stood with her tiger at the dock end of the ramp.

"Where's Yancey?" he asked.

"Inspecting the runabout.*" Her tone screamed, *Yancey is crazy.* She inhaled deeply, like a cobra rising to strike, then jerked a finger over her shoulder. "I'm sorry, but we need to cross to another docking corridor. You won't need any Prism guards other than me today."

He followed her. The spaceport seemed to be the only safe haven for Earthers on the planet. A short walk on the docks didn't bother him, but most of his friends would balk at the idea. Earth's privileged mega-rich travelers expected a level of sycophancy in their employees. He hadn't seen the tiniest bit of that trait in his pilot. Maybe Prism bred that out of its prisoner settlers.

When people found out he was making the trip to Prism, several voiced an interest in going somewhere *new*. Building a resort might turn a profit. A huge profit. But if he were to open Prism to tourists through luxury liner flights, the pilots and guards would need extensive re-training to meet Montgomery Travel's standards for client treatment. He made a note to gather additional research when he returned to Earth.

She halted beside a highly polished skimmer large enough to have its own real gangway. "This is it." She led the way up the ramp. "Full restroom aft, with a pull-down showerhead. Galley here amidships. Your lunch, snacks, and drinks have already been stowed."

There were four seats in the passenger cabin, arranged in two facing rows with plenty of legroom. She motioned to the small doorway forward. "Separate pilot compartment for your complete privacy." She touched a switch on an armrest. "Intercom system to communicate with me. Check before you release your safety restraint, to be sure we're not approaching an area with air currents."

Yancey emerged from the restroom. "Everything looks fine, sir."

"Thank you, Yancey. And thank-you, O'Neill, for snagging this luxury ride. We were pretty cramped yesterday." He heard movement in the pilot compartment. "Is Solo already up front?"

O'Neill looked at the deck.

She's hiding something.

"Co-pilot. Today you'll take a hike through the Crystal Forest in the Mountains. You'll stop for lunch at Soldier Beach on the return trip. You aren't allowed to swim in the ocean because of the crystals and strong currents. Most Prismers aren't. It's S.O.P. But you can enjoy the crystals on the shore. If you find a broken crystal you like, you can take it home." She looked everywhere but at him.

"S.O.P?" he asked, hoping she'd decide to tell him what she was trying to hide.

She met his gaze. "Standard Operating Procedure."

"Uh-huh." Something was bothering her, and she wasn't good at hiding that fact. He craned his head forward. "Can I meet the co-pilot?"

Her eyes widened. "You want to talk to Ensign Novakov?"

So it was the same one as before. "Sure, why not? If he's going to occupy Solo's seat..."

"Oh, Solo is still going with us." Her chin jutted forward. "Ensign Novakov, could you come aft, please?"

The man ducked through the cockpit door then straightened. His blackened eye had lost a little of its puffiness. "Da?"

Jericho offered his hand. "You're O'Neill's backup. I'm surprised you're willing to sit next to her all day without your friends around."

Novakoff shook Jericho's hand and chuckled. "At work, she is picture of good conduct. Da?" He looked at her for confirmation.

She gave him a sharp nod. "Don't you need to verify our flight plan with the dockmaster?"

Why was she out of sorts?

Hand thumping his chest, Novakov said, "Back to number two chair for me," and ducked through the cockpit door.

She stepped toward the cockpit. "If you sit and fasten your safety harnesses, we'll get started."

He stood beside his seat. "Two things, first, if I might."

"Yes?" She frowned.

"If there is a time during our flight, and it doesn't breach security protocol, I would like to ride up front with you."

"Why?"

"I have some questions to ask you to help put together my contract offer. I need more facts, and your opinions and insight will help me make an offer fair for both sides."

Her lips pursed like she'd bitten a sour lemon candy from Earth. "From the Crystal Forest to the beach you don't have to be in blackout. Certain areas of Prism are blacked out to all passengers to keep flight patterns secure. You can ask Novy for information. I'll tell him to cooperate. What's your second question?"

He smiled. If she agreed to his second request, he had his *in*. "If it would be more comfortable to have Solo ride back here with us, I'd enjoy spending time with a tiger. They're rare on Earth. And no one's pets."

"There's plenty of room for Solo up front." She paused, then sighed. "I'll think about it."

"Thanks. I appreciate that. There won't be any problems." He sat and buckled his harness. "Ready, Yancey?"

F rom the personal log of Liam Neill: Exile Year 25, Day 193

If Jocko's alive and I ever get my hands on him, I'm going to bloody his face for putting O in danger. She arrived at the compound this morning with the data chips from our Earther contact. Thank goodness she had the good sense not to tell anyone about them. Thack Washington says the first chip looks like the usual news, but the conglomerate media continues to paint a darker picture of us, saying the pittance they send us twice a year takes away from Earth's needy. There was a mention that the translithium quota was not met in the last shipment. Lying fraggers. One article suggested sending a mercenary army here. Thack is decoding the encrypted messages from our friends around Earth. Looks like we need to speed up our preparations.

IT TOOK them two hours to fly to the Crystal Forest, over a flat plain scattered with identical white crystals no taller than a man. The monotony of the landscape encouraged Jericho to add new details to his contract offer.

After landing, O'Neill conferred with her co-pilot, then sprinted away, Solo beside her. Apparently some parts of Prism, those far from Convict Town, were not so dangerous. Good to know for potential tourism, if the planet held sights worth the trip. A small but steady tourism trade would substantially up his profit. Corporation owners would pay for bragging rights to a vacation others could never take. Like *Freedom*, their yachts had cryo-pods for deep sleep during long trips through space. Would the Joint Committee approve of renovation to the spaceport if Mongomery Conglomerates footed the bill?

Novakov walked to Jericho and Yancey. "O'Neill runs to train for Battle. I am your guide through forest. No problems here." He trotted down a path of shimmering powdered crystal dust woven between the natural crystal structures. Jericho followed, but Yancey trailed, capturing holographic images for a Montgomery promo about Jericho on Prism. Even if he didn't win the shipping bid, footage of him on Prism could be used to sell anything. His image was well-known and trusted on Earth. His father had been careful to keep Jericho separate from any of the uglier, unpleasant side of corporate dealings.

Random wispy clouds streaked the blue sky above. Not the straight patterns of the chem trails of the air tankers on Earth that seeded clouds, released pharmaceuticals, and delivered nutrients to barren land.

He followed Novakov through the narrow opening between two monolith formations resembling giant jeweled trees. Sunlight through the faceted prisms presented ever-changing colors dancing around them. Jericho slowed to rotate and take in a beauty he'd never experienced. "What is this Battle that O'Neill is training for?"

Novakov whistled. "Is competition begun by first gen military leaders."

"Who pays for it?"

"Everyone here. Shipping contract. Not my area of..." Novakov shrugged. "Expert?"

"Expertise. If I land the shipping contract, I'll return in six months. I'd like to know more about life on-planet."

"Much happens here that never reaches Earth."

Jericho hadn't thought about the lack of news about Prism. He'd follow up with his pilot on that later. "Tell me about O'Neill."

Novakov's back tensed, but he kept leading the way through straight-sided brown crystals that tapered into dark green spikes with small green prisms dangling high above. In the breeze the leaflike prisms struck together with a tinkling bell-like quality. *Why don't they shatter?*

If there were secrets on Prism, he needed to know them before he offered a contract. Unknowns could add huge costs on his end, but if he gained O'Neill's trust, he hoped she'd share potential problems with him. He tried a different tactic. "Why is the Battle so important to her?"

Whatever had tightened his guide's back muscles melted. The Battle and his pilot weren't off-limits for conversation. "This is her first Battle. Chance to win boon is objective."

"Boon?"

"Winner asks for boon from community. Or supplies to be ordered from Earth. Warden approves request for Earth goods. Joint Committee approves request for boon. Is powerful reason to train and then suffer through pain of Battle."

"Tell me about this Battle."

"First gen military leaders started Battle to give purpose for all to train and work together. Is athletic competition with military..." He rotated his hand from his wrist. "Twist?"

"Yes. How's that?"

At the sound of Yancey's approach Novakov stopped and pointed down the trail. "This is largest crystal tree in forest. Is twelve meters tall and over five meters in circumference."

Jericho nodded. "Yancey, you all right?"

The man rounded a bend in the trail. "Yes, sir. Getting some good holos. Do you need me?"

"No, I'm fine." He looked at Novakov and lowered his voice. "I want to know more about the Battle."

"Da. But good time for water stop, in and out." The guide took a long pull from the tube looping around from his back. "You okay if I step away for leak?"

"Sure. Is it okay for me to do the same?"

"Is fine." He stepped off the path. "Careful not to touch, uh, man parts on crystals. May burn sensitive skin."

"Thanks for the warning." Jericho took a step in the opposite direction toward a small *tree* and relieved himself.

When finished, they returned to the trail.

Novakov tapped the water bladder on his back. "You drink?"

"Going to right now." Jericho flipped the tab of his water tube. The water had been warmed by his body heat but quenched his thirst. He checked his watch. They'd been hiking more than an hour. "When do we head back to the skimmer?"

"Trail circles to landing. We are more than halfway."

Yancey rounded the curved path. He peered up at the shimmering crystals. "Wow, this is a big one."

Jericho knelt and looked up, then posed for some pictures. "Make sure you get it from all angles. We've got another hour or so on this trail. You okay with us going ahead?"

"Yes, sir."

"By the way, if you take a leak, be sure not to let your jewels touch the crystals."

"Copy that." Yancey lay on his back, positioning the holo-cam.

Novakov strode down the trail.

"What does the Battle consist of?" Jericho noticed small blue grass-like crystals growing nearby.

"Full day competition. Three events. My father says like old Earth Olympics. Swimming, flying and melee this year—all combatants fight together on field. Cal coaches O'Neill since her father disappeared."

Jericho nodded. "Sounds tough." No wonder she was angry about interrupting her training schedule. Maybe he should offer the holo program in *Freedom*'s gym. He needed her savvy for his contract offer, and he wasn't going to win her over by screwing her chances for winning the Battle.

"Are all the girls on Prism like her?" The question escaped before Jericho realized he'd thought it out loud. He would have cringed if Novakov hadn't started laughing.

"Thanks be to all snow on Siberian plain, no. She is, uh, out of ordinary."

"Meaning?"

Novakov halted and turned to face him, without his easy smile. His eyes squinted as if his whole body had tightened. "After kidnapping, O'Neill not same laughing, happy girl."

"She was kidnapped?"

Novakoff spat. "Earthers."

"Stench and pollution! Why?" Who would have been so bold as to try that? And why capture a little girl? But then, parents in many corporate areas of Earth sold their children into what they were promised would be a better life.

Novakoff's lips thinned. "Her father off exploring so she was easy target. Earthers hid her in tunnels, attached wristlock and metal wire through cheek to tether her to rock." He poked a finger deep into his cheek. "They wanted location of translithium mine."

Electricity shot through him like he'd put his foot on a live current. "Good God. The scar..." He clamped his teeth together to stem the wave of nausea that slammed his gut. Why kidnap a child? If he could, he'd find out who had been so ruthless and take them to the World Board.

"She yanked out wire and escaped. Jocko found her on Great Plain."

Brave. Independent. His impression in Cornelia's office had been correct. "What happened to the kidnappers?"

"We think her father finds them. Three Earthers at mine entrance. Throats slit."

"Was it reported? What did the Earth authorities do?"

Novakoff spat. "Da. Nothing. But her father finds Number Two

Mine on that trip. He demands tiger with protein rations for life as his finder's prize."

"O'Neill's father discovered Translithium Number Two? He owns the mine?"

"*Da* and *nyet*. All own mine. No, that is not right. Jocko say share mine, share labor. Mine no good to just him. He finds mine Number One also, with Cal's father. He works for better life for us."

"And Solo is the only animal on Prism?"

"*Da*. O'Neill says she is zookeeper of smallest menagerie in galaxy." He grinned and touched his side. "Girl has funny ribs."

Jericho smiled. Questions cascaded through his mind, but Yancey joined them.

Novakoff checked his watch. "We jog to ship now. She worries if we be late."

Jericho took a sip of water and settled into an easy pace, jogging between the two men responsible for his safety.

Since her father had discovered the translithium mines, would a corporation have sent undercover agents to kidnap or kill him a few weeks ago? Why now? Would another corporation target Jericho if he got the shipping deal?

Now he understood why O'Neill was so hard on him. Prism was not safe.

For anyone.

———

O'NEILL RETURNED to the skimmer before the three men, giving her time to complete the pre-flight checks. Sweaty from the heat and exertion, she was debating taking a quick shower when Solo looked toward the Crystal Forest and sniffed the air. Seconds later Novakov led the Earthers out of the clusters of spires. She slapped the gangway control and felt the shudder of the mechanism lowering the ramp.

Rising from the pilot seat, she ducked through the cockpit door and walked to the access port to pop the hatch. They sprinted toward the skimmer in formation, Jericho in the middle. She frowned. He had no protection from the side angles. She scanned the little group's left and right flanks.

Once the entire Prism population knew the son of Gatfield Montgomery was on-planet, some fool might try to kidnap him. She needed to have a private conversation with Yancey to see how he dealt with this possibility on Earth.

Novy stopped at the bottom of the ramp, allowing Jericho to board first.

"Those formations were amazing. The wind whistling through the forest could have been a modernesque symphony." There was a sheen to the Earther's skin and his shirt was damp in spots, but he wasn't gasping for breath after the run to the shuttle. "The sun made the crystals glitter like jewels. Do artisans here set the crystals in jewelry?" His tone was filled with childlike wonder.

"We have no metal for baubles, and there are too many crystals on Prism for them to be valuable. Translithium, that's different."

"I'm sure there would be a market for them on Earth."

"Scoop up a bucketful and take them home. A woman in Convict Town makes jewelry, but it's not considered *valuable*; it's only for decoration." She stepped aside and motioned to the small restroom in the rear of the skimmer. "You'll have plenty of time for a shower before we get to the beach." She looked at Novy. "How far did you run?"

"From Grandpa's Tree."

She couldn't help sneaking another look at Jericho. He was in damn good shape for a run that distance. When he pulled his shirt off, her breath caught. Muscles rippled across his back, and when he turned, his chest and abdomen appeared as hard as the sculptures in the pictures of Earth museums.

What the frag was she thinking? *Seven days before the Battle and this is what you're concentrating on? Being distracted by Jericho equals having to move in with Mother—and Ray Reagan.* She forced herself to turn away. "Your housekeeper provided a couple of changes of clothes for each of you in the aft closet. I'll keep the bumps to a minimum."

"Thanks." Jericho ducked into the bathroom.

His bodyguard stepped through the hatch. Yancey's shirt looked like an old-fashioned water-catcher cloth. He could have wrung it out and had a whole glass of sweat to purify into drinking water.

She nodded to Novy. "Let's get to work, Ensign."

He secured the gangway then followed her to the cockpit behind Solo. They lifted as soon as he strapped in.

Jericho stuck his head through the cockpit door fifteen minutes later, asking if he could "ride up front."

Before O'Neill could say no, Novy unsnapped his safety harness and stood. What had happened today that made Novy like the Earther? She needed to have a talk with him to remind him that, as pilot, she made the decisions. Not that she needed a co-pilot on this hop.

"Thanks, Novakov. Can I call you Novy?"

"Your wish." Novy sidled around Jericho, ducked into the passenger compartment, and closed the door.

Jericho settled into the co-pilot seat and patted Solo before snapping his safety harness.

"Do you know how to fly a skimmer?" she asked.

"No. I don't even drive."

"Drive?"

"A car. A four-wheeled Earth vehicle that rolls on the ground."

"Doesn't sound very efficient to me."

"It's an old form of transportation. Requires upkeep of roads, but it's handy for short trips in the city or between neighbors. Of course, our vehicles are armored and we travel in convoys. There are a lot of disgruntled citizens at home."

It sounded like Earth was no safer than Prism. "Hang on, the currents can be tricky here, and I don't want Yancey to fall if he's still in the shower."

She increased her altitude and concentrated on skirting a vibra-

tional current above the flat plain below. The swirling clash of
surface wind near the ground would have shaken loose every rivet
in the skimmer.

Jericho took advantage of the higher perspective, twisting in
his seat for the best views of the variegated green crystal landscape
climbing the rolling hills.

"If you look in that direction," she pointed, "you can make out
the blue of the ocean."

"This is a beautiful world." His words sounded like a prayer.
"I'm beginning to see why my mother fell in love with this planet."

A chill scraped across her jacket-covered arms. She swallowed.
"Your mother fell in love with Prism?"

"She was an archaeologist before she married my father. Even
though the expedition didn't find artifacts from an ancient civilization here, she told me stories about the planet. And the people she
met. She had a pilot who showed her the crystal forest and the
caves. Sometimes I think that if she hadn't been married to my
father, she would have found a way to return to Prism."

Had her father known Jericho's mother? After all, he'd discovered the alien-looking tunnels under the Great Plains, and the
Warden had sent Dad's sketches and the rocks with strange markings back to Earth. Dad had talked about the excitement
surrounding the arrival of the group of archaeologists from Earth in
the days when Prismers still held boiling fury in their guts for
Earthers. "Too bad they didn't find anything." She would have
given anything to be able to ask her father more about the dig.
How many times would she want to be able to ask for his advice?
Her stomach tightened and she flexed her fingers into a fist.

"Life would probably be very different here if they had. You'd
have a settlement of *dirt diggers*, as my mother called her friends.
More support from Earth..." He chuckled. "And I may not have
been born."

She glanced at him. "Why do you think that?"

"My father missed my mother the eight months she was gone.

So much so that as soon as she returned, he whisked her off for a second honeymoon. And here I am."

"Lucky you." She wanted to ask him if Earthers needed a fertile field to make babies, but the properties of the crystal fields weren't discussed with offworlders. Her father told her that the corporations started the war because they didn't want the governments to control what they did to the land or the pollution they caused.

If Earthers knew details about the Fertile Field or the Healing Field, Prism could be overrun with people who would care even less for her planet than they did for their own. Those crystals were alive with energy, and broken off pieces couldn't heal the body or help make babies. The first gens had tried that decades ago.

After a few minutes of silence, she flipped the intercom switch. "Status check."

Novy stopped whistling. "No bounce in Current Alley. Sad your passengers get no thrills."

"I like it that way." She switched off the intercom.

"You're a good pilot." Jericho seemed sincere. "You watch me as if I were your child. The mine manager called you Smooth Landing. You're very serious about your job."

She snorted. "Serious doesn't guarantee safety."

"I think you'd take it personally if I got hurt on Prism."

His words hit her like a fist in her chest, right above her heart. More than her pride would be hurt if any of her passengers were injured. She rubbed the spot. "No one gets hurt on my watch." Her father had instilled that command responsibility, drilling it deep into her heart every time they worked together.

"So I've heard."

"You've been asking about me?"

"No. Just listening."

"If you've got questions, go ahead and ask. If I'm not performing to your needs, you have to tell me. I'm no psychic."

He uncapped his water tube and took a long swallow. He

replaced the cap. "Your father discovered Translithium Number Two. Why didn't you tell me?"

"It was a long time ago. How is that relevant to my being your pilot?"

"The discovery of that mine should have changed your life."

A long-suffering sigh escaped her lips. "It did." But she wasn't going to tell him about how she was kidnapped while her father was finding that mine, how her mother deserted them a month later, how the Healing Field hadn't been able to erase the scar that knotted her inner cheek so, that with every swipe of her tongue, she remembered her childhood terror.

"Tell me how. Did your father have to supervise the mine?"

For all his study, he knew nothing of Prism economics. "No. The mines allow us to work. Having a job means an extra meal every day and credits to order supplies—like work boots, better clothing, specialties like hydroponic equipment and plants—from Earth. The administrator coordinates the miner schedules, assigns the shuttle pilots, and orders mining supplies and extra rations. Workers receive credits, which they can spend by turning in requisition requests to the leader of their group. My RR's go to an assistant to the leader of the soldiers."

"No bank or planetary system to store your credits? Administrator Schultz is not involved?"

"No. I'm responsible to track my own."

"What if someone makes a mistake?"

"The leader of the group settles it."

The Earther looked like he was going to make a comment, but decided against it. "Want to tell me more about your life here?"

"Not while I'm on duty."

"Then sometime when you're not on duty."

Not going to happen. "I don't fraternize with Earthers." *I could make an exception for Jericho.* Where had that come from?

"Why not?"

She flipped the autopilot switch and swiveled her seat to face Jericho's confident smile. He was used to getting what he wanted.

"The few Earthers who come to Prism, are here for the short term. They never come back. I'm sure you recognize a personal investment with no chance of return."

"But it's not prohibited?"

Why was he pushing her? Couldn't he tell she wasn't interested? "As long as the Earther doesn't complain."

He nodded, but the set of his mouth said he wasn't in agreement. "To strengthen my proposal, I need to know how life, jobs, leisure time, credits work here. I'm serious about winning this shipping contract, and I need the best offer to do that. If you don't want to *fraternize*, can you arrange a meeting with someone who will talk to me?"

Clouds skittered overhead. A shadow moved across the cockpit dials. If Jericho wanted information, the Warden had said it was her job to supply it. "The registered mine locator has the right to request a boon from the corporation that receives the shipping contract. The usual boon request is for Earth goods for use or barter. Clothing, food, electronics, liquor, building supplies, even a personal skimmer. The amount is determined by the nature of the goods and the space available on the next cargo shipment. A yearly supply drop can be requested."

"Your father requested Solo?"

Cheeks heating, she struggled to remain detached from the past. Novy was going to pay for giving no-need-to-know information to Jericho. "I think you already know the answer to that."

He covered her hand with his. The concern in his eyes stopped her from pulling back. The only person who looked at her exactly like that was her father. Not that Cal, her friends, even her mother, didn't study her with worry at times. But their looks were tinged with judgment and a desire for her to be what they wanted her to be.

"Sometime I'd like to hear about your kidnapping if you're willing to share the story with me." He squeezed her hand gently.

Her brain froze. So did her body. She couldn't pull her hand away. But she wouldn't talk with an Earther about something she tried to forget.

He smiled. "I have a lot to learn about life on Prism and not much time to do it. I'd appreciate any help you're willing to give me."

The door opened and Novakov entered the cockpit. "Is almost time for to darken windows." He stared at her seat facing Jericho and her hand in his and ducked his head. "Excuse interruption."

O jerked her hand back, swiveled forward and flicked the autopilot off. "I'm sorry, Mr. Montgomery, but you'll have to return to the passenger compartment. Policy. Ensign Novakov and I have to discuss need-to-know parameters."

Novy's cheeks pinked. No more from that source of information, and O'Neill made sure the Earther knew it.

Mr. Montgomery. That wouldn't give her the distance she needed to forget what made this Earther so different from all the others. He valued her opinion. He treated her as an equal. He cared.

Precious few days until the Battle. I can't afford to lose my focus.

While the men switched places without disturbing the sleeping Solo, O tried to settle the fluttery feeling in her throat. This Earther should have come with a special gyroscope to keep her world oriented in the right direction. Whatever that course was, it couldn't include Jericho Montgomery.

8

E
arth, Present Day
        Journal of Gatfield Montgomery/RETINAL
SCAN REQUIRED:

*Twenty-five years ago we shipped those military and govern-
ment losers to PRISM, and we're still dealing with the leftover
agitators. The damn rebels are getting reckless. Yesterday they
used a missile to take out our air tanker releasing a bio-trial over
New Philly. Not a deadly new disease, but an uncomfortable one
that we've made the antidote for and can race in to cure the population of the city. We'll look like their saviors. Now we have to pick
a new target and divert one of the other tankers. Private conversations with other corporate heads have convinced me there is a
global underground. Looks like it may be time to move up the
timetable to take back Prism. That will divert the attention of the
masses.*

IN THE PASSENGER COMPARTMENT, Jericho sat, snapped his safety
harness, and closed his eyes. He didn't want to talk to Yancey. He
wanted to replay what had just happened with O'Neill.

When he'd reached out to her in a gesture of concern, he'd expected her to pull back. She hadn't. But she froze like an ice princess when her co-pilot intruded.

He could feel the trace tingle of her fingers. So much life in that hand. Like the vibrational currents on Prism that he'd read about but not yet experienced. He rubbed his palms together. Maybe the Prism-born had altered DNA.

He opened his eyes to Yancey's concerned look. "I'm fine."

Yancey's raised eyebrow said *nice try*.

A light bump signaled the skimmer was down. She must have let her co-pilot land.

Novy entered the cabin, opened the hatch, extended the gangway and left the skimmer without a word.

O'Neill ducked through the cockpit door and stood, leaning against it. "Welcome to Soldier's Beach, gentlemen. I'll bring your lunch in a moment. You can enjoy it at your leisure and beachcomb for crystals if you'd like. You'll notice a difference between Earth sand and Prism sand. I'm told Prism sand has the consistency of your sugar. Swimming is strictly off limits to Earthers. There are rogue waves and dangerous crystals and currents in the water. Most Prismers only wade in to their knees.

"Wear your sunshields at all times to protect against the sun's reflection. If you have questions, Novakov will be happy to answer them. You'll have a little more than an hour here."

Yancey rose.

Jericho fumbled with his harness. "Yancey, why don't you take the lunch? I'll be out soon."

Yancey took the bags from the storage cooler and exited the skimmer.

Jericho stood and took a step toward her. "Are you staying inside?"

"No, I'm going for a training swim."

The little skimmer shook, boots pounding up the gangway.

Novy rushed past them. "Incoming. Single ship."

"On it." She looked at Jericho. "Get Yancey inside."

She darted into the cockpit as Yancey scrambled through the hatch.

Crap. Are we being attacked?

He felt the tremor in the hull from the gangway retracting. Novy secured the hatch and moved to an aft locker. He opened it and passed Yancey an old-fashioned missile launcher like one Jericho had seen in a historic weapons museum.

O'Neill shouted. "Single ship on approach to Soldier Beach. Identify yourself. Repeat, identify. You are not flightplan approved for this location."

The speaker hissed static for several seconds.

She repeated her order. More static. She yelled some numbers at Novy and powered up the engine.

More static and a hiss. "Relax, O. It's Cal. I tried to ID, but this snafu radio fritzed."

"Stand down, Novy," she called over her shoulder, shutting down the engine. "It's Cal." She turned toward the passenger compartment and gave Novy a hand signal that looked like a variation on an obscene Earth one. Her jaw was set in that stubborn angle Jericho remembered from the bar. She swiveled and returned her attention to the radio. "Frag you, Cal. You nearly crystalized my blood. You'll be fined if anyone finds out you made this unauthorized hop. What are you doing here?"

More static on the radio before, "I know you're going to train, and I don't want you swimming alone. I'm off today, so I'm your lifeguard. And training coach if you've forgiven me."

A tap on his shoulder forced Jericho's attention away from the radio conversation.

Yancey held a blanket. "Shall we go outside for lunch, sir?"

Jericho wanted to hear O'Neill's response but reluctantly followed his bodyguard.

The sand glistened like tiny diamonds, shooting rainbows of dancing light into the air. Near the water, small clear crystals poked through the fine translucent sand. At the tide's edge crystals grew in clumps standing two feet above the water's surface. The water was clear, clean. In the space between the crystals, waves lapped on the sand like a hungry child licking sugar off a plate. Occasionally a large wave crashed against the shore, creating a long divot in the shimmering sand. "Yancey, did you bring the holo gear? I want to get some shots of this beach." *And our pilot swimming.*

He'd helicoptered over a fish-fouled oil-covered shore on Earth, but that was the closest he'd ever been to a shoreline. No one swam in the polluted oceans at home. But he'd been on the swim team, in an indoor pool, during high school. Maybe Cornelia would let him break the rules so he could swim here.

A very small skimmer landed nearby. Its canopy slid back and Cal climbed out. After a quick survey of the beach, he strode toward their skimmer. The guy didn't lack confidence.

Jericho hadn't paid a lot of attention to Cal and the other guards during the day at the mine. They'd stayed at the back of the shuttle, talking to each other in hushed voices. Except when he'd given them lunch. After what Novy told him today, Jericho would pay a lot more attention to Cal.

O'Neill walked down the gangway, towel in hand, heading for the surf. She'd changed clothes.

Jericho watched her, surveying long, trim legs from her ankles to her mid-thigh khaki shorts. Rubbery-looking slip-ons and a worn white tee-shirt completed her outfit. If she stayed on her trajectory, she'd beat Cal to the water.

Cal changed course to intercept her. He shouted for her to wait, but she ignored him. He jogged to catch her.

O'Neill pulled the tee over her head and slid out of her shorts. Underneath she wore a serviceable bright yellow swimsuit cut like samples in the company's fashion museum. It did amazing things for her body. *Truly amazing.* He made a mental note to sketch the suit when he returned to *Freedom* and to tell the company designers to study the old fashions.

She folded her shorts and placed them on the towel she'd dropped to the sand. She pointed at Jericho. "Stay with Novy.

Don't go in the water." She walked into the surf. Solo leapt into a wave behind her.

Cal ran. "Wait for me!"

O'Neill disappeared beneath another cresting wave.

"Damn stubborn girl." Cal stripped off his shirt and followed her into the water, wearing cut-off shorts and shoes of the same gel-like material.

Novakov walked up behind Jericho. "He is going to have interesting life."

"Why's that?" Jericho scanned the water for O'Neill.

"My older brother has a new wife who will not listen to him. Cal and O'Neill are much same."

Jericho's gut rammed his heart. "Cal and O'Neill are married?"

"No. Poor, frustrated Cal. O'Neill is skittish like Earth donkey."

"Donkeys are extinct. It's horse. Skittish like a horse."

"Four-legged Earth animal. All extinct here, except Solo." He laughed. "O'Neill wants same freedom, same life as always. This cannot be. Her father dead. She must surrender control of her life to a new protector, man who keeps her safe. She must raise family. Cal is best match for her."

No mention of love. At least his mother had loved his father when she married him. What had that gotten her but a life of solitary privilege?

They strolled up a hill where they could observe the swimmers. Cal had managed to catch O'Neill, stopping her for an arm waving, apparent shouting match before she swam away toward the horizon, leaving the poor guy to plow through the waves after her.

"You are big star of games on Earth, yes?" The co-pilot's easy smile hid something.

"If you mean high school and college sports. Montgomery Conglomerates used photos and footage of me in numerous ad campaigns, but I wasn't a big star." When the Russian's brow creased, he added, "No professional teams tried to recruit me."

"Cal and Washington saw interview after you won award." He

shrugged. "We get one news holo with every shipment to show good life on Earth."

He'd won awards and been interviewed so many times they blurred together. His father took advantage of every opportunity to put his heir in the news. Still, he'd like to see one of the holo programs. It was probably as carefully edited as was every program shown to the public.

Novy's jaw worked side to side. "Cal said Earth ladies drip off you like sweat."

Jericho choked off a snort. "Not exactly. They just want to be seen with me. They're hoping for something more."

It was the Russian's turn to chuckle. "*Da*. You give them more?"

"Not if I can help it." Thank goodness they'd reached the picnic spot. "Here we are." He hoped his tone ended the conversation.

They settled on the blanket Yancey had spread and enjoyed a lunch of roast beef with spicy mustard on croissants, mango with pineapple salad, and frosted brownies while monitoring their pilot's swim. Novy hadn't worried about Jericho's explanations about the food. He'd attacked everything with enthusiasm that would make his cook preen. Jericho handed Novy a soda.

The guide rolled the package to activate the instant-cool feature then popped the tab. He guzzled the contents as if he'd not already downed two packages. "Flavored bubble water from Earth." He sighed. "One of my favorite luxuries. Thank you for feeding me."

"You're welcome." Sending the Russian a case of the stuff could be a good investment. Besides, Jericho liked the guy. "Does she enjoy soda as much as you do?"

"I doubt. Have never seen her use any Earth thing. Except general rations."

O'Neill disliked the luxuries he could offer her. How would he win her support?

Jericho ate his sandwich without tasting it.

O'NEILL STOPPED PULLING water at the turnaround point. She'd half grown up in the water, swimming at this beach with her mother and father before she could walk. But long-distance swimming wasn't Cal's strength. Every time he'd tried to talk to her, she'd stroked faster.

Even Solo had trouble matching her anger-fed pace. Chin raised out of the water, he paddled behind her. She slowed.

Cal pulled abreast, breathing hard. They treaded water together in silence until he could speak. "You aren't really thinking of finding a new coach for the Battle, are you?"

"No."

"You're not quitting, are you?"

If the ocean water hadn't been lapping at her chin, she would have opened her mouth in disbelief. "I'm out here training, aren't I?"

He swiped at the dripping lock of hair in his eyes. "I'm a fool. In more ways than one." He reached for her hand. "When you said you would find a new coach I couldn't think of anything but somebody else training you. It drove me crazy, picturing another guy's arms hugging you after a workout or touching you if you got hurt." Water dripped down his forehead and he swiped at it. "You winning the Battle will make starting our life together easier, but if you don't, I don't care. All I want is to get married and live with you."

She couldn't look him in the eye, so she stared at the horizon.

"O, the Battle is prime important. Now that your father is dead you can't wait to declare me as your protector."

"He's not dead." The words ground between her teeth. "Wash's mother told me Dad isn't dead." She shrugged off Cal's arm when he tried to wrap it around her shoulder.

"Yeah, well, Wash's mother may tell fortunes, but you know better than to get your hopes up on what her cards say. Even your dad couldn't survive this long on the Great Plain without provisions."

The minerals in the water weren't the cause of her eyes stinging. She ducked underwater, then surfaced, smoothing her hair back. "Slower pace on the way back?"

Cal's hands bracketed her waist and he pulled her nearer. She let him.

"O, babe, I can't imagine what I'd do if I'd lost my father." He kissed her forehead. "You don't have to worry about anything. I will take care of you."

She wasn't ready to declare anyone as her protector. Not even Cal. But she didn't want to fight with him in the middle of the ocean. "You always have."

His arms wrapped around her and their legs intertwined. They'd done this underwater dance before, but this time O tensed. She tried to relax. With one arm supporting her back and the other her neck, Cal kissed her. The slow kicks of their legs became even slower as their bodies melded together.

Nothing. Her father had told her his heart sang every time he'd kissed her mother. Her heart had never raced at Cal's touch or sung when he'd started stealing kisses years ago. Perhaps her heart just didn't sing. She'd never kissed another second gen, so she had no comparison. Maybe she should ask Novy to kiss her.

Cal groaned. Right before they sank under the water.

They broke apart and bobbed to the surface, sputtering. Laughing.

"You are dangerous to my health, woman." He reached for her, kissed her hard and let her go. "I love you, O. Whatever it takes, I'll make you happy." His hand tapped her butt under the water. "Race you back to the beach." He swam away from her, kicking water up around her.

He loves me. She watched him. She'd loved him since she'd been old enough to toddle along behind him. But she didn't love him like he loved her. Could that change?

He does love you.

"Dad? Where are you?"

You don't have to shout. I'm right here, in the air next to you, above the water.

She saw a circle of sunlight shimmering on the water near her. The surface of the water seemed to be trying to bubble up in a some kind of a fairy dance. She'd never seen anything like it before.

You'd better start moving or he's going to beat you back to the beach. I'll try talk to you tonight, but I have to return to my body now to renew my energy reserves.

"Don't leave, Dad." The shimmering circle was gone. Why couldn't he have talked to her when Cal was with her? If Cal heard her father, she'd know she wasn't crazy. She wanted to swim around the area and look for other perfect patches of sunlight.

She thought about her father. Had she just talked to his ghost? Would he be able to talk to her tonight?

She'd given Cal such a head start that he might beat her back. But not without a fight. She stroked hard for the beach.

———

THOUGH HE'D TRIED to appear disinterested in the swimmers, Jericho had positioned himself to watch them. They spent a long time treading water very close together. How close together he couldn't tell without distance goggles, and he didn't want to ask Novakov for the case.

Cal swam toward the beach, O'Neill trailing. She dug her arms deep into the water and fast-kicked as if she hadn't already swum a few kilometers.

Yancey and Novy repacked the hamper, stowing the extra food and trash, while Jericho watched O'Neill's long strokes draw her nearer to the beach. Cal's steady style kept him a little ahead, but she'd changed her approach and had a shorter angle to the shore.

"I'm going down to the water," Jericho said.

Novy straightened. "Do not go in ocean. Strict rule."

"No problem." Jericho loped down the hill, reaching the sand when O'Neill walked out of the water. He stooped to retrieve her towel. "Impressive." He didn't know whether the word came to him because of her swimming prowess or her body. He held out the dingy, rough cloth.

When she reached for the material, he saw the glitter of a small golden O on her wrist.

"Thanks." Her response was distracted.

Solo clambered out of the water nearby and gave a mighty shake. Droplets sprayed Jericho.

Breathing hard, O'Neill dried her hair. After a quick look over her shoulder she said, "I'll see you in the skimmer." She sprinted like something was chasing her. Solo loped behind.

Cal emerged from the water. "O, wait!" He looked like he was going to take off after her, but with a shake of his head, he bent to pick up his shirt instead.

"That was quite a workout. How long is your route?" Jericho looked for a tattoo on Cal's wrist but saw none.

Cal watched O'Neill jog to the skimmer. "We only did one round trip, about three thousand meters. Usually we do two trips. Record is four."

Food hamper in hand, Yancey veered toward the skimmer.

Novy approached them.

Cal buttoned his shirt. "Let's have some fun," he whispered, giving Jericho a conspiratorial wink as his friend closed the distance. "Sorry, Novy. She's pissed at me for showing up. And at you for telling me she'd be here. Not going to be pleasant in the cockpit for the return."

Novakoff rubbed his bruised, crooked nose. "How much pissed?"

Cal smiled. "Not enough to break that ugly thing again." He looked at Jericho and shrugged. "No worries for you."

Jericho returned the grin. "I wasn't worried."

The two friends looked like they were going to shake hands, but they grabbed each other's wrists.

"Safe return," Cal said.

"You, as well," Novy replied.

Cal pointed at Jericho before heading toward his skimmer. "I'll be seeing you again."

"We go into tiger den." Novakov slumped toward the gangway. "Do not mean Solo."

Jericho laughed.

She waited for them at the top of the steps. "Novy, you ride with Yancey. Jericho has some questions he wants answered on the turnaround." She nodded at Jericho. "You're riding up front with me."

She wasn't pissed.

In fact, she winked at him.

9

EARTH: Present Day
    Journal   of   Gatfield   Montgomery/RETINAL
    SCAN REQUIRED:

*I should skin every one of those scientists and boil them alive.
The third set of geosynchronous satellites was deployed above that
fucking planet last week. Unlike the first two sets, we're getting
signals. The satellites work, but they're sending back crap. Instead
of being able to map the surface, we can't even use the heat-
seeking capability to locate one of the prisoners. My scientists talk
about the frequencies of the crystals jamming signals. I couldn't
see the damned spaceport, the biggest building on the planet. And
pinpointing the translithium mines? Not a chance. Jocko Neill put
in safeguards that my bribes haven't been able to get around for
twenty-four years. I need the location of those mines. And by God,
whatever I have to do, I'm getting them.*

O'NEILL LISTENED to the pitch of the engine and checked the
instrument panel. Situation optimal. Cal thought everything was
back to normal with them after the swim. He couldn't, or wouldn't,

understand her need for independence, no matter what her argument. In his mind, they belonged together and sooner was better. If felt to her like he was taking advantage of the urgency of her situation. His not considering her perspective, her feelings, her need for more time, drained her.

She should relax and see what questions her passenger had. Thoughtful of him to bring her share of lunch to the cockpit for the return flight, but she never ate in the air. "Thanks for stowing the extra food in my pack."

"Sure you wouldn't like a soda?"

"No, thank you." Some rare treat shared with a visitor might make her forget her hatred of all things Earth. Clothing and hygiene products were helpful, but she could make do without them if she had to. Without protein bars and powders from that planet, she couldn't survive.

Jericho cleared his throat. "Novy sure likes soda. Doesn't seem to matter what flavor."

"Novy likes anything he can eat or drink. You had questions?"

"What do you think the Joint Committee members want from the new shipping contract?"

"What they always want. More rations. Ways to produce food on planet. Equipment and electronics. Building materials. Earth products to make life easier here."

"Why don't you grow your own food?"

"Hydroponically, we can. And we collect our own, uh," she looked away from him, "uh, body waste as a nutrient source for containers. It works, to a point."

"The original colony was supplied with farm equipment and seeds. What happened?"

Did he really not know? "Your research didn't tell you?"

"The official history states that the prisoners refused to grow their own food. But I'd like to hear what really happened from you."

"Fragging corporations." She wanted to let loose with a string of expletives but swallowed her Neill temper. "My grandfather told me about the beautiful plants and fruits the first gens grew."

"First gens?"

"The original prisoners. My grandfather and my dad are both first gens, like everyone who arrived on the cryoship twenty-five years ago. I'm second gen because I was born on Prism."

"Your grandfather is still alive?" The disbelief in his tone surprised her.

"Yes. He said that when people started eating Earth plants grown in Prism soil, they got sick. He burned his crops, but lots of people wouldn't. The more people ate, the sicker they became. Our medics said they died because their organs crystalized. Between the fighting for what supplies didn't get slagged and those poisonous crops, almost sixty percent of the first gens died before the first supply ship arrived. That doesn't include the suicides."

Jericho's brows furrowed. "Slagged? Suicides?"

"The captain of the colony ship offloaded the first six-months of supplies into two jumbled heaps the size of small mountains. When he lifted for Earth, he angled the engines at one heap and melted all the metal containers together, destroying the contents. Luckily, most of the food was in the untouched heap, or no one would have survived until the next delivery day."

"Shit." He made the word sound more disgusting than it was. "There is no record of that on Earth. The captain should have been up on charges for his negligence."

As if the corporations cared. "I'll bet a lot of things that happened in the early years here—heck, even now—have never been reported on Earth."

Jericho angled to face her. His gaze searched for answers in her eyes. "Would your grandfather be willing to talk to me?"

She wanted to say no. She wanted to lie. She couldn't.

Her grandfather was one of the three members of the committee who would award the shipping contract. How could it be that Jericho Montgomery didn't know that?

She shook her head. "Maybe. I'll ask him when I see him."

He nodded. "Thank you. At the beach I noticed the golden O on your wrist. Is it a tattoo?"

"Yes. The first babies were often stolen by the convicts, so parents made sure their children could be identified."

"Are they all gold?"

"No. My mother was a chemist on Earth. She blended the ink for mine." As a child she'd cherished that special golden ink. Now it was a constant reminder of her mother's betrayal.

"Cal doesn't have one."

She grinned. "Not on his wrist."

He held up his hands. "Not asking how you know that."

She would have told him about the blue outline of the Earth state he was named for on the bottom of Cal's right foot, but a knock on the bulkhead door interrupted. Novy called, "O, you mean to run along shoreline whole trip?"

Crap. She should have turned inland before now. She hadn't been paying attention to the flight plan.

"I'm sorry, Jericho. You'll have to return to the passenger compartment now. Novy needs to get back to work."

"I'd like to ask your mother questions about a first gen's requirements for a fair contract proposal."

Of all the first gens he could talk to, why did he want to question her mother? O knew her mother would love the chance to entertain an Earther in her home, and Jericho would make an excellent buffer between her and her dickwad stepfather the next time she had to go to dinner. "I'll ask her and let you know."

He stood and squeezed around Novy, heading for the passenger compartment. She caught the wink he gave her co-pilot.

———

AFTER RETURNING Jericho to his ship, O'Neill flew Novy to the Soldier Compound and made what she hoped would be a quick stop to relay Jericho's request for a meeting to her grandfather.

After she asked to speak with him, he'd cleared the soldiers out of his office. This wasn't going to be as fast as she'd hoped.

"Thanks for seeing me, Granddad. I have a problem. Actually, two problems."

He raised his chin. "First one?"

"The Earther wants to meet you."

"Why?"

"He's here to negotiate the shipping contract for Translithium Three, but he doesn't know you have a say in that. He didn't ask to meet you until I told him about the slagheap. He seemed genuinely upset about what that pilot did. He says he wants to talk to first-gens about the beginning years. I don't know why, but he wants to meet my mother."

"Are you going to take him to Sunday dinner?"

"Yes. I think it will make everyone happy."

"Good camouflage for you, too, to hide from Reagan."

She stared at a crack in the flooring. "Yes, sir."

"Your Earther came all the way here to negotiate the shipping contract. Are you sure he doesn't want to talk to me because I'm Liam Neill?"

"He's not my Earther." She would have propped her hands on her hips if she were younger. "I don't think he knows you're on the committee. His intel isn't always reliable."

His pursed lips quirked up. "Or he's acting dumb. Gatfield Montgomery's son must be smart like the proverbial fox. Cornelia probably briefed him."

Her grandfather's smile faded and the furrows in his forehead deepened. "His grandfather, Perseus Montgomery, owned Montgomery Arms and Shipping, the major agitator for the global war. His corporation wasn't a conglomerate at the time. He was a minor player then."

"Warden Schultz said something about Montgomery Conglomerates, and his father being the richest man on Earth. I thought it was an exaggeration."

Her grandfather rested his elbows on the table, clasping his hands. "If he is the grandson of Perseus Montgomery, he may be looking for answers to long-buried questions. And I may get some answers from him. Bring your Earther to morning practice tomorrow."

Long-buried questions? About what? And how could Jericho have answers to any of Granddad's questions? "I told you, he is not *my* Earther."

He chuckled. "Good thing you weren't born into a politico family with that face. And it's a really good thing your father never taught you to play poker."

"Why would you want to talk to a rich, spoiled Earther?"

"Someday he's going to run Montgomery Conglomerates. It would be good for Prism to have a powerful ally on Earth. Do you know his mother owns half of Thørsongud Shipping, the company that made the cryo-ship that brought the first gens here?"

"She died recently."

He looked away. "Then he owns her shares now. I'll have tea with him after practice and we'll get to know each other."

Get to know each other over tea? Had her grandfather lost his mind? Why would he want to know anything about the Earther? She put her palm to her forehead and shook her head.

"It won't be that boring. I may even come up with a story you haven't heard before. Now, what's your second problem?"

"I need your advice about asking someone to be my protector."

He sat back in his chair. "I had hoped you'd worked beyond your fear. Cal seems the obvious choice."

"I want to ask one of the soldiers living in the Citadel. That way I could live in my home and continue much the same as now. Would you support my request?"

"Which soldier?"

"I don't know. It doesn't really matter. I get along with all of them."

Elbows propped on the table before him, he rested his chin on steepled fingers. "Sounds to me like you're trying to take advantage of your father's old mates. Tell me again why Cal is suddenly unacceptable."

"It's not that sudden. Since Dad went missing, Cal acts like I can't take care of myself. He's been trying to boss me around." *Even though he says it's only about my safety.*

Granddad tried to hide his smile. "How has that worked?"

"Not well. He's frustrated and I'm angry. But if I declare him as my protector, I'll have to do what he says. And he's already acting like a jailer." She pulled her bottom lip between her teeth.

"Married people don't always agree. They have fights. They make up."

"Dad and Mom didn't make up."

His eye focused on a point far beyond the wall of the building. "Now we're getting to the real reason you don't want to declare your protector. Are you afraid you'll end up like your mother?"

"No." The hard vehemence in her answer stunned her. "I won't be my mother."

"Reagan hasn't been the best example of a protector, has he? And he's Cal's uncle." He studied her face. His eyes hardened. "Don't paint Cal with that brush, O. He's more of a man at twenty than his uncle will ever be." He stood, signaling that their time together was over. "Anything else?"

"Yes, but it will keep." She'd have to tell him about hearing her father, but not today. That revelation might land her with an instant protector.

———

BENEATH THE AFTERNOON SUN, O'Neill jogged halfway down the mountain to the building where she lived, the Citadel. She'd taken short pushing steps going up and small choppy steps going down to build her stamina. Solo kept pace at her side. "You've got a nice dinner waiting for you, big guy. I have to wash my uniforms tonight, then we'll snuggle, play *Save the Princess*, and wait for Dad to show up." Because if he didn't, she would declare herself crazy. The more she thought about it, talking to her missing, body-less father was not the act of a sane person.

Standing alone on the steep mountain, the Citadel looked like the fortress it was built to be. Seven floors of living quarters made it the tallest building on the planet, besides the spaceport. Bricks made of sparkling Prism soil made it look like pictures she'd seen of an old Earth castle.

She walked around to the side of the building that faced Convict Town, avoiding the covered deep pit and the net trap. At the barred door to the stairwell, she placed her thumb on the pad and spoke her name. A metallic click signaled the locking mechanism had disengaged, giving her ten seconds to pull the door open. She held the door wide. "In you go." She followed Solo into the small entry space and up the stairwell. Because she usually came and went in a skimmer, she rarely used the front door.

The security measures on each landing had been designed to defend the building against invasion from the inhabitants of Convict Town. They had yet to be tested, which was probably a good thing. They had no gatekeeper and few reinforcements if a serious group of intruders attacked, so they'd settled for designing a different security block at every floor to slow the access of the enemy. The families could flee to the roof and escape by skimmer if necessary.

Miguel sat on the second landing, leg crooked to balance his body during meditation. The sole of his lone boot had a hole. His clothes were ragged but clean, like the rest of him. Wrinkles surrounded weary brown eyes set in darkly tanned skin. "Welcome home, *cara*."

"*Buenas tardes*, Miguel. I've got something for you." She reached into her pack and handed over the food Jericho had insisted she take. "I think you're going to like this. Earth food."

"I can't take this. It's your dinner and way too expensive for someone like me."

"The only mechanic my dad allowed to touch his skimmer?" Miguel hadn't been a member of the Aussie Brigade at the beginning of the Earth war, but had been assigned to them after their mechanics had been fragged at their base. On Prism, her father had paid him to keep the skimmer battle worthy. She'd have to allocate credits for that now.

A pride-filled light shone in the old soldier's eyes. He stood, wobbling with the aid of his cloth-wrapped crystal crutch. Solo allowed him to lean against his flank for support.

After her mother deserted her husband and child, the first-gen had taken care of O for days at a time when her father left on one of his exploration trips. He'd held her when she cried herself to sleep at night, missing her mother. To distract her from pining for her mother's return, he told her stories about taking care of her father's fighter planes during the war. Miguel deserved her loyalty.

"I am grateful." He accepted the food. "You are too generous."

"*I* am grateful." She brushed her lips on his weathered cheek. "You know you're welcome to bunk on the roof."

He nodded toward the apartment door. "I'm pulling a little security detail tonight."

He could have stayed in the Soldier Compound, but Miguel didn't want the charity or pity he received there. The occupants of the Citadel allowed Miguel to perform small jobs for credits and shelter after he'd lost his leg last year in a skimmer crash. The Aussie Brigade took care of their own.

"Thanks for guarding the 'well." She punched in the day's code to unlock the door to the upper floors.

After a buzzing sound, the panel swung open.

At the third floor landing, she bent and looked into the retinal scanner her father had "liberated" from a docked supply ship. A portion of the wall recessed. She followed Solo through and waited until the wall closed before trailing him up the stairs.

At the next barrier she bent and pulled up a section of the flooring. She was feeling for the switch when the door to the fourth-floor home opened.

A young boy stood in the doorway. "Hi, O. Mom says you can join us for games tonight."

"Thanks, Richie, but I'm going right to bed. I'm working early tomorrow."

"Oh, darn. I wanted to hear stories. I'll pass you through if you don't want to use the switch."

Each home had a security pad as an emergency bypass to the next level. The squadron had designed redundancy into their system. "Thanks." She replaced the flooring and waited for the seven-year-old to enter the code correctly on the pad inside his home. It took three tries.

Solo waited for her on the top step. She squeezed around him. The stairwell narrowed here and the booby-trap security on this floor often malfunctioned.

She took a long step to the outside wall then tapped the panes of the high-set window in the proper sequence. She thought she might have to bunk on the landing, but then a squeal of metal on metal pierced the air, making her wince. Quincy had better oil that mechanism before it failed.

A plazsteel plate creaked out from under Quincy's door to cover the space in front of the stairwell security door. When it had fully extended, she stepped on it, stated her name and after the seconds it took to verify her voice and weight, the security door clicked open. Solo followed her.

At the top of the stairs she whistled her father's favorite song, and the door swung open to the only home she'd ever known. Her father and mother had made a home here for three years before she was born. They'd welcomed their daughter to the Citadel almost eighteen years ago and lived and played—and loved each other— until her mother ruined their happy family twenty-five hundred and thirteen days ago. Solo walked past her to perform his usual security check.

She set her pack on the floor, next to the crystal pillar holding a large triangular flat rock, the table in the center of the room that served as kitchen, living, dining, and storage room. A long cloth hung from the ceiling to separate a corner into her bedroom. The bathroom and her father's bedroom lay behind a closed door.

A crystal resting in the middle of the table filled the room with a luminous glow. From a bag on a shelf above the sink, she took out a long stick of leathery, dried protein and gave it to Solo. He curled on the rug her mother had braided out of bits of old material years ago. Lengths of her father's favorite old shirt twined with her childhood play dress and her mother's nightgown near the tiger's thumping tail.

Pulling retractable stairs from the ceiling in the far corner of the room, she climbed to the roof, the largest "room" in the Citadel. The Aussie Brigade's job was intel. They watched Convict Town, recorded meetings, street conflicts, and tracked traffic, both foot and air, between Convict Town, Soldier Compound, and the Politico Compound. Richie's mom was responsible for filing the daily report with Granddad's second in command.

"Hi, Quincy," she said to her neighbor. "Anything happening?"

"Hey, O." He pushed the distance goggles to his forehead. "Couple of minor skirmishes in Convict Town. Some air traffic between Soldier and Politico Compounds. You doing okay?"

"Yeah. Just got home. I need to eat before I start my watch, but I wanted to check up here first. Can you lube the security plate on your floor? I thought I was going to have to sleep on your landing when I came up."

"Sorry. Been meaning to get that taken care of."

Her father's three-seater skimmer occupied the middle of the roof, making it invisible from the ground–a security precaution so attackers wouldn't know if the flyer was there.

On one side of the roof was her pride, a garden that supplied her with fresh berries and tomatoes year-round. Her mother had started it, but O had taken it over after Francine left them.

Damn. She didn't have time to tear up over her mother teaching her how to pick tomatoes almost eight years ago.

Quincy rose from his stool on the corner. "I've got your watch tonight." She started to protest, but he raised a hand. "The Citadel hasn't had a Battle participant in years. You need your rest. Between running grid patterns searching for your father, your training, and your job, you've got to be falling-down tired. We had a confab and we're covering your watches until after the Battle." He sat down and lowered the goggles. "Non-negotiable. 'Bye, O."

"Thank you." She swallowed. "And thank everyone for me, will you?"

"We got your six, O. Now get some rack time."

How lucky she was to live in a building with her father's men. They'd always been kind to her, treated her with respect. Now she felt like she was one of them, even though she'd never been to Earth, let alone fought in the war that got them all exiled to Prism.

She went down the stairs and pulled the trapdoor closed. Solo was still gnawing on his dinner. "Tasty, boy?"

After replacing her jumpsuit with a nightgown, she heated some water to mix with the protein powder. She took the steaming mug into her father's room and set it on crate next to his bed. After she planned the Earther's day for tomorrow, she pulled the holo-reader from its hiding place in the closet. Settled cross-legged in the middle of the mattress, she flipped the power switch, then took a trial sip of her dinner. Still too hot, she set it back on the crate.

"Okay, princess, let's see what you've got." The hologram girl sat in a tattered dress at a wooden table. The plate in front of her held a furry piece of food. O'Neill had found the food the last time she'd played, along with a knife, which rested beside the plate. She gave the command for the figure to cut up the food. A rough hard object was in the center, so O'Neill had to figure out the directions for cutting it out in case it wasn't edible. She decided to scrape the food from the furry skin then let the princess taste it.

"Yummy. That was delicious. Now I need a nap." Wide-eyed, the princess looked around the small room that acted as the stage for the hologram.

O snickered. Who took a nap after eating a meal?

I used to.

"Dad? Are you really here?"

He chuckled. *I am. I'd say in the flesh, but that's not true.*

Someone would have said she was talking to herself, but she

wasn't. Her dad was here. In his bedroom. She had to believe that. "I have questions."

I'll bet you do. I'm getting stronger every time I visit, but I don't know how much warning I'll have before I have to leave.

"You're alive?" How could that be, if she could hear but not see him?

Yes, sweetheart. Different, but alive.

How different? How was he alive? Could she visit him? "Where are you when you aren't with me?"

In a tunnel under the Great Plain. And, no, you wouldn't be able to find me, so don't try.

She swallowed against the tightness in her throat. She didn't feel like she was dreaming, but she pinched her arm anyway. She felt the sting. "Will I ever see you again?"

I'm working on it. Right now, I'm what the Ancients call an energy body, like them. I have a consciousness, but no material essence. We're working on reuniting my life force with my body, but they don't know all the requirements to repair the physical matter of the human body.

Jericho's mother had come to Prism to look for artifacts left by an ancient society. But the expedition found nothing and returned to Earth. "You found the Ancients? They're not a myth? What are they like?"

Yes, and I didn't find them. They found me and rescued me after the crash. When I woke up I was lying on a stone plinth in one of their tunnels. I was looking at my body, but I wasn't in it. I couldn't move or feel a thing. I looked pretty banged up. We haven't exactly had a long conversation. I didn't know they existed.

O felt like the room started to spin. She grabbed the edge of the bed. Her dad was living with the Ancients. He was alive, but not in his body. If she told anyone, they'd lock her up so she couldn't hurt herself.

The warmth of another hand covered hers. She gasped, then squinted at a shimmer of air that hovered over her fingers. "Dad, can you feel my hand?"

Warm, prickly sensation. What's it feel like to you?

"The same. Nothing solid." Disappointment laced her words. This conversation with her disembodied father seemed like the casual chats she used to have with him over dinner. Anyone else would say she was talking to a ghost.

How's the Battle training going?

"Okay. I'm going to melee practice at Granddad's tomorrow morning."

Good. How's Cal?

She didn't want to tell him. Could he read her mind? What could a *ghost* do? What did he know? "He's acting like he owns me. Wants me to declare him as my protector now."

You've always known that was going to happen someday. What's the problem?

"I'm not ready to get married. I don't want a protector. I don't need one." She couldn't see her father, but she felt him smile.

You may be right. It's a lot to take in, I know. But now that I'm on the mend, I'll be around more.

How? As a shimmer? A voice only she could hear? It didn't matter. She had her dad back. "Promise?"

I'm stronger. I still have a lot to learn about controlling this energy body of mine. I connect with your energy, then I can pop into your mind and talk to you. I didn't know I could touch you until I reached for your hand.

Soul-deep relief comforted her, even though she had no idea if his *recovery* would restore his body and if he could climb back inside that human shell. "I have so many questions for you, but could we just play the game for a while?"

Sure. I'm glad you got your birthday present.

"About that…"

Later. We're playing the game now.

The bubble chips would have to wait until after the princess' nap.

10

P RISM - Present Day
       Private Journal Notes of Administrator Cornelia
       Schultz:

The World Board news summary doesn't look good for us. There are outbreaks of rebellion in each of the conglomerate areas. The corporation owners are desperate enough to work together to identify the underground connections between their fiefdoms. Populations are rioting for food, medicine and jobs. They've had to start conscripting their military forces. It's not going to be long before the supply ships stop coming. Or a battle force lands on Prism. Not much the exiles can do with their slingshots, no matter how accurate they can shoot. Rocks are no match for blasters and missile launchers.

THE NEXT MORNING, after a long night of number-crunching, Jericho followed O'Neill down the skimmer's ramp inside the wall-enclosed "soldier compound." The military exiles had settled far, a two-hour-jog, to the west of Convict Town. Before they landed, he'd glimpsed the Politico Compound, another two-hour run beyond the Soldier Compound.

He should have stayed on *Freedom* to review the numbers for his revised proposal, but O'Neill had agreed to take him to a Battle training session today and introduce him to her grandfather. Even his father would agree that talking to a first gen was worth the time investment. And spending time with O'Neill—that was becoming a pleasure he looked forward to every morning. He wouldn't say no to spending time doing anything with her.

He'd already devoted too many hours trying to figure out the puzzle that was his pilot. Why should he be nervous about meeting her grandfather? He ran his fingers through his hair. He'd never worried about being introduced to the parents of girls he'd dated. He wasn't dating O'Neill and yet he wanted to run away. Maybe it was the idea of coming face to face with one of the eight hundred exiled by the World Board twenty-five years ago. Would O'Neill's grandfather be a broken, bitter old man?

The street was just a width of dirt between two rows of one-story buildings built of large adobe-style bricks made from the sparkly Prism earth. Yancey walked nearest the long row of houses and "single barracks." O'Neill kept pace on Jericho's other side. Her gait was more relaxed than the day before, even though several people walked toward them, milling about the street. She waved in response to greetings and welcomed an occasional quick hug.

Solo trotted ahead of them, head swinging right then left. From the assessing looks Jericho got, he wondered if everyone knew who he was. The walk gave him an idea of Prism's meager standard of living. Shanty-town style lean-tos made of thin sheets of salvaged metal and large shaved slices of crystal lined the tall wall enclosing the camp.

Laughing children, dressed in clean clothes, chased each other like they had no worries or fear. When the kids saw O'Neill and Solo, they dashed toward them. The tiger allowed little hands to dig into his fur while a brave girl nuzzled his neck. He licked a wet stripe up her face.

"He kissed me!" She ran away squealing with delight.

"Okay, that's enough. Solo is working." O'Neill's voice was firm but kind.

The children got in their final rubs then backed away. Only then did they notice Jericho. The shortest pointed. "Who dat?"

"A visitor."

O'Neill's answer must have satisfied them. They scattered away like leaves in an autumn breeze on Earth.

"These are homes of the first-gen soldiers and their families," O'Neill said. "The original convicts stayed close to the drop zone, now the spaceport, for proximity to supplies." She waved to a group of children. "The Burnt Engine is on the outskirts of Convict Town. The military exiles built this compound as a buffer between the convict settlement and the politicos, who built and occupy the prime location beyond." She jerked her thumb to the left, though he couldn't see over the protective wall.

"Who is the leader of Prism?"

"There is no one spokesperson for us, although Warden, I mean Administrator, Schultz does her best to convey our needs and wants to the World Board on Earth. Matters that concern all three groups are decided by the Joint Committee, which is made up of one elected person from each of the three groups." A smile lit her face. "You can talk to Cal about the politicos. He's one. And Wash lives with his parents in Convict Town."

He filed her smile with the first bit of information she'd given him about one of her friends and her Battle coach. "Where do you live?"

"In the Citadel."

"Sounds very military. Is that where your grandfather lives?" He scanned the area for a tall building, but saw none.

"Hardly. The Citadel was built by a squad who wanted to get out from under the military rules in the Soldier Compound. The seven friends built the first apartment, then added a floor for each of them as time and credits allowed. My father's was built last, so it's the top floor. Made sense because he had his personal skimmer by then and the roof is a secure landing pad."

He let out a low whistle. "How did your father get his own skimmer?"

O'Neill shrugged as if a prisoner being given a shuttle was not remarkable. "He and his best friend discovered the first translithium deposits together. Each of them received a personal skimmer as part of the first translithium shipping contract with Earth. My dad argued that he could cover more territory with a skimmer than he could on foot. Earth was definitely interested in him exploring for more translithium. They bargained for extra daily meals to keep up the strength of those who volunteered to mine the crystals. And credit bonuses for increased production."

Jericho had fallen a step behind, taking everything in, but lengthened his stride to catch up.

The wall enclosing the Soldier Compound was made of thick blocks formed from white Prism dirt embedded with small glinting crystals. At regular intervals, ladders led up to what had to be watchtowers atop the twelve-foot walls. Two sentries, military exiles by their looks, stood on each covered platform.

Yancey slowed, examining the guards, probably looking for weapons. Jericho saw none.

O'Neill stopped outside a long, low building in front of a metal panel that was only four feet tall.

"Be careful when you enter." She gave each of them a warning stare.

"Short on doors when this was built?"

"I don't mean be careful to duck. Be careful when you step into the room."

Following the cryptic warning she entered. Solo followed.

Jericho looked at Yancey and shrugged. Bending, he opened the closed corrugated metal door and stepped through. The room was almost dark. Something pipe-like slammed into his shin. Hard. "Cripes!"

Yancey followed, shoving him aside.

Jericho's eyes adjusted to the lack of light. A very old man, missing one eye and a few teeth, leaned on a crystal staff that was the right size to have delivered the blow to his already-bruising leg.

Rows of Prismers, from six-years-old to gray-haired Earth-borns, knelt on mats spaced in orderly rows in a very large, windowless room. Not one moved. Or looked in his direction.

O'Neill whispered, "Welcome to my grandfather's school. Meditation now, then training. After that we'll join him." Pride and something he couldn't identify spiraled around her words.

Whoa. Meditation? That was the last thing he expected from soldiers deemed lethal enough to be banned from Earth forever. He reached for O'Neill's hand, but she moved it behind her back. He would have liked to touch her, for her to anchor him in this unusual place. Hell, he just wanted to hold her hand.

"Follow me. Do what I do." She crossed the room, removed her boots and stored them in an open cupboard with other assorted footgear.

Under her watchful gaze, he did the same. Yancey took a post next to the entrance.

She pulled two mats from her pack, then tossed the worn bag near the wall, lining the mats up with the others.

He took the mat nearest the wall and settled into the feet-under-butt, hands-on-thighs position she assumed. She closed her eyes, but he looked around the room.

The man on the raised platform sat in the same position, but he watched the other latecomers enter, giving them each a subtle nod. He had graying hair and a whipcord body that appeared lean and muscled beneath shirt and pants that were almost military-tailored. His calm, kind face radiated power and strength. Jericho couldn't think of a single reason why the Prismer looked so familiar.

Solo sprawled in front of the paper-thin wall. It was the first time he'd seen the big cat settle in to sleep.

A gong sounded. The man in front straightened. "Welcome. We'll begin this morning with Body Like a Mountain."

Metal chimes rang twice. Everyone in the room began their

silent meditations. He watched their chests begin to rise and fall in unison.

"Feel the stability of Prism below you."

Jericho closed his eyes. Billions of people on Earth meditated, but he wasn't one of them. Sketching relaxed him. He only shared his fashion sketches. The others, in his leather-bound sketchbook, were for him alone. A treasure chest of memories, rarely opened, seldom indulged.

He felt the hard, planked metal floor through the thin material of the mat. What he wouldn't give for his mother's thick, cushioned yoga mat right now. If this was a popular planetary hobby, he could offload Montgomery Conglomerates' extra mats in his contract offer.

In an effort to relieve the weight on his knees, he shifted— and had to use both hands to brace himself when he over-balanced. He fought to keep the smile from his lips as he pictured his silent row falling like surprised dominoes if he'd crashed into O'Neill.

His thigh muscles burned. His feet threatened to cramp. He glanced at O'Neill, who looked like she might levitate soon. On his other side, Solo let loose a tiger snore.

Finally the chimes rang once, twice, and everyone stirred. The man on the platform, hands together at his chest as if praying, bowed from his seated position. The group returned the bow, but no one stood.

"Today's physical training, melee practice, will be held in the courtyard for Battle participants and those willing to teach them some lessons. Wild goose practice will be in here, by age groups. Form on your instructors, now."

Wild goose practice?

The leader stood and hopped from the platform, pausing to chat with people rolling their mats. When he reached O'Neill's side he hugged her. Jericho finished rolling his mat and stood, holding the material in his left hand.

The man released O'Neill and she turned. "Grandfather, this is

Jericho Montgomery. Jericho, I'd like to introduce you to my grandfather, Liam Neill."

That man was dead, according to the history books. Jericho's jaw dropped. The man before him didn't look old enough to be O'Neill's grandfather. And he couldn't be *the* Liam Neill, who'd been the commanding general for the Earth Union of Nations in the war against the corporations. The general who lost the planetary civil war twenty-five years ago.

Jericho reached for the ghost's outstretched hand. A warm, firm grip returned his.

No wonder the man looked so familiar. The commanding general, along with the leaders of the Union of Nations, made a rogues' gallery in the surrender-signing picture in every history book he'd ever read. Along with the footnote of Neill's death six years after transport. The historians had that fact dead wrong.

The man before him was tall and lean, hiding his seventy-five years, looking more like the man in all the historic pictures with an addition of a long, straight scar that disappeared under his square jaw. His eyes matched the color of the giant Montgomery Sapphire in the family museum.

"You're the first shipping contract negotiator I've met," Liam Neill said.

"And you're the first, uh, first generation soldier I've met." He released the hand of a contemporary of his own grandfather, dead years before Jericho was born. Thanks to pollutants, genetic food mutations, and assassinations, no one on Earth lived past seventy. His own father was perilously old at sixty. His mother had died before her fiftieth birthday.

Jericho tried to put together a cohesive thought, a question, but his brain was a dry, shriveled sponge. O'Neill had said she was a second gen. So what did that make her father? The prison colony was only twenty-five years old, so the man must have fought in the war with his father. Liam Neill, the commanding general of the Union of Nations forces. "Uh, I'm pleased to meet you, ah, sir."

The old man's lips parted, displaying a complete set of perfect, white teeth. *Like a hungry Solo might.* Liam Neill's eyes never left Jericho. The general patted his granddaughter's back. "Go on outside. Your Earther and I will get acquainted while you accumulate some bruises."

O'Neill left Jericho amidst the hubbub of a roomful of children, Yancey, and a sleeping tiger.

The old man made Jericho nervous. "Liam Neill is dead," he blurted.

The man flexed the fingers of both hands, then ran a palm across his stubbled chin. "Hadn't heard that one. Wouldn't be the first time the World Board lied." Stone-still, he stared at Jericho.

In an attempt to fill the awkward silence between them Jericho said, "I brought dinner. She gave it to the men who secured the skimmer."

"Earth hospitality. After all these years, I still miss sitting down to a real meal with a group of friends."

He motioned to two simple, cushionless chairs made from lengths of crystals. "You'll probably be more comfortable sitting than squatting on your haunches."

"Thank you."

They moved their chairs outside on a terrace overlooking a large courtyard where more than a dozen very fit-looking adults greeted each other with bear hugs and handshakes.

"Why would the World Board lie about your death?" Gatfield Montgomery had to know the truth. Why hadn't he said something?

The former general gave Jericho a hard look. "There must have been some reason the Corporations wanted Earthers to believe that whale dreck. Maybe they were told the fragger was successful."

"Fragger?"

A young man Jericho's age mounted the steps. "Excuse me, General. By your leave, we're ready to begin. Any additional orders?"

"No, Corporal. Make it count."

"Yes, sir." He gave a sharp salute and returned to the courtyard.

The General is still very much a general.

O'Neill stood with two other women, laughing. Had he ever seen her laugh?

While the practice participants arranged themselves into two lines, he tried again. "What's a fragger?"

"Infiltrating a fragger became a common Corporation practice toward the end of the war. They recruited volunteers, trained them in assassination techniques, and sent them on suicide missions to take out our battle group leaders. They promised the fraggers that if they were successful, their families would be supplied with food and shelter for the rest of their lives." He snorted. "I doubt they ended up any better off on Earth than we are on Prism."

The history books said nothing about *fraggers*. The super-confidential Montgomery Conglomerates files held no mention of fraggers. What other omissions was he going to be hit with? What other unforgivable corporation and World Board crimes had been hidden from the public? *I'm screwed.* The Joint Committee would never give him the shipping contract. "Then, later, they sent an assassin here to murder you?"

The man's attention didn't stray from the courtyard. "They never expected us to survive the first six months."

"Why not?"

He turned and studied Jericho's face as if he were counting eyebrow hairs. Finally he sighed. "The megacorporations wanted freedom from the laws that protected our citizens and our resources. They started the war to grab control. They turned families against each other with their lies of their corporate desire to make the Earth a healthier, better place to live."

"It became a global civil war." Jericho hadn't been alive during the war, but he'd seen pictures of cities and countries before the war. Cities that had supported the governments had paid the price for that loyalty. And Earth's resources, in general, had been used to benefit the corporations. His mother had taken him to places served by her charities, bemoaning the pollution that had grown much worse once governments no longer regulated industry.

The general nodded. "The governments lost the war and the corporations exiled us here because the world population threatened to revolt if they executed us all. Three-hundred military leaders and their personal squads, three-hundred political leaders and their government scientists and contractors, and unknown to us or the general Earth population, two-hundred psych-ward convicts. Not enough supplies or food, because the captain burned up half of them with the drive exhaust from the last shuttle. No security forces or authority. We were left on our own. Prism was a battle zone in the early years. You could only trust people you had personal history with."

"Two-hundred psych-ward convicts?" With a start, Jericho realized he'd said it out loud.

"They were a surprise to me, too. The corporate crew unfroze and offloaded them first."

He shifted his body and attention, closing the subject.

Now was not the time to press for details. Instead he asked, "You still have all your teeth, and you can probably beat me in a race. You're, what, seventy-five?"

"Seventy-six." Neill focused on the courtyard. "Prism is kind to the human body."

Solid thunks of crystal staffs hitting each other drew Jericho's attention. Pairs traded blows in what appeared to be a choreographed routine.

"They're warming up with a kata before they free fight. This will be O's toughest event in the Battle." He watched a moment longer. "I've answered your questions; now I have some of my own."

"Fair enough."

"Why are you here?"

"I wanted to meet an original settler."

"We're prisoners. Prism doesn't hold colonization papers." The curt words held decades of anger.

"I'm sorry. Everyone on Earth refers to Prism as a colony."

"In twenty-five years no new *colonists* have arrived. Any prisoner finding a way to leave Prism would have a summary execution order issued." He spat then cocked his head toward the courtyard. "That goes for the youngsters, too."

"Surely the original deportation orders didn't apply to descendants of the prisoners."

"The order says that no one living on Prism, except the warden, may leave the planet without being under penalty of summary execution. We can't even shuttle up to the re-supply ship. Now, why did you come to Prism?"

"To negotiate the shipping contract for Translithium Number Three."

"Hardly worth six months frozen in a flying can." He shouted encouragement to the closest group of combatants. "No one has ever bothered to travel here for negotiations."

"I hope that personal involvement will give me an edge. I can talk with the miners, get a sense of what might be useful to the colonists ..."

"Prisoners. That's why you wanted to meet me."

Jericho noted the tension in the old general's clenched hands and frowned. "I didn't know her grandfather was *the* General Liam Neill. Her name is O'Neill, after all, sir."

"I'm not your C.O." He paused, peering at the activity in the yard. "Footwork!" he yelled before turning back to Jericho. "Her last name is Neill. My son could only say, "Oh," over and over when he first saw her. He named her O. Family and her close friends call her O. Everyone else calls her O'Neill." His gaze returned to the courtyard. "This is going to get interesting. Watch."

The corporal stood on the sidelines in the space between two lines of staff-wielding soldiers. And O'Neill. "Charge!"

The groups ran toward each other from opposite ends of the training field, yelling and brandishing their staffs.

Jericho looked for O'Neill and found her long ponytail of bouncing white curls amid the chaos of bodies before him. She blocked one blow, then another. A man came at her from behind.

Jericho leapt up.

O'Neill whirled and thrust the end of her pole at the man's chest. He crumpled onto the dirt. A staff cracked across O'Neill's back.

Jericho winced, but she spun and blocked a second blow from a man who was a foot taller. While she was occupied with him, a woman cracked her weapon across O'Neill's left side. A blow to the back of O'Neill's knees drove her to the ground, where she stayed, unmoving, for several beats of Jericho's heart. He wanted to run onto the field, scoop her up and carry her to safety. She'd probably break that crystal rod against his skull if he tried.

Her attackers moved on, still fighting. O'Neill pushed herself up with the aid of her staff and limped to the edge of the field.

Jericho knew he had no right to be angry. He wanted to hit something anyway. He yelled at her grandfather instead. "She's hurt. How can you let her do that?"

"How many days have you known her?"

The general-voice didn't faze him. Jericho's feelings did. He cared about O'Neill. Was it only because she'd kept him safe? He hedged, counting that first night they met in the bar. "Five."

"Do you think anyone could tell that girl she can't do something she wants to do?" The general's voice gentled a bit.

Jericho recalled the fight in the bar. He wouldn't want to take O'Neill on. "You have no medical facilities. And she risks broken bones doing that." He waved toward the few participants still fighting.

The general-mask cracked, the grandfather peeking through with Liam's chuckle. "Oh, I'm sure she'd rather not get hit. But I'm equally sure she's willing to take whatever physical punishment might be necessary to get what she wants."

"What is it she wants?"

The question hung in the air long enough for Jericho to feel uncomfortable. It was a personal question, the first one he'd asked.

Age flickered across the old man's face. Age and sadness. "She wants to be happy."

I could give a rat's ass if you're happy. The anger-spewed words his father had shouted in their last conversation reverberated in Jericho's skull.

Raising his chin, he focused on O'Neill to distract his thoughts. Focused on the scar on her cheek. Imagined what she'd gone through. She deserved to be happy. "That's all she wants?"

Her grandfather's icy stare froze his racing emotions. Jericho's face heated. The old man probably thought he was a fool. Hopefully, that was all he thought.

"Happiness is all that's important. Money won't buy it. What else is there?" The general sounded like he must have when he talked to his troops, the dense ones. "O thinks she wants what the politicos want. Independence. But she doesn't care about independence from Earth. She wants her personal independence. She wants to make her own rules. That's what will make her happy." A rush of air escaped his chest. "She's just like her father."

Maybe Jericho had more in common with his guide than he'd thought.

Independence. A curse word in Gatfield Montgomery's vocabulary. *Control. Dominance.* Those were the words his father worshipped. But only if they were in *his* hands.

Jericho hadn't noticed it so much when his mother had been alive. Hadn't noticed how over the years, he'd learned to buffer her from her husband. Hadn't noticed how he'd tried to limit his father's control and dominance over his mother's independence.

Now he noticed. His father maintained control of Jericho's life. Always had, and Jericho had never pushed back, let alone fought for his freedom. Did his father really want Jericho to succeed? *Not if success meant independence.* Jericho clamped his jaw shut to keep from screaming. Hell, Yancey was probably his father's spy, reporting everything back to Gatfield. Jericho had less independence than that corporal who'd started the melee.

The fighting ended. Participants shook hands then dispersed toward buildings surrounding the courtyard. O'Neill straightened, squared her shoulders and walked toward them. Trails of sweat streaked the crystal dust crusting her face. She dropped her staff in a box with others.

Her grandfather rose and in four strides he faced her. Jericho followed.

"Better. But you still have to use all your senses to anticipate an attack. Bring Cal next time. I'll work with the two of you on body positioning and strategies so you can practice with him."

Jericho wanted to yell, "No, teach me. I can help her," but he kept his mouth shut. He had no history, no trust, with O'Neill or her grandfather. But he could work on that. He would offer to train her with the holo programs on *Freedom*.

"Thanks. I need all the help I can get." She brushed her wrist across her sweaty forehead.

"And on how to take those body strikes." He put one arm around her shoulder and hugged her to his side.

She melted against the older man.

In Jericho's years of observing body language, he'd never seen that combination of trust and surrender. But his body remembered. Remembered when, as a small boy, his mother had pulled him against her side like a mother bird with her chick. His throat tightened. *God, I miss you, Mom.*

Solo padded to O'Neill and nuzzled her hand. She dropped to her knees and wrapped her arms around his neck.

"Let's get you to the house so my medic can fuss over you with his salves." The general nodded at Jericho. "He brought lunch. I'm sure you're hungry."

O'Neill stood. Raised eyebrows creased her forehead. "I thought we'd just have tea after training. I'm tired and dirty. And I hurt." She pulled her lower lip between her teeth, looking like she was fighting tears.

"The lad brought lunch. You need to eat. So do I." While her grandfather's tone wasn't harsh, it left no doubt that they would all sit down together to eat the lunch Matilda had sent.

Instead of putting his arm around her to offer comfort, Jericho looked at O'Neill in silent apology.

"You didn't ask if you could bring lunch."

Yancey coughed.

Neill gave the bodyguard a nod. "You probably want to talk about compound security." They fell into step, walking away.

"I'm sorry, O'Neill. I didn't mean to cause trouble."

She pressed her lips together and looked away. "It would have come up anyway, sooner or later. Granddad's right. I need someone to practice melee with. Cal's the obvious choice."

"I can help you."

"You?" Surprise, and maybe hope, washed across her face. "How?"

"I have a gym aboard *Freedom*. There are hologram programs for many sports. I've tried one for Kendo, an ancient martial art that looks a lot like your melee." She just stared at him, as he kept talking. "You can use the program on my ship. I can practice with you."

"You know how to fight in a melee?"

"No, but I can learn."

She laughed. It was more of a snicker. "Not fast enough to help me, but thanks. You gave me a little hope for a moment." She motioned at her grandfather's receding back. "We need to get moving."

He walked next to her. If he had his way, he'd give her a lot more than hope. He'd give her results from training with him. "Why don't you come onboard tomorrow morning and try it?"

She stuffed her fists into her pockets.

Time to close the deal. He touched her elbow to make her look at him. "You can invite your friends."

11

——————

From the personal log of Liam Neill: Present Day

 The commanders are briefing the troops with plans to build shelters and store supplies on the Great Plain, at the edges of each field. While those preparations continue, my staff and I are planning defenses and reviewing strategies to repel the forces that I've always known would arrive. My soldiers are ready to fight.

O SET plates and glasses on the "war table." Three plates, three bowls, three glasses, three forks, knives and spoons. Good thing it was a big table. Big enough for a dozen first and second gens to gather every day to pass information. She didn't call this a dining room; it had always been the war room.

 Her grandfather's assistant walked into the room. She held foot-wide squares of cloth and wore a dress and "flats." O could, on the fingers of one hand, count the number of times she'd seen the woman in a dress instead of her uniform. Ex-military aide to the former President of the Union of Nations on Earth, now Anne took care of "administrative details" for O's grandfather.

Nodding approval over the table arrangement, Anne folded the squares into little hats and put one at each place. "Napkins." She had a disconcerting tendency to answer O's questions before she asked them. "Your grandfather didn't say anything about your Earther bringing lunch."

He's not my *Earther.* "I thought we were only having tea in the wardroom after the melee training."

"His bodyguard is eating in the kitchen with the corps."

The corps. The men who had been her grandfather's trusted captains in the war. If Yancey had secrets, he wouldn't have them by the time they finished with him.

"Enjoy lunch. It's a special treat." Anne chucked O under the chin. "Don't look so sour."

O forced her lips into a thin, hard smile. Anne wasn't responsible for O's stinging bruises or her confusion about Jericho. How could she be drawn to the Earther when she knew he was leaving soon? He was not the solution to her protector problem. "I'm not really hungry."

"Go tell them we're ready. I'll bring the food to the table."

At Anne's insistence O'Neill had showered and changed into the nicest civilian clothes she'd ever worn—black pants with a pink top sporting a scooped neck and thin-strapped metallic sandals that Anne had insisted on loaning her. She'd braided her wet hair and twisted it on top of her head, securing it with two crystal chopsticks. Other than at Soldier Beach, she'd always worn her uniform with her hair stuffed under a cap around Jericho. Her passenger.

Why did he skew her gyroscope? Maybe it was because he seemed to care about her. He seemed to understand her problem. But then, she'd seen all her friends shirtless, and she never bothered to take a second look. Jericho shirtless on the shuttle after his run, that had been worth a second look. Her cheeks heated and she swallowed, trying for a mask of nonchalance before walking into the sitting room.

Jericho couldn't see her enter from the kitchen. She heard him chuckle. When she walked into his view, he jumped from his seat. Whatever he'd been saying to her grandfather slid into a stammer of "Uh, uh, um."

His admiring stare surprised her. She didn't know what to say. Could civilian clothes make such a difference in her appearance?

"You look lovely," Jericho said.

Lovely. No one had every called her lovely before. Maybe he meant the clothes. Wasn't he in charge of fashion in his father's conglomerate? "Thank you. I hope waiting hasn't made you too hungry."

Hungry? Not with her stomach doing barrel rolls. Breaking her personal fraternization rule was nothing compared to putting herself in a social situation with Jericho. How would she compare to the girls on Earth? Why did she care?

He offered his arm. "I'm fine."

Her grandfather's jovial smile wavered. Was he displeased that she was out of uniform? "Lunch ready?"

"Anne's putting it on the table."

"Been twenty-five years since I've had a meal made entirely from fresh Earth food."

Why didn't he sound as excited as he had before? What had changed during his visit with Jericho? They'd been laughing when she'd come in to get them.

She entered the war room, where she'd spent plenty of time as a child playing on the floor when her father came for meetings. Usually a dozen or more officers surrounded the table littered with papers, electronics, crystals and inventions. Wash's dad worked for her grandfather, fixing broken electronics, configuring translithium crystal arrays as a power source for the Soldier Compound, and building new devices from savaged parts. The dishes, utensils and napkins gave an alien flavor to the room.

Her grandfather sat at the end of the table and motioned Jericho to the lone place setting to his right. "You sit here." O sat to his left. He nodded to Anne. "Thank you, Staff Sergeant. You're dismissed."

"It looks delicious, Jericho. Reminds me of when I was a boy." Granddad winked at O. "Except for the napkins."

He made a show of shaking out the intricate folds and placing it in his lap. She pulled the corners of her cloth and smoothed it across her thighs. She'd never used a napkin before and wondered what else she was supposed to do with it.

Jericho picked up a plate stacked with some of their lunch. "The sandwiches are turkey, pear, spinach and gouda cheese on grilled Bush Damper with cranberry spread." He appeared pleased with himself when he passed them to her grandfather.

Sand witches again. She had no idea what she was about to eat, nor did she know how to eat it. She watched her grandfather gather the stacked food between his fingers and transfer it to his plate, then she tried to copy his moves.

"I made Bush Damper—that's a rustic kind of bread, O—when I went on walkabout as a young man." Granddad waited until everyone had a sandwich then took a large bite. "My sangers never tasted this good."

"I asked my cook to prepare dishes that were favorites in Anzac, Britannia, and North America."

Jericho must have found out her grandfather was on the Joint Committee. He was trying to impress Granddad with the lunch.

"So it's Anzac now? The corporate name substitutes for the land names? We're talking about Australia and New Zealand. Hell, Australia is a continent and it's been reduced to one letter in a corporation name." Granddad jabbed at fruit slices from a metal platter reeling off the names for her benefit. "Apple, kiwi, banana, orange, strawberry, melon."

She wouldn't be able to connect the fruit with its name by the time lunch was over. She'd refused to eat Earther food since the kidnapping and didn't remember tasting any before that. But she knew from Granddad's reaction, this lunch was very special to him, in a way far-removed from simply the food. She suspected her grandfather was reliving distant memories of other meals, other times on Earth. Very happy memories, from the noises escaping from between his lips. She smiled, happy that Jericho had made the effort to re-create an Earth meal for Granddad.

Her grandfather's fork hovered above a slice with a fuzzy edge. "And peach." Reverence surrounded the word. He put the juice-filled bit in his mouth, closed his eyes and chewed. Something like a groan sounded deep in his throat. "How did you get this fruit here in such fresh condition?"

Too bad her father wasn't here to enjoy all these tastes from his youth. She wondered if anyone else would be able to hear him. The sad wish sent a shiver from her shoulders to her fingertips.

Jericho noticed. "Are you cold, O'Neill?"

"No. Just reactions to all these foods. Thank you."

"You're welcome. But you haven't tried any of the fruit yet." He eyed her as if he didn't believe her words, then shifted his attention to Granddad. "There's a small hydroponic garden onboard my ship. I picked all the fruit this morning."

Her grandfather up-ended his beer. *In a glass bottle.* After several swallows, he clunked the bottle on the table and ran his thumbnail down the frosty ice on the outside of the glass. "Ice cold beer. Never thought I'd have one again." He pushed the fruit platter toward her. "Fruits. Try them, O."

She lifted a slice of each fruit onto her plate. Spearing the peach with the fork, she tried it first. And couldn't help closing her eyes when she bit into the juicy pulp. Flavor unlike any bar or powder she'd ever had tantalized her taste buds. The strawberry was the only fruit she'd tasted before, since she grew them in her rooftop garden. It tasted different, though, like it had been infused with more strawberry essence.

The tines from her fork resisted the skin of the next slice. She pushed the fork hard into the fruit.

"That's an apple," Jericho said. "From a tree outside my bedroom window at home, hydrogen-preserved for freshness."

"My mother made me eat an apple every day," her grandfather said. "She swore it would keep me healthy." He held a slice between his fingers and bit. It crunched.

O tried the apple and the rest of the fruit. Jericho supplied the names as she tasted each. Her favorite was the apple. She took three more slices of it.

While she ate the fruit, she watched Jericho eat his sandwich. "Take a bite of your sandwich. It's the protein source. And there's dessert."

She held it tight, afraid it would fall apart when she moved it to her mouth like he'd done.

Granddad showed her. "Honey, pick it up with both hands and take a bite. If something falls out, that's okay. The best sandwiches are messy."

A blob squirted from Jericho's sandwich, falling on his pristine blue shirt. He looked up to see if anyone had noticed, meeting O's gaze.

She could have laughed at the mess the richest heir on Earth had made, but she didn't. It was nice to see him make a mistake, spill his food. He was a person. A person who didn't always get it right. Like her.

Giving her an embarrassed grin, he reached for the cloth on his lap and swiped his chin before rubbing the spot on his shirt. "It really is good."

Her grandfather nodded. "Aye on that, Montgomery."

O gathered the crispy Bush Damper and squeezed hard, trying to hold everything inside. Bits fell out onto her plate. A pinkish glob gathered on the edge of the bread. She waited for it to plop onto the plate, then took a bite. A bigger bite than she'd intended. She didn't want to look like guys in the soldier dining hall shoveling food into their mouths at the annual Remembrance Day dinner, but she was certain she did. A quick glance at Jericho's warm smile relaxed her worry.

"Montgomery, if word gets out that you have food like this on your ship, we'll need to triple dock security." Her grandfather popped the last bite of his sandwich into his mouth.

She chewed. And chewed. Finally swallowed. Crispy bread scratched at the roof of her mouth while the smooth sauce coated her tongue with a cool softness. "It's a wonder there isn't a riot every time an Earth ship docks."

Her grandfather's fork froze midair. He speared O with a look. Her thoughtless, offhand comment had killed his jovial attitude. He didn't need to remind her of the deadly riots at the landing of every supply ship in the early years. "Wonder indeed." he said.

After the awkward minutes that followed, Jericho said, "My cook, Matilda, makes meals that rival anything I've eaten on Earth. Sometime if you'd like to have dinner aboard *Freedom*, I know she'll pull out the stops."

His offer met silence. There was nothing wrong with his courtesy. He didn't act like he was better or above them; he was being kind—offering to share what he had.

Granddad paid way too much attention to the last bites of food on his plate. Why couldn't he acknowledge the offer then decline it? Something between hurt and question flickered across Jericho's face before he addressed his remaining food. The Earther deserved better than to be ignored.

"I'd like to see your ship." She'd blurted the words like she'd apply salve to a wound. "Well, the engine room, anyway. And maybe that hydroponic garden." Why was she babbling about specifics? Now he'd think she *was* interested in his ship rather making an effort to defuse table-talk gone bad.

He put his fork down. "Really? I thought you didn't fraternize with passengers."

Her grandfather set his empty beer bottle on the table with a thunk. "Someone mentioned dessert?"

O stood. "I'll clear the dishes." She felt guilty about leaving Jericho alone with her brooding grandfather, but she had no choice except to gather plates and utensils and leave him to fend for himself. The faster she moved, the sooner she'd rejoin the men. She hoped there would be no blood to clean up.

———

JERICHO WATCHED O'Neill's very nice backside disappear through the kitchen door before forcing his attention back to the table. Too late.

Her grandfather had seen his appreciation. The man glared and cleared his throat. "You're very young. Very rich. Very privileged."

His spine straightened and he prepared for a lecture. He knew all the signs of an incoming verbal beat down from his father. "Yes, sir." His tone was a mix of cool and get-on-with-it.

"There's probably nothing you've wanted that your father's money hasn't bought for you."

Jericho met her grandfather's icy glare. If the man only knew how many times Jericho had tried to show what he could do on his own, without any assistance from the Montgomery name or influence. There was brittle hardness in his answering stare.

No more grandfather. A general now. "Your father's money won't work here."

"Sir?"

"I was young and randy, many years ago." He raised his strong, square chin. "You want that shipping contract? You leave my granddaughter alone."

The man thought he wanted to seduce O'Neill. *Goddammit all.* He met Neill's gaze. "Sir, it's not like *that.*" And it wasn't. He didn't want a one-and-done with O'Neill. But he did want something that included her. Included her skill, her confidence, her sass. Yes, and her amazing body.

Not fair to her. He was leaving after the shipping contract winner was announced. Less than two weeks. He couldn't ruin what she had with Cal. Heck, they were practically engaged. *Shitfuckhim.*

The man's tanned hand lifted off the table and closed into a fist. "Don't look me in the eye and lie, Montgomery."

Before he could formulate a reply, O emerged with the special dessert he'd brought for the man. Jericho needed time to hash things over with her grandfather. He would have welcomed Liam

Neill's advice on the contract bid. On O's training for the Battle. On O herself.

She set the plate of cookies and a container in front of the general, gave Jericho a questioning look, and took her seat opposite him.

Her grandfather didn't look at the food. He looked like he wanted to rip Jericho's head off. Maybe he thought he could scoop out the crap that passed for Jericho's brain. The brain that flashed a warning signal: This is not the way to win friends and influence important people. He inhaled a long calm-down breath.

Neill harrumphed and mumbled something about soldiers giving chocolate bars to children. "Ice cream and biscuits." He raked Jericho with a glance that promised physical punishment if they were ever left alone.

Jericho lowered his chin in a message of no contest. How had this meeting veered out-of-bounds so quickly?

The general's gaze softened when it fell on O's lovely face. He shrugged. "Well, dish it up evenly. It'll probably be another twenty-five years before I eat ice cream again. I'll be right back."

Jericho watched him walk through the door into the kitchen. He had no idea how to turn the evening around. Didn't the man know his granddaughter could take care of herself? That no one could do anything to O'Neill if she didn't agree?

She gave him an uncertain smile. "Everything okay between the two of you?"

"Your grandfather loves you very much." He scooped the creamy dessert, giving a full bowl to O, setting one in front of the general's empty chair and taking the last bowl for himself.

"You didn't answer my question."

"Sure. Everything's fine." *I wish.* "Why wouldn't it be?"

"No reason. You're still breathing." She gave him a brilliant *gotcha* smile and picked up her spoon. "Don't wait for Granddad."

Jericho peered over his spoon at her. Head cocked, she just stared back for what seemed forever. He was comfortable with no words between them. While he waited for the general to return with what—weapons of torture?—he was content to stare at O'Neill. What did that mean about him? About them?

O dipped into her dessert. "Oh, this is delicious." She took another spoonful. "And cold."

It was so easy to smile around her. "I'll send you a container before I leave. I'd like to talk about what trade goods you think would be best received here. I can open up trade with Earth. Prism's beautiful crystals would sell well at home. Any Prism product would be an instant sellout as a novelty. There are no laws about importing goods from Prism to Earth." He dug his spoon into the ice cream. It hit a hard nut and the spoon slid sideways to clang against the bowl.

"No shipping proposal has ever included personal trade goods." The inflection of her words made it a question.

He nodded. "No negotiator has ever visited here before. Trade will be good for everyone."

The kitchen door swung and the general returned to the table, his face unreadable even to Jericho. "Enjoy your dessert, O. Two escort skimmer details are forming up. One will take your wombat and his bodyguard back to the spaceport. The other will get you home to the Citadel."

Wombat? Wasn't that an Australian rodent? He must have really pissed her grandfather off.

Her mouth formed a perfect O before she closed it.

She reached for a cookie. "I can get home by myself."

"You're bruised and tired." Her grandfather raised his palm. "Humor me."

Solo trotted in and surveyed the table. He walked to Jericho and waited. Jericho scratched the place on the tiger's neck that had made the big cat practically purr on the skimmer, then Solo ambled around the table to O'Neill's chair and sat.

Jericho felt heat radiate from the general. Who knew the damn tiger could get him in more trouble? He stood. "Thank you for your hospitality, General Neill. I'm ready to leave now."

O'Neill stood.

Her grandfather sat, waving her into her seat. "Sit down, O. Let's finish our dessert. The corporal will show the Earther out."

O'Neill swayed for a moment, as if she wanted to go with him, but a uniformed man entered the room.

Jericho gave her a quick nod.

"Good-bye, Montgomery." Her grandfather stayed seated and didn't offer his hand.

"Good evening, sir."

Jericho was pretty sure he and Yancey wouldn't make it back to *Freedom* alive.

12

O**fficial Montgomery Corporate Earth News, Twenty Years Ago**
The prisoner society on Prism is developing their own economic system of credits based on working in the translithium mines. With a day's work in the mines, a prisoner receives a fifty percent increase in daily rations. In addition, they receive credits to purchase supplies, such as building materials, clothing, hydroponics and luxuries such as Earth food. Possession of weapons and technology not related to translithium mining continue to be punishable by death.

Personal Journal of Gatfield Montgomery/RETINAL SCAN REQUIRED:

I don't trust the exiles. I wish I could make them dig with their hands and fingernails and trek across the planet to the translithium mines on bare feet. I was outvoted because the rest of the World Board wants that damn translithium to calm their citizens. I hope the day doesn't come when I have to say, "I told you we never should have sent them shuttles." I didn't want to send them hydroponics. We need to keep them totally dependent on us for food. Then they'll be our marionettes, and we'll pull their strings. Damn

*translithium makes them think they're the puppet masters.
Screw them.*

THE NEXT MORNING while she was dressing, O'Neill wondered why her grandfather had gotten angry with Jericho. Had he called Granddad a liar about something written in an Earther history book? She hoped they hadn't talked about Cal. Or her need for a protector. The guard had whisked Jericho off to a skimmer so quickly, she'd barely been able to say good-bye to him. And that was wrong. He'd gone to a lot of trouble to spend time at the Soldier Compound and meet her grandfather. He'd supplied a delicious lunch, with thoughtful details geared to Granddad's past.

Normally her soldier escorts joked with her or with each other, but on the flight to the Citadel, the men refused to say a word—not even to answer her questions or talk to each other. Had Granddad ordered their silence?

What the frag had happened while she was in the kitchen getting dessert? When she brought the cookies and ice cream into the dining room, Granddad looked like he wanted to use Jericho for melee practice. He'd called Jericho a wombat. From what she knew of the Earth animal, it was a nocturnal rodent that could get over, around or through any fence. Her dad had told her that you always knew when a wombat had been thieving during the night— by all the shit it left behind.

What had Jericho said that made her grandfather compare him to the farm pests of Granddad's youth? Was Jericho hiding that he was trying to steal something? Why would he want to lift anything off Prism? Too bad she wouldn't get a chance to talk to him until tomorrow. Her day had been co-opted for another duty.

She arrived at the spaceport early. The pilot and copilot assigned to the mining shuttle were ill. According to the Dockmaster, who made the flight schedule, O was listed as first backup. There was no second. She'd be in the cockpit alone today. Not standard ops, but she could handle the job by herself.

After completing the shuttle's pre-flight, she strode down the empty dock toward Jericho's yacht. She had to be honest with herself that she was disappointed that she wouldn't be working with him today, so she was happy to be able to talk to him and let him know the change in plan. But she was nervous about what had happened at lunch with her grandfather and if Jericho would blame her. Why did she care so much what the Earther thought?

Solo padded beside her. Three people could have walked abreast up the yacht's gangway. She touched the access pad.

Within seconds a male voice said, "Yes, Lieutenant O'Neill?"

Of course they had visual.

She spoke into the audio screen, even though she probably could stand anywhere on the gangway and be heard. "I'm sorry, but I've been assigned other duties today. Will you tell Mr. Montgomery when he wakes up that I'll take him to Translithium Two tomorrow morning?"

"I'm awake." Jericho sounded like he was standing beside her. "I'll be right there."

He didn't have to come to the hatch. Did he want to see her? She smoothed her flight suit. Because his appreciative stare made her heart flutter yesterday. *Why do I care what he thinks about how I look?*

There was no need for discussion. Even Administrator Schultz couldn't change her assignment. Mining shuttles had top priority. Miners had to work to make the planetary quotas and to get their bonuses of extra rations. Once, when a shuttle was grounded for repairs, the miners rioted. They'd gotten a "spare" shuttle from Earth to be sure that never happened again.

The access panel slid open. Hair wet and slicked back, stubble on his chin, Jericho finished buttoning his shirt. His tired eyes took her in. "Sorry, I wasn't expecting you so early. Would you like to come aboard?"

Yes. "No." Did he get ready fast, just to see her? Even with wet hair and unshaven, he looked amazing. "I have to pilot a miners' shuttle today, but I'll be available whatever time you'd like to start tomorrow."

"Perfect. I'll go with you. I'll have lots of time to talk to the miners on the way out there, without their supervisor. How much time do I have before we leave?"

Had he gone deaf? Did he think she'd take the risk of his safety when she didn't have a co-pilot, didn't have her friends to guard him? "You can't ride on a miners' shuttle. It's a four-hour ride each way with no amenities except two restrooms for a hundred-and-fifty miners with no manners. You'd have to ride with them, since security rules preclude anyone but authorized pilots in the cockpit."

"No problem. Yancey will be with me." He bent to scratch Solo between the ears. "Solo can eat anyone who gets too close." He winked at her.

Did he think his security details were a joke? Just because nothing had happened to him didn't mean it couldn't. Frag, she'd been attacked in Convict Town with her friends. "Solo can't eat a hundred and fifty men."

Jericho chuckled. "I don't think there will be a problem."

"You think wrong. If Solo attacked to protect you, those men would rip you apart, then Yancey, and finally Solo. I'm not taking that chance." She pursed her lips. "With Solo." She threw a look at the spaceport's ceiling girders and tried to exhale some of the heat of her temper. "It's against all security protocols. If they figure out who you are, they could hold you for ransom." She shook her head. "Not good for my reputation, Jericho."

"What if you procured appropriate clothing for Yancey and me so we'll blend in?"

He thought *clothes* would make him pass for a Prism miner? She snorted a scoffing laugh. "You can't pass for a second gen. Your hair isn't the right color." He cocked his head, but before he could open his mouth, she added, "In case you haven't noticed, all second gens have white hair."

"I've noticed." He gave her a tight smile. "And an intriguing shimmer to your skin."

Intriguing shimmer? Did he really think he could sweet-talk himself onto her shuttle? "Miners know each other. You don't know anything about mining tools, techniques or living arrangements."

A determined set of his chin replaced his smile. "Precisely why I need to go on this trip. This is much better than sitting at a table asking questions of managers. I can listen to the miners' conversation and learn. I'll be able to ask relevant questions." He gave her an I-will-make-calls look. "I'm going to get that shipping contract. I need this opportunity to gather data."

"I can't guarantee your safety."

"I'll sign a waiver absolving you of responsibility."

A waiver? On Prism? The fool wasn't going to back down. Didn't he realize *she* was accountable for getting him back to his ship every night? A ludicrous waiver wouldn't negate that.

"Let's see what Yancey says." His lips thinned into a grin. He thought he'd already won. "Yancey?"

Yancey appeared at the hatch way too fast. "Yes, sir?"

"O'Neill is concerned that you can't protect me on a miners' shuttle."

Heat flooded her cheeks. "I never said that."

Jericho raised one eyebrow. "Close enough. What about it?"

Yancey considered. "If we introduce you as a Prismer with an interest in improving the mines…"

"Won't work. They'll ask you questions about your politico family, where you spent your mandatory mine time, why Yancey is with you, why your hair isn't white. You won't be able to give a satisfactory answer to any of them. Miners get lit easily, and when they figure out they've been lied to, Solo doesn't have enough teeth to protect you."

Jericho's eyes narrowed. It was the closest she'd seen to him getting angry. But then, like a spoiled child, he'd probably always gotten what he'd wanted on Earth. "What do you suggest?"

"I suggest you relax here today."

"No." He turned and motioned her aboard his ship. "We'll figure it out inside." He followed Yancey through the hatch.

Solo followed the two men, leaving her no option but to board *Freedom*. She had precious few minutes of wiggle room in her liftoff schedule. *Arrogant son of a corporation.*

The access hatch closed silently behind her. She stood, gawking like an Earther in the crystal fields for the first time. Sofas lined a room as large as her home. The walls were covered in what looked like polished wood. Flowering plants and pictures of Earth scenes lined the room. There was no evident lighting source, but the sun could have been shining inside.

She followed them through an open, beamed door into a corridor much too wide for a ship. A woman the age of a younger first gen dashed past, murmuring apologies. Yancey went after her.

What was her job and why she had apologized? Passing through a sizable salon with a variety of seating and tables, she spied what, from pictures, looked like a piano. *A piano on a ship?* Jericho stopped in a room with a clear tabletop balanced on what looked like a large clump of clear crystal spikes. He motioned her to a chair made of the same clear material.

She pulled out the seat, almost tipping it over, it was so light. Sitting carefully on its fluffy white cushion, she scooted to the edge of the table. She tapped it with her nail. It was made of thick glass and had to have required several men to lift it. The crystal shape beneath had no vibration. Probably glass, as well.

"How much time do we have?"

Jericho's words jarred her. She'd been acting the tourist, ogling the ship's fittings. "Shuttle boarding starts at oh-eight-hundred. It will take ten minutes at least to get to the dock. But you aren't going."

He tapped his watch. "That gives us twenty-five minutes to figure out a plan and implement it. Ideas?"

Frag him. She wasn't going to put him in danger. She wasn't going to pick up bloodied pieces of his body. She was his protector.

He had to do what she said. Ironic that in her role as Jericho's protector, she was as pissed-off and high-handed as Cal was with her.

Yancey coughed as he entered the room. "The Administrator has cleared your request. We need to have proper clothing delivered."

"What?" Her voice slid up a whole octave on the word. "I can't believe the warden agreed. I don't have his guards, and even if I did, that would put him at higher risk because everyone would know he's important." She crossed her arms over her chest.

Yancey had the survival skills to look apologetic. "I did convey the circumstances. I believe her exact words were, 'The Lieutenant is a smart girl. She'll figure out how to make it work.'"

And she'd started to believe that *this* Earther was different. His charm must have turned the warden's brain to mush. Like Cal, Jericho thought he could tell her what to do. Blood pounded at her temples. Was this what people called a headache? *Frag him.* "You'll need used miner's coveralls. Preferably with some stains. Send a request, urgent priority, to the dockmaster's office." If she was lucky, this whole discussion would end with the lack of adequate camouflage.

Jericho nodded at his bodyguard, who rose and left the room.

"I strongly advise against this trip," she said. Her father would have been able to talk Jericho out of going on a mining shuttle. *Where are you when I need you, Dad?*

Great. Now she was talking to him, asking for his help. And, uh, nothing.

"Noted. But this trip is why I'm on-planet. I've done this sort of thing on Earth. I've traveled to some dicey locales. I've taken some self-defense classes and can hold my own."

His earnest face relayed truth, but O'Neill couldn't imagine his father allowing the heir to Montgomery Conglomerates being exposed to any danger. Jericho must trust Yancey. And she trusted her miners. Onboard, the miners were her hostages; they might get rowdy, but they wouldn't create a security problem for her if they weren't antagonized—*if they didn't think they could profit from holding, or hurting, the Montgomery heir.*

His identity had to remain secret. There was no time to get Wash, Hoshi, Novy and Cal to the spaceport. She had the authority to include or exclude passengers on the mining shuttle. And the responsibility for her decision.

She sighed. "I'll introduce you as an Earth representative here to complete the annual inspection of the mines and conditions. Yancey will be your assistant. They'll buy that, even though no representative has ridden in the miners' shuttle before. They may have heard about your visit to Translith Three. Do you remember what name you used?"

"Easy to remember. My mother's brother is Price Thorsøngud. I introduced myself as Mr. Price. That's the name I use on Earth when I want to travel under the radar."

She knew the name of the premier shipbuilder on Earth. So that was his uncle. The cryo-ship that brought the first gens was a Thorsøngud ship. "Okay, you're Mr. Price. All Earthers have the same first name. Mister. You'll answer to nothing but Mr. Price. You'll be spending much longer with the miners than you did with Robinson at Translith Three."

"What about Yancey?"

"Yancey will be addressed as Mr. Price's assistant. He has no name of his own."

The bodyguard entered the room and took his seat. "Clothing will arrive in ten minutes."

Frag. She'd hoped lack of clothing would have stymied them.

The woman from the corridor entered, balancing a tray of food and a couple of carafes. Jericho introduced her as Matilda. Yancey rose to help her.

"You can't leave without some breakfast." She removed the lid from a covered platter. "Warm croissants with ham and melted cheese. And fruit skewers." She distributed plates, napkins and utensils before pouring cups of a steaming aromatic brew.

Jericho and Yancey began eating. She wasn't going to ruin her uniform with one of the *sandwiches*, even though they were stacked high on the plate and they smelled delicious. A couple of the fruit cubes looked familiar. Hands clasped behind her back, she tried to remember the names of the fruit.

Matilda set the carafe on the table. "I'll prepare box lunches."

O'Neill stared at the volume of food. "No lunches. Just water packs and two protein bars each. If you have any."

The woman looked at Jericho for confirmation.

Between bites, he nodded. "Whatever she says."

"Well, then, I'll get those ready." She took the empty tray and left.

"Help yourself." Jericho motioned to the plate, then reached for another fruit skewer. "How long is this trip?"

"Four hours in and four hours out. One bar each way." Maybe he'd change his mind if it meant missing his Earth meals. "You won't starve. If you pull out Earth food, you'll create a riot on my shuttle. Two regulation bars each, that's it. If you don't have any, I'll give you mine."

"We've got 'em. Why don't you help Mattie, Yancey?"

The bodyguard left, munching on his croissant.

"Are we done? I need to finish cleaning up." Jericho popped the rest of his breakfast into his mouth and poured a dark steaming liquid into her cup after he stood. "Go ahead, try something. And have some coffee."

"Don't shave. You'll fit in better." She took a sandwich, making a flaky mess by holding it too tight.

"Try it."

When O'Neill bit into the layers of dough, more flakes fell onto her uniform. She didn't care. Something warm oozed over her tongue, coating it in thick, creamy richness. The flakes melted in her mouth, and she chewed on a salty layer of something that married the flavors and textures together in tasty little explosions. Five days after meeting Jericho and she'd succumbed to the delights of Earth food. *Frag.*

Jericho chuckled. "Enjoy it. The coffee, too. I'll meet you in the entry in ten minutes. Can you find your way back there?"

Mouth full, she nodded. God help her if Jericho kept feeding her. Resolved to refuse any more of his Earth food, she finished her croissant and burned her lips and the inside of her mouth with the coffee. She'd never had anything that hot in her entire life. She drank it all.

Ten minutes later, she waited on the plush sofa beside the access hatch. She hadn't ever been so full, even when she'd eaten all her mother's rooftop berries when she was seven. Now she understood the contented sounds Solo made after a satisfying meal.

"Ready?" Jericho entered from the forward corridor, unshaven, wearing a clean but crumpled light blue coverall with a stain across one thigh. No matter what he wore, he looked like... well, the second gen females would eat him up like that yummy sandwich.

Behind him, Yancey wore an older version, patched at the elbow.

She hoped they'd return with no blood splattered on the borrowed clothing.

———

JERICHO STOOD a step below O'Neill on the narrow ramp that passed for a gangway to the miners' shuttle. Yancey and Solo stood behind him.

"Okay, you dirt diggers. Listen up!" She shouted at the miners who, duffels in tow, pushed into a crooked line. "We've got a couple guests from Earth on this flight. They're here to check on safety and production upgrades. If you're real nice, they might listen to your suggestions." After allowing a few muttered comments she said, "Here's your safety lecture. Same rules as usual. No pissing or puking anywhere but the heads. No fighting, no blood in my shuttle. If I have to hose down the inside between trips, I'm doing it with you inside. It gets rowdy, I make it real rough going in. Questions?"

"Will you marry me, O'Neill?"

"Has that tiger had breakfast?"

She ignored the questions, waving the Earthers inside to take the seats by the cockpit door; then she moved to the top of the ramp, greeting each of the one hundred forty-two miners on her roster by name. She'd covered this run often enough to know them all. And they knew she meant business. She'd only had to use the fire hose once, long ago.

"Hi, Maury. How's the wife?"

"She left me for Ben." He jerked his thumb toward the end of the line.

"I'm sorry."

He smiled, revealing two missing teeth. "I ain't."

The men pressed forward.

When all her passengers were aboard, she manually retracted the gangway and closed the hatch, dogging it tight.

She stepped to the front of the windowless cabin. "Belts fastened and snug. Check your neighbors, boys." Everyone laughed, but complied, pulling the safety harness of the person next to them. "Water, protein bars okay. Anything else you got on you waits for the privacy of your tent. You unclip your harness only to use the head."

Bored assents met her announcements.

"If I have to come back here to settle anything, you're going to regret it."

"Promises, promises," someone shouted, sparking scattered laughter.

She turned and opened the cockpit door, visually checking that Jericho and Yancey were properly belted in. Jericho winked at her and grinned.

He had to be crazy to look forward to this flight. But then, he'd made the three-month voyage to Prism in the first place. She hoped he'd be grinning at the end of the flight.

———

JERICHO HAD to credit the designer of the craft for efficiency of space. The shuttle rows faced each other with a half aisle between. It afforded a third more seats than conventional rows would have allowed. Liftoff, following a flashing red light and one buzz, had been uneventful.

Some of the miners were already asleep, either passed out from their last night in town or catching rest before their first shift. He would have liked to pound some Zs after working on his proposal into the early morning. The pair sitting across from him, however, were wide awake, staring at him like he might end up on their dinner menu. One had a nasty scar that ran from his forehead, across an eye and under his chin, as if a giant cleaver had hit his face.

"Name?" Scarface asked.

"Price. Yours?"

"Where you from?"

"Virginia."

"Your mother was a virgin?"

Jericho wanted to smile, but sat forward like he'd been insulted. "Better than a whore."

Scarface looked surprised, then grinned. "North American Union, huh?"

"Yeah."

"My people came from Colorado. Mines there, too."

"My boss is from there. Says it's pretty country, away from the mines."

The man spit on the worn deck, then looked around and rubbed his shoe across it. "Damned corporations. Ruined the land and the farms. Polluted the rivers and killed the animals. All to make a bankful of credits. Damn them all to hell."

Jericho kept his face neutral. If all the men in this shuttle felt the same, O'Neill was right. Her tiger wouldn't have enough teeth to protect him if they knew his true identity. "They got everyone by the twin bags for sure."

Scarface's brow wrinkled like the folds of a brain.

Jericho held his breath.

"Welcome to Prism. What d'ya do to make your boss send you here?"

"Low guy at the bottom of the heap." Jericho told him his job was to find ways to boost mine production and research bonuses that would entice miners to work harder. Scarface and the man beside him had plenty of ideas, a couple of noteworthy ones.

When Jericho got up to use the head, Scarface stopped him. "Use the portside one."

"Thanks. Other one doesn't work?"

"Works fine. We don't use it until after O'Neill does. Should be twenty more minutes, at the halfway point."

O'Neill's instructions ignored, men stretched out on the deck asleep, legs encroaching into the now almost nonexistent aisle. He stepped across bodies and duffels. Those who were awake watched him.

When he reached the two heads, the man in the last seat jerked a finger to the port panel. He nodded. When he came out, three men waited in line. The starboard head remained unused.

Back at his seat, two different men sat across from him. As soon as he secured his harness, they introduced themselves as shift leaders and started talking business. They had some ideas worth looking at to improve production and safety. The corporations may not own the mines, but improving production improved profits, so every proposal included safety and technical upgrades.

He was so engrossed in the story the men were telling him about extraction of large tracts of translithium, he missed the opening of the cockpit door until Solo shifted, settling on Jericho's feet.

O'Neill emerged, scanned the compartment then looked at him. He gave her the thumbs-up. She walked down the newly cleared aisle. When had that happened?

A few minutes later, she returned. "Everything all right, Mr. Price?"

He nodded. "Yes, thank you, ma'am."

She stepped into the cockpit and secured the door. Solo moved back to his spot guarding the panel.

As if on theatrical cue, twenty men jumped up and dashed aft for the heads, jostling each other, lining up in front of both doors.

Jericho couldn't help chuckling.

The man across from him nodded. "Little girl has that effect. You just want to take care of her."

He felt that during her melee practice. "Seems to me she can take care of herself just fine."

"Knew her father. He discovered Translith One, you know."

Jericho nodded.

"He used to bring her on these runs. We've watched her grow up. She's the best shuttle pilot on Prism."

The man seemed proud of O'Neill. Proud that he knew her father. This conversation wasn't what he'd expected from a miner. "That's comforting."

"She was a tough little grunt even before—"

"Before?"

"Before she earned her scar, damn Earther kidnappers. She was only ten." He started to spit on the deck but looked at the cockpit door and stopped. "Fraggers."

Jericho nodded his head. "Anyone who hurts children…"

"Should be strung up by his balls." The miner nodded. "Since Jocko disappeared, she's held her own. Damn brave for a girl her age not to declare right away. Lives alone now."

"Really?"

"Well, except for that tiger. And a building full of trained killers."

She lived with assassins? Had they taught her their skills? "That sounds like pretty good protection to me."

"Lot of people care about her. Are betting their credits on her in the Battle." The man studied Jericho like he was a translithium crystal in the rock matrix. "If anyone took advantage of her, he probably wouldn't make it offplanet."

Jericho raised both hands in surrender.

Yancey laughed and pointed at Jericho. "His wife back home would kill him. She's my sister."

The Prismer relaxed into his seat and gave Jericho a toothy grin. He looked a little less like a hungry shark.

Jericho took advantage of the rest of the trip to make a mental to-do list at the mine. But his thoughts kept straying to that cleared aisle and unused starboard head. And the men's pride and certainty in O'Neill's skills. And the not-so-subtle threat of bodily injury if he did anything to harm her.

Her grandfather's men hadn't been subtle. It seemed to Jericho that she had a whole planetful of men protecting her. Was this because they'd liked or they'd owed her father? What made her so special?

O'Neill's importance to everyone he'd met intrigued him. He'd give his quarterly dividends to know why his rough-acting guide was becoming important to him as well.

———

THE RETURN TRIP had been uneventful, with miners, tired from a weeklong shift, sleeping most of the way to the spaceport. They hadn't been interested in Jericho or his questions.

That night he initiated a burst laser call to his father, who yawned while tugging his bathrobe closed.

"Good evening, Dad."

"What's so fucking important you had to drag me out of a warm bed?"

Good to hear your voice, too, Dad. "I have some ideas for the contract that you might have to sell to the World Board."

His father's eyes narrowed and he leaned forward. "I'm too tired for you to swing me around by my dick. Why did you call?"

"I want to propose transporting three scientists to Prism."

The image on his screen seemed to freeze. He thought the connection had failed, until his father shouted, "Have you lost your mind? No one will agree to that."

"Food is the primary concern of everyone on the planet. After their early attempts to grow crops proved fatal, nothing else has been tried. Legal can build a case for a second try with new seeds, new technology and on-planet research to prevent repeating the first disaster. An agro-engineer, a medical researcher, and an entomologist could arrive on the next supply ship with equipment to begin their work."

"No one will move to that wasteland."

"You taught me that everyone, given enough incentive, *will* do anything. A young, hungry researcher will jump at an opportunity like this if it's presented in the right light."

His father nodded, steepling his fingertips. "It might be helpful to have them on Prism when we take it back. But the cost comes out of your end."

He shouldn't have to pay the costs of the agreement out of his profit, especially if his father thought the scientists were a good idea. "When we take it back? What do you mean?"

"There's a glitch in our connection." His father's tone changed, like he had something to hide. "I'll have legal clear it with the Board members. Might take some credits to grease the skids—out of your end as well. You just get us that contract, or be prepared to have a very different lifestyle. I'm going back to bed."

"But–"

The screen went dark.

Damn. *What the hell is that jerk planning now? And why am I the last to know?*

13

O fficial Montgomery Corporate Earth News, Twenty-one Years Ago
Well, it's finally happened. The first baby was born on Prism six months ago. (Include picture) It's taken the prisoners four years, but it looks like they're claiming their planet for a second generation of Prismers.

Personal Journal of Gatfield Montgomery/RETINAL SCAN REQUIRED:
How the hell did this happen? Every shipment of food has enough anti-birth meds to make a thoroughbred stud turn up his nose to a mare in heat. And enough fetal poisons to cause sponta-neous abortions within hours of conception. I had hoped to reclaim the planet, with its enhancements courtesy of the World Board and the other conglomerates, once the prisoners were all dead. This prolongs the process, but I'll figure out a solution to this second generation problem.

PINK and purple streaks of dawn lighting her way, O'Neill saw Wash jogging toward the Citadel. She sprinted to him. They ran toward Convict Town and loped along the outside perimeter of the sleeping settlement. Boots crunching on pebbles and broken crystals, they settled into the rhythm of their twice-weekly early-morning runs.

Wash glanced sideways at her. "Talked to Cal yet?"

"Are you worried about losing a bet, too?" She hurdled over a mound of trash, circling back to leap it again. Jumping a mountain of trash would be easier than trying to get the protector law overturned.

Wash kept pace while Solo followed behind. When she encountered a long, dented steel pipe that hadn't been turned into a home, she ducked and scuttled through it, reversed her course and tried to better her time. She leapt onto a four-foot high, corrugated box and ran, then side-stepped and hopped on one leg along its length to practice her balance while Wash jogged in place. Jumping off the flat roof, she hit the ground and rolled to a stand, ending face to face with a bent-over, toothless old man.

"Wat'chu doin' on my roof, crazy girl?" He cocked his head, sheltering his eyes by squinting against the rising sun. He pointed at Wash. "You should be in his bed this time o'day."

"Not today, Mister. Not this year." She gave him a quick salute and ran on.

After the second circuit, they sprinted across ground to the slope that rose to become the mountain upon which the Citadel was built. Wash turned to continue toward the Soldier Compound.

O ran up the six flights of stairs, whistling her father's favorite song. She recognized that she no longer had to break the tempo of her run to struggle for breath.

Today, Jericho wanted to see the tunnels that the Earther archaeologists had explored over twenty years before. That expedition had been the only time a large group of Earthers had landed on Prism. They'd stayed for almost two months. The researchers thought that the tunnels her father had discovered were not natural phenomena, but no evidence of the hoped-for ancient race was discovered.

She'd wandered those tunnels with her father, and right now, thinking about them, she could feel him with her. Dad, his body, was somewhere here, under the Great Plains. His vibrational energy held her, like his arms used to when she was frightened. But she'd never confess hearing his voice or feeling his energy to anyone. They'd force her to move to her mother's for sure.

Maybe the old man in Convict Town had been right. Maybe she was crazy. Crazy to think she could win the Battle. Crazy to want her independence. Crazy to believe her father was still alive. Crazy to hear his voice. But she was certain she'd heard him.

Okay, maybe just in her head, but she hadn't imagined him talking to her. It was like he was there in the room with her. And he sounded like himself. He just didn't stick around long enough for her to ask questions. Had she lost her mind during the long days of searching—and hoping?

Last night she'd scanned his logs from the days of the archaeological expedition. It had been more than a year since she'd been to the tunnels. She scoured the detailed maps with his side notes about diameters of tunnel openings, hazards, times it took to get from one point to another. He'd added humorous thoughts about the Earthers and what they did.

The biggest surprise was finding several paragraphs he'd written about Jericho's mother. Bryn had been his passenger, and he'd been her personal pilot, guide, and protector on Prism. From what he'd written, he'd liked her. A lot. His descriptions of her included words like brilliant. Beautiful. Dedicated. Vivacious. She'd only heard him use words like that about her mother or herself.

Had her father fallen for Jericho's mother? Would he have written about her in his log if he did?

He'd told her long before her mother left that from the moment he'd seen her mother on Prism, he'd directed all his energy to winning Francine. His future. His love. He wasn't the kind of man to stray from a mission. But it took five years before her mother agreed to declare him as her protector. Her husband.

It took two more years after they married before she went to the Fertile Field with him. He hadn't dictated his will to her mother. Hadn't taken her to the Fertile Field the first night of his protectorship. He'd encouraged his wife's independence, just as he'd encouraged O's. Except her mother left her father for a tyrant. A bully who made her mother cower beneath his will, who forced her go to the Fertile Field the night she left her family. Maybe it was finally time to ask her mother questions about that night.

She fed Solo a brick of dried animal protein and set out a big bowl of fresh water. Sometime soon she would take Solo to the lake so the tiger could have a good swim while she ran around it.

She grabbed a protein bar from the shelf, not caring what kind. Three bites and breakfast was done. A lot more efficient than the yesterday's croissant. Okay, not as interesting. Not as tasty. Frag the flaky crumbs, she wanted another warm croissant. She was turning into Novy.

After a shower, she pulled on her last clean uniform. She sniffed a pair of socks. "Laundry detail tonight." She filled her water pack at the kitchen sink, strapped it on and took a drink. Her ready-pack leaned against the entry door, as usual. She hefted it, feeling the extra canteen's weight. The tunnels would be hot and dehydrating.

"We're flying in to work today, Solo. Roof."

The tiger walked up the stairs, waiting for her to push the trap-door open at the top. She emerged into the sunshine and allowed her eyes to adjust to the bright light.

"Morning, O." Miguel rose from the tent-like awning in the corner.

"No need to get up, Miguel. I left the door open so you can rest inside. I'm flying out to the tunnels today, so I won't get back until late. You're welcome to bunk here again if you want."

"Thanks. Appreciate it." He jerked a thumb to the row of pots near the edge of the roof. "You're going to have some nice bunches of berries in a couple of days. I'll water them for you."

"Thanks. I didn't get to eat any of the ones I took to Sarge's last week." She climbed up the side and slid back the canopy of the flyer.

"I fine-tuned the translith crystals last night. Worked on smoothing the radio static, too. She's ready to go."

O'Neill tapped the hull. "Up you go, boy." Solo used the small metal step that jutted from the side to propel himself into the rear seat. "Thanks, Miguel. Love you."

"Back at'cha. Safe journey, kid."

She climbed into the cockpit, pulled the canopy shut and fastened her safety harness before flipping switches. When the engine rumbled to life, she headed for the spaceport, thinking she should take Jericho to the tunnel that her dad and Jericho's mother discovered. They'd kept it a secret by not noting it on any of the maps. It hadn't occurred to her before to wonder at that.

How was her father able to communicate with her—visit their home? What did that mean? Would he ever be able to walk among his friends and be seen, be touched? If he wasn't dead, could he be her protector as, what did he call it, an *energy being*?

And why had the Ancients saved him?

———

AN HOUR LATER, squeezed with Solo behind O'Neill in the cockpit of the tiny flyer, Jericho looked down, afraid he'd made a bad decision.

They could have taken the larger skimmer and left it outside the tunnel entrance with Yancey guarding it. The two of them would hike more than a mile inside to reach the maze of tunnels. But O'Neill's smaller flyer would fit inside the outer tunnels and fly deep into the caverns, allowing them more time to explore on foot.

Yancey had argued that Jericho's safety was his job, but Jericho had decided to travel alone with O'Neill and Solo. His pilot hadn't joined the heated discussion. She'd leaned against a table and listened. His safety was her responsibility—not just her job. He'd stood his ground, motivated by a need for privacy for some of the questions he had for her. And he sure didn't want to re-hash the debacle with her grandfather in front of Yancey.

Even though she'd acted the same as usual, he was going to use this expedition to clear the air between them from that meal. He'd been attracted to her, and he was pretty sure she'd been attracted to him. He had no idea how that would play out, but he wanted to explore the possibilities. And he wanted to invite her back to *Freedom*.

He shifted in his seat. At his feet, Solo twisted and growled.

"Not much further." Her voice came through his headset. The engine was too loud for conversation. A food hamper rested up front with her. No protein bars for him today.

She flew the craft like it was a bird. Soaring high, then dipping low to check the ground. Occasionally she pointed out something of interest, but he most enjoyed catching snippets of her humming a tune his mother had sung to him as a child. He would have joined in, but he enjoyed listening to her off-key rendition too much. He smiled. He'd discovered something his competent pilot wasn't good at. But there was heart in her voice, even when the notes fell flat.

"There they are. The tunnels extend under that plain."

Powdery dust covered the flat, crystal-free mesa. Reflected light stabbed at his eyes. Bleeding off speed, the craft descended. Once they were low enough, the glare disappeared, and he saw a small hole in the ground. The closer they flew, the larger the hole got. It couldn't have been much bigger than the length of the flyer.

The engine pitch changed and the craft shuddered. He took a deep breath. They fell straight down to the planet.

"It may seem like we've stalled out, but my father modified this flyer for the tunnels. It takes a minute for the system to reset itself. Close your eyes. It'll be easier for your first time."

He didn't comply. He wanted to see the entrance. It loomed in front of them. The opening was small, only large enough to—maybe—. Too fast! His body tightened. He slammed his eyes shut.

He felt suspended in space with only Solo's rump against his cramping legs. His safety harness and a ragged dragged-in breath reminded him he was still alive. He gulped air and opened one eye. Darkness enveloped him, but a beacon lit the way through the tunnel ahead.

"There's not much worth looking at the entrance, but further in it gets interesting. I'll fly to the turn-around point. We'll walk from there." When he didn't answer she asked, "You okay back there?"

"Yeah. We're okay." He wasn't, but he refused to confess that fact.

The deeper in they flew, the narrower the tunnel became, with more and more turns. More than once he caught himself holding his breath, wishing O'Neill had a little less confidence in her piloting ability. It would be worth the cost of transporting her to Earth to fly Montgomery Shipping's trickier cargo runs through the jungles of the Southern Americas.

Finally, the ship slowed and hovered in a cavernous space, settling to the ground in a flurry of dust.

O'Neill clicked her safety restraint and twisted around to look at him. "Welcome to the tunnels of Prism. Maybe you'll be the lucky one to find an alien artifact." She chuckled.

He released his harness while she popped the canopy and deplaned into the darkness. Solo padded across his lap and jumped to the ground. The tiger wasn't only big; he was heavy. Jericho knew he'd have paw-shaped bruises on his thighs tomorrow.

His exit was less than graceful, but O'Neill didn't comment. Good thing she'd left the flyer's exterior light on so he didn't fall. Once his shoes bit into the dirt, she ducked around to the other side of the plane, returning with a large shielded crystal that glowed with the power of a million-candle spotlight. She set it on a rock near the flyer and slapped a switch on the hull. The beacon on the nose of the craft winked out.

It took a few seconds for his eyes to adjust to the bright light illuminating the high rock walls.

"Let me grab my pack and the food, then we'll be off." She

pulled herself up to the ledge-step below the cockpit and, leaning in, snagged the straps of the bags.

He positioned himself below her. "Drop them to me."

Half expecting her to haul both bags down herself, he was surprised when her pack grazed his shoulder. He barely had time to set it on the ground before the food pack followed.

She hopped from the ledge, landed next to him and bent, reaching for both bags.

"I'll carry the food." He reached for the container. His hand grazed hers, and she released the bag as if it were on fire. Did she have a no-contact rule? "You okay?"

"Yes. Today you'll figure out why it's better to carry just a bar in your pocket."

She pulled two glowing crystals from her pack before slinging it over one shoulder. "Put this light crystal in your pocket until you want to examine something. Mine is all we'll need for walking through the access tunnels. Watch the ceiling and mind your head. Ready?"

He adjusted his water tube then hefted the food pack, reminding himself to tell Matilda to pack lighter lunches. "Let's go."

She walked to one of the six openings. He followed, with Solo behind.

"Do you have a map of all the tunnels?"

She tapped her head. "My dad explored them long before I was born. I played in these tunnels when he was mapping them."

He ducked at the low entrance, hunching his shoulders to fit in the narrow passageway. "Why'd you pick this one?"

"I checked my father's logs for the months your mother was onplanet. He was her pilot. And her protector."

Jericho missed a step. "Your father knew my mother?" He bumped his head trying to regain his stride. "She never talked about any of the people she met. Never mentioned names. She just told me stories about the planet. And working in the tunnels."

"The dig happened before my parents were married. I never heard them talk about it."

"Do you think your father and my mother were friends?" *Like us? Are we friends?*

"Probably not. Prism was still rough then, and the exiles didn't care much for Earthers."

"I wish I could ask her about her time here."

"Yeah, I wish I could ask my dad about a lot of things he never told me. Like the rest of that scientific team, they found nothing of significance. But the two of them did find one tunnel that no one else knew about."

"How was that?"

She turned around, a grin lighting her eyes with a mischievous glow. Was that a dimple? Was she flirting with him? "You'll see."

They went left at a fork in the cramped corridor. The ceiling angled down but the floor remained level, forcing Jericho to squat as he shuffled forward. The weight of the food pack screwed with his balance. He had visions of a turtle on its back with legs flailing. Hunched over, all he could see was her behind. He knew a few women on Earth who would give their quarterly dividends for that butt.

Solo followed close, sometimes near enough that Jericho felt the moisture in the big cat's breath. Though his pilot carried her glow crystal at her side, lighting ahead and behind, he was far enough back that it didn't help much. The ground before him was in shadow, but he wasn't going to try to get to the crystal from his pack. He tripped on a rock, grunting an oath when he hit his head on the wall.

The light ahead stopped. "You okay?" Her words echoed.

He fingered a sticky patch of scalp. "You may have to break out the med kit to sew up my head." He reached one hand to run along the wall and one above his head to measure the space before he stood, still hunching over.

The light brightened. She didn't stop until she was close

enough that her breath ruffled his hair. She lowered the crystal in front of his face.

He squinted.

"Are you bleeding?"

"Not much."

"Oh, frag." She dropped her pack. "Where?"

"Top of my head. I rammed it against a rock when I tried to straighten up. It's not bad, just a scratch."

He heard air whoosh out of her lungs. "Well, I can't send the poster boy of Montgomery Conglomerates back to Earth with a scar." She looked at the top of his head, her fingers threading his hair. "Looks like the bleeding's slowed. It could take a stitch, maybe two, if you want."

"I'm fine. Let's keep going."

"How many fingers am I holding up?"

Two fingers appeared in front of his nose. "I never noticed you had six fingers."

O'Neill gasped. She jerked her hand away and fell back on her rear, dropping the light crystal.

He laughed and reached to help her to her feet. "No, I was wrong. Two very lovely fingers."

"You jerk." There was a grudging smile in her voice. She shifted away and the light crystal glowed between them. "I told you to be careful."

"I was." He shrugged. "An uncoordinated moment."

"I have trouble believing that." She stood and resumed her path down the tunnel.

He was able to straighten when the floor of the tunnel began to angle downward.

"Novy, Wash and Cal have done nothing but talk about your athletic achievements. They've watched the news holos that are delivered with every supply ship. They call you the Grid Iron Star. I think they'd like to play that Earth game with you. Cal in particular."

"Football?"

"They think I'd enjoy watching."

"Would you?"

"I don't have time to watch games. But Cal and Novy want to team up against you and Wash."

"What, Wash got stuck with me?"

"More like Cal and Novy want to beat you."

"That wouldn't be hard. I had ten excellent players on the field with me. Without them, I wouldn't have this unscarred face." As soon as he said the words, Jericho wanted to inhale them back before they reached her ears. But they did. He knew because she froze, as if she'd gotten stuck in the narrow tunnel.

"I'm so sorry, O'Neill." When she made no comment, he would have gladly swapped places with Harvard's tackling dummy.

He wanted to tell her he'd forgotten all about her scar. That was the truth. When he thought of her, he'd never pictured it. But he knew to try to explain his way out of his mistake would only make matters between them worse.

She inhaled a deep breath and started moving. "Not your doing. What's the Earth expression? No harm, no foul? Ah, we're here."

She disappeared from his field of vision. When he stepped out, he saw that the tunnel opened to a tall-ceilinged cave with giant stalactites and stalagmites wider than his body, shining in iridescent hues in the light crystals' illumination. Solo nudged him forward.

"I should have brought the holo recorder."

She turned and looked at him, chewing on her bottom lip again. If only he could read what her eyes were trying to tell him. She gave him a small smile and shook her head. "Yeah, it's pretty. Only three people knew about this room—my father, your mother, and me. Now you."

Why had she decided to share this place with him? It meant a hell of a lot to him, but did it mean that much to her? "I'm honored by your trust."

She crossed to the maze of spires and ran her fingers across the surface of one. "It's not like you could find your way back here alone."

"I wouldn't want to. I can't imagine being here with anyone but you."

She raised a brow and continued through the maze.

Maybe he'd overstepped a boundary with last comment, but he meant it. Even if he got the shipping contract and started small tourist expeditions, this cave would remain their secret. He followed, slower because he couldn't help gawking at the beauty suspended above him. "It's beautiful. I'm … , well, I'm speechless." He caught up to her and cupped her elbow. "Your friends don't know about this place? Not even Cal?"

She looked at the powdery dirt at her feet. "Never came up. They aren't interested in the tunnels, anyway, even if some people believe they were made by a species that evolved here. Or an alien race."

He ran his palm along the smooth, glittery wall, trying to find words to convey his appreciation. "You didn't have to bring me here. I'm grateful you did."

She leaned against the opposite wall. "It seemed like the right thing to do, since our parents spent a lot of time exploring these tunnels. I'd appreciate you keeping this one our secret."

"Of course." It was the first thing she'd asked of him. And it cost him nothing. He'd never been around a girl for seven straight days without her wanting jewelry, a business favor, credits or, more often, his body.

Behind a giant, faceted boulder she pointed at an exit to the small room. "It gets better." The inflection in her voice broadcast her excitement, and her step was lighter as she threaded her way across the cavern floor. "Mind your head. I mean it, Jericho."

She ducked and entered the oval opening. It angled so sharply down that Jericho was glad it was dry so he wouldn't slip in the deep powder of the floor. She didn't talk and he didn't try to start a conversation. Between the lunch and his gear, he had started to huff and puff like the wolf in the story his mother used to read to him when he was little.

Three tunnel branches later, O'Neill dropped to her hands and knees and crawled. He did the same, thankful there were no rocks to cut his palms. Fifty yards later she flattened onto her belly. "Two more minutes."

And then what? Crawling half the length of a football field had taken a lot more energy than running that length for a touchdown ever had. The food pack caught on the ceiling, so he unstrapped it and pushed it ahead of him. Whatever they were going to see had better be worth all this trouble. Wriggling in the tunnel like a worm, he had dust in his hair, dust in his clothes, and dust in his lungs. He longed for the whirlpool in *Freedom*.

Light flooded into the end of the tunnel. She rested on one knee, arm stretched toward him. "Good job. We're here."

He crawled forward, grabbed her hand and she helped him up. Not letting go, he stared at her. They were both flushed from exertion, but he was pretty sure she blushed, adding another layer of beauty to the picture of her that he kept refining in his mind. He released her hand and brushed at his clothing. The material shimmered like the clothes of the locals.

Solo dashed past him and Jericho heard a splash. He straightened and gaped. Head like a periscope with paddling paws, the tiger cruised the surface of an underground lake. The ripples made by four hundred pounds of animal joy sent rainbows of light through the air. Glow crystals, naturally embedded in the walls of the cave and under the water, gave enough illumination to reveal the underground room's beauty. A narrow beam of light speared into the middle of the lake. He looked for the source but couldn't find it.

"A tiny opening to the surface."

She could read his mind. Good thing he hadn't been thinking of her in a bathing suit.

As if a decorator had intentionally placed them, tall crystals of every color lined the walls of the room. Smaller crystals rested in clumps on the floor.

Solo emerged from the pool, gave a mighty shake, then stretched on a clear crystal slab near the water's edge.

O'Neill put down her pack. "I don't know about you, but I need a swim more than I need food." She leaned against a clump of green, transparent crystals and pulled off her boots and socks. "Last one in gives a boon!" She untabbed her flight suit and shrugged it down her hips, stepped clear and sprinted for the water.

Mouth open, Jericho stared at O'Neill's back like a boy who'd never seen a naked girl. Only she wasn't naked. Her camisole and boy shorts covered a whole lot more than any bikini on Earth. What his eyes saw wasn't being communicated accurately to his lower half, because the word *naked* kept pulsing from his brain, ordering a major diversion in blood flow.

O'Neill had practically stripped in front of him. What did that mean?

He closed his mouth, divested himself of his clothes faster than his broker sold off bad stock, and strode to the lake in his designer boxers. Thank God his mother had taught him to swim.

And never go anywhere without clean underwear.

He dove into the most stunning body of water he'd ever seen.

14

Jericho's face broke the surface of the water of the underground lake. He shook his head and opened his eyes. Him swimming in the sparkling grotto was the kind of photo opportunity the Montgomery Conglomerates media specialists snapped up. *Can't you let business go for one afternoon?*

"Beautiful dive." O'Neill sounded surprised. She rolled to her back in a lazy float on the water.

It took only three easy strokes to come alongside her. "I told you I could swim."

"Well, there's swimming and there's *swimming*." She back-stroked away from him.

Catching her ankle, he pulled her to him across the surface of the water. Her wet camisole stuck to her skin, outlining a heck of a lot more than a swimsuit would have. "What does that mean?"

He released her foot when she laughed and went vertical. She stayed just beyond his reach, teasing him by moving her arms and making lazy ripples to keep afloat. "It means you're better than I thought." Definitely flirting with him. *Thank God.*

How many days had it taken to get a compliment from her? He grinned. "Better at what?"

Eyes widening before she flung a handful of water at him, her cupped hand sliced through the water, digging deep to race away. "Swimming." Her feet fluttered spray in his face.

She had no chance of winning this game. He noted her direction, put his face in the water and swam like it was the finals of the Ivy League Championship. No way was she getting away from him. His leg muscles propelled him forward with the smooth speed of an ocean predator.

He pulled into her path.

She didn't see him in time and crashed into him.

His arms instinctively circled her.

He'd only meant to stop her, but holding her body close in the cool, clear water, his chest pressed against her breasts and her waist pulled close to his, shocked his lower body into fast-growing awareness. His heartbeat thudded against hers, paced like they were racing together to meet at some unseen finish line. Her tight curves felt damn good nestled against him. He would have sworn he felt her stomach ripple with laughter when she grinned.

Water streamed down her hair when she blinked, orienting herself. Then she went still. Worse, her body stiffened.

"You need to let go of me, Jericho." Not a command, not a request.

He didn't want to, but he pulled his arms away and backed off to give her space, watching her expression for a clue to her feelings. He let her sort through the emotions that flickered across her face. Surprise, attraction, desire, embarrassment. When her jaw set, he said, "I'm sorry."

She cocked her head as if measuring his sincerity while her tongue traced her lips, grabbing beads of sparkling moisture. She probably had no idea how alluring she was. He was pretty sure Earthers shouldn't kiss their pilots, but he was willing to chance it. Even if he ended up wandering the underground tunnels alone.

She twisted a wet curl around her finger. She could drive him crazy. Maybe he already was. Her mouth opened, but a heartbeat passed before she spoke. "You can swim. I'd heard most Earthers can't."

Being compared to other Earthers wasn't what he wanted her thinking about. "I'm not *most Earthers*. My mother insisted I learn. We had a long pool for laps rather than a decorative grotto pool that's only good for parties."

"A pool for *laps*?"

"You swim back and forth the length of the pool. I swam thousands of laps at school."

"At school?"

"Off-season sport. Football in the fall. My father believed sports would promote my business career. Visibility. Company photographers used my pictures to promote sales of athletic equipment, sports supplements, even underwear."

She wasn't impressed, unless studying him like he was something growing on a glass slide meant she was. "There are holos of you in your underwear?" She looked way too thoughtful.

"I'm not a model or a sports jock. Those were my images, not my identity." Maybe he should mention his charitable work. Maybe he should get out of the water now and let her look her fill at his *underwear*.

"Could you teach me to swim for a competition?"

She wanted tips on her stroke?

His feet paddled under the water without making a ripple. "I'm guessing it's safe to swim here even though the beach is off limits?"

"There's no current, and there are no dangerous crystals on the lake floor." O'Neill brought her arms out of the water and rested them on the rock edge. "Let me watch you swim a couple of laps."

What guy didn't want to show off for a pretty girl?

He swam hard and fast to the opposite side of the lake's rock edge. It was longer than his lap pool. Flip-turning off the edge, he swam back to her.

"Your kick is more powerful than mine, and you do something different with your arms." She tried to recreate his form. "Show me how you hold your hands."

He raised his cupped hand out of the water, and she imitated his position. It was a little off so he corrected it and showed her how to pull through with the outline of her body for more power. He tried not to get too close to her, but he took as much advantage of their positions as he dared.

"I have to practice that." She gave him that look again, like he was a bug and she was deciding whether to flick him off.

He had numbers to run, more questions and data to collect before he could finalize his contract bid. He needed a chunk of time at his deskcomp. But he was in no hurry to leave. "Your ocean is very different, with its tides and current. I've never swum with those variables."

"But your technique will improve my speed. I know it will."

Her lips didn't beg. Her eyes didn't beg. But she wanted to practice now.

"You can swim a few laps and I can help you with your form." He rubbed the top of his head with a wet hand. He was going to have trouble keeping his hands off her form. He needed a distraction. "So...can I read your father's logs?"

"He just recorded locations, drew maps, and put down times between landmarks." She hadn't said no, and she'd looked like she didn't want to. That was a good start.

"He didn't mention my mother?"

It was hard to tell in the shifting light, but it looked like her cheeks had turned red. Her stare made him feel like he'd walked in on something very private. "He thought she was beautiful."

"She was." His whisper sounded disconnected from his body.

"And brilliant." Her words were softer.

"She was." He kept his arms under the water, but stroked to move closer to her. "What else?"

She watched him narrow the gap between them. "Vivacious." She swallowed. "He wrote that she was vivacious."

His mother had loved life, but fighting with his father had taken a toll. She had been on Prism, taking a *vacation* from his father. Things had to have been better between them when she returned to Earth, because she got pregnant and delivered Jericho nine months later.

"She was. Her eyes sparkled with joy." *When my father wasn't around.* "Thank you for sharing that with me." He breathed in a long breath. "It must have been hard to go through your father's things."

O'Neill's hand found his under the water and he squeezed it. "You know. You've had to do it."

And it had taken months to get through all her personal and legal documents. He'd read too many pages before learning when to stop before he fell apart. His mother's loss had taken a chunk of his humanity. Had given him a hard edge, like the one he saw in O'Neill. No doubt it would have been better with the support of his father but, as far as he'd seen, his father hadn't shed a single tear. And he didn't cut Jericho any slack in his business duties for mourning.

He didn't know if O'Neill's hardness had encased her long before her father had died, but it couldn't have gotten better after his loss. He took her other hand and brought it to his lips. "I wish I could make it easier for you."

For precious minutes they treaded water, spoke with their eyes and held hands. If they'd been on a street, Jericho would have hugged her, without thought of their state of undress. This was comfort, two hearts connecting in loss.

Finally O'Neill moved them into the tiny beam of light hitting the center of the underground pool. Professional experts couldn't have made her look any more beautiful. Water beaded on her lashes, making them fuller, longer. The natural shine of her skin translated into a healthy glow in the underground chamber.

An air of reluctance surrounded her when she released his hands. She glanced down at the water then looked at him with a shy smile. "Let's swim a few laps and you can give me some tips. We'll eat lunch afterward while our clothes dry."

———

O'NEILL SAT, resting her back against the smooth wall of the underground chamber. It was nice to take a day off from worrying about the Battle and thinking about a protector. She watched the rhythmic rise and fall of Jericho's chest. Thinking about her father, she hadn't trusted her voice not to crack when Jericho had thanked her for telling him about his mother, and had ended up swimming more laps than she'd intended while he trained her before lunch.

He'd fallen asleep stretched across the ledge next to her, after swallowing the last bite of brownie. He hadn't complained when her "few laps" turned into a fast-paced training session. He swam with her, pointing out ways she could change her kick or her stroke to be more aerodynamic. He showed her a more efficient way to breathe. He teased her when she slowed. At least that's what she thought that "ice breaker" comment had meant.

The hint of a snore rumbled in his throat. It sounded like a contented Solo, rolled on his back while she rubbed his belly. She couldn't help a smile.

Something shimmered at the corner of her vision. Her chin jerked toward the sight, but there was nothing to see. Was the cave a little brighter?

O.

Had she heard her name? "Dad?" Nothing. Could he find her in the tunnels?

It's called telepathy.

Watching Jericho's deep breaths, she stood and moved away, then covered her mouth and whispered, "You know what I'm thinking?"

Though she didn't hear his voice, she felt its tone. Gentle. Not finger-pointing. He knew that she knew what telepathy was. They'd joked it would have made communication so much easier when he went exploring. *You don't have to speak the words for me to hear them.*

She pressed her lips together and thought, "Okay."

That's it. But you don't have to concentrate so hard. Pretend I'm sitting at the kitchen table with you. Just think what you want to say.

"Okay."

He chuckled. *That's my girl. I'm glad you brought Bryn's son to our lake.* A pause. *You like him.*

It wasn't a question. "You're in my head". Even though she only thought the words, they sounded mean. Spiteful.

No need to bristle. I'm not rooting around for your deepest secrets. Telepathy doesn't work that way. That you brought him here speaks volumes. You've never brought Cal here.

There were a lot of things she wanted to talk to her dad about, but for now, she wanted the luxury of sinking into his comfort. Whether or not he could hug her. In the back of her brain she worried that talking with her father was a fantasy, something she'd made up to cope with his disappearance.

"I don't want to waste our time talking about Cal."

Her father's laugh sounded strange in her head, like it ricocheted around inside her skull.

"Tell me about the crash. Where are you now?"

I don't remember much about the crash. My vision blurred, my gut burned, and my legs and arms were paralyzed. It happened so fast, I barely got the Mayday off.

"So your skimmer didn't malfunction?"

He shook his head. How did she know that?

I don't think so. The mechanics will find anything that went wrong if the pieces are big enough. As to where I am, I'm in tunnels that are not connected to any we explored. They're walled off to prevent discovery. The Ancients literally walk through the walls.

So much for searching for him down here. "You weren't sick

before you left, and if your skimmer didn't malfunction, then what happened?"

I've been thinking about that. I don't want you to be frightened, but you need to know. I think I was poisoned.

Poisoned? "By whom?"

No idea. I spent an hour at the Burnt Engine the night before I left. Could have been anyone there. Or maybe some contact poison was in the cockpit.

She started to shake and couldn't stop. The sensation of an arm settling across her shoulders made her look. The same shimmer hovered above her arms. Her skin prickled, but she stopped shaking.

You need to be very careful. Check the cockpit of anything you fly. You could be a target, too.

"Why did the Ancients save you?" Would they save her?

As near as I can understand, they've been watching us since the first shuttle landed. I match their energy in love for Prism, so they could rescue me.

"Are you hugging me, Dad?"

You can feel it?

"Yes."

I'm going to have to leave you. I love you, Baby Girl.

"I love you, Daddy."

And he was gone.

She shook her head and sat for awhile before walking to her folded clothes. Jericho hadn't moved. She pulled on her jumpsuit, socks and boots, watching the slow rise and fall of his chest, remembering how quickly his arms had gone around her when she'd crashed into him. How they'd wrapped her securely for a few heartbeats longer than necessary. Although she'd been in no danger, she felt safe in his embrace. Better than safe.

Her heart had raced when she thought he would kiss her. She'd wanted him to. Was that why the fleeting sadness when his support had dropped away? She'd never been tempted by anyone other than Cal. She hadn't known she could be—was—tempted by Jericho.

She stared across the still, shining water. Not at all like her muddled thoughts.

"A penny for them." Jericho's voice startled her.

"What?"

"Old Earth saying, old Earth form of credit. I'm sure your thoughts are worth much more than a penny." He reached for his clothing. "Thanks for stacking them within reach." He pulled his pants over his expensive underwear.

She watched him finish dressing. She'd watched many men follow the same routine after a swim, but she'd never been interested in how they put their clothes on. Watched their legs disappear when they pulled their pants up. Watch a stomach disappear when the hem of a shirt got tugged into place. Jericho had become too interesting to her.

At her two-note whistle, Solo stood and stretched, giving a mighty yawn. Did all males nap after a meal?

She smiled. "At least the food pack is lighter."

He positioned it across his back. "It would be empty if you'd eaten your share."

"I've eaten more food in the past sixty-three hours than any other time in my life. I haven't been hungry for three days."

"Are you usually hungry?"

"I wouldn't say hungry. I'm lucky. I grew up on three rations a day instead of two, since my dad could draw extra proteins for piloting and exploring. I'd be hungry if I didn't get three bars. I never felt full like this, though." She raised the side of her hand to her forehead. "Fed up."

His smile brightened the dark grotto. "Just full. Fed up is entirely different." He bent to grab her pack and handed it to her. "It's hard to believe that your dad and my mom swam in this lake twenty-three years ago." He scanned the room as if memorizing every crystal, every rainbow reflecting from the water. "Thanks for sharing it with me."

The space seemed to shrink, or maybe he filled more of it. Being in the tunnels with him made her feel closer to him. Not like how she felt close to Hoshi, Wash, Novy. Or Cal. There was something about the way he appreciated *her*, not just what she could do for him—her Earther passenger—that warmed her heart.

She adjusted the straps of her pack. "They stayed down in the tunnels for days at a time, exploring. I bet they were really happy to discover this lake." Grabbing the handle of the glow crystal lantern, she dropped to her hands and knees at the tunnel entrance and led the way out.

Before she finished the crawl to the large tunnel, something squeezed her ankle. "Ugh." She jerked her foot, hitting the sole of her boot on the tunnel wall. "Back up." She tried to turn around in the tunnel, but there wasn't enough room.

"Easy. I'm sorry. I was going to tease you about something alive down here."

She made a noise that sounded like a very unprofessional snort. "Why would you do that?"

"To save you."

What? He thought she needed saving?

"Sorry. Bad idea." When she didn't comment he added, "I know you didn't need saving back there in the lake, but it felt good to… Like I said, sorry."

Should she respond to his confession? She'd liked the feel of his arms around her. She'd wanted him to kiss her, for frag sake. "It was nice to be saved, even when I didn't need it." She sighed. "But don't pull a stunt like that again or you might get a fist in your eye. I don't want anyone to try to save me."

"I understand and I will not surprise you again with a *stunt*. But if I warn you first, it will be okay?"

"If you warn me first, I won't warn you until after my fist connects with your jaw." But if he forewarned her, she wouldn't coldcock him. Would she run? She lowered to her belly and scrabbled forward. "Get moving. And no funny business. We're going uphill on the exit, but we should be able to make it to the skimmer in the same amount of time it took to get here."

"Yes, ma'am. Roger that, loud and clear." He wasn't chuckling but, frag, his laughter rang in her head.

She didn't wait to offer a hand when she pulled herself clear of the tunnel. Crouched over, she hiked up the steep slope of the larger space, pushing herself, telling herself she was training. And he kept pace with her. Not so close that if she stopped suddenly he'd run into her, but close enough that she could hear his ragged breathing over her own as they stood and neared the skimmer. Solo was so quiet, if she hadn't known better, she'd have wondered if the big cat were still behind them.

"We're here." The glow crystal she'd left in the large cavern lit the space around the skimmer. She circled the craft, checking that everything was just as she'd left it. Dipping under the hull, she stuck out a hand. "I'll stow the food pack, Mr. Montgomery."

"Jericho. My name's Jericho." He extended the bag, but when she tried to take it, he hung on. "I think after today, you should use my name."

She gave the pack a small tug and he released it. She wanted to call him Jericho. She thought of him as Jericho, but using his name was so…personal. Before she ducked under the hull, she stared at him. He didn't look angry, but he was irritated. She looked at her boots. "Okay. You're the boss."

"Oh, no. Don't pull that on me. You've never given in to me before, even though, technically I *am* your boss."

Wrong. She'd given in to him yesterday when he forced her to take him on the mining shuttle. "So what do you want…Jericho?"

"I'd like for you to tell me the rules of this game you're playing. Every time I think you're relaxing that *I don't fraternize* stance, you snap tighter than a clam."

Not knowing exactly what "snap tighter than a clam" meant, she sensed his frustration. She nodded, feeling it, too.

"Hell, you brought me somewhere magical today. A place you haven't taken the guy who everyone says you're going to marry."

She couldn't look at him. "Cal isn't interested in crawling through tunnels."

He ran a hand through his disarrayed hair. "I don't know what your experience of Earthers is, but I'm not going to jump you. I'm not going to push you up against a wall and do what every second gen male on this planet would love to do with you."

Did he think anyone other than Cal was interested in her? Was Wash? Was Novy? They'd joked, but never tried to hold her hand or kiss her. "What do you want?" She hadn't meant to snap out the question. His outburst—no, that wasn't fair, it hadn't been an outburst—caught her by surprise. Had he been as affected by that hug, that almost-kiss, as she had?

He took a step back and shook his head. "I just would enjoy a friendly face. What do I want? I want you to think of me as Jericho. Just. Jericho."

From what he said, he'd been thinking about her and Cal. And he'd been thinking about *fraternizing* with her. What would that mean? What would it feel like?

She bobbed her head. "Okay. Jericho." While she stowed the gear, he climbed into the backseat. After boosting Solo, she swung up onto the side step. She hesitated before throwing her leg over the side into the cockpit. Thrusting her hand at him, she gave her passenger a grudging grin. "Jericho. Truce?"

He smiled and took her wrist, helping her up. "I've never been at war with you, O."

O? Ha, he'd just won a skirmish. He'd appropriated her first name. And she was going to let him. Because her name sounded good rolling off his tongue. She cocked her head and pursed her lips. "Good thing. You've wouldn't have survived. Jericho."

His smile told her he knew he'd won that round, but he also knew better than to push his luck. "So what's on the agenda for the ride home?"

She hadn't planned anything but a simple return to the space-port, but maybe she'd stretch the rules, the law, just a bit.

Warden Schultz had approved Jericho to go anywhere within

the bounds of his guaranteed safety, so she could fly him over any part of Prism. Including the Fields. She couldn't tell him their importance, since field details were not shared with Earthers, to keep them from coming to Prism to use them for their own personal gain.

Without the Fertile Field, there would be no second-gens. Something about the planet's energy made the exiles unable to conceive. The first three years, no one got pregnant. After a couple spent the night in the Fertile Field, and nine months later the first second-gen was born the rush to create families started.

When she'd received her full-pilot status, she'd flown a bit into it to test the feelings with her friends. Those *feelings* hit them fast and hard. The field definitely *put you in the mood*, as Cal said.

He'd decked Novy when the Russian tried to lip-lock her. She'd bugged out fast after that, but Cal had been all over her—hands covering her breasts, mouth kissing a path from her ear to her neck to…She would have enjoyed it, except it was her first time flying over the field and she'd been afraid she would crash the skimmer.

She'd have to fly through the Fertile Field for part of her flight route for the Battle. It wouldn't hurt to try a little of the route she'd have to take. Maybe an Earther, *her* Earther, was immune to the vibrational energy. But maybe he wouldn't be…

Although she'd have to fly deep into the Retching Field for the Battle, she didn't want to subject him to that—though she might tease him a bit. And she wouldn't take him to the Healing Field, which served as their hospital. If you were ill and spent the night within the boundary of the Healing Field, you were better in the morning. Much better. The politico scientists said it was the vibrational energy of the giant crystals adjusting the vibration of the body's cells. Which was good, because Prismers had to rely on soldier medics for all things health related. The corporations hadn't included medical care for its exiles. Jericho's notes to himself about medical care wouldn't mean anything in his proposal. But she wouldn't tell him that.

And she wouldn't take him across the Retching Field after declaring a truce.

"You wanted to see more of the planet, so today we're going to fly the skimmer across some crystal fields and view them from the air. We'll be trying out part of the route I'll be flying for the Battle. We won't be hiking through them, but you'll feel their energy."

"Above the ground in the skimmer?"

"Trust me, you will feel the planet's energy."

"We'll see."

It would be her pleasure.

15

Private Journal Notes of Cornelia Schultz (Present Day):

It's a good thing Prismers are close-mouthed about their "fields," although I'm not sure what good the Retching Field will ever be. But the Fertile Field saved them by producing a new generation and hope for a future. And the Healing Field is better than Earth's most advanced hospitals and medical research facilities. Heaven help us if the World Board finds out about them. Those fields may end up being worth more than our translithium mines.

AFTER AN HOUR CROSSING what O'Neill called the Great Plain, Jericho wasn't sure if he'd missed what he was supposed to sense. "Will Solo feel the vibrations?"

She waited for a fraction too long before answering. He'd surprised her.

"Nice of you to consider him. He'll feel it. Don't worry, he won't throw up on your shoes. There's a shub in the pocket under your seat."

"Shub?"

"Stomach Heave Up Bag."

Crap. She expected him to puke.

His father had subjected him to the Screamin' Reamin' ride at Monty's Wonderland when Jericho was tall enough. They'd stayed on the ride until Jericho could no longer scream, his throat was so raw. His father had slapped him when he discovered Jericho had pissed his pants. "A Montgomery is afraid of nothing."

Forgetting she couldn't see it, he gave a curt nod. He wasn't going to scream, piss himself, or vomit.

But he noticed a growing tension in his body. A tension not at all related to his muscles.

He closed his eyes to concentrate on what his body communicated to his brain.

Nothing related to his digestive system. Lower. He had the sudden urge to put his arm around O and pull her to him. His breathing became heavier. Did the energy affect Earthers in a different way?

Oblivious to whatever affected him, she scanned the landscape of orange crystals running below the skimmer.

His breathing quickened even more. At least his pants were loose, but if this went on much longer, he'd need something to cover his lap. It was too late to tell her to change course. And that wouldn't have been what he wanted, anyway.

He wanted O and he wanted her now. Naked, under him. Skin sliding across skin. He reached across the back of her seat for her shoulder.

She grabbed his fingers and squeezed, pulling his hand to rest on the top swell of her breast. Her neck was flushed, and with his forearm on her shoulder, he could tell she was breathing hard, but she stared straight ahead and flew the damned skimmer instead of landing.

The craft banked into a sharp climbing turn. His safety harness dug into his side, jerking his arm back to his lap. He wanted to climb over the half-wall between them. She could fly and he would try not to distract her too much with kisses and touches.

"A few more minutes for the effect. We're on our way back to the spaceport."

Just peachy. If they landed in less than fifteen minutes, he'd have to ask for a book to read so he wouldn't embarrass himself getting out of this crate. "How long?"

"A few more minutes."

"Until we're home?" His voice cracked like he was in junior high again.

"No. Until you won't feel the vibrational energy."

"Well, thank fuck for that."

"Excuse me?"

"How long until we land?"

"A little more than an hour. Are you all right?" She certainly wasn't, by the pitch of her words.

"I'll get back to you on that." Right now, he just wanted to relax and feel the ebb of the energy. He closed his eyes and rested his head against the padded cushion behind him. The mating imperative lessened, but his pain-filled lower half hadn't gotten that message yet. He could have satisfied every one of the sex-crazed Harvard cheerleaders, and maybe even given them a second round.

After a long time he finally put his hand back on O's shoulder and squeezed. "What the hell was that, O?"

"You felt it, then?"

"Yeh, and you did, too. Horny as a lab-enhanced rabbit."

"I don't know what that is."

"Put him in a pen with female rabbits and he'll kill himself trying to screw them all."

She stiffened. He saw it in her neck and felt the tension in her shoulder.

"I'm sorry. I wasn't sure you'd…"

"Must make for a hell of a date."

"Excuse me?"

"You go there often with Cal?"

"That was uncalled for." She exhaled hard, three times. Like she was practicing a ritual. "Only once. And that was on a dare. I had just gotten my full pilot status, and I flew Cal, Novy, Hoshi and Wash there."

"That must have been fun." His toned screamed, *Not in this century.*

"They were older. I was stupid. I didn't know that much about it. I bugged out of there as soon as I realized what was going on."

He'd gotten upset at the idea of her there with Cal and Novy. That was a first. He couldn't remember getting jealous about any of his girlfriends on Earth. O was *not* his girlfriend. And she never would be if he didn't get his emotions under control. "And you've never been back?"

"Nope. Just corner overflies to cut flight times somewhere else. Always alone."

His heart quit hammering like it was trying to beat its way out of his chest. As it slowed, he calmed. He couldn't put a name to what he felt; it was too new and different.

"The spaceport's ahead."

She landed the skimmer and popped the canopy. He watched her swing her leg out to the hull step and hop out. Still feeling the effect of the vibrational energy, he stared at her as if he were a glutton at a feast. Solo followed her; then Jericho levered himself down. She waited for him on the dock, holding the food pack. Wearing an embarrassed half-smile.

He glanced around. All the workers were gone for the day. "That skimmer with the autopilot? Can you get it again?"

She looked at him like she was afraid he'd gone crazy. "Yes."

"Good. If you ever want to give that energy a fair chance, reserve that shuttle and I'll go with you. Alone. I'm all for experiencing whatever you think I should while I'm here."

Sweet O, she looked like a frightened little rabbit. "Oh, I don't think…"

"You don't have to think." He wrapped his arms around her

and pulled her close, like he had in the underground lake. He touched her forehead with his. "You are amazing, O."

"That's just the after-effects of…"

"No, that's you."

She scanned the empty dock. "I should get you back to your ship."

He took her hand. She let him. "It's just down the corridor. Why don't you get in and go home?"

"No. It's my job to see you safely back to your ship."

He smiled. Thorn, one of his teammates would have called it a shit-eating grin. "Are you angling for a good night kiss at my hatch?"

The shock of his suggestion reflected in her wide eyes. "No."

He squeezed her hand. "Too bad. My loss. Let's get me back so you can go home."

Solo followed as she walked beside Jericho to *Freedom's* hatch. It opened as soon as his foot touched the ramp.

"Goodnight, Jericho. I," her gaze dipped to the ramp before looking back at him, "hope you enjoyed today as much as I did."

He could have swept her up and whirled her around in a circle. But she knew Yancey would be watching and he wouldn't embarrass her. "There is no way you could have enjoyed it as much as I have. I'm looking forward to seeing you tomorrow. Good night…O."

He walked through the open hatch and hit the pad to close the door. On the security hatch's monitor, she looked at the closed door for a few seconds before she turned around, petted Solo, and walked away. He leaned his back against the hatch and smiled. Even though he'd gotten no work done on the shipping proposal, today had been a good day.

A very good day.

———

THE NEXT MORNING, O's muscles protested the underground swimming lesson. She rubbed the last of her mother's homemade liniment into her legs, shoulders, and arms. It smelled better than what her grandfather would have given her.

It was strange how comforting the act of rubbing the liniment into her calves felt. Almost as if she were receiving a tiny bit of the nurturing she'd craved from her absent mother. She'd need a whole container full after the Battle. So would every other competitor. Francine's remedies were prized and carefully hoarded. Ray Reagan didn't like his wife *working*, so there was always more demand than supply for her concoctions.

Her skin prickled. O would have to ask for another bottle. Asking her mother for anything grated, and not just because it made her mother happy to be able to give something that O would accept. Asking for anything reminded O that she wasn't self-sufficient. Wasn't independent.

Her mother had concocted the mix for her father's aches and pains. When O was little, she was convinced her father would ask for the stuff just to have her mother massage it into his muscles. Most of the time, before the fragrant liquid had disappeared, O was sent downstairs to play for a while. Her parents had been so in love. How could her mother have walked out on her father without a backward glance? It was time to find out.

She'd accepted this bottle almost a year ago. Dad had warned her that her mother would have a birthday gift for her, and that he expected her to accept it. *With grace.* To the best of her ability, she'd unwrapped the present, muttered something about how she could use it, and gritted out a thank-you. Maybe she would try to do better this year. That would make Dad happy.

She finished dressing and Washington joined her on the jog to the spaceport. "Need any help with Jericho? I'm off duty today."

"Why the sudden interest?"

"Thought we could spend some time at the beach."

"Just the three of us?"

"You're invited. Hoshi, Novy and Cal will meet us."

Her fist tightened. "Whose idea?"

Wash almost tripped. "Cal's." Color rose from Wash's neck to his face. "He saw a holo sales promo of your Earther in his underwear."

She thought of those bubble chips. One or more of them could have carried Earther news. "How'd he get that?"

"He said a news disk was floating around the Politico Compound. He's mentioned them before. This one had a, what did he call it? Oh, yeah, an *advertisement* between stories about increased food production and a new miracle drug."

"Oh, hell, Wash. He's not my Earther. Just come aboard and ask to see him in his underwear if you want to. I'm sure he won't care, since billions on Earth have seen that holo." But he was her Earther now. She'd already seen Jericho in his underwear. Seen and felt that underwear up close. Very personal. And she'd like to do it again. Frag her, she had to bury those memories.

He sputtered. "No. No, that's not it. Cal thought…"

She quit running and planted her feet wide. Cal had put him up to this. What was the politico thinking? Was Cal going to use this as a way to convince her she needed him as her protector? To remind O that she was his, and had been since her birth? "Stop right there."

He did, but out of her attack range.

"You guys want to fraternize with an Earther?" She spat, but a bitter taste stayed in her mouth. She'd done more than fraternize yesterday. What she'd done felt like a betrayal. But who or what had been betrayed was beyond the reach of her bewildered brain. "Why would I want to spend time with Jericho at the beach? The pack of you could have asked me. I don't know why you decided to get caught up in a politico's machinery, Wash, but I'm telling you, if you *ever* try to outflank me for Cal again, you'll get worse than what Novy got. And you can tell Cal I'll give him the same. No beach. No balls. Get it?" She shifted her pack and jogged away.

Wash caught up to her. "Come on, O. We just want to see what Jericho's got."

She kept running. "I'm not sure what he's got. I haven't seen it.

Not my business. But I'm pretty sure it's the same as what you've all got." She turned and ran backward. "Except he's still got his brain in his skull and yours has apparently moved below your waist."

"I thought Cal had talked to you about the day. I didn't know he was trying an end run."

But that's exactly what he'd had done. Ran behind her back to get what he wanted. A chance to show off in front of her, and to let her know he had power over her. Maybe he hadn't lied to her, but long ago Cal's father had lectured them both about sins of omission when they'd answered questions about a prank they'd pulled, but hadn't told the whole truth because they hadn't been asked the right questions. And when she got home, her father had started in on her about duty and honor.

Her temper heated, boiling her gut juices. She'd have to teach Cal the lesson he hadn't learned that day.

Within sight of the guard tower, she finished her run to the spaceport entrance alone. Wash had followed Cal into the land of crazed male. Were Novy and Hoshi next? Why had she never seen this before? If the tower guard hadn't been watching, she would have planted her butt on the ground, pulled up her knees, wrapped her arms around her liniment covered legs, and had a good think. Instead, she waved at the first gen and entered the building.

Jericho met her at *Freedom*'s access hatch. "How are you this morning?"

He looked good. Better than good. Her body felt drawn to his like a magnet. She pretended her boots were nailed to the ramp so she wouldn't step into his arms and beg for a kiss. Whew. Veiled parts of her had came alive. She'd never been afraid of what she might do around Cal. No wonder he wanted to compete with Jericho—while she watched. Wait, Jericho had asked her a question that she hadn't answered. It took a moment to recall his words. "A little sore, nothing debilitating. How's your head?"

"A little sore, nothing debilitating." He winked. "Follow me."

He led the way to the room with the table. A large bowl of bite-sized pieces of yellow fruit mixed with red, round plump ones and a plate of many rolled sandwiches waited, along with a sweating pitcher of orange liquid. So far, her stomach hadn't rebelled against his Earth meals, but she'd been careful not to overdo. Even so, her body had welcomed the extra calories.

There was way too much food for the two of them. And one, two, three,… six plates. Frag. He was expecting everyone. They'd already invited him to Soldier Beach. Without asking her.

She was the one in command of Jericho's schedule, and they thought they could take charge? Either she'd dropped into a parallel universe or her friends' brains had fallen into their asses. They needed a refresher lecture on respect and chain-of-command.

He pulled out a chair and motioned her to sit.

"I'm hoping today's itinerary is less active."

"It will be." After she settled, he dropped a kiss on the top of her head. What was she supposed to do, to say, in response? She stifled the sigh that crept up her throat. If she couldn't tell whether the sound was a response to wanting more or not knowing what to do, how would Jericho?

"I hope you're hungry." He sat next to her. At the head of the table. In the same place her dad sat at home. And she was in her mother's place.

Maybe humor would defuse her tension. "I live on Prism. I'm always hungry."

"Try the fruit?" He put a spoonful on a plate after she nodded. "Pineapple and cherries. Sweet and tart."

She couldn't resist touching the pitcher. Expecting it to be hot, she jerked her fingers back from the cold surface.

"Iced orange juice. Fruit and Eggs Benedict wraps." He poured them each a glass of the orange liquid from the frost-encrusted container, then added half a *wrap* to the plate and offered it to her. "We may as well start while the wraps are still hot. They must be running late."

She studied the full plate, wondering if the wrap might be too much, then glanced up to him studying her. "I didn't think all this food was just for us. Who are you expecting?"

He put his fork down. "I thought this was your idea."

"What did you assume was my idea?" Her tone matched the icy exterior of the orange juice.

His brows creased. "The Dockmaster delivered a message from Cal last night. He invited me to play football at the beach with the guys. I invited everyone here for breakfast before we leave. Are you saying they didn't invite you?" He reached across the table.

She pulled her hand into her lap. "No, they did *not* clear it with me."

His fingers drummed the glass tabletop. "Well, I'm inviting you. You deserve a day to relax."

After a long inhale and an even longer exhale, she twisted a loose strand of her hair around her finger. "I'm not going." She put up her palm to stop whatever he was going to say to sway her. "They didn't talk to me about it. Not when they planned it, not when they invited you. They know all schedules go through me. This is a breach of security. A breach of protocol." How was he going to take being told she wouldn't let him go?

"Crap, I had no idea." He ran his tongue across his lower lip. "They overstepped. I get it." He nodded. "It's happened to me more often than I like to remember. Older managers, supervisors who wanted to put me in my place, whatever they thought that was." His gaze hardened. "I'll meet them at the hatch and tell them the party's canceled." He stood.

Not the reaction she'd expected. He didn't argue to spend the day playing ball with her friends. He didn't try to talk her into forgiving them, or worse, convince her they'd done nothing wrong.

He looked like he was trying to put together the pieces of a puzzle. "This is part of that protector law, isn't it?"

"Sit." She waved a hand. "The problem is my sudden need for a protector when my father went missing. Cal is sure he's the only one for that job." She looked at him and her eyes softened. "Then there's you."

He pulled out the chair alongside hers, turned it around and straddled it. "I've created a problem for you. I never..."

"You haven't created *their* problem. Specifically, I think Cal's got a problem with you."

A smile grew as understanding lit his eyes. "Oh." He put an elbow on the back of his chair and rested his chin on his palm. "This could get interesting."

He might think he could have fun with the situation, but she wouldn't. "No, it's just going to get more difficult for me. I need to handle this."

"I'll be right beside you." He paused, then sat back. "If you want me there, that is."

Did she? It might be nice to have a wingman, but she didn't need him. If she didn't need a protector, she had to be able to deal with Cal on her own.

Yancey peeked into the room. "The guards are approaching the ramp, sir."

Jericho stood and pulled out her chair. "Thank you, Yancey. We've got the hatch."

"Yes, sir." Yancey returned to wherever he came from.

They walked in silence to meet her friends. Jericho was probably making plans, running scenarios, trying out alternatives. She only wanted to keep her Neill temper under control. She didn't want to give them a reason to say she couldn't handle a simple change in plans.

A kernel of an idea popped into her awareness. Maybe there was a way to teach them all a lesson. But it wasn't going to be easy on her. And there might be a lot to clean up.

———

THE HATCH SLID OPEN. O'Neill stood next to Jericho.

They hadn't talked about who would speak first, but Jericho waited for her to take the lead, so she did. Except Cal cut her off before she got started.

He stood in front of Novy, Wash and Hoshi, feet apart, hands clasped behind his back, like he'd been taught at the Soldier Compound classes. "Good morning, O. I'm sorry signals got crossed."

She took her time looking him over. "No, you're not. And your signals didn't get crossed." He opened his mouth, but she cut him off. "I'm not going to cite your errors in judgment in public." She stood aside, Jericho moved with her. "Come aboard so we can talk."

They filed through the hatch and stood in the center of the small reception room.

"Welcome to *Freedom*, gentlemen." Jericho looked at her and inclined his head toward the dining room, as if asking a question. She nodded. "If you'd follow me into the dining room."

They acted as if they'd been given a reprieve from a mine sentence. They exhaled as a group and followed Jericho, jostling each other good-naturedly, thinking Jericho was on their side, and with a little sucking up, they'd be off to the beach.

She pulled her shoulders back and watched them take the seats Jericho assigned them. He put Cal directly across from her, with Hoshi on her right. Wash sat next to Cal, and Novy was opposite Jericho, at the other end of the table. Her friends eyed the pitcher, the bowl of fruit and the platter of wraps. She hoped her quick look conveyed her agreement with Jericho's seating arrangement. He didn't offer them the food. He gave her the same slow blink Solo did when he wanted her to know he was watching but wasn't planning to act.

She narrowed her eyes at each one of them, starting with Hoshi and continuing counterclockwise—ending with Cal. "Okay, you jerk-offs."

"Hey."

She continued over Cal's interruption, pointing to Novy and Hoshi. "Your behavior is inexcusable. You understand the chain of command, correct? You know I am the commanding officer here.

And you allowed him," she pointed at Cal, "to act like your C.O. I should put both of you on report."

"Listen, O, I didn't mean…"

"Shut up, Cal. Your turn is coming." She targeted Wash, and his smirk, next. "You aren't officially a soldier, but you've gone through soldier training and drilled with us. You had to have known this would come back to bite you on the butt." He nodded. The smirk disappeared. "But at least you had the sense to give me a heads up."

She leveled her pent-up anger, on Cal. "You. You're just an assbrain." Saying the word released the confused emotions that had given her so many sleepless nights the past two weeks.

His jaw tightened. The muscles in his neck flexed. He was trying hard not to respond.

"I can't believe you fragged me last night."

That rolled him over the edge. He pushed up from the table and leaned toward her. "I. Did. Not. Frag. You. Last night or any other time. What the hell are you talking about?"

She stood, mirroring his position. Her face was maybe six inches from his. She could feel his quick, hot breaths. "You did frag me. You took over my command, disregarded any plans I'd made, turned my troops against me." She paused and looked at Hoshi, Novy and Wash before glaring at Cal. "You wanted to play a game with my Earther." She pulled back and sat. "Now, tell me what part I got wrong."

Cal gave Jericho a death glare before reclaiming his seat. "He's not your Earther."

She couldn't keep the corners of her mouth from quirking up. "That all you got?"

"None of what I did was meant that way."

"And if I brought it to the court-martial board for review, would they see it from the politico side?"

He shook his head. "You know they won't."

"Words like traitor and betrayal come to mind."

He looked at her without his previous superiority. "That's harsh, O."

"Maybe. Words like that in your record won't help get you elected to anything."

"I was just looking out for you."

Novy's chin tilted toward Jericho. "Maybe best to not wash laundry in front of Earther."

Jericho, who could have passed for a statue until then, looked at her. "Want me to leave?"

It was his ship. Yet he gave her total control. "No need."

She peered around the table. "Do you all agree to abide by my decision on this, or do I write up the incident?" She gave them the choice of an informal soldier-solution. She hoped they would take it, because she couldn't put them up on charges.

Hoshi slapped his hand on the table. "Agree."

Wash gave her a crooked smile and did the same. "Agree."

Novy nodded. "Jewels in sling. No choice." His hand slapped the table. "Agree."

Cal's fingers rubbed back and forth across his lips. He took in the hands on the clear table. "Under protest..."

"Not good enough. Either you agree that you planned to hijack my authority or you don't. Which is it?"

"You haven't been yourself since your father disappeared. It has nothing to do with your authority."

Her hand slapped the table. "The hell it doesn't. You've been walking around the last two weeks like you're wearing your little brother's underwear."

Wash's other hand couldn't hide his chuckle. Hoshi shook his head.

Elbows propped on the table, Cal's forehead rested in his cupped palms. "Agreed." He lowered one hand to the table in the soldier-solution sign of surrender.

For the first time in her life, she'd confronted the formidable collective force of her friends. Her chest expanded with a long, unrestricted breath. She'd *done her lolly*, gotten angry, stood her ground. And they'd backed down. "Fine. I declare you all guilty of violating Section 5, Article 1, Paragraph 4 of the Earth Union Military Code of Conduct by ignoring chain-of-command regulations. California Reagan, as leader you bear the greater responsibility and the greater sentence. Are you ready to hear your penalties?"

They sounded like a hologram choir, answering yes in unison.

"Hoshi, Novy, and Wash, for the next month you will protect me from anyone who, without my permission, declares that he is my protector. You will use whatever means are necessary that will not land you in the brig or under the ground."

The three looked at each other. They hadn't been expecting that sentence. Relief bled through their smiles. They didn't believe they'd have to do a thing, but she knew they had just become her unofficial protectors from Cal or any other unwanted protector. "Agreed?"

Three hands reached toward her. She shook them each before turning her attention back to Cal, who looked like he wanted to argue, but had resigned himself to what he hoped was a smarter course of action. "California Reagan, you are to cease and desist from all overt and covert actions as if you are my protector. You are tasked with devising ways to support my wishes and plans without usurping my power."

Cal leaned forward. "For how long?"

Wash whistled. "Shut up, Cal. She went easy on you. Take it."

"How long?"

"One month."

He smiled and nodded. Looked like he'd won.

"I'm not finished. One month if you agree that you will *never* become my protector." Jaws dropped around the table. "Forever, supporting me without exercising control, if you want a shot at that job." The second option would give her a protector in name, but he could do nothing without her consent—including marrying her.

Now he was pissed. "It's a protector's job to evaluate requests based on safety issues."

"So you're taking the one month option, then." She tried to

sound disinterested, but she had to ball her fists to keep her hands from shaking. And even that didn't help much. Maybe she'd pushed him too harshly.

"Frag, no. I'm not agreeing to anything that keeps me from being your protector. And for the record, I've always supported your wishes and plans."

She swallowed to steady her voice. "One month or forever, Cal?"

He stood, walked around the table and faced her. Serious. Fire in his eyes. "Forever."

She'd forgotten to breathe. She forced her arm forward. "Agreed."

He threaded his fingers through hers and pulled her against him. "Frag that." His lips crushed against hers. "Yes, I'm yours forever."

No. That wasn't her offer. She'd wanted to keep him from forcing her to marry him, then carting her off to the Fertile Field. But he thought she'd meant something else.

And so did Novy, Wash and Hoshi. Her friends clapped. Novy asked if it was time to eat. Cal returned to his seat.

In the excitement, Jericho leaned over and whispered, "I think you've just agreed to a protector for life." He wasn't smiling.

She wasn't hungry.

She was well and duly fragged.

16

Official Montgomery Corporate Earth News, Two Years after the prisoners landed on Prism
The World Board archaeological expedition left today for Prism. The prisoners have discovered tunnel systems suspected to have been made over a thousand years ago by an ancient race. We're excited about the possibility of the expedition's scientific and medical discoveries that may improve our lives beyond our wildest dreams.

Journal of Gatfield Montgomery/RETINAL SCAN REQUIRED:

It's costing me a half year's profits to underwrite my soon-to-be ex-wife's dig, but the public relations during the divorce will be much easier to sell. With her desertion to pursue her academic interests, the bleeding heart public will finally empathize with me. And they'll cheer when I announce my engagement to wife number seven, an exotic, guaranteed fertile, daughter of the PanAsian conglomerate's owner. With her, I'm getting a new market for the conglomerate along with a young wife, willing to stay home and care for the sons I plan to fill her with. Did I mention she's a twenty percent shareholder in PanAsian?

As soon as they'd finished breakfast, O announced that instead of a beach party, they would all fly with her over a part of the circuit that she'd have to fly for the Battle. Jericho cringed and pulled her aside, concerned about her safety with six horny-as-hell males. She only had time to tell him they weren't going to the same area before her friends caught up. Still, he'd claimed the co-pilot seat, pulling the *Earther-as-Tourist* card. Cal hadn't been happy, but he'd backed off at her pointed look.

Everyone settled in for the one-hour flight to their destination. Since the other guys looked glum, he was pretty sure he wasn't in for a repeat of yesterday.

She looked over her shoulder into the passenger compartment. Yancey was kicked back in a reclining seat, looking like he was sound asleep. Hoshi sat next to him, meditating. Cal, Novy, and Wash sat close together, whispering, with the occasional glance to be sure no one was leaving the cockpit.

Jericho cleared his throat. "I was ready to commend your nego- tiating skills, right up until you got yourself a protector for life. I sure didn't see that coming." And now he had no chance with her.

"That was not my plan." She sounded distressed. "I just wanted him to agree to stand down. I'll fix the misunderstanding."

Yeah, good luck with that.

"I didn't intend to go so far into the Battle flight plan yesterday. I've never flown so deep into that crystal field—only danced around the perimeter. It's part of the course, so I thought I'd try it out. But I got caught in the vibrations and…" Her voice trailed off.

He wanted an answer, even if she didn't want to give it. "And what?" His voice was soft, coaxing.

She turned her face away. "I wanted to feel the vibrations. With you."

The skimmer engine sounded like it was humming the ancient song *Praise the Lord, Now Pass the Ammunition*. He smiled at the random joys of a world-class undergraduate degree in American history and slid his hand to O's fingertips. His smile turned into a lighthouse beacon. He still had a chance with her. He brought her hand to his lips.

Her gaze rose from where he kissed her knuckles to his eyes. "One of the events for the Battle is to fly a route marked only by four fly-over beacons. I'd hoped to reach the first one yesterday. I'll try out a few ideas on this flight, but I won't make you miserable."

"Today's flight is training for the Battle. Do what you have to do so you'll win."

"No. I was going to do that to them," she jerked her thumb toward the passenger compartment, "but I can't do it to you."

"I said I'd help you train and I meant it. Keep to your original flight plan. What am I going to feel?"

"You're going to throw up your breakfast."

Great. "You'll give me warning?"

She pulled her hand out of his. "It won't help." Her face scrunched. "I'm sorry. I wanted to make them pay, to give them something to remember, but this was a bad idea."

He leaned toward the open door to the passenger compartment. "Yancey, the good news is that soon we'll be puking our guts out. Grab your shub." He pulled his sack from its mesh pocket and shook it open. "Let's make this interesting, O. How about a little wager on who loses their breakfast first?"

"I'm supposed to bet on you or Yancey?"

"No. You and me."

Lips apart, she stared at him like he was crazy. Maybe he was.

"Not a fair bet. Earthers get slammed by the energy. Prism-born have some resistance to the vibrations."

"Another kiss says you'll fill your shub before me. If I fill mine first, I'll give you a case of dried protein snacks for my friend, Solo."

Her cheeks pinked. "A kiss is hardly worth a case of protein snacks."

"You're right; your kiss is worth a cargo hold of protein snacks."

She spared him an assessing look. "Not a chance of you winning. Anyway, it would be irresponsible of me to endanger you by getting sick myself."

"So it's a crapshoot. A fair bet. Can't you program the autopilot to bug out when you grab your bag?"

"Yes, but I didn't eat as much as you." As if on a preset cue, her empty stomach rumbled.

My first bet with her, and I'm going to lose. I doubt that puking into a bag is going to be a good look, from any angle.

———

FIFTEEN MINUTES later O'Neill spotted the ugly brown spires of the Retching Field. Her gut tightened reflexively. "Three minutes to threshold. Two after that for first effect. That's the time to ready your bag."

Only one time had she played Puke and Perish with Hoshi, Wash, and Novy. Novy had piloted his extended family's skimmer far into the field. Nobody won that game. Novy's father made them scrub the inside of the craft three times to get rid of the stench. He still wouldn't let Novy borrow it. Her father had punished her lack of judgment with a month of poop patrol for the Citadel's reclamation system.

"Is the tiger going to puke?" Yancey called.

"No, Solo will be fine. At least, he was last time." She noted Jericho's raised eyebrow. "You don't want to know."

Dark brown crystals passed under their low-flying ship. "Entering field. Two minutes to event horizon. Mark."

She gave directions to the autopilot to clear the field should her right hand lose contact with the board. She waited.

"I see a puce green, misshapen crystal ahead." Jericho sounded sick already.

Her left hand slipped into the mesh pocket and felt for a bag.

Nothing. She'd be all right. Her Earther should start throwing up just about ...

"Fuck!" Yancey retched. And kept retching.

Jericho gave her a thumbs-up, then slanted his thumb to horizontal. He didn't open his bag.

Her stomach lurched; then twisted tighter. Sweat popped on her forehead. Frag! She punched the autopilot and grabbed Jericho's bag. *Just in time.*

The added pressure of the skimmer's tight turn didn't do anything to calm her heaving stomach. At least it hadn't been full.

Over the rim of the half-full bag she caught Jericho's eye. Jaw clamped tight, skin green-tinged, he shook his head once. Of course he didn't want his bag back. But how had he managed not to throw up?

They raced toward the clear crystals at the perimeter of the field. She folded the top of the bag three times before she heard the snick of Yancey's safety harness unlatching.

"I'm going to the head." His voice was weak.

She'd wanted to visit the head herself to get rid of the bag.

"Give it to me," Jericho said. "I'll take it back while I check on Yancey."

"No, I can't have you ..."

"In the months before my mother died, when we were alone, I dealt with worse than the shub." He nodded at the sack. "Give me the bag, O."

She gave it to him.

"We're crossing into neutral territory now. I'll hold her steady until you're back in your seat."

He unhooked his safety harness and squeezed out of the cockpit.

He'd started calling her O in the tunnels. Only her friends and family used just her first name. She had a weakness for the way he said it. There'd been a softness in his voice that wasn't there when he called her O'Neill. She liked it. What did his friends and father call him? Jerry? Ric? Rico?

A few minutes later when he returned from the head, Jericho leaned close and whispered, "The guys don't look so good. I think you made your point."

She started to protest but let the words die in her throat. She'd frozen when she thought he was going to demand his kiss in front of everyone. But he wouldn't do that to her; he knew it would make her uncomfortable. Yesterday, she wouldn't have thought she'd subject anyone to what she did to Jericho over the Fertile Field, yet today, she barfed into *his* shub over the Retching Field.

He was a good sport. What had he said about his image not being his identity? Was her image her identity? She wasn't even sure what that meant.

"You're awfully quiet." His palm cradled her elbow. "Are you okay? Do you need to use the head?"

"No. Yes." She checked the autopilot and released her harness. "I'll be right back."

On the way aft, she gave Yancey a shy smile. He didn't return it. In fact, his glare could have burned a hole in the hull. "I'm sorry it got so rough today, Yancey."

After using the head she brushed her teeth with her finger and the paste stocked for long trips. She wet a cloth with cool water, pressed it to her forehead, then wiped it across her face and neck. Refreshed, she started up the aisle to the cockpit.

Yancey looked like he wanted to spit on the deck. "I can hardly wait for your next surprise."

She walked past him, bent and stroked Solo, who answered with a throat rumble. Standing, she slipped through the door and resumed her position in the pilot's chair. Restraints latched, she disengaged the autopilot, setting a course to the spaceport.

"Tell me one more time why you took me on yesterday's flight."

She sorted through simple answers. Because it wasn't far from the tunnels. Because it was on the Battle route. Because she was curious. A simple answer wouldn't do for Jericho. Her throat narrowed, almost squeezing off her words. "I'm certain you could learn to love Prism, if you take the time." Where had that come from?

The corners of his eyes crinkled with his smile. "You may be right." He smoothed an escaped curl behind her ear. "I think you've spent a good deal of time around the wisdom crystals."

She laughed. "There are no wisdom crystals."

"They just haven't been discovered yet." He glanced over his shoulder at the passenger compartment and then leaned across the armrests. After brushing a quick kiss against her cheek, he sat back in his seat. "I've wanted to do that since you showed up at the hatch this morning." He grinned. "Well, days ago, to be honest. I'm glad your friends weren't watching."

She felt as if Solo's tail tickled the insides of her stomach. And her head seemed light enough to float away. Crawling around in the tunnels with Jericho yesterday must have crystalized some of her brain cells.

He was watching her. She smiled, hoping he couldn't tell it was for show. "We'll be back to the spaceport in less than an hour."

"What did you have in mind then?"

———

BACK AT THE spaceport O'Neill's friends scattered to their other duties, but not before Hoshi and Novy reaffirmed their pledges, followed by Wash who'd given her a sly smile before swearing to save her from all false protectors. Cal had sworn to nothing, merely tried to kiss her, and chucked her under the chin when she'd turned her face to the side. He'd declared, "You've always been mine, O. You always will be."

She'd let him walk away without calling him on his controlling words and possessive actions. Like always. He'd done things, said things, which she didn't agree with. It was easier not to confront him. Because *she* hadn't been willing to start one, they'd never had an argument.

It was going to take a long talk, probably with shouting on both sides, to set him straight about their agreement. He hadn't sworn his pledge to her, which was a requirement for a *soldier solution.* Of course, Cal wasn't a soldier. She'd heard enough talk growing up that politicos fought with words, not blood, and that they'd surrender their honor to get what they wanted. She hadn't put Cal in that group.

She ran through the post-flight skimmer routine while Jericho and Solo watched. He probably could see the angry steam coming from her ears. She thought she'd been clear, but Jericho didn't understand her logic. That talk with Cal had to be soon, before he told everyone she'd all but asked him to be her protector.

Jericho followed her to the other side of the hull. "Thank you for today."

She smiled to cover her embarrassment. "I'm sorry about the ride."

"Because you lost the bet?" He ducked under the wing.

Did he plan to collect his kiss right here on the dock? "Uh, no. Because that ride was an irrational reaction to the derailment of my plan."

"Your plan to…? I'm not sure what you needed a plan for." Head tilted a bit to the right, he looked interested.

"They ganged up on me. Left me out. Went behind my back. They're working under my command. They're supposed to be my friends."

"And you ended up threatening them with a court-martial if they didn't agree to whatever terms you gave them. Doesn't sound friendly on either side to me." His head tilted and his brows bunched in a question.

She thumped her clenched fist against the hull.

"Thank you again for yesterday and showing me the tunnels my mom explored with your dad. It made me feel closer to her."

O's chest went tight. She wondered what it would be like to be close to her mother. But her mother had abandoned her to go live with Ray Reagan. To have his sons. She'd walked away from the love of her family. Her mother had cried, saying that she loved O, but she'd refused O's tearful pleas to return home. O had stopped asking her mother to come home. In all the years—and dinners—since, O had stonewalled the woman like the traitor she was.

Even though her father always arranged for someone to watch O when he couldn't take her with him, she'd chosen to sit alone on her bed in the safety of her corner of the living room. Straining to hear the engine of his skimmer landing, afraid he might leave her, too.

She focused on pulling open the panel to the translithium crystals so Jericho couldn't see her face. "I'm glad you're happy with what you're seeing on Prism."

He moved to her side. "I'd like to see more. More of Prism. More first gens." He touched her arm. "More of you."

Yes. She breathed in a deep breath, then another, but didn't turn to him. Because every time she wanted to reach for him, she had to remember that he would return to Earth soon, and she'd be left on Prism, missing a chunk of her heart. Already, just knowing this made her chest hurt. "I'm your pilot. You tell me where you want to go and I'll make it happen. That's my job."

He put his other hand on her elbow and gently moved her to face him. "Really? I'm just a job to you?"

She looked at her boots. It wasn't her nature to lie, but breaking this off now would make it easier. If he didn't, then she had to have the strength for both of them. She pushed her chin up and tried for a casual slouch. "Sure. You're here for a job. I'm here for a job. Except when it's done, you'll go home to Earth, and I'll still be here on Prism."

Before she saw him move, he bracketed her shoulders by resting his hands on the hull of the skimmer above the open panel. She couldn't see around him, couldn't return his look; a look that had the intensity of a laser torch. He was close. Too close. She should have felt caged. Even as he towered over her, she felt admired. Cherished. Wanted.

"You aren't just my pilot. In the tunnels, I was exploring with someone who was more than just my friend." His gaze softened. "We're at least friends, aren't we, O?"

She let her back slump against the hull for support. How could she be *friends* with the son of the richest corporation owner on Earth? "Kind of a long-distance friendship, don't you think? You're going back to Earth in, what, a week?"

His lips pressed together. "When I win the shipping contract, I plan to return to Prism on the first supply ship."

"In six months? What did you have in mind for me then?"

He looked surprised. "I haven't thought that far."

"I'm not going to Earth. Ever. I doubt you want to move here and eat protein bars for the rest of your life." Her tone could have cut the trans-steel of the hull at her back.

"I don't feel like you're my employee. Yancey is my employee. You aren't."

"But I am." Was he trying to manipulate her? "You pay Soldier Compound for my services. My piloting services."

"And I'm happy to do that. But I'd like our relationship to be more than that."

She felt heat rise in her cheeks. Her heart kicked into turbo mode, ready to fight or run. "You won a bet and you want your kiss." Her body was as brittle as her voice.

He took a step back and raised his hands like he was surrendering. "I could give a goddamnfuck about our bet. Here's the deal. I'm by myself here on Prism." When she started to respond, he waved her off. "Oh, there are lots of people around, but it's like at home. Everybody's nice to me for a reason, for a paycheck, for a favor. I'd just like to have a friend. Someone I can trust, someone I can talk to. Someone who will stop me from making a fool of myself.

"I didn't intend to come between you and Cal. I'm definitely not trying to get you into my bed then leave you." He ran his fingers through his hair and sighed. "I'm trying to tell you that if you could take a chance on me, take a chance that maybe you can trust me a little bit—not like you trust Novy or Cal—but enough to…" He shook his head. "I don't know. At home I'd say loosen up. Joke around. Relax around me."

He looked hopeful, confused. He looked like he needed a friend.

Could she do it? Could she relax around this Earther? Could she trust him? Could she be his friend? She wanted that. Maybe she wanted more. Her hesitation had nothing to do with anything between her and Cal.

The tightness in her chest loosened as the silence between them lengthened. She hadn't expected this. This strange, unsure feeling of wanting him faced off against entrenched post-kidnapping childhood beliefs about Earthers who only came to Prism to hurt her.

He studied her face. His was open, laying his emotions before her to do with as she wished. "How about dinner tonight?"

His soft invitation made her want to give him the world with an affirmative answer. But she had her standing commitment to fulfill, even though her father wasn't there to enforce the visit. "I have to train, then I'm going to my mother's for dinner tonight."

"I'd like to hear the viewpoint of a first-gen politico. Do you think she'd mind if I came with you?"

He did feel at ease with her if he was inviting himself to her mother's. How could she, as a *friend*, subject him to something she dreaded every week? Although, having someone else with her would be a good buffer. Her mother wouldn't be able to badger her about moving in with her and Reagan. *Or do I just want to spend more time with him?* "You'll have to deal with the twins."

His brows hunched. "You have siblings? No problem."

It felt like he'd tossed a bucket of cold water on her. "Half brothers." They loved her without reservation and looked forward to her visits. Still, it was hard to see the boys run to her mother for a hug or to share their child enthusiasm with her. "She had them with her new husband. They're six. They're…good kids." And they were. Turned out Ray Reagan was a pretty good father. Absolutely vile as a stepfather, and she suspected the man was a crappy husband. Her mother always looked worried, afraid she'd make him angry. She never looked happy or laughed like O remembered.

Jericho's features morphed into playfulness. "Perfect. Kids love me. I need to meet more first gens. Families."

"Oh, yes, because that went so well with my grandfather." She covered her mouth and coughed.

He brought his forefinger to his temple and moved his thumb, like first-gens did when they'd done something stupid. "I can be persuasive with the ladies if I try."

"I've noticed." What she really noticed was how relaxed her body was now. She was fraternizing with an Earther, and it felt good. Had Prism tilted on its axis? It was only one dinner. A dinner that she would rather skip. She'd see if he could run interference for her with that oaf of a husband married to her mother. "Okay. Dinner tonight at my mother's. I'll send word to ask her if I can bring a guest. If you don't get a cancel message from me, I'll pick you up at your ramp at seventeen thirty."

His shoulders settled. His smile was brighter than a fresh glow crystal. He looked like she'd given him the world. Or at least a little corner of it.

———

FROM THE SPACEPORT O'Neill flew to the Soldier Compound. She entered the meditation room through the small door, and after a few minutes of solitary contemplation, she peeked into the wardroom.

Novy coughed behind her. "Your grandfather is at Politico Compound eating lunch with Cal's father."

"Probably talking about the shipping contract."

"Or the Battle."

Only four days until the Battle. Today's training would help.

They bowed to the guard at the short entry and ducked through the entrance to the outside of the compound. Novy jogged ahead of her down the hill toward the center of Convict Town to pick up Wash. From his house they'd cut across to the plain.

When she caught up to him, Novy picked up the pace. "You are ready?"

She lengthened her stride. "Some mornings I've run zigzags on the mountain and around the perimeter of Con-town. I flew near one of the beacons yesterday, with you, and I've flown into the Fertile Field, too."

"You up-the-chuck yesterday. Not go crazy in Fertile Field?"

"The Retching Field wasn't as bad as that time you dared us. And no, I didn't go crazy in the Fertile Field." She smiled at the memory of the short ride with Jericho.

"My father not forget. Two more months, then I borrow skimmer again."

She waved at a couple of dockworkers walking to the spaceport before they turned on Wash's street. Wash stood outside his house, in conversation with his mother. He spotted them, hugged his mother, and jogged to meet them. "You're late."

Novy chuckled. "*Dobroye utro* to you, Washington."

Wash led them down a narrow, deserted side alley. "Sorry. Good morning. My mother took advantage of the time to deliver one of her lectures about my future."

Novy had her six. "How is bad? Her cards, her leaves, her crystals tell her what comes."

Wash combined a rude noise with a Russian curse. "She doesn't predict. She prescribes for potential problems."

O grinned. "Okay, guys."

Even though she couldn't see him, she knew Novy was shaking his head.

Wash skirted a stack of rocks.

She jumped a pile of something that smelled.

Wash nodded, approving her clearance. "Must be my cue to pick up the pace." He did.

The three of them ran in silence until they were well outside the perimeter of the town.

Sweat ran down her forehead, but thanks to the cloth she'd tied at her brow, it stayed out of her eyes. She took a sip from the water tube attached to the pack on her back. Wash sprinted ahead of them while Novy stayed even with her.

"I'm taking Jericho to dinner at my mom's tonight," she said.

Novy's gait faltered. "Why?"

She stopped to shake out her limbs. "He wants to meet her."

Wash circled back to them. "What is this? The ladies' gossip circle? Are we running?"

"Good luck." Novy left them and ran toward the horizon.

"Good luck? What are you up to, O?" Wash jogged in place, blocking her path.

"When I fly you and your mom home from the Politico Compound tonight, we'll have a guest with us."

A sly smile preceded his wink. "So, Cal's taking you for your weekly dinner with your mom and then you're taking him home with you. For dessert?" A broad grin showed his teeth.

She balled her fist and jabbed his shoulder. Hard. "You. Lech." She sprinted away as if the race had started in earnest.

It took two seconds for him to catch her. He matched her pace. How could he run, look sideways at her, and raise his eyebrows at the same time?

"Congratulations." He could have been sitting at a table in the Burnt Engine.

"You should write fiction stories."

"You haven't decided to declare for Cal, have you? I thought he took your *forever* ultimatum the wrong way."

Wash might clown at times, but he always knew what was going on.

"No, asshole. I'm taking Jericho to dinner with me so he can ask my mother what a female first gen wants from the shipping contract. I'll clear up Cal's misconception the next time I see him. I'm not going to be forced into declaring him my protector."

Wash stumbled. "You're taking the Earther to your mother's?"

"It will keep her from lecturing me."

"You like your Earther. Have you kissed him yet?"

She misstepped and bumped into him. "Wash!"

"You don't have to answer. Might not be a bad idea for a comparison. So you know how good Cal is for you."

She stopped running and he circled back to her. "Wash, have you kissed Cal?"

He spit. "Frag, no. I'm not his girlfriend."

"How do you know he's such a good kisser, then?

He scratched at his cheek. "Uh, geez, O, he's a guy. He's kissed a few girls. They practically fall at his feet in the Politico Compound. Doesn't mean he doesn't love you. Only you. He's never been serious about anyone but you. He knows you're a catch."

She sprinted past Wash, to keep him from digging a deeper hole when it came to Cal, who'd been kissing *other girls*. "Thanks for the intel."

"Cal's right about lot of things."

He'd been kissing other girls. How many? How often?

Frag. She's never thought of herself as the jealous type, but Cal was lucky he wasn't within arms reach. She wanted to hit something. His jaw would have been perfect.

Wash caught up with her and they overtook Novy. She ran as fast as she could for twenty minutes. Finally, she surrendered and bent over, panting for breath.

"Two clicks further than when we began training. Good job." Wash sucked big gulps of air through his mouth. "If all girls ran like you, there'd be no need for protectors."

Not so subtle, Wash. He wanted to draw her out and talk up Cal as her protector, but she wasn't falling into his trap. Shooting him a glare, she let the comment die, but filed it away. He was right. She could take care of herself better than most second-gen females.

Novy raised his hands. "I say nothing about protectors."

Wash took a long drink. "Ready to head back?"

She toed the ground. "Okay." They loped abreast, with her in the middle. "You know, I've been thinking."

"Danger. Female thinking." Novy shot her a wide, toothy grin before jerking his hands in the air. "Only joke. You smarter than us, with exception maybe of Cal."

His nose still looked horrible. She let the comment pass with only a huffed-out breath. "I've talked to some of the girls in Soldier Compound. We don't think all second-gen females need a protector. We're smart enough to know when we need an escort." She raised a hand to keep them from interrupting. "First gens, yes, they had to. But Prism is civilized now."

Novy's smile disappeared. "You talk of changing prime rule." He shook his head. "You know how hard would be?"

"Getting the Joint Committee to agree to anything is next to impossible." Wash slowed. "Look how long it takes them to decide on a shipping contract. And they've got a lot of incentive for that. Prism is still a dangerous place. That's why Warden Schultz pays us to guard Earthers."

Wash sounded sure of himself.

But he was not a woman; he would never have to give his independence away to a protector. He couldn't understand.

They ran fast enough escorting her to the Citadel to make talking difficult, giving O the time for serious thoughts about a plan to earn her independence if she lost the Battle.

17

C oded Burst Laser Message from Gatfield
Montgomery to *Freedom*, at dock on Prism
Present Day

Yancey, it's going to be tricky, but I need you to get the coordinates of at least one of the translithium mines before you leave. Promise my agent whatever you need to as an incentive. I've hinted that he'll take over Administrator Schultz's job once we reclaim the planet. Tell him you'll give him a contract before you leave if he delivers all three mines. I will continue to communicate and pay him in the usual manner.

AFTER RUNNING costs of shipping schedules, freighter capacities and candidates for the scientific team he wanted to propose, Jericho was more than ready to leave *Freedom* for dinner with O'Neill's mother. He settled Mitzi on his bed then walked to meet O and Solo at the entry hatch. Yancey had already put the gift for her mother in the skimmer, along with a bottle of chilled wine.

Her clothes didn't have the sheen of the all-prevalent Prism dust. She'd washed her hair and twisted it on top of her head. She looked like an ordinary Earther girl. Well, not ordinary, by miles of ticker tape. In a military uniform, in civilian clothes, she would make plenty of his colleagues on Earth take a second, and a third, look. He was lucky to get to spend the evening with her. And her mother. "Did you have a good afternoon?"

"Yes. Wash, Novy and I had a long run." She took her time taking in the detail of his suit. "You didn't have to dress up."

"I'm meeting your mother. I want to make a good impression."

"Why?"

He shrugged. Why indeed? Her mother's opinion of him meant nothing. Except he wanted her mother to like him. And dressing up to meet someone showed respect. "For you."

Lips slightly parted, she shook her head. "Yancey's onboard already with Solo. You ready to leave?"

"Yes, ma'am." He followed her down the ramp to the neighboring berth. "How far away does your mother live?"

"My father and I used to jog there, but it's too far for you, and you'd need more protection than Yancey and me, particularly returning to the spaceport after dark."

"But you could?"

"With a protector. I'm trained to take care of myself. And you." She dogged the hatch. "You want to ride up front?"

"Does a bear…" She wouldn't understand the old Earth expression. "Sorry. Yes."

"Shit in the woods?" She smiled at him. One of those smiles that lit her whole face. "Wash's father talks about camping on Earth. And running from bears. He uses that saying all the time. He tells us about rafting down rivers, climbing rocks, roasting mushmellows."

"Marshmallows."

"I'll never see one of those animals."

She thinks a marshmallow is an animal. She was so innocent.

O walked up the aisle. "His dad spent a lot of time hiding in the wilderness. He was a tech wizard. He got exiled because he hacked into corporation servers and stole money and secrets. I bet he'd be interesting for you to talk to."

They settled in the cockpit. When Jericho snapped his safety harness, he felt for the shub in the pocket under his seat. He smiled. She'd replaced it.

"You won't need it tonight. This is a short hop, no vibrational energies." She looked over her shoulder.

"Strapped in," Yancey called.

She powered up the engines, used the headset to get clearance from the dock master, then lifted.

Jericho sat back. "Tell me about your mother."

She took a long moment to reply, as if deciding what to share with him. "She likes to cook. She makes crystal powders for medicines and, uh, beauty."

"She has her own business?"

"She doesn't have a shop or anything, but I guess you could call it that."

"You told me she sews. What does she make?"

"Clothes, mostly. She sells some of her designs, too." She pointed ahead. "There's the politico stockade."

A fence made of crystal spires enclosed a large area dotted with close to a hundred small one-story buildings made of Prism-dirt bricks.

"Looks like they have individual homes."

"They do. They don't share barracks like the soldier community does."

Was that disdain in her tone?

"Do you see your brothers often?" He'd wished for a younger brother for years. Until he made the mistake of asking for one for Christmas, in front of his father. He hadn't scooted off Santa's lap before Gatfield backhanded him.

"Half-brothers. No. Just once a week at dinner. There isn't a lot of interaction between politico families and soldier families." She picked up the handset. "Neill for Ray Reagan."

"Pad three, Neill for Ray Reagan."

"Copy that." She clamped the unit on the dash.

They set down at the edge of an open area near a half dozen small skimmers. She shut down the engine.

Jericho followed her onto the ramp but stopped to stare at the buildings. They were fancier than the soldiers', with painted trim and carved ethnic decorations. Some even displayed faded national flags. "Do they have more credits?"

She waited for him at the bottom of the ramp. "More credits than what?"

"The buildings look more, uh, more prosperous than the ones I saw at your grandfather's."

Her eyes narrowed. "They barter their artistic skills with each other and spend time beautifying their surroundings while soldiers train to protect everyone. Politicos value things differently." She closed her mouth fast, as if biting off something more. "My mother's house is in the second inner circle."

Yancey followed them down a wide street. A long line of women stood outside an official-looking building. They appeared relaxed, talking and laughing with those next to them.

"What's going on?" he asked.

"Sunday-go-to-meeting."

"Can't everyone fit inside? Or do the women have to wait outside?" He'd never understood why some Earth religions barred women from the sanctuary.

"They're waiting their turn." Her sigh was long-suffering. Or she didn't want to talk about it. "For what?"

"Wash's mother is having her weekly sessions to answer questions." She waved toward the covered porch.

Wash leaned against a pillar. He waved to them. Well, he waved to O.

"Every Sunday after I have dinner with my mother, I fly them back to the spaceport. This is his mother's service to the politico community."

"Is she a teacher? How much do they pay her? What kinds of

questions does she answer?" Maybe she would answer some of his, help him fine-tune his proposal. "I should talk to her."

"I'm not sure if she accepts payment for what she does. Wash's mother is a fortune-teller." O's tone conveyed no negative judgment. "We don't have time to wait in line. We have to get to my mother's."

A fortune-teller on Prism? He considered psychics and such for entertainment value, not as credible resources. "Why was she exiled?"

"You can ask Wash for more details, but, from what I know, one of the corporate owners talked to her regularly long before the war started. She knew too much about his plans and his under-handed dealings. He was too superstitious to have her killed, so he sent her here. She met Wash's dad on Prism."

Interviewing a first gen *convict* might be helpful. "What does Wash's dad do here?"

"I'll let him decide if he wants to tell you."

Her tone and her answers became more terse the further they walked into the center of the Politico Compound. Even her normally loose gait had tightened. More questions would be useless. "I'll ask him. Thanks."

Solo led the way to a small house made of the ever-present crystal-dust bricks, with large windows and a metal door. The door swung open and a tall, Prism-thin woman wearing an apron stepped out. Thick, gray-streaked brown hair in delicate curls framed her beauty. The woman could have made a fortune as a model on Earth when she was younger. She was the first woman he'd seen on Prism who wore eye makeup and lip gloss. Of course, he hadn't seen all that many women in a social setting.

The woman cocked her head, staring at him and Yancey. Her smile faded.

"Hello, Mother." O closed the space between them, but held back, out of reach, body stiff, arms at her sides. "This is Jericho Montgomery, the Earther I've been flying around the planet. And his bodyguard, Yancey."

No hug. No kiss. And it wasn't because he was there. The woman didn't try to bridge the gap until she reached out and touched O's elbow, drawing her aside.

Jericho strained to hear the woman's whisper.

"When you asked if you could bring a guest, I thought you meant Cal."

O's lips pursed. "I thought you might enjoy talking to Jericho. He's responsible for Montgomery Conglomerates fashion and entertainment divisions." Her harsh tone surprised him.

The woman adjusted her smile, directing it at Jericho. "O knows I'm not a fan of surprises. I'm sorry for my confusion. Please come inside. Welcome to our home."

O rolled her eyes, but not at him. He swallowed his laugh in a cough and walked through the door. Yancey entered the house next. O let Solo in, then followed. The screen door slapped shut.

"Let me add some more plates." Her mother looked nervous. Maybe she didn't have enough food for two extra guests.

"Ma'am, I'll take my meal in the kitchen," Yancey said.

Her mother looked to O, who gave a brief nod. "All right. My husband will be home soon, Mr. Montgomery." She led them into a small but homey room furnished with fabric-covered chairs and a cushion-covered metal rack that served as a couch. She motioned Jericho to the best-looking chair.

Her husband must make decent credits, or whatever they use for money here. He hadn't seen O's home, but he'd walked through the Soldier Compound and been inside her grandfather's sparsely furnished house. This place could have been the home of a team leader on Earth. He sat. "Please, it's Jericho, Mrs. Reagan." Yancey handed him the bottles of wine then stood by a window overlooking the backyard.

Jericho offered her the gift. "I brought these for you."

She studied the labels. "Wine from Earth. From California. And one is very cold." She smiled. "I'm from France. My father missed his Bordeaux more than anything else from Earth. I'll open the red for it to breathe. Thank you."

Before he could tell her to keep the wine for herself, she was out of the room.

"Well, she's going to love you now." Bitterness charged O's voice.

"Is there a problem with giving her alcohol? I'm sorry, I should have checked with you."

"It's okay. She values expensive things, and a bottle of wine from Earth is very expensive. My father could only afford to requisition her favorite once. I think that's one of the reasons she left him...us. Ray Reagan is in charge of supplies for the Politico Compound, and he can requisition specialty items for his family. Well, for himself."

Eyeing her crossed legs and arms–he hadn't seen her cross them before–and her clenched jaw, it didn't take an expert in body language to know she didn't share her mother's values.

"I brought her something else, but I don't have to give it to her."

"I don't care. Let her have it. It will give her something to show off to her neighbors." She flicked a hand like she was swatting away a pesky insect.

Her mother came back with four glasses. Thick, utilitarian thumbprint juice glasses. "Here we are. Would you do the honors?" She lowered her voice. "I didn't know if your employee would imbibe, but I brought a glass for him."

Jericho cleared his throat. "Yancey, would you like a glass of wine?"

"No, thank you, sir." He turned from the window. "Mrs. Reagan, would you mind if I went outside to check security?"

"Oh, goodness. There won't be any problem inside the compound." She smoothed her skirt. "Of course, you must do your job. Please don't mention it to my husband, though. He'd be offended."

"Thank-you ma'am." Yancey left.

Her mother pointed to the bottle. "Do you know how to open that?"

"Of course."

"None for me," O said.

"Just try a sip, dear." Her mother's voice shook, but not with anger.

The woman was keeping something inside. Something she was afraid to let out. Was it because *he* was here?

He looked at O and raised his brows in question. She said nothing, just shook her head, so he poured two glasses half full of wine and handed one to her mother. "I understand you are an entrepreneur, Mrs. Reagan."

"Oh, nothing in your league, Mister, uh, Jericho." She tasted her wine. "Mon Dieu, this is delicious." She sipped some more. "Over the years we've splurged on a few bottles, but nothing as good as this." At the nodding of his head she added, "My husband earns many credits as the supplies and distribution manager here in the compound."

O looked at the ceiling.

This is going to be an uncomfortable night. He took a sip. Fruity, a tad sweet, but dry. "Tell me about your crystal concoctions."

A knock sounded on the front door. O'Neill and her mother rose.

"I'll get it, dear." Her mother hurried to the door.

O followed. "Jericho's safety is part of my job, Mother."

He wondered why she didn't trust the security within the politico fence.

"What are *you* doing here?" O's tone had nothing to do with protection.

He set his glass on the metal crate beside his chair and stood, listening to the hushed, harsh voices at the front door, ready to lend a hand if there were a problem.

Mrs. Reagan returned. Her raised chin and straight back told him all he needed to know, except who was at the door. "When O asked if she could bring a guest, I thought she'd invited Cal. Yesterday I mentioned something about seeing him at dinner tonight. They're working it out now." She watched the hall as if waiting for a bomb to explode. "I'll go set another place at the table."

He couldn't make out all the words, but he did hear the expletives. He'd like to add a few more of his own. His night had just gone from uncomfortable to shot-to-hell. He wasn't going to get much of an opportunity for private talk with O.

She stomped into the room, followed by Cal.

"Mother invited him." She looked at her mother like she wanted to shake the poor woman. "By mistake."

Jericho extended his hand. "Glad you could join us, Cal."

Her wannabe protector took Jericho's hand, shaking it like the pissing contest had already begun. Jericho countered the tug designed to pull him off balance and matched the strength in the grip. Cal looked as unhappy to see him as O was to see Cal.

He hoped her mother was a good cook. And that dinner would be served before a war started in the sitting room.

18

Official Montgomery Corporate Earth News, Present Day
    The prisoners have developed their own economic system of credits. Of course, they all receive two meals a day, three for every day they work in the translithium mines. In addition, they receive credits based on their productivity. With those credits, they can requisition luxury items from Earth, like specialty food or clothing, or private building supplies. No one prisoner owns a mine, which, to our way of thinking, creates havoc with their system. This means profits are shared by the community in the form of requisitioned extra food, supplies, and materials for leisure activities. However, we've heard there is fighting after supply ships arrive. Maybe they need to adopt our conglomerate system.
    Private Journal of Gatfield Montgomery/RETINAL SCAN REQUIRED:
    I've started the media campaign to reclaim Prism. If I've read the population correctly, they'll not only wildly support our conglomerate's takeover of the planet, they'll gladly pay for it. I just wish I could be on that troop ship so I could personally execute every one of those military bastards.

O watched Jericho and Cal shake hands. *What a cluster fuck.*

Cal's back was to her, but Jericho looked stiff, wary. They gripped each other's hands much longer than a usual handshake. *Frag.* She didn't have time to handle any problem they had with each other. Dealing with her mother was going to be bad enough. Bringing Jericho to dinner hadn't been a good idea. In fact, it was a helluva bad idea. And Cal should never have set foot in the house.

She had to have *the talk* with him before he told her mother O had said *protector* and *forever* in the same sentence. She'd hoped to talk with him alone, maybe on a run. Coming to her mother's house always put her on edge, and taking her bad temper out on Cal would be unfair, but she couldn't act like everything was good with them.

She glanced into the sitting room. Jericho and Cal sat alone, not talking. *Frag.* She'd rather be anywhere but here. Her feet felt like she was wearing lead boots when she forced herself to walk to the room. She pulled on a neutral expression—it wasn't easy—and shuffled to join them.

———

JERICHO SAT in the chair Mrs. Reagan indicated. She left and O entered, perching at the opposite end of the couch from Cal—stiff, silent, and eyes studying the floor as if there were an intricately designed carpet instead of clean-swept rock tiles.

Cal watched her like she was a bomb ready to explode. She was doing a good job trying to hide her anger, but the guy was right. Jericho wasn't going to supply the spark to her short fuse. He'd play the level-headed mediator if necessary, but he wasn't going to be impartial. Even though she wouldn't acknowledge him as one, his pilot had an ally.

Her mother returned. "Dinner will be ready in fifteen minutes. That will give us time to get acquainted."

O gave her an I-already-know-everyone look. She tapped her foot and studied a button on her jacket.

Cal started to say something but closed his mouth.

Her mother straightened and forced a smile. "You wanted to know about my crystal powders."

"Yes, I do. O told me you're something of an entrepreneur."

Mrs. Reagan's smile of gratitude, whether for the diversion or for his interest, made a lump form in his throat. Didn't O know how lucky she was to be able to sit in the same room with her mother? He'd give anything for one more dinner with his mom.

"I can show you my lab."

"You have a lab?" He stood.

"Mrs. Reagan," Cal said, "would it be all right with you if O and I go outside? I have something new to show her for the Battle."

The woman spread her hands as if surrendering. "I'll let you know when it's time to wash."

Yes, his night had definitely gone in the crapper. And he'd provided the opportunity for Cal to get O alone. No resistance on her part, though anyone could read that don't-tell-me-what-to-do face. She was halfway to the back door already.

"Well, it's just the two of us, then." Her mother looked like she'd just discovered her hands.

He reached into his jacket. "I brought this for you."

She accepted the flat package, wrapped with a voile ribbon. "The wine is too much already." Her fingers fumbled with the knot, and excitement on her face grew. "Anything from Earth is such a treat. Even the packaging is a gift." Lifting the lid off the box, she gasped. "Oh, my. What an array of seedlings!"

"I asked my cook to choose a selection of herbs that she couldn't live without. Basil, oregano, thyme, dill, and more. Their labels are on the paper they're attached to."

The woman looked like she might cry. "Even the paper is valuable. Thank you."

The paper was valuable? So was packaging? Of course they were. Anything besides two rations per day had to be earned, somehow. The Prismers had developed an economy that he needed to understand if he planned to suggest opening up trade with them. "I am grateful for your invitation to dinner, Mrs. Reagan. Could I see your lab now?"

Box hugged to her chest, she led him through the sparsely furnished house to a room no larger than a plate closet at home. He squeezed in behind her.

Her hand cupped a small stone bowl resting on a square metal table. "This was my father's mortar and pestle. He brought them from Earth. He was a government chemist, as was I. My mother was not allowed to come here with us."

Her simple statement was like his father slapping Jericho's head with a notebook when he hadn't been paying attention. He'd never thought about how the families were separated, how the lives on Earth had been destroyed by the exile. Everyone on Prism had left a family behind. And hundreds of people on Earth never saw or heard from their loved ones again. None of them knew how the others were or if they were still alive. Hell, O's grandfather's family believed he'd been dead for two decades.

No wonder the World Board was still battling resistance movements around the globe. When you took into account the soldiers and citizens on the government side, there had been a lot of pissed-off people at the end of the war. And that was before things got tough with crop failures, factory sabotage and crime.

"My raw materials, used for everything from cosmetics to medicinals." Mrs. Reagan's voice brought him back to the tiny room. One wall held shelves stacked with jars carved from rocks. She waved a hand at the crystals lining the shelves on the other wall. Pride filled the tiny space.

"Tell me about them."

"Well, let's start with my favorite."

He tried to stay focused on her enthusiastic details of each product. A lip stain, rouge, a powder to smooth hand and face skin. "Does anyone else use the crystals to make products like yours?"

She shook her head. "No. My father and I were the only chemists who were exiled." Her eyes focused on the blank wall in her tiny lab. "We developed weapons for the French government and, when the war started, the Union. He died two years after O was born. I wish she had a memory of him. He loved her so."

Her slight accent had grown more pronounced. No wonder she'd been sent to Prism. Her knowledge could have been put to use by the resistance movement that formed after the war. It must have been hard for a researcher to live in these conditions. As a woman, it had to be even harder. He wondered how she'd ended up with O's father, but he didn't ask. It was too personal a question, considering she'd been living with another man for years.

"I have powders with medicinal properties, too, if you're interested. I developed a lot of them when I, uh, when I was with O's father. He was always getting hurt and needed things to relieve pain and ease his muscles." Her accent was thick now.

The truth was he'd already made up his mind to purchase everything she had to sell, even if it never hit the retail shelves on Earth. The money wouldn't impact his budget, but this was O's mother. The extra credits would help the woman. And maybe even O.

"Mrs. Reagan, if that wall contains all your stock, you are going to be very busy. I'm buying everything here to take back to Earth for our most exclusive boutique."

"Mon Dieu. Let me tell you more about what I think I can compound."

He nodded, but his mind kept wandering to what Cal and O were doing outside.

———

O BALANCED on her right leg, the left stretched behind her, reaching for the rock at her foot. Bending at the waist wouldn't get her low enough; her arms weren't that long. She bent her knee, lowered her butt, and reached for the rock. Destabilized, she wobbled and fell. "This isn't easy."

How could she complete a balance exercise when everything

about tonight was so out of balance? Her stomach twisted when she thought of Cal and Jericho. Her muscles clenched at any stray sound that might signal Ray Reagan had come home. What a nightmare.

Cal, in better humor since they'd come outside, chuckled. "Yep, I lost a bet with my sister when she could pick up a rock more times than I could without falling." He waggled his eyebrows at her. "I'm really going to miss that blue shirt."

She reversed her motion and lowered the rock to the ground. "You never liked that shirt." Balancing on her left leg, she repeated the exercise. "But you'd better make sure K.C. doesn't wear my mother's creation in front of her." She overcorrected and had to plant her right foot hard enough to raise dust. Her proximity to Cal wasn't helping her balance. She needed to set him straight about what she'd said.

"I don't think your mother will mind that I've passed it on to my sister. It was too tight." He positioned a rock at his feet. "I've included this in my daily practice. Watch what I've been able to do in just one week."

He wobbled once, retrieving the rock a dozen times without having to lower his other foot to keep from falling over.

She clapped. She'd always done that when he'd shown off for her. It had been the normal thing to do with her *friend*. It didn't feel normal now.

He wiped beads of sweat from his forehead. "I don't know whether it's the concentration or my leg muscles, but I sweat enough to fill a holey bucket every time I do this."

She tried another one-legged squat. "Give me the turbo on the technique while I practice."

He put his hand under his chin. "It is my pleasure to coach you to win the Battle, Lieutenant Neill. For a price, of course." He tapped his lips.

She pushed him over.

He grabbed her wrist and tugged her with him to the ground. It was like old times, but it didn't feel right. She gave him a sharp push and stood.

"California Reagan, this morning I said you were to cease and desist from all overt and covert actions acting as if you are my protector. I asked you to devise ways to support my wishes and plans without usurping my power."

"Geez, O." He pushed himself up and faced her. "What's your problem? I said yes. Forever."

"You said yes to wanting a chance at the job of being my protector. You've got to stop acting like you're already my protector. You can't tell me what to do. I didn't ask you to be my protector this morning. I asked you to stop acting like you already are."

He reached for her. "I'm sorry you're upset. I know we weren't planning on this happening so soon, but it will be fine. I will take care of you."

She swatted his arms away, throwing her hip into him when he wrapped an arm around her. "You don't get it. I don't need you to take care of me. I. Can. Take. Care. Of. Myself." She gritted out the last words like missiles fired from the planes her father had flown.

He stared at her like she'd grown an extra head. "Who else is going to be your protector, then? We belong together, O. Since the day you were born. You're mine."

"I don't belong to you." She turned toward the house, but he grabbed her shoulder and spun her around. Her feet tangled and she started to fall. Strong fingers wrapped around her upper arm.

WHEN JERICHO and O's mother left her lab, she went to the kitchen to check on dinner, leaving Jericho to watch O and Cal outside. Jericho flexed his fist watching them roll in the dirt, opened his palm and forced himself to relax. Their laughter floated to him, but their words didn't. Whatever O seemed angry about had been resolved. They seemed more than chummy now. He was surprised how much that chafed.

Jericho looked at the ceiling, not wanting to see more. Telling himself O and Cal had been practically engaged didn't improve his mood.

"Did one of the boys throw something that stuck to the ceiling again?"

Startled, he turned to see her mother walking toward him. "How old are they?"

"The twins are almost six. I caught them in here last week with their slingshots." She examined the ceiling then glanced out the window. "Oh, they're practicing again. She's very committed to her training. I don't know why winning the Battle is so important to her." She stared at her daughter. "Maybe it's because her father won it. Twice. Once for him, once for me. To get the building materials for our home."

The softness in her voice betrayed what her face didn't. She still cared for O's father.

She stepped to the window. "Oh, my."

Jericho stared outside. O hip-checked Cal with an ease that showed she'd done it many times. Cal wrapped an arm around her waist, though she didn't need steadying, and she didn't push him away. His hands were all over her.

Jericho wasn't aware he'd walked outside until he heard the door behind him slam.

Back to him, O was talking. She sounded upset. "I don't belong to anyone."

She tripped over her own feet and he reached for her arm to keep her from falling. "You okay, O?" He steadied her.

"She's fine, Earther. Take your hand off her."

"Cal!" She brushed off her backside and turned around. "This is exactly why you are not, and will never be, my protector. You. Don't. Own. Me."

Jericho wanted to do a little victory dance. Hell, a big, towering pyramid with a hundred cheerleaders pumping pompoms during a leaping end-zone victory dance. She must have told the sucker that he'd misunderstood her this morning. Good for her. He beamed his approval.

Cal smirked, brushing at the dirt on his pants. "You finished with the makeup, Earther?" An unspoken "Sissy Boy" hung at the end of the question.

Jericho's fists tightened. Now he was *Earther*? Ready to trade more than barbs with Cal, he paused. Realization struck him like a water cannon. Cal had to have sensed the change in O's relationship with Jericho. The politico thought if he got Jericho out of the picture, he'd be back in with O. Jericho worked for his neutral expression. But knowing that he had a chance with O made the corners of his mouth curl upward.

"Everybody okay?" Yancey opened a gate and stepped into the yard.

Cal's fist covered his mouth. "Lifeguard to the little boy's rescue."

O's mouth opened and her fist connected hard with Cal's shoulder. Hard enough to move him a little off-center. Hands on hips, she raised a finger in front of his face.

"O and Cal, go wash." Her mother held the door open. "Mr. Yancey, would you help me get dinner on the table?" She smiled at Jericho. "Why don't you relax in the sitting room?"

Cal grabbed O's finger, wrapped his fingers around her hand and tried to tug her toward a side door.

"I know where to wash up, Cal. You don't need to drag me to the wash tub." She shook her hand free and didn't move. "I'll wait until you finish."

Chin raised and eyes narrowed, Jericho threw Cal a "Game on" stare. Its Earth meaning was probably lost on the jerk. From the set of O's mouth, she understood completely.

———

AFTER DIRECTING everybody to their seats, her mother escaped to the kitchen while Solo settled on the floor behind O's chair. O wondered at her mother's willingness to risk Reagan's wrath in putting dinner on the table before the man returned home. Under cover of her lashes, she saw Cal prop his wrist on the table's edge and make a fist. Jericho raised his chin like that would deflect Cal's ire.

She was sick of Cal and Jericho dueling with their eyes across the table. "Jericho, did my mother answer all your questions?"

He shifted his attention to her. "Yes, she's very knowledgeable. There might be a market for her powders on Earth. I'm taking everything she's got for a test study. I've placed an order that will require her to hire a couple of assistants."

O's empty stomach tightened. Jericho's credits would make her mother's husband ecstatic. He was all about credits.

Cal fingered the metal knife at his place setting. "Don't think you can buy O with your credits, Earther."

"Cal!" *Did Cal think she was for sale? Did Jericho?* He knew she wanted nothing from Earth. "Make any more trouble during dinner and I will take you outside and hose you down for your rudeness. Jericho hasn't done a thing to you."

Cal sulked. Jericho said nothing but appeared ready to jam his fist down Cal's throat.

She sighed. Cal had never had a rival for her attention, but it was clear that he saw Jericho as one. How could he think that, when Jericho would return to Earth in a week? She didn't have the time or inclination to play referee between them. "Can you throttle it back during dinner? Once we leave, you can beat each other senseless for all I care. Just make sure Wash is around to pick up the pieces, because I won't."

Jericho sat back into his chair. "There's no need for it to go that far, is there, Cal?"

Cal leaned forward. "I wouldn't do anything that would get O called into the Warden's office. I care too much about her."

Jericho looked like he wanted the last word, but Yancey

entered with a platter and her mother followed close behind with a large bowl. Who knew her mother could save her?

"Thank you, Mr. Yancey. That platter goes in front of Cal. It's his favorite."

Cal perked at the thinly sliced tomatoes sprinkled with the herbs grown in her mother's garden. "I'd marry you myself if my uncle hadn't snapped you up."

Her eyes sparkled. The front door opened. The sparkle dimmed.

"I'm home, and I'm hungry, Francine." The deep, loud voice carried over the footsteps approaching the dining room.

Without warning, the smell of the food turned O's stomach. The hair on her arms stood up as if the tiny strands could run away.

Her mother set the soup bowl on the table and turned to greet him.

"You've started without me." He frowned, sounding irked. He glared at Solo. "What's that doing in my house?"

"We're just setting things on the table, dear. You know Solo goes everywhere with O." She gestured to Jericho. "Ray, this is O's Earther, Jericho Montgomery of Montgomery Conglomerates."

Confusion flitted across the man's features, but he extended his right hand.

Jericho rose and they shook. "Pleased to meet you, sir. I hope you won't be angry with me, but your wife is going to be very busy for the next six months. She's agreed to produce powders for our cosmetics division. On a trial basis, of course."

Granddad had been trying to convince his ex-daughter-in-law to do some kind of research for him, probably on a new crystal. Now, with Montgomery credits on the line, Reagan wouldn't let her.

A smile lit Reagan's face. "More credits in the coffer, right, Francie?" The man glanced at O then wrapped his arm around her mother's waist, pulled her to him and lip-locked her.

"Ray! We have guests." Her mother pushed against his chest.

O's hand went to her mouth, and she caught herself scrubbing her lips.

Ray winked at Jericho. "Got to keep the ladies happy. Right, boy?"

"So my father tells me."

Yancey cleared his throat.

Her mother's husband looked at him. "I'll take care of the bodyguard, honey. Don't wait for me. Go ahead and start while the food's warm."

Her mother watched Yancey and Reagan leave the room. Confusion showed in her worried eyes.

O reached for Jericho's bowl. "Let me give you some soup."

They passed plates and dug in, murmuring appreciative comments about the meal.

After a nervous glance toward the kitchen, her mother stood. "Ray's taking a long time. Maybe I should see if he needs me."

The man sailed through the door, holding the open wine bottle aloft. "The bodyguard said Montgomery brought this."

The top of the liquid was way below the lip. He'd obviously helped himself to some in the kitchen.

He filled his glass, then proceeded around the table, pouring half a glass for everyone else. He set the bottle in front of his plate, dropped a kiss on her mother's neck and slid into his chair.

O's stomach turned. He always made a point to maul her mother when O was around.

"Tell me about this soup." Jericho gaze didn't leave her.

O could have kissed him for the distraction. She looked down at her bowl and smiled. She didn't need a reason to kiss Jericho. His kisses made her want more.

Her mother fussed with the ladle. "Since O and Cal are training, I used extra protein rations–along with fresh onions, squash and herbs from my garden."

"It's delicious."

Her mother's husband puffed out his chest. "Too bad the boys aren't here to enjoy it."

Jericho appeared unfazed at the mention of her half-brothers. "Where are they?"

"They're spending the night with a friend." Her mother's voice cracked.

The twins never missed dinner with her. She wanted to ask what the occasion was, but her mother looked scared, so she remained silent.

Reagan threw down his napkin next to his empty plate and rose. "I'm off to a meeting. I'll see you again, Montgomery." After gulping the last of his wine, he put his hand on Francine's shoulder then slid it across her clavicle to her neck. "And I'll see you when I get home. We've got the house to ourselves tonight, so be ready for some of this." He gave her a sloppy kiss, dropped his hand to her breast and squeezed it before he left.

O exhaled a long breath.

So did her mother. She used her napkin to wipe her mouth.

Cal patted O's hand.

Did he not see how embarrassing his uncle's treatment of her mother was?

The look he lobbed at Jericho could have been a fragging grenade. He pulled the pin with his next words. "Man's got to earn his credits, O."

Jericho's easy smile didn't mask the contempt in his eyes.

"Why did you come to Prism?" Cal's tone could have matched one of Solo's snarls.

Jericho's smile widened, showing his perfect white teeth. "It's no secret I hope to win the translithium shipping contract. I think my bid will make life here easier. Better. If I can do that, won't it be worth the profit I make?"

So much for the dinnertime truce. Would Cal be a problem on Jericho's protection detail? She had to have to a serious talk with her Battle coach in the morning. She wasn't about to let something happen to Jericho because of Cal. And it wasn't because of her reputation and job. She genuinely liked Jericho. Without thinking, the heel of her hand rubbed hard against her sternum.

Against the pain she knew was coming when he returned to Earth.

Her mother rose. "You young men work out your politics. O, help me clear the dishes."

O looked from Cal to Jericho, not sure she could leave them alone without bloodshed.

"We'll be fine, O." Jericho stared at Cal as if he were challenging him to disagree.

Swallowing her misgivings, she picked up their plates and followed her mother into the kitchen.

19

Official Montgomery Corporate Earth News, Present Day

We're hoping that Jericho Montgomery finds something of value on Prism to bring back to Earth. Maybe the prisoners have taken up artistic hobbies to fill the days when they vacation from mining the translithium, which we so desperately need here. Maybe he'll discover that the prisms that litter the surface of the planet are diamonds or other precious gems. We've rooted for Jericho to win on the playing field and in the pool. Let's hope he scores a big win on the prison world—a big win for all of us.

Private Journal of Gatfield Montgomery/RETINAL SCAN REQUIRED:

If that boy is stupid enough to bring anything but the shipping contract and more translithium home from that godforsaken hellhole of a planet, I will personally kick his ass across space to get back there.

IN THE KITCHEN, O set the dishes in the sink.

Her mother gave her a quick hug and released her, stepping back, eyes welling with tears.

O had been mean enough to make her mother cry almost every week during dinner the past seven years. But those tears weren't because of something she'd said. For the first time, she felt sorry for her mother and the life she'd chosen.

"I begged him, but Ray wouldn't bring me to you. I'm so sorry about your father. I wish it had been me instead of him."

Blindsided by her comment, O stared. This was the first time she'd seen her mother since her father was declared KIA. "Why?"

"I know how much you loved him."

"*Love* him."

"If I could trade my life for his, I would. You don't need me, but you needed him."

For seven years she hadn't talked about her father to her mother—not because O hadn't tried. This sentiment from the woman was entirely new. And uncomfortable.

"I made a mistake when I left you both that night seven years ago."

What?

Shocked to her core, O didn't breathe. When she finally gasped in a lungful of air, she wasn't certain she'd heard her mother correctly. But Francine stood opposite her, unmoving. Watching O as if she might shatter into a million tiny shards.

Right after her mother left, during their first weekly dinner, O had begged her to explain why she deserted her family…and to return home. She'd asked so many times she'd lost count of the silent refusals. Jocko had been declared dead, and *now* Francine wanted to confess her *mistake*? It felt like a giant crystal had lodged in her throat, filling it so she might choke. She concentrated on getting words around it. "Why didn't you tell Dad?"

"I couldn't. He would have killed Ray, and then I would still have lost your father. Lost the love of my life."

The love of her life?

"But now that Jocko is gone, you deserve to know the truth."

How could her mother have done what she did to *the love of her life*? O shook her head.

"I know you hate me for leaving you and your father." Her mother's eyes seemed to look through the wall of the kitchen at something far away. "I was so afraid. Afraid he wouldn't come back from one of his explorations. Afraid he wouldn't come back every time he left the Citadel." She blew her nose. "Then you were kidnapped. I could not forgive him for that. I was so angry with him, even though he found you and brought you home." Tears in her eyes, she touched her fingers to O's scarred cheek. "We argued more after that. I started confiding my anger and fear to Ray. He'd wanted to marry me before I fell in love with your father."

O remembered raised voices coming from her parents' bedroom. She tried to clear her throat. "You could have worked things out. He loved you."

"And I loved him. But he became moody. Ray listened. He was kind to me while your father had changed into a silent, angry man."

O tried, but couldn't think of a time that her always upbeat father had ever been moody around her.

Her mother shook her head. "He offered to help, to give me a safe place to think. That night when you were at Liam's with Jocko, Ray showed up at the Citadel in a skimmer. He listened to my sobs and convinced me to leave with him."

"How could you do that? Were you already sleeping with him?"

"No! He was just a friend. I thought he was taking me to Patrick's for the night. I needed to talk to your father's best friend. I thought he could tell me how to help Jocko with his guilt and how to live with my fear."

So far, her mother hadn't said anything that would absolve her from what she'd done. O felt her heart hardening to her mother's self-made plight. "I need to get the rest of the dishes." She left the kitchen.

At least Jericho and Cal weren't rolling on the floor pummeling each other. They'd scooted the dishes to the side of the table and Cal was looking at an electronic tablet. Jericho nodded to her.

She grabbed the large platter and stacked dishes on top of it. "My mother is waiting for these."

Jericho stood. "I can help."

Cal looked surprised and rose. "I will, too."

"Both of you sit down. I'll be out in a minute. We have to leave soon, Jericho." She carried the dirty dishes to the kitchen and set them beside the stack her mother had begun to rinse.

Her mother's fists were balled and she looked angrier than O had ever seen her. "Ray didn't take me to the Politico Compound. He took me to the Fertile Field."

What?

"The next morning he brought me here. Your father was frantic; he'd been looking everywhere for me all night. Patrick told him I was at Ray's and your father came to the compound, demanding I go back to the Citadel with him."

O's skin prickled. *I should kill Reagan.* "What happened?"

"Ray acted like the peacock he is, bragging that he'd taken me to the Fertile Field, and that I belonged to him. Your father said he didn't care; he insisted that I belonged to no one, and he wanted his wife back home." She put her face in her hands. "Jocko loved me so much he would have taken me back even though we all knew I had to be pregnant with Ray's baby."

How could her parents have kept this from her all these years? "Why didn't you go home with Dad?"

"Ray threatened to hurt you if I left him. He threatened to make sure Jocko wouldn't return one day. I was frightened."

"You didn't trust Dad to protect us." The cold truth almost made O shiver.

"I knew your father would die protecting the two of us. I couldn't let that happen. I loved him too much." She straightened. Strength that O had never seen radiated from her mother. "I've loved him, and you, every day I've lived in this house."

O closed her eyes. She knew even less about love now than she thought she had known this morning. "Mama, go to Granddad's. Reagan can't touch you there."

"He can. I won't do to the twins what I did to you. What I need is strength to live with the mess I've made of my life—and yours."

Her mother's fierce expression stunned O. No wonder she hadn't shared what had happened that night. Her father would have done whatever was necessary, even physical violence, to bring his wife home had he known the truth. And she knew that O would have shared the truth with him.

O folded the dishtowel and set it on the counter. "I'm sorry for the things you've had to survive under this roof. You should have told Dad. He was your protector. He would have made things right."

After a sad shake of her head her mother dried her hands. "I was terrified for the two of you. Ray can be a brute when he's crossed."

And even when he isn't. O remembered his visit on the rooftop of the Citadel. She opened her arms and hugged her mother.

It had been so long since she'd felt her mother's arms wrapped around her. Francine clung to her, quietly choking back sobs. If only she'd stood up to Reagan years ago and returned home with Dad.

After their tears stopped, her mother stepped back and studied her. "Jocko has done such a lovely job with you. You are so strong, so confident. I know you will win your Battle." She kissed both of O's cheeks, then smiled and added one more on O's nose, like she used to do.

Your Battle. Did she know about the trouble with Cal?

O returned to the living room, where Cal and Jericho sat like statues at opposite ends of her mother's precious fabric-covered couch. "It's time to go. We need to pick up Wash and his mother at the meeting house. Cal, can you finish washing the dishes for my mom? I think she needs to sit down by herself for awhile."

"Sure." He didn't look happy about her request. He probably wanted to walk her to the skimmer.

"Thank you."

Her mother came into the room, untying her apron. Jericho stood and smiled.

"I'm sure there is paperwork for me to sign about the sale of my products?"

"I'll have Yancey deliver a contract and arrange for the transport of your products to my ship, Mrs. Reagan. I'll transfer the credits into your account as soon as the formalities are complete. Thank you again for dinner."

"You're most welcome, young man. I hope my merchandise does well for you." She extended her hand, palm down, like when they'd played princess years ago.

The perfect prince, Jericho took it between both his own. "I have no doubt we will have a profitable partnership, Mrs. Reagan."

She turned to O. "If you ever want to talk about your father…"

"Cal is going to finish washing the dishes so you can rest." She glanced at Cal and received a nod of confirmation. "Thank you for dinner. Good-bye, Mother." O couldn't get through the front door fast enough. She was not going to cry again.

Jericho followed. Yancey wasn't far behind.

"Your mother has very little accent, even though she said she was French. Why does Novy have such a distinctive accent?"

Of all the questions Jericho could have asked about the evening, this one kept the tears at bay. *Bless him.* "My father used to joke that the whole Russian navy was sent to Prism. There are a lot of them, that's for sure. They have their own barracks and primary school. Novy's dad was their Admiral. I met Novy when I was five. He couldn't speak a word of English, even though most of the first-gen Russians understood it well enough. He speaks English only outside of his home."

"Makes his speech colorful."

"His accent makes the girls crazy, too."

Jericho nodded. "He's a charmer."

O smiled. "Yes, Novy's Lady Stare is becoming legend."

"But it doesn't work on you."

She walked faster. She didn't want to think about how Jericho's glances worked on her.

"Are you okay, after whatever happened between you and your mother in the kitchen?"

His greatest fault was being too perceptive.

"I'm fine." She wasn't ready to talk about how her relationship with her mother had shifted tonight. She walked faster.

"If you want to talk about it…"

"We're late." It really didn't matter. No one would leave the meeting hall until Wash's mother departed. But the fast pace might keep Jericho from asking questions. She had way too many of her own questions to answer any of his.

Without effort he matched her strides. "What is Wash's mother's name?"

She should have known he'd have more questions. "Esmeralda."

He repeated the name like he'd heard it before. "Wash lives in Convict Town. Were his parents convicts on Earth?"

"Yes." *Will you ever stop asking questions?*

"And she, what? Teaches people? Tutors them? Answers their questions? Tells their fortunes?"

"In a manner of speaking." Wash's mother was a no nonsense woman, sure of her gift, her insights.

"What was her crime?"

She stopped. "Knowing too much. Here we are." *Thank God.*

Wash's mother sat in a rocking chair with thirty or so women sitting cross-legged on the ground. She was laughing, bouncing a baby on her lap. Wash leaned against the porch rail, away from the circle of females. He pushed off at O's approach.

The women stood and scattered, nodding at O as they passed.

One paused and hugged her. "I'm so sorry about your father, O. We'll support whatever declaration you want to make. You know how much we love you."

"Thank you, Mrs. Reagan." O stepped back, and the woman walked down the street.

Jericho watched her. "Mrs. Reagan?"

Could he stop asking questions she didn't want to answer?

"Cal's mom. My mother's husband is Cal's uncle."

He brushed a stray curl behind her ear. "I bet that makes things difficult for you."

"Uh-huh." Thank goodness, Wash had already moved the chair to the porch and was escorting his mother toward them.

"Good evening, Madame." O inclined her head. "This is Jericho Montgomery from Earth. He and his bodyguard will accompany us to the spaceport."

Wash's mom extended her fingertips to Jericho, who touched them and bowed. "I'm pleased to meet you, Madame." He smiled at Wash. "I've enjoyed the time I've spent with your son." He crooked his arm and offered his elbow. "May I?"

Esmeralda linked her arm with his. "You are on a long journey."

"Yes, Earth is very far away."

Wash looked at O, then to the sky. He was used to his mother's roundabout conversations.

His mother said, "That distance has nothing to do with your journey. You have reached the fork in the road, but your journey doesn't begin until you choose your path. It will be a long journey, not without danger."

O shook her head and prayed that Wash's mother wouldn't say another word. She could make anyone nervous with her pronouncements, and O had no idea what Jericho would make of her. The skimmer was just ahead. She tried to change the conversation. "I want to thank you for allowing Wash to run with me in the mornings, Madame."

"He is old enough. I cannot stop him, and he is your friend. But this one, Jericho, he is not your friend."

Jericho's not my friend? He didn't seem like an enemy. What did Madame mean?

Jericho opened his mouth, then must have thought better, closing it without a word.

O and Wash reached the ramp first. He mounted the steps and opened the hatch while O stood at the base. "Jericho will ride up front with me, Wash." No way was she letting him sit in the back with Esmeralda. He could ask a hell of a lot of questions in an hour-long ride. She knew from experience.

"I'd like to sit with Madame if she agrees. I have some questions for her."

I bet you do. "I'm sure Madame is tired after her long day."

Wash's mother started up the ramp. "I will answer his questions." She looked at O. "Then I will answer yours."

Lord have mercy. Wash's mother had never volunteered to answer her questions. But the woman had thrown out comments, made pronouncements, told O to do certain things—all without explanation. There were so many things O wanted to know. How many questions could she ask? Were some topics off-limits?

What should she ask? *Too bad Madame couldn't read minds. Cal's been acting like such a jerk. I'd like to know what he's thinking.*

When was Jericho going to collect that kiss she owed him? Would she be allowed to live without a protector?

So many questions…

20

P ersonal Journal of Gatfield Montgomery/RETINAL SCAN REQUIRED:

It's too bad my father sent that witch seer of his to Prism. I could use her skills now that I'm coming down to the wire to reclaim the planet. Perseus thought he was cutting off Medusa's head by exiling her, but whatever tricks she used, she knew what was going to happen and advised us on ways to avoid the worst.

SETTLED next to Wash's short, chocolate-skinned mother in the skimmer, Jericho wondered about Wash's ebony skin and the man's father. He chatted about why he'd come to Prism, asked her what she thought was important in a shipping contract, listened to her version of the first days on the planet and how she met Wash's father.

There wasn't much time left in the flight. He'd never talked with a psychic before and had no idea how to proceed. Did he even believe in fortune telling? "What did you mean that I'm not O'Neill's friend?"

Short curly black locks fringed her heart-shaped face. She pursed dark, full lips. "You are not her friend. But you want to be."

He nodded.

"And you will be. More than a friend."

He couldn't help a frown. "What do you mean? How do you know?"

Her laughter tinkled like the silver bells on the winter sleigh his mother had loved. "I have always known more than I should. More than I have a right to know." She sighed. "That is why I was sent to Prism by your grandfather."

His original questions slammed to the edge of his brain, piling into each other, crowding his skull. "My grandfather wasn't a judge. He couldn't have sentenced you to Prism."

"Oh, but he did." She looked at him like he was a lost puppy. "Because he didn't like what I read for him."

"You read to him?" Jericho's grandfather had died before he was born, but his father had talked about Perseus Montgomery. Jericho had pored over everything he could find about his grandfather's rise as a corporate world leader during, and after, the global war. He'd built his company into a corporation and then, a conglomerate.

"I was his seer. He did not like what I saw."

"He couldn't banish you here for that."

"He did. In the confusion and terror the first weeks after the fall of the governments, it was simple. He thought it would be bad luck to kill me, like he did most of his enemies. But he didn't want anyone to hear what I saw, so I was one of the first put into a cryo pod."

He'd never heard about this. "What did you tell him?"

"The truth."

"Touchdown in five, four, three, two, one." O's voice.

Wash stepped through the door of the cockpit before the engines cut off. "Ready, Mama?"

She unlatched her safety harness and stood. "I have something to tell Jocko's girl."

O came out of the cockpit. "You know something about my father. Where he is?"

"Do not waste more time looking for him. You will not find his body. Even he is looking for his body. But he will find his way back to you. He is learning how to talk to you, isn't he?"

O leaned against the bulkhead, her face ashen.

"And you *will* marry Patrick Reagan's oldest son. Have no doubt of that."

If Wash hadn't been between them, Jericho would have wrapped his arms around O in support. She looked just as shaken as he was.

Lips quivering, O was making a massive effort not to cry. She sucked in a sob.

He kept his arm around her on the walk to *Freedom*. She leaned against him for support. How would she make it to her skimmer under her own power? "Would you like me to walk you back?"

She sniffled. "No. I'll be fine."

At the bottom of the ramp, her arms went around him in a hug. Whether she was trying to claim support or strength from him, he didn't know, but all he had, he would gladly share with her. Madame's pronouncement about O marrying Cal had blindsided him. He didn't want her to end up in a situation like her mother. "Would you like to stay here tonight?"

Her breath hitched. "I can't do *that*."

He put his hand under chin to raise it so she had to look at him. "I didn't mean it like *that*."

"No, I need time alone. Time to think. I thought I had everything figured out. I don't like being wrong."

"Maybe you're not wrong. Maybe Wash's mom is."

"She never has been before."

"First time for everything."

———

O WASN'T sure how she made it back to the Citadel's rooftop after Wash's mother dropped her bomb. Esmeralda knew her father was talking to her. *What the frag?* The shock blew up her questions about how to get around the First Law.

Madame said, again, that she and Cal would get married. But Cal was acting more and more like his uncle, telling her what she couldn't do. Jericho made her want more, more of something she couldn't describe. As soon as the Joint Committee chose a shipping contract he'd be gone, and she'd never see him again. She couldn't make decisions about the rest of her life thinking about him.

She hadn't had time to figure out how she felt about what her mother had revealed tonight. Her whole world, everything she'd believed for the past seven years, slipped sideways. Her mother still loved her father. O needed a protector. She liked an Earther. Everything she'd believed about her life had landed in the crapper. Her head should be spinning a three-sixty on her neck.

She pressed her lips together, but that didn't stop the sobs that racked her body. One truth played over and over in her brain. Wash's mother never made mistakes.

She stared at the trapdoor in the ceiling. Well, she'd better figure out what to do so she didn't end up like her mother, unhappy and married to the wrong man.

The first step was to double her efforts on her training and winning the Battle.

Cross-legged on the floor, she completed her breathwork exercises and was settled enough to focus on her immediate problem: what to do about a protector. An appeal to Warden Schultz or the Joint Committee for an exemption from the First Law? In the morning she'd make an appointment to ask the warden for advice.

Her resolve solidified. She would do whatever she had to do to preserve her independence. If that meant convincing the Warden to get involved in a discussion about the need for protectors and what they could demand, she'd risk an insubordination charge. She wasn't going to be a victim of an obsolete law. And she wasn't going to be forced to choose between living with her mother and marrying Cal.

She had a much better chance of winning the Battle. She'd developed the strength and stamina to hold her own in the swim and the melee. But to win the Battle, she had to win the flying event.

Her gut seized. She stood and paced the track Solo had worn into the braided rug around the kitchen table. Curled at the base of the ladder to the roof, the tiger eyed her. "I don't want to get married. To anyone." Talking to her mother had crystalized that realization.

Since she was born, everyone—including her—had believed she would marry Cal. And she'd accepted that as truth. But this reality was cracking around her like dead crystals. Tomorrow she'd start pushing against some of her other long-held beliefs. Maybe she'd start finding answers instead of more confusion.

Wash's mom was going to be wrong, for the first time.

Jocko Neill was alive. Her father would help her.

———

Jericho rose early the next morning, even though his appointment with the Joint Committee wasn't until eleven. He wanted to review the details of his offer one more time. And maybe one more time after that.

Though his father vetoed a team of scientists in the proposal, Jericho had included them, along with their research equipment. He was the negotiator, so the contract would be legal and binding, regardless of what Gatfield Montgomery wanted. His study of the Joint Committee requests over the years showed they wanted more opportunities for the planet to become self-sustaining.

Food production remained the sticking point. If just one supply ship didn't arrive, the Prismers would starve. They had to know that and so did the corporations. The only thing that had saved the original exiles was the threat of global revolution. The conglomerate supply ships still delivered rations because of that continuing threat. And, of course, there was the translithium.

He selected his clothes with intention. A classic light blue shirt, red-and-blue diagonally striped tie, a not-too-modern navy suit. Polished black shoes. He studied his reflection in the three-D mirror. The tie wasn't right.

Sliding the Windsor knot down, he removed the expensive length of cloth. No one wore a tie on Prism. If he wanted to beat out his competitors, he needed to convince the Joint Committee, whoever they were, that he wasn't afraid to get his hands dirty. That he was alongside them in this venture.

He pulled off the fancy jacket and pants. The dress shirt would suffice to convey that the meeting was important. At some point during the presentation he'd unbutton the cuffs and roll them back to show that he was willing to work with the people of Prism.

A pair of blue slacks, not too dressy, along with the boots he wore for sightseeing, looked much better. He felt more comfortable, more relaxed in them, too.

His father would rail at him. Attending a business meeting attired in anything less than the most expensive suit in his closet was not acceptable. But Gatfield Montgomery wasn't on Prism. Besides, Jericho knew his audience far better than his father ever would.

Since the meeting was in the spaceport, O didn't need to fly or protect him. He would have liked to talk to her, ask for her opinion on his clothes. Who was he kidding? He wanted to see her before his presentation. He wanted her to wait for him so he could dissect what had happened during his meeting with the committee. But that wasn't her job. She was probably flying the mining shuttle today.

The ship's intercom chimed. He punched the button.

"Sir, you wanted to leave in five minutes." Yancey paused.

"I'll meet you at the hatch." He closed his black leather brief-case and glanced at the picture of his mother. He wanted to return to Prism. To O. That meant he had to secure the shipping contract. "I understand why you fell in love with this planet, Mom." He stroked her cat's fur. "And its people."

He left the cabin and strode down the short corridor.

Yancey waited at the open hatch. "Good luck today, sir."

"Thanks, Yancey." He stepped onto the ramp and paused. He had hoped O would be waiting there for him. Starting his day without her didn't seem right. He shook off the superstitious thought.

A man in an Earth suit stood on the dock. "Good morning, Mr. Montgomery." He nodded to Yancey. "My name is Quay. I'm Administrator Schultz's assistant. It's my pleasure to show you to the conference room." He offered his hand.

Jericho gave him a firm handshake and fell into step beside him. "Can you tell me anything about your Joint Committee?"

"I suppose it's all right to tell you that it consists of the leaders of the politicos, soldiers and convicts. By the way, your bodyguard will not be allowed in the elevator."

Jericho glimpsed Solo loping toward him, weaving through the dockworkers still working to remove and store six months of supplies. His heart stuttered; then beat to some ancient tribal rhythm. *Kuh thump. She's near. Kuh thump. She's here.* His next question dissolved on his lips. He saw O'Neill, wearing formal pants topped by a buttoned, matching double-breasted jacket. Shiny shoes and a black military style hat on her head completed what must be her dress uniform.

She stopped to speak to a man who touched her elbow, giving him a brief hug before resuming her journey down the dock, ducking between the crush of people. Watching her, he realized he'd fallen in love with the serious, opinionated, talented, beautiful pilot. His heart didn't stop to worry how his love could work. His mind didn't either.

Their eyes met. He accelerated to a run. *She came for me. She cares.*

"Mr. Montgomery," Quay called after him.

Jericho nearly knocked over a dockworker. "Sorry." He cut off a spaceport official with, "Excuse me." Stuck behind a group of people in stained jumpsuits, frustrated at the impediment to his progress, he barely kept from shouting, "Pardon me."

He jostled his way toward her, glimpsing her curly hair and uniform between the others milling on the docks. When they finally faced each other, he stopped and stared. "It's really you. You didn't have to be here. Are you okay?"

She nodded. "I'm fine. You look nice." She gave him a lop-sided smile and the once-over.

Keeping his arms at his sides was the hardest thing he'd ever had to do. "You look amazing. All the workers are stealing covert looks at you."

She took a quick look to the side. "I don't see anyone staring at me."

"That's the whole idea. They wouldn't be covert looks if you saw them."

Additional words eluded him. He winked at her.

She gave him a shy smile. "I'm sorry about last night. If I didn't have to go to those family dinners, I wouldn't."

"You don't have anything to be sorry for. I've endured my fair share of less-than-loving dinners with my family."

"Well, Wash's mom can be uncomfortable. I should have arranged another way to Convict Town for them."

His brain was still gnawing on what the woman had told him about being his grandfather's seer, being shipped to Prism because the man had been afraid of what she'd seen, and her pronouncement that he wasn't O's friend. "No reason to do that. She had interesting information about my grandfather."

"Well, I don't care what she says, you are my friend."

He took her hand. Wanted to do more, but the dock wasn't the right place. And now, well, he didn't have the time to do it right.

Solo rubbed against his leg. "Guilty, as charged. I am your friend. Where could I find another sass-talking pilot who can land a skimmer without a bounce?"

A conspiratorial smile lit her face. "Don't say that around Novy or Cal." She glanced down the dock behind him. "You ready to meet the Joint Committee?"

"I'm ready to pitch this proposal and close the deal. Have lunch with me, so we can talk about what happens when I return with the next supply ship."

"You're coming back?" She sounded surprised.

"Yes. I thought I'd told you." He released O's hand before Yancey and Quay caught up to them. "We'll talk more about that later.

The four of them walked in silence to a single elevator large enough to hold a couple of pallets of supplies. Yancey handed Jericho his briefcase. "Good luck, sir. I'll wait here for you."

Quay, O, Solo and Jericho boarded the elevator. Quay pressed his thumb against a lighted panel then tapped the keyboard.

The elevator went down, deep underground. He shouldn't have been surprised. The administrative complex was only two stories tall. The corporations wouldn't have installed an elevator for one flight of stairs, but they would have built a bunker in case they needed one.

The door slid open to a circular foyer with six cushioned, metal chairs fanned out in the space in front of a metal desk with electronic equipment and an empty chair.

Quay seated himself at the desk. "I'll let them know you've arrived."

O grabbed his hand and squeezed. "Good luck." She walked to Quay's desk. "May I speak with you?"

The man looked surprised. "In a moment." He turned to Jericho. "They're ready for you." Quay stood and crossed to the handle of one of the huge metal doors.

The biggest pitch of his life, and he hadn't thought about it for twenty minutes. He tried to remember his opening line, but he couldn't. He glanced at O, who gave him a thumbs-up and a radiant smile.

At his nod, Quay pulled the door wide.

Jericho stepped into his future.

The room was small, round, and unimposing. Thin, brushed metal walls enclosed a long crystal table that could have seated six. Three non-smiling men sat behind it. Jericho's breath hitched. Between a man in an outdated business suit and another in a patched jumpsuit sat O's grandfather, wearing military fatigues.

He should have figured it out. His face heated. Embarrassment that he'd overlooked the obvious mixed with growing anger that O'Neill hadn't cared enough to tell him Liam Neill was on the committee. But her loyalty was to her grandfather, not to him.

The former general inclined his head. "Good morning, Mr. Montgomery. Mr. Reagan, representing the politico interest, is on my left. Mr. Simms, on my right, looks out for the well-being of the convict community."

Mr. Reagan. Cal's father? She could have at least told him he'd meet Cal's dad here. He was screwed, or rather *fragged*, as they said on Prism.

Jericho strode to the table, reaching across it to shake their hands. Simms' assessing eyes could have squealed that he looked out for his own well-being first. The convict representative would expect a hefty kickback.

There was no table, chair or podium for his use, so he returned to the center of the room. If dinner at her grandfather's house was any indication, his only hope was winning the other two men to his side. Looking at Mr. Reagan was like looking at an older version of Cal. That didn't make it any easier to smile at the man.

He set his briefcase at his feet, failing to remember his carefully crafted opening argument. "Gentlemen, Earth needs the translithium from your mines. You need supplies from Earth. A contract with Montgomery Conglomerates will allow everyone to profit in ways you haven't thought possible."

Simms looked like he wanted to spit on the floor. "Yeah, and your fraggin' rich daddy will profit the most."

Jericho ignored the insult. "My proposal is based on a fair return for everyone, including the miners and the communities that support them." He moved a step closer. "I rode on a miners' shuttle to Translithium Two. I spoke with the workers about ways to improve their productivity, new tools in development on Earth, and what they would like to receive in bonuses. I've also spoken with five of your second gen guards about their needs and what they want for their lives. I've toured Prism."

The politico representative interrupted. "Why did you come here? Why not just ask Administrator Schultz for answers to your questions?"

"Mr. Reagan, I came to Prism to see for myself what I would be committing the corporation to. To see the facilities, meet the people. My mother told me stories about Prism, about her archaeological dig here the year before I was born. I was more than intrigued."

Reagan straightened, folding his hands on the table. "What is your mother's name?"

The cloth around Jericho's neck tightened. "My mother was Brynhildr Thorsøngud Montgomery." He tried to keep his voice steady. "She died last year."

The man's exhale sounded like *Bryn*. His lips thinned.

Did Reagan know my mother?

"Get on with what you're going to give us," the convict leader said.

"My proposal is designed for the long-term benefit of Prismers. Fresh food seems to be a priority. I understand in the beginning years of the colony you tried to grow food, but only obtained deadly results. I will contract a biologist, a medical researcher, and a marine environmentalist to live here, on Prism, and I'll supply lab equipment to research methods to grow and harvest your own food. I will commit the resources of Montgomery Conglomerates to find a beginning solution. Of course, it will take decades to build thriving agriculture and animal production, but by then, hopefully you'll have achieved colony status and a freer exchange of goods, people and information."

"The World Board will not allow this." The general's lips turned down.

"It will be in their best interest. As the colony ages, a case can be made for the rights of your descendants. They've committed no crimes. Another part of my proposal is to lobby for Colony Citizen Status now for the children and future grandchildren of the original settlers. This will open the planet for additional colonization and more business opportunities."

Reagan's brows shot up.

The convict representative snorted. "Original settlers. Ain't that a nice spin on it? But what's in it for us? The original *prisoners*?" He spread his hands, indicating the other two men.

Jericho bent to retrieve his briefcase. "If I may?" He stepped to the long table. His thumbprint and a code of six letters and digits cleared the locks. Opening the lid, he pulled out three identical data pads and distributed them. "These are yours to keep. The details of my proposal are contained in the contract file. I've included other files for your interest." He gave each man a frosted soft-plaz carrier containing the data pads. "If you have questions as you read through the terms, my ship's com codes are on the lower corner of the screen."

He closed his briefcase, returned to the middle of the room, set the briefcase on the floor and waited.

The men accessed the file, scanning his offer. Twice O's grandfather frowned and looked up at Jericho. Reagan ran his fingers down one screen and smiled, shaking his head. At one point he and Neill put their heads together, whispering and pointing to the proposal.

Hopefully they were happy with the additional rations, electronics—even though what he offered was out of date on Earth—and vastly expanded trade opportunities, to and from Earth. And only three months between supply ships. Administrator Schultz would have authority to requisition supplies she felt necessary to support a thriving colony. He'd promised to explore the possibility of third gens, the grandchildren of the original exiles, to have the opportunity for a university education on Earth.

Simms scanned the pages and, making a rude noise, reached the end first. "What will you give me for my agreement?"

Neill and Reagan pinned him with their stares.

"There is a clause about usual considerations for accepting the proposal." He hadn't put into writing individual offers for fear of insulting the committee members, but his father had been adamant about using bribes to secure their signatures on the contract.

O's grandfather turned to the convict representative. "Gordon, this appears to be an all-inclusive contract. If you expect Mr. Montgomery to buy your vote with a bribe, I'll be sure your people know you received it." He refocused his attention on Jericho. "We have at least three other offers to consider. We'll discuss what you've given us and contact you if we have questions. You'll have our answer within seven days. You're dismissed, Mr. Montgomery."

Jericho was stunned. He wanted to argue the advantages of his plan, explain the salient features that would benefit all Prismers. He wanted to convey how he felt about the planet. He wanted to leave feeling that his proposal stood a chance.

You can't always get what you want. Don't oversell.

He gave the committee a short bow. "Thank you for your time and consideration, gentlemen."

He turned and made for the metal door. It opened before he reached it; Quay held his escape route open.

Jericho pulled his shoulder blades together, raised his chin and kept his eyes forward. Still, he felt like he was slinking away. If he didn't get the contract, he could deal with his father's fury. But he couldn't stand the idea of his mother's charities failing for lack of funding. And the thought of not returning to Prism, never seeing O'Neill again, was like someone forced a fiery poker down his gut.

The elevator waited, doors open. O stood beside the gaping

hole. Too bad he couldn't step inside and rest his forehead against the wall in privacy on the long ride topside. He didn't want her to see his anger, and he wasn't sure he could keep a mask of indifference in place.

He made an effort to smile at her while wondering if he'd ever had a chance of convincing the three men of the worth of his plans. And why she hadn't shared the small fact that her grandfather and Cal's father were on the committee.

21

PRISM Administrator Report from Cornelia Schultz to
World Board (Seven years ago)
Re: Kidnap attempt

*Information item: The daughter of Jocko Neill, who discovered
the translithium mine, has been kidnapped. The rumor is that
crewmembers from the supply ship are responsible and that they
are demanding the location of the translithium mine. I have seen
no ransom letter.*

Private Journal Notes of Cornelia Schultz:

*The soldier community has mobilized to search for O'Neill.
The soldiers have ripped apart Convict Town, and last night I
received complaints that they were in the process of trashing the
Politico Compound. Liam Neill received a demand for the mine's
location in exchange for the girl. Jocko Neill is on an exploration
expedition. I pray the girl is found before he returns. Hell, I just
pray that sweet little thing is found alive.*

O LEANED against the wall next to the elevator door. *I should have
told him my grandfather is on the panel.* Maybe she should have

told him Cal's father was, too. But her grandfather had asked her not to share that information with *the Earther*. Her Earther.

Her stomach growled. Solo's ears perked.

The longer the committee questioned him, the better his chances were for winning the shipping contract. And she wanted him to win that contract. Wanted to believe that he would return to Prism. To her.

She pushed off the wall, intending to sit on a chair and eat her first protein bar of the day, but Quay stood and went to the giant doors. He'd agreed to make an appointment for her to meet with Administrator Schultz to discuss the Protector Law, but he'd pursed his lips and shaken his head when she told him why she wanted to see the warden.

Jericho stepped out and forced a smile. He avoided meeting her gaze. Even though his clothing was freshly pressed and his shoulders were stiff, he looked drained, as if he'd just run for miles. He'd only been with the committee for twenty minutes. That wasn't a good sign.

"I'll walk you back to your ship." She boarded the elevator beside him.

They rode up in silence. The trip took a minute longer than forever.

They exited and she fell into step beside him. Yancey hung back.

Walking next to Jericho was like walking next to a silent ghost. He'd been the one to keep the conversation flowing. Her heart was breaking—for him, for her—but she didn't know what to say.

Head down, he strode toward his ship as if he were walking against a strong wind. They were well into the spaceport when he said, "You could have told me."

It wasn't hard to guess what he meant. "My grandfather asked me not to."

Jaw clenched, he squeezed around a container and continued toward the dock where his ship was berthed.

O matched his stride, waves of betrayal searing her skin.

Because he seemed so easy-going, she'd fooled herself into thinking his reaction wouldn't be so harsh. What kind of friend did that make her? His contract proposal was like the Battle for her. He needed to win the contract. Not for the profit he'd make. Something inside her stomach gnawed to get out. She suspected it was duplicity.

He had a right to be angry. He'd been blindsided, and it was her fault. But they could talk, she could explain. Jericho had always been level-headed and rational. He'd forgive her. She'd have to give him time. And understanding.

She grabbed his elbow. "I'm sorry." She laced her fingers through his. "I *am* your friend, Jericho."

He sighed. "I know." He balled his other fist and settled it over his heart. "This contract is so important. It hurts to think I may lose it. If I do, my chance to preserve my mother's legacy is gone." He studied O's face.

She held her breath until his fingers tightened on hers. They did need to talk. And to listen to each other. "Do you think knowing that my grandfather and Cal's father were on the committee would have changed your proposal?"

He didn't look at her. "Absolutely. And it would have saved me the embarrassment of feeling like I was holding my dick during the introductions." They walked side-by-side up the ramp.

The entry hatch opened, revealing his cook. "Welcome back."

"Thanks, Mattie. Can you bring lunch for two and a meaty bone for Solo to my father's office?"

"Certainly, sir."

The interior corridor was wide enough that she could walk next to him. They passed two doors on the right before he stopped in front of double doors at the end of the passageway. He freed her hand and placed his palm on the scanner. The doors recessed and he stepped through.

She followed Solo inside.

Jericho's shipboard office was as large as Administrator Schultz's. The huge, clear plazglass desk, with three chairs in front of it and a throne-like seat behind, hardly made a dent in the floor space. To one side of the room, two full-sized sofas bordered a low table. On the other side, a reclining chair, with a small table at its side, faced a wall of security monitors which showed the activity on the dock around the vessel. One focused on the empty entry ramp.

"This is how you knew when I was at the hatch."

His lips moved like he might smile, but he didn't. He pushed a button on the desktop and a bulkhead rolled up into the ceiling, revealing shelves filled with bottles and glasses. He took two soft-plaz containers off a shelf, rolled one between his palms to activate the cooling feature, popped the lid and handed it to her.

"Thanks." She took a careful sip. The frosty, tart liquid had a hint of sweetness. "This is very good."

He'd already downed a good portion of his. "One of my favorites."

A yowl punctuated his statement. It sounded like someone had pinched a baby.

"What was that?" She wondered if someone needed help.

Solo paced before of the door to the adjoining cabin.

Jericho waved a hand in dismissal. "Mitzi. It's her naptime, but she's heard us and wants some attention. She'll be fine."

"You have a baby?" How could she not have known he'd brought his child?

Another shriek, this one more emphatic.

She stepped beside Solo, who sniffed the floor in front of the door and starting scratching at it. "You need to see what the matter is." Solo growled in agreement.

"I can't let her in here with Solo."

What, he thought Solo would eat a child? "I'll hold on to him. Open the door."

Jericho checked to see that her fingers were fisted in Solo's neck fur before palming the door pad. He bent and scooped a ball of fluff into his arms. "This is Mitzi. My mother's cat."

Solo nudged Jericho's arm. The cream-colored micro version

of Solo, with dark ears and tail instead of stripes, looked over Jericho's elbow at the big feline below her. A tiny, soft trill counterpointed Solo's deep-throated rumbles.

She coaxed Solo to sit beside her. "I'm not sure he isn't looking at your mother's cat as lunch."

"My thoughts precisely. I'll put her back in the cabin." He crossed to the open door, bent and released the cat.

Before he could palm the doorpad, the cat ran back into the office. Solo leapt out of O's grasp.

"Solo. Stop!"

The only two animals on Prism froze a foot apart, noses sniffing overtime.

O couldn't breathe. It would be so easy for Solo to close his big teeth around the little cat's body. A solid bite and she'd have to pry its limp and lifeless carcass from Solo's jaws. If he didn't eat it.

"Don't move unless Solo goes for her." Jericho edged along the wall to get closer to Mitzi.

His cat took a tentative step toward Solo. The big cat shifted his weight to his rear.

"Easy, boy," O murmured. She could lunge and grab some of his fur. She hoped.

The cat rolled on its back in front of Solo. He dipped his snout to her belly.

Two bites. Jericho's cat was only big enough for two bites. And Solo hadn't been fed today.

Her tiger nuzzled the cat's stomach, rolling her over. Mitzi stood, walked closer and flopped before him again. She reached a paw to his nose. Solo laid down, belly on the carpet, and rested his paw across Mitzi's body. Mitzi purred. Solo exhaled what sounded like a purr, though she'd never heard him make that particular sound. Now O understood the difference between *purr* and Solo's sub-vocal roar.

Was Solo lonesome for his own kind? Even if that kind was significantly smaller?

O exhaled.

Jericho tiptoed around the back of the desk, his gaze never leaving the cats.

She joined him.

"At the beginning of this trip, I wouldn't have cared if she'd been his appetizer," he said softly. "But she's grown on me."

The door chime sounded.

Solo raised his head and wrapped a protective paw around Mitzi.

Jericho touched something on the desk, and the door panel whisked open.

Mattie stood outside with a tray of food. Her eyes went wide, staring at the cats. "Oh."

"It's okay." He walked to the door, took the tray, and thanked her. She closed the door from the outside.

Solo sniffed.

Jericho set the tray on the table between the sofas. "My bet is the finger sandwiches are for us and that plate with the cut-up raw steak is for Solo."

She knelt beside Solo and put the plate under his nose. He stood and began eating.

Mitzi inched toward the food. Solo stopped eating and stared at her. The little cat pulled a small piece off the plate and chewed it. Solo watched for a moment then went back to eating from his side of the plate.

She took a deep breath. "I guess they're friends."

Jericho nodded. "The two of them figured that out in a lot less time than it's taken us." He sank his teeth into one of the small sandwiches. "Now that I've made my proposal, you don't have to babysit me anymore."

Was he telling her to leave? Is that what he wanted? She hadn't taken a bite of anything, but she swallowed. "Granddad asked me not to tell you who was on the Joint Committee. I could have asked him why, but I didn't. I'm sorry. If that makes you lose the contract, I'll talk to him, plead with him. I'll talk to Cal's dad, too."

"No, don't do that. Your grandfather didn't want you involved, and I don't either. I keep telling myself that your failure to share the fact that not only was your grandfather in that room but Cal's dad was, too, was more about loyalty and love for Liam Neill than disregard for me. If I'm wrong, set me straight."

"You're right. But you need this contract. Just like I need to win the Battle." *How did I not see this before?* "Not because we won't survive, but because we will. Losing may put out the fire inside each of us." What would his father do to him if he lost the contract? She couldn't imagine Jericho bitter. Broken. She didn't want to be the cause of him losing his zest for life.

"Winning the contract is the fastest route to fulfill my dreams, but there are other ways." His smile didn't reach his eyes. "I'll get what I want; it just may take longer."

He seemed so confident. She could use some of that optimism. "We've never talked about your dreams. Why is the shipping contract so important that you made the trip here?"

A faraway look stole across his eyes like a high, fast-moving cloud. She wasn't sure he would give her an answer.

"When other people ask that, I reply that my father will relegate me to the entertainment and fashion division."

Whatever he did would be amazing, but she couldn't picture him designing clothing and playing holo games for the rest of his life. "And the real reason?"

"I'm here because I want the enormous profit of a shipping contract."

Her breath caught. He'd never acted concerned about credits.

"My mother supported many charities with the billions of credits my father gave her every year. When she died, he stopped the contributions. I have a good income, but not enough to maintain what she started. To maintain her legacy."

Billions of credits to charities? In his mother's memory. "What kinds of charities?"

"Educational foundations, food for children and mothers, clean water for communities, medical treatment, training for self-sufficiency, protecting wildlife, rescuing domestic animals. If there was a need, my mother tried to fill the gap. She believed my father should have used the conglomerate's clout to better the lives of the people in our region."

"No wonder your proposal is so important to you. I'm sorry I didn't ask before."

"Now that you know, don't try to influence anyone on the Joint Committee. I have to do this myself. I have to do this for her. Whatever it takes."

Like she had to win her own independence from the First Law. For herself, and for her father. Whatever it took. She nodded, not so much for Jericho but because she was beginning to understand that her struggle included much more than just herself.

"I'm glad you're my friend, O. It means a lot to have someone here who cares about me."

Her heart smiled, it's warmth spreading through her body. They'd established a deeper bond. He'd forgiven her for not revealing the committee members.

She picked up a sandwich that had green leaves spilling out the sides. "Tell me what happened with the committee."

———

CONCILIATORY LUNCH FINISHED, O accepted Jericho's offer for a tour of *Freedom*. They left the napping cats curled together in his office.

After peeking into two luxurious guest cabins, both larger than her entire home, she told him she didn't need to see the other six. Next, he led her aft to the engine room, with its gleaming, burnished steel. All he knew about the faster-than-light engines was, "They're big and they work."

He lived amid so much wealth. Excess like she'd never imagined. The shipping contract mattered to him as a way of preserving his mother's charitable legacy, but he didn't need the credits, even if *Freedom* wasn't his. He planned to come back to Prism, but if he did, he couldn't live on the planet. He'd have to live here in his ship, as he'd done this trip, with Mattie to cook and clean for him. Could he live as a Prismer for just twenty-four hours? She'd been crazy to dream that he'd want to.

He knew a lot about the hydroponic garden. They walked through rack upon rack, row after row of green growth, sporting colorful fruits and vegetables and little flowers that would develop into future food. She recognized the tomato and raspberry plants but none of the others. There was even a raised bed with spiny plants in Earth soil.

"My father loves pineapple. They don't grow well hydroponically, so he had the dirt beds installed."

Her dad had loved her strawberries. He'd joked that if she could grow enough of them, he'd make himself sick eating them just like he had as a boy on Granddad's farm. She walked between racks of plants at different stages of growth. "Who cares for all this?"

"It's fully automated, but Mattie or Jamie walk through daily, and I visit as well."

She followed him down an aisle to the corner, where individual trees stood in large pots with nutrient-rich bubbling water bathing their roots. She'd seen trees in similar containers at Hoshi's house, but none as tall as these.

He put his hand on one of the trunks. "This is a Meyer lemon. Less tart than regular lemons. Too bad there are no blossoms for you to smell."

"What's your favorite?"

"The oranges." He nodded to the far corner. "The smell of the blossoms, picking the ripe fruit, popping juicy sections into my mouth. Since I was a kid, I've loved eating them right off the tree."

He brushed aside a branch. "Ah, there's one. You want to pick it?"

"I've never picked anything from a tree. I don't know how."

"Just put your fingers around it, twist and give a gentle tug. If it doesn't pull free, it's not ripe yet."

She leaned in and reached for the fruit. It was just beyond her fingertips.

"Here." Jericho shifted closer to the tree. His hip pressed hers. Stretching, he pulled the branch forward. "I think you can get it now."

She had to lean across his body for her fingers to wrap around the pebbled skin. She pulled, but nothing happened.

"Twist it, then give a quick tug."

The warm breath behind his words wafted across her ear, sending a tingle of electricity down her arms.

When the orange separated from its branch, she wobbled, off balance, not just physically.

His arm wrapped around her waist, steadying her. It stayed there a moment longer than necessary. She wouldn't have minded if he'd left it there longer. How could she decide to distance herself from him when he wasn't around, then change her mind so easily when she was with him?

She examined the fruit instead of her emotions. "Do you eat it like an apple?"

"Let me show you." He extended his palm.

She gave it to him. Her fingers seared where they touched his.

He gave her a funny look. Did he feel it, too?

He dug his thumb deep into the skin of the orange.

A fine mist sprayed across Jericho's hands. Then the smell assaulted her. *Orange.* She rolled her tongue along the roof of her mouth, finally understanding the first-gen expression, *made my mouth water*.

He pulled back a piece of thick rind. "You don't eat the skin, but it can be used to season food, and it can be candied." He continued stripping the skin from the membrane surrounding the orange, placing the peel on a plate resting on a small table nearby.

She watched his beautiful hands, their sure motions, and inhaled the strong, sweet aroma. A strange feeling pooled at the bottom of her stomach, as if she'd discovered a new vibrational field. What was happening to her?

"Then you break it into sections." He pulled a piece away from the sphere. "Open your mouth." He held out a section dripping with juice.

She opened her mouth and he popped the fruit inside. She closed her eyes and bit down. Sweetness squirted across her tongue as the pulp crushed between her teeth. "Mmmmm." She chewed slowly, swallowed the delicacy, and opened her eyes.

Jericho was staring at her, like he'd shared her private delight.

A drop of juice ran down her chin. She reached for it, but he was faster.

"Let me." His thumb brushed across her chin, gathering the juice. Still staring at her lips, he licked the juice off his thumb. "Oh, this is a sweet one."

He's not talking about the orange. How had she not noticed the room's heat before? Too bad she'd already taken off her jacket. She stared at his hand moving back to her chin. A furtive glance at him made her heart race. Her flight muscles wouldn't engage.

Intense. The only word that came close to describing his eyes, the set of his mouth.

He's going to kiss me.

Not a shred of fear, even though her heart tried to clamber up her throat. Her skin tingled. She moistened her too-dry lips. And watched his face grow larger. Her eyelids slid shut.

His thumb and forefinger bracketed her chin, which he tilted. The barest touch of his soft lips on hers. She wanted more. Wanted it to last longer. Then the pressure was gone.

"It'll be better if you open your eyes." His voice was lower in pitch. Leashed.

It took every ounce of will she possessed to pry her lids apart, though she wouldn't have said they were open. The best she could do was to gaze at him through her lashes.

"You have no idea how much I've wanted to do that again." He sighed and shifted his stance, pulling her close. When her eyelids started to close, he whispered, "Look at me, O."

She did. Longing, determination, tenderness filled her vision. "Oh."

He pulled her flush to him, one arm across her back, the other cradling her head. His lips met hers, tender at first, then more insistent. Who knew a kiss could be so sweet while stoking something inside her, something that threatened to sear her from the inside out?

He watched her watching him. What could be so interesting? She wasn't moving. Didn't want to move out of his arms or move away from his lips.

One of them groaned. She was too close to tell whom.

When his tongue ran across her lips she raised her palms to his shoulders and beyond, wrapping her arms around his neck. Lost in his embrace, she kissed him back as if his kisses could keep her from drowning. Because she was drowning in his arms. In his love.

Somewhere in her brain a warning light flickered. She wanted to ignore it, but there was no ignoring the love conveyed by that kiss. That kiss was the promise of more. More kisses, more of his love, more time with him. His tongue explored the seam of her lips and a ragged breath escaped her. She needed oxygen. She needed him.

She moved her palms to his shoulders and pressed. And was sorry she had when his arm left her back and his hand stopped cradling her head.

He took a half step backward, watching her as if she were a grenade. With the pin pulled.

Frag. Her body already missed his touch, his support. *He's going home to Earth soon.* What had she been thinking? Her home was on Prism. His was on another planet. She blushed, and knowing that her face was turning multiple shades of red made it worse.

He shifted his weight. "I should apologize, but I'm not going to." He pulled another section of the orange free and offered it to her in the flat of his palm. "Unless you want me to."

She didn't want an apology. *I want another kiss. Right now would be good.* She'd heard of people begging for food on Earth. She was in danger of begging for kisses. Jericho's kisses.

"You are amazing."

She shook her head. She wasn't amazing; her face was on fire.

He opened his mouth like he wanted to say something more, but he just smiled. Smiled like she'd given him... a kiss. Probably not that great of one since she hadn't practiced with anyone but Cal. And not that much with him. Maybe she would have kissed Cal more if she'd had this reaction.

She stepped back and patted her palms against her thighs, needing time and distance to control her actions. And feelings.

Her emotions bounced up and down like a skimmer buffeted by strong winds. Not that long ago, she'd decided to back away from their friendship. Now she was counting the hours until he had to return to Earth. Could she wait six months for his return? That kiss. A kiss could change everything. What did she know?

Nothing about love.

He passed her pieces of the orange while he showed her the flower garden. She was careful with the juice. His matter-of-fact discourse on hydroponics allowed her to regain her composure. *How had he regained his so quickly?*

She had not been impressed by his wealth, however, viewing the plants grown merely for their beauty did the trick. There were at least three whole rows of *ornamental* plants. Yellow daffodils, blue iris, pink tulips. Air ferns, sword-leaf ferns, maiden hair ferns. She hoped he didn't plan to test her after the tour. Even if her brain cells weren't still scattered from his mind-exploding kiss, she would have been hard-pressed to remember the names of all these plants.

"Why is it so important for you to win the Battle?"

How could someone with so much freedom, so much independence, understand her answer?

"It's not so much about winning, as it is about the prize."

"Sounds like me winning the shipping contract."

"In a way. But I'm not interested in credits or supplies from Earth."

His brows drew together. "Then what's the prize?"

"The winner can ask for those things and more. But I want a boon."

"Which is…?" He studied her face.

"Something that doesn't cost anything to give."

"Seems like you're going to a lot of trouble to get something that's free."

"Oh, it's not free. I'm going to ask to keep living in my home, on my own, without a protector."

"Can you get around your First Law that way?"

"I don't know. No one has ever tried."

"What exactly does the First Law say?"

"That every female needs at least one male protector to guard her from kidnap and rape."

Jericho looked thoughtful.

"Usually girls my age marry their protectors. Cal wants that. If I declare him as my protector, he can make me marry him. I'd have to move to the politico compound, live by their rules and do what Cal says."

"I'm not a fan of Cal when it comes to you." He took a deep breath and walked to another shelf of pots. "This flower is called a rose. Roses are beautiful, but they have thorns, sharp bits on the stem that can poke through your skin and make you bleed. Like your protector law. It sounds like it was designed to keep you safe, but the thorn is the loss of your independence." He plucked a yellow bloom from a low-lying bush and offered it to her. "Smell."

She took the stem, put the bloom to her nose, and sniffed. The scent made her think of sunlight and happiness. She smiled.

"This variety has no thorns." He cocked his head, a serious look settling on his features. "Maybe a new law can be written that's thorn-free."

"No one wants to change it, especially the men. They like the power that the First Law gives them. Most of the time, there isn't a problem. Maybe my mother wouldn't have stayed with Reagan if there was no First Law." Her heart was suddenly heavy.

His fingertips raised to her cheek, but he drew a breath and stopped before he touched her. "Come with me. I've saved the best for last."

He was wrong. His kiss was the best part. Nothing that he showed her would be better than the feeling of his lips on hers. Nothing could feel better than being held in his arms.

Jericho hurried her along the port bulkhead. After three doors and more guest cabins, he stopped before a larger panel and touched the entry pad. "Go ahead."

The panel slid soundlessly aside to reveal a large room. Colors, painted like rectangular rugs, decorated the white, cushioned floor. Metal contraptions stood against one wall.

Hand at the small of her back, he urged her forward. "You can train for the Battle in here."

Not likely. It wasn't as large as her home combined with the rooftop. "How many times will I have to run around the room to get fives miles in? And where's the ocean for me to practice swimming?"

"Trust me."

22

P ersonal Journal of Adminstrator Cornelia Schultz
(Present Day): Retinal Scan Required
*I'm looking at the packet that arrived seven years ago
from my best friend on Earth. She told me to give it to her son, if he
ever visited me. I'm pretty sure it's not a present for him, since
there are conditions on my delivering it. I don't know what to do.
All I know is that I can't open the file or it will go up in smoke. Not
literally, but close enough. He's a nice kid, and this might ruin his
life. Bryn loved him so much. She would have died for her son.
Maybe that's what happened, at the hands of her bastard husband.*

JERICHO WANTED to touch more than her waist. He wanted to kiss
more than her lips. He wanted more than her friendship. But he
didn't want to scare her off. He reined in his craving. It wasn't
easy. He might not be able to change the law, but he could give her
this. He could invite her to train aboard *Freedom* until the Battle.

He pulled back his hand, afraid its heat might sear her—or him.
Although he would, at some point, love to let her skin sear his. He
needed to workout, work his muscles to fatigue. "This is the gym.

A complete strength circuit, cardio equipment, free weights and state-of-the-art flooring and video-sound system." He stopped rambling and tried to compose himself.

She surveyed the room. The corners of her mouth turned up in what he thought of as her obligatory smile, the one that said she had no idea what she was looking at. She'd never seen a gym before. There was no need for one on Prism. Surviving on Prism was a workout.

"Anything you can think of, except swimming, can be done in this room. You can train here, in safety and with all the benefits of scientific research."

"Really? I can take a five-mile run in here?" Her tone teased him. "How many times will I have to run around the room?"

He directed her to a large red rectangle. "Get ready to run."

"Okay." Her brows lifted.

He took a step back. "Red treadmill, gradual startup to three miles per hour."

The rectangle moved half its length before she started walking. "The floor is moving."

He nodded. "Keep walking. You can control the speed and elevation by telling it what to do. Red treadmill, increase elevation five degrees. Red treadmill, gradual increase speed point one mile per hour. Limit four mph." The front of the rectangle rose and the belt moved faster.

She started an easy jog. "Can it go faster, higher?"

"Red treadmill, gradual increase elevation and speed to my pace." He waited for the machine to adjust. "Say decrease to lower the elevation or speed."

She smiled like a kid on Christmas morning at one of his mother's centers. "I'll be fine. Go ahead and do what you need to."

He crossed to a cabinet and pulled out a couple of fluffy white towels and two water bulbs, then returned to her. "Here you go."

A T-shaped towel holder rose from the floor. O's mouth gaped while he hung a towel over it and placed a water bulb on the tray. "This is a lot more convenient way to train. I would have offered it days ago if you hadn't been so concerned about fraternization." He lowered his voice to dramatize the last word.

She sighed. "I didn't like Earthers then. But I like you." She looked at the red rectangle. "This sure isn't the same as jumping garbage in Convict Town."

He grinned. "I'm going to use a rowing program. If you'd like to try one of my jogging programs, I can load it for you. It will seem like you're running through some of my favorite Earth terrains."

"Sure, show me what you've got." An enigmatic smile lifted the corners of her lips. Lips that he vowed not to touch until she'd finished her workout.

"Load *Jericho's Travels, Waterway Path*." He walked to the blue rectangle and sat. The foam molded to his butt while footpads and plas-glaz oar handles rose through a slit that opened in the floor.

The lights dimmed and on the blank walls of the room, a three-hundred-sixty-degree panorama of a river with a running path alongside appeared. One of his favorite motivational songs began playing through the sixteen speakers placed in the walls.

O stumbled. "Oh. This is what Earth is like?"

"A few places. Keep jogging," he called.

She recovered quickly and settled into the pace of the program. "Are you just going to sit there?"

"Nope." He pulled off his shirt, tucked his shoes under the restraining straps attached to the foot bar that had appeared and grabbed the oars, and peeked over his shoulder. As he'd hoped, she was staring at him. He winked at her then began pulling on the oars. A whooshing sound of water added to the music. On the wall in front of him, the bow of a crew shell cut through the flat, blue water of the river. Glancing to his right he saw the familiar, protective, manmade jetty with its running path. He settled into the rhythm of the music, pulling with strong, sure strokes, losing himself to the synchronicity of his body, the machine, and the program.

When he saw the float in the distance he stopped rowing.

"Program paused," said a mechanical voice. The music kept playing but the picture on the wall froze.

He glanced at O.

Arms pumping, she was running up a steep hill.

"Ready to stop?" he shouted, to be heard over the music.

Startled, she kept running, but nodded.

He disengaged himself from the rower and stood. By the time he was alongside her, the floor was just a floor again.

Sweaty and winded, she pulled in big breaths. "That river is gorgeous."

"One of my favorites. Not many places like that left." At her questioning look, he added, "Too many people and too much pollution."

"I thought that the corporations vowed to fix those problems after the war."

"The war took care of the immediate population problems, but people are unwilling to sacrifice to the degree necessary to reverse the pollution."

She grabbed the towel from the stand, wiped her face, and took a long drink. "I thought the corporations could make people do whatever the World Board wanted."

He shook his head. "Hasn't worked that way yet, but my father keeps trying. The corporations replaced the governments, but they aren't any more successful at getting citizens to follow a corporate agenda than a political one. Conditions were better after the war, at first. But now…not so much." He grabbed the other water bulb and drank. "Did you enjoy your workout?"

"This is an amazing room."

"You're welcome to use it whenever you want."

"I should have let you give me this tour that first day when you offered." She looked at the floor and sighed, regret mingling with sweat.

"Now that I've presented my proposal, you don't need to play tour guide anymore. Let's plan on you training here tomorrow. You won't get in trouble for that, will you?"

"No, but I really need another swim."

"I can take care of that."

"We'll need to take the guys to the beach."

"I haven't shown you everything. Come with me."

"There's more?"

"Oh, yeah." *And we won't need your friends around for protection.* He threaded his way through the racks of free weights, past the wall of mirrors and tapped on a door pad.

A large panel retracted to reveal a lap pool and sizeable hot tub.

Her jaw dropped. "You have a lake in your ship." She stepped through the door.

He followed her. "A lap pool. It's only twenty-five feet long, but it gives me the opportunity to swim."

"What's that?" She pointed to the round Jacuzzi.

"It's a hot water tub with jets." *Go easy. Don't press her. Don't act like getting in there with her would be heaven.*

"Jets in the water?"

"Not jet engines like the skimmer, but a pump that forces hot water through small holes to make it bubble around you. It soothes sore muscles."

She leaned forward like she wanted to test it. He knew from the set of her chin she was arguing with herself.

"There are spare suits in the changing rooms."

She shook her head. "I should go home. I'm expected before dark."

"I can have Mattie prepare special training meals for you. High protein for your muscles, but easy to digest. I ate them when I was training for sports."

Bottom lip pulled between her teeth, she tilted her head, undecided.

He struck a muscle pose. "What, you don't think good nutrition works?"

She pushed at his abs, but he saw it coming and she didn't

move him. He grabbed her hands and wrapped them around his waist, pulling her to him. "I want to support you. I want you to win and get your boon. Hell, I'll give you all the profits I'll make on the shipping contract if it will help you to be your own protector."

She looked up at him. "You need those credits for your mother's charities."

"There is that." He couldn't help himself. She was so sweet, so honest. He dropped a kiss on her forehead, then released her hands. "How about this? We swim until our arms threaten to fall off..."

She gave him the laugh he was trying for.

"Then we'll relax in the hot tub. I'll have Mattie pack up your training dinner so you can be home before dark. You show up here first thing in the morning and we train all day. If you want, you can let your protectors know that you'll be late tomorrow night." *He was rooting for later. Way later.*

Her hand went to the back of her neck. "Okay."

"You sure about this?"

She grinned. "Frag, yes."

———

O took the swimsuit from Jericho and walked into the small, mirrored room in the gym to change into it. When she emerged, Jericho was in his swimsuit, waiting for her with a hair clip—bless him— and an armful of thick, fluffy-looking towels. He was crazy if he thought she needed all of those. One cloth, half the size, took care of her showers and hair for a week. She followed him into the lake room, where he dumped the towels on a long chair that he called a *recliner*.

"I'll get everything going, then we can climb in. We can swim until you're ready to stop."

The noisy machinery started, pushing the water in the *lap pool* toward her. He adjusted switches and dials until he pronounced it perfect for training.

Hand in hand, they stepped into the end of the pool. The water wasn't cold like the ocean at Soldier Beach. It was just the right briskness for exerting energy without draining it. They continued down the next steps, until her feet touched the smooth, flat bottom. The water reached above her waist, all the way to her breasts. She peeked at her chest and stifled a groan when she saw the waterline cut right across her nipples. The formfitting swimsuit accentuated what looked like a pebble in each of the molded cups.

Releasing Jericho's hand, she dunked below the water, then rose and checked the front of her suit again. When the suit was entirely wet, where she stuck out wasn't so pronounced. She followed Jericho's lead and walked to the middle of the pool, pressing into the strong current. It didn't take long to get the hang of staying in the same place while stroking and kicking.

She strained against the *wave jets* at the end of the pool. Concentrating on her form, remembering what Jericho showed her at the underground lake, kept her from being pushed back by the fast-flowing water. Soon after they starting swimming, Jericho stood beside her, studying her movement like she imagined his coaches had watched him practice.

He stepped closer, adjusted her arm and told her to try the new position. Then he concentrated on her form and offered a suggestion for a small change that relaxed her tightening muscles. He stopped her occasionally to nudge her body into a more efficient pattern and swam parallel to her for ten minutes. He stood. "Enough for today? I don't want you to overdo it; you can't end up with sore muscles before the Battle."

She could have worked longer, but he had a point. "Okay." Before she had her feet under her, he'd swept her into his arms and was carrying her to the steps. She slapped at his hands, but didn't really try to get away. "Put me down. I'm not so tired that I can't walk under my own power."

He gripped her tighter. "Stop trying to make me drop you." She quit struggling right before his foot hit the first step out of the pool, and he made a sound in his throat that sounded like one of Solo's deep throat-rumbles. "If I ask nicely, will you put your arms around my neck?"

He didn't have to ask.

Water dripped onto the floor while he carried her to the round tub. "The water's going to be hot. Ready?" He waited for her nod before he stepped into the pool, slowly lowering them into the water. "You okay?" At her quick nod, he dipped his head and kissed her. Unlike in the hydroponic garden, there was no tentative testing to this kiss. He claimed her and she claimed him back.

More sure of herself, she met his exploration of her lips and a vibrational energy zinged through her body. She slowed to take stock of what had just happened, and he pulled his face away to inspect hers. She smiled and ran her finger up his throat. "Better now."

He groaned. "You're going to kill me, O." He kissed her again —unhurried, thorough— before setting her on her feet. "But I would die a happy man."

She found a molded seat and settled into it, resting her neck on the ledge that rimmed the tub. The surface gave, cradling her head in firm softness. Thousands of bubbles burst around her, and she smiled. Who knew bubbles could make her happy?

Jericho settled into the seat next to hers, raising his elbows and stretching his arms on the edge of the pool. If she did the same thing, they could hold hands. But the bubbles had started working their magic on her legs and back. Her arms and shoulders wanted those healing bubbles.

"You like?" Jericho let his head tilt so it rested against the soft pillow-like surface.

"Very much." Although she wasn't sleepy, her voice sounded dreamy.

"Just relax. The jets will shut off in twenty-minutes. You'll have plenty of time to change, grab your dinner and get home before dark, Cinderella."

Her mother had told O the French fairytale, complete with sketches of dresses, a castle, and a *pumpkin*. Did he really think her skimmer would turn into a giant orange squash? She let her eyes drift shut.

THE HOT TUB jets cut off, waking Jericho from a dream where he stayed on Prism after the supply ship left. O was still asleep. He hadn't thought about her as Cinderella until he'd worried about her getting home on time. *As if she'll lose a glass slipper.*

He smiled and touched her arm, floating on the top of the water. "Time to wake up."

"Ummm. Dontwanna, Daddy." She'd been dreaming, too.

He waited for her to open her eyes and watched while she took in her surroundings and her brain connected the dots.

"Ugh. Sorry." She sighed. "It's only been twenty minutes?" She pushed off the seat and stood. She wobbled and he offered his arm. "Thanks, I've got it."

She followed him out of the pool, and he handed her one of the towels he'd stacked near the edge. Before he finished toweling himself dry she'd already secured her towel around her hair. She pointed to the material. "Do you have a brush I can borrow?"

He gulped the chuckle that rose. Hadn't she seen all the guest staterooms? "Only a couple of dozen."

She groaned. "I just need one."

In separate changing rooms they stripped off their wet swimsuits and put on their workout clothes before heading to check on Mitzi and Solo. The cats were still curled together sleeping, but their positions had changed. Not wanting to wake them, Jericho and O left quietly for the dining room. He seated her before saying, "I'll be right back after I talk to Mattie." He left her and ducked into the galley.

When he returned, O's head rested on arms folded over the clear tabletop. Asleep again, she looked so unguarded. He went back into the galley to wait for Mattie to finish making their protein drinks. He carried the tall glasses and a bowlful of supplements to O.

She was stretching her back like she finally was fully awake. Eyeing what he carried, she watched him balance their dinner. "That's it? That's my protein-laden special meal?"

"Don't judge it by its looks." He set the bowl next to his place and put her glass in front of her before sitting. "I picked out some fast-acting supplements for your muscles, joints and tendons. And energy." He sorted the pills while explaining the benefits of each. "You don't have to take everything, but I don't think there's anything here that could cause a problem."

"I know some of the Battle competitors take lots of supplements from Earth." She nodded then took a careful sip of her drink. "You're right. This is better than it looks. I've never seen a dark green, thick liquid."

"That's from all the fresh vegetables that are blended together. Three of these a day for a week, and I feel a real difference in my performance."

She swallowed more. "You're happy about making me sorry again that I refused your tour that first night?"

He latticed his fingers, turned his palms outward and stretched. "Not me. Just wish we had more time." When she lifted the glass he added, "You may want to take those pills with that."

She looked at the bowl, pulling her bottom lip between her teeth. "How do I do that?"

Fighting an angry reaction that she'd not had access to simple meds, he showed her how to take them, coaxing her through a predictable first gagging reflex before he went to the galley for a couple of waters.

Standing by her chair when he returned, he offered the water and she gulped half of it. "Thanks. It got pretty thick there at the end." She sipped the rest of her water then checked the time." I'm sorry, but I've got to get back to the Citadel."

"You are well within your mission parameters, Lieutenant." *Where did that line come from?* Judging from her smile, it calmed her. They retrieved Solo from Mitzi's mewling good-by and walked to the entry hatch. He hesitated before palming the pad. "I had a good time today."

She looked at the deck before meeting his gaze. "Thank you. I did, too. I'll see you a bit later in the morning. I have an appointment with Administrator Schultz."

"Anything I can help with?"

"I wish, but no."

He wanted to pull her to him for a kiss to remind her to hurry in the morning. "I'll be here." Before he could reach for her, she placed her palms on either side of his face.

"And I'll be back." She tilted his chin down and kissed him.

His hands moved to her waist, pulling her closer as he deepened their kiss. He smoothed his hands down her hips and ended the kiss. Before he could start all over again, he slammed the entry pad, turned her around and tapped her butt. "Go."

————

AFTER O LEFT Jericho she still had time to fly to the Soldier Compound to check in with her grandfather about her appointment with the warden. She stopped off at the noisy community-dining hall and found Hoshi, Novy and Wash engaged in a lively discussion with other second gens. When she approached their table, the conversation stopped. "Can I talk to you?" She jerked her head to the door, indicating she wanted a private discussion.

They nodded and followed her outside.

Wash eyed her. "Got a problem?"

"Nope."

"Do you know how Jericho did with the Joint Committee?" Hoshi dealt with his four younger sisters, so he was usually more tuned in to her feelings.

"They didn't go easy on him, even though he's the first negotiator who's bothered to visit Prism. He wasn't happy I didn't tell him Granddad was a member."

Novy's I-know-what's-best look had always been harsher than Cal's. "Being pilot is not being spy."

"I didn't come here to hash over his contract proposal. I came here to let you know that I'm training for the Battle aboard *Freedom* tomorrow. There's an amazing room with a moving floor and something called a lap pool. I trained there this afternoon."

"Cal knows?" Novy's frown said he bet Cal didn't know.

"No. Why should he?"

Novy drilled her with a stare that said he thought he knew exactly why she didn't want to talk to Cal. Wash looked at the ground. Hoshi, thank goodness, nodded and said, "Novy, remember our oath."

She grabbed his hand. "Thank you." Releasing his hand, her gaze took in the three of them. "What had your table so rowdy in there?"

Silence. More silence and aggressive I-don't-want-to-make-eye-contact.

"Frag. Were they talking about me?"

Wash whistled. Off-key.

"Were you betting on someone else to win the Battle?"

"No. We have complete faith in you." Hoshi's solid response heartened her. "The table was debating the pros and cons of doing away with protectors and the First Law."

Good. She needed all the help she could get. "Anything interesting?"

"Females mostly in favor. First gen females, too." Novy looked like he'd been told he had to spend three days in the Retching Field.

"And the males?"

Hoshi jumped to answer. "Divided opinions."

"Uh huh." She had a pretty good idea where those divided opinions ran with her friends.

"Dropping in for dinner?" Her grandfather walked toward her. He sounded pleased.

Her friends murmured their goodbyes and went inside.

She jumped off the porch and strode toward Granddad, hoping he didn't already know about the mess hall gossip. But he'd know. He knew everything going on in the Soldier Compound and beyond. "I already ate. I was looking for you."

He motioned to the steps, then sat. "What do you want to talk about?"

She plopped her butt on the step next to him. "I have an appointment with the Warden tomorrow morning."

"Know what she wants?" He didn't look worried.

"I made the appointment with her. To talk about the First Law."

"Schultz wasn't here those first years. She doesn't understand the necessity. Only a first gen does."

"Then why not call a vote and let the first gens decide if we still need the First Law? There are plenty of women who probably agree with me. There are first gen females who flew missions during the war, but their protectors won't let them fly here. There are no enemy missiles to worry about, so why can't they pilot a mining shuttle?

"Better yet, let second gens vote, too. Prism is civilized now. From what Jericho says, we have fewer problems here than they have on Earth."

He looked down, interlaced his fingers and frowned. "For twenty-five years we've used the First Law to keep our women safe. I know there are problems with some men taking their protector role to dictator status. But if we throw out the First Law, families will break up. There may be physical fighting." He unlaced his fingers and his right hand curled into a fist before he looked at her. "Now is not the time for this, O. But, I promise, when the timing is right, I'll bring it up at the Joint Committee myself."

How could the timing not be right when his own granddaughter was in danger of losing her freedom? Twenty-five years and now was *not the time*? Did he have any idea of what Ray Reagan intended to do to her if she had to move in with her mother for just a few days?

He stood, nodding to a couple of second-gens who froze while stepping around them to walk down the steps. "As you were." He let them pass.

She rose and bit the inside of her scar. "Maybe if there hadn't been a First Law, my mother wouldn't have left Daddy. If she had, maybe they could have gotten back together. I'm still going to see Administrator Schultz."

"I didn't order you not to. Now, I'm going inside to listen to the debates you've started in my mess hall." He hugged her, went up the steps and through the door.

At least he hadn't ordered her to stand down. He knew she would defy that command. He was the leader of the soldiers, but he wasn't her protector. She didn't have to do what he said when it came to her personal life.

23

P

ersonal Journal of Brynhildr Thorsøngud Montgomery: (Twenty-three Years ago) Archived in the Oslo Museum of Nature History

Prism, Day Twelve: It's disappointing, but no one on the team has found the tiniest trinket from a previous civilization. Even though we're working in different areas of the vast tunnel system, there hasn't been a pictograph, a pottery fragment, or even a bone to indicate life in the tunnels. But the tunnel system is too precise and uniform to be a natural phenomenon. My pilot (and protector) assures me that these tunnels are the only ones he's found on the planet. Well, under the planet. Sometimes I get the strangest feeling —like electricity sparking over my skin—that someone, something, is watching me. It's only been two weeks.

THE NEXT MORNING, in a spotless, flawless jumpsuit, O'Neill sat on the bench outside the Warden's office, reviewing her reasons to kill the First Law of Prism. She thought of her mother. If women chose to leave their protectors, it would be because they had good reasons. Yes, children's needs would have to be taken care of, but those details could be worked out. If husbands loved their wives, they'd figure out how to live without being tyrants. The men would complain at their loss of power, but when their wives were happy, the protectors would be, too. And what woman didn't want control over her own destiny?

"She'll see you now." Quay jerked his thumb toward Administrator Schultz's closed office door.

O'Neill had been parked long enough that the "go ahead" signal had her on her feet before the assistant finished speaking. She pulled the door open and looked straight ahead at Administrator Schultz's desk. She wasn't there.

"Come in, Lieutenant Neill, and close the door." The warden's voice sounded less harried than usual.

O stepped inside, securing the door behind Solo, to find Cornelia Schultz sitting on the sofa, shoes off, feet tucked under her. "What's on your mind, young lady?"

The carefully thought-out arguments now jumbled together in shocked disarray, leaving O speechless. She'd never thought of the representative of the World Board as a real person. A real person who might get tired or be willing to talk freely with a second gen about her individual concerns.

Schultz patted the leather. "Have a seat."

O sat on the edge, literally, her spine locked in place like landing gear.

"Relax. I don't bite." A muted chuckle set off a genuine grin of amusement. "You are a serious one."

"Yes, ma'am. I have a lot to be serious about, since my father died." She gulped. May as well lay out her problem. And hopeful solution. "I don't have much time before I have to either declare a protector or move in with my mother and Ray Reagan."

"And...?"

"I don't want to live in Reagan's house, and I'm not ready to get married."

The warden shifted against the end of the sofa, angling herself toward O. "I'm not surprised that you don't want to live with your stepfather as your protector. He's not at all like your father."

"He's a wicked, evil man. He's threatened me. Solo, too."

"Has he? He's too sly for witnesses, correct?"

"It was on the rooftop of the Citadel when I was on watch. No one heard him say he planned to sell Solo for steaks." The tiger leaned against her legs. "He said he was going to arrange for me to go to the Fertile Field, as if he would sell me to the highest bidder. He said I would have a bastard." Her voice was almost a wail.

The administrator straightened. "Raymond has always been a controlling dickhead. But I thought you and Cal got along well. Isn't he your coach now for the Battle?"

Besides her daily reports, the woman knew all the gossip in the three compounds. She had to have eyes and ears everywhere. "Yes. But I'm not ready to trust my independence to him." She took a deep breath. "I want you to help me find a way to get around the First Law."

That got Schultz's attention. She stared at O with a frozen look in her eyes that O could not read. After more time than it took to swap out a mining shuttle's translithium crystals, the woman laughed, closed-mouth at first then full on laughed. "You would. Your father changed life on Prism with his discovery and now, after twenty-five years of the First Law, you want to change things up. Good for you."

O steeled herself for the power-it-down refusal before the *Good for you* made it to her brain. The warden agreed with her?

"Oh, honey, I've argued for the dissolution of the First Law for over two years. Prism can make a better case for colony status if there is no appearance of lawlessness and danger on the planet." She dipped her chin. "There is no longer a reason for protectors. Earth is more dangerous than Prism."

O's mouth was open, poised to lay out her logical reasons for throwing out the edict. No words formed. No words were necessary. The warden agreed with her. She sighed deeply.

"You know I can't do anything about the First Law. The first gens agreed to it twenty-five years ago. If I were you, I'd talk to your grandfather and Cal's dad. You know only the Joint Committee can make the change. But don't ambush them publicly. Men tend to jump into their bunkers when women confront them about changing their minds, especially when there's an audience." A knock sounded on the wooden door. "Dang." She bent, picked up her shoes, and moved behind her desk. "I've enjoyed our conversation. Anytime you've got something on your mind, drop by, O'Neill. My door is always open for you."

O stood and left the office in a daze. Solo padded alongside her, looking up like he wanted to ask a question. What had happened? Had she said good-bye or thank-you?

The Warden is my ally. She'd never envisioned the warden of Prism as a possible friend.

———

AFTER HER BRIEF meeting two floors above the docking area, O walked up the ramp to *Freedom*. Her stomach knotted, and it wasn't because she hadn't eaten. Ideas she hadn't given a credit's chance of getting past the warden hadn't been squashed. Now, she had to figure out how to best put together a formal request for the Joint Committee—before the Battle.

And Jericho? He was the fourth protein bar in her day's rations. A special treat of abundance and…joy. He would help her.

The hatch slid open. Jericho had been watching for her.

"Good morning. Hi, Solo." He stepped aside for them to enter. A smile lit his eyes before he kissed her cheek. He put his palm under her elbow and guided her to the right, toward his office. "Mitzi misses Solo. I've got breakfast for them. In separate bowls."

"Solo is not going like when you leave and he doesn't get his fresh proteins."

"What about you?" His hand snaked around her waist.

"Maybe. I can get cranky when I'm hungry. You saw me at the

Burnt Engine." She put her hand on his and squeezed. "Did your proposal happen to include shipments of fresh Earth food?"

Jericho palmed the pad one door short of his office. "No, too expensive. Besides, shipments of fresh food wouldn't hold up well on the trip. Without refrigeration, it won't last more than a couple days here, anyway." The panel slid into the wall, but he pulled her to him instead of letting her walk through. "You okay?"

"Yes."

"Good." He gave her a fast, solid kiss. "Come inside."

Solo trotted past them. It was a sleeping cabin, even larger than the guest cabins she'd seen yesterday. The adjoining sitting area was almost as large as the main room of her home. With delicate furniture and colors, it had a definite feminine air. Mitzi rose and stretched on the quilted gold fabric covering the bed before jumping to the deck to greet Solo by rubbing against his leg.

"This was my mother's cabin. Now it's Mitzi's."

"All this space for a little cat?"

Solo bent his nose to the tiny feline. She rubbed her whiskers against his muzzle.

"Who knew she was such a flirt?" He ruffled her fur. "Okay, it's feeding time at the zoo." He crossed to a cabinet and removed two filled dishes, one large and one small.

Both cats followed him. Mitzi screeched a yowl.

"Okay, okay." Jericho put the dishes in front of them and patted Mitzi. "I'm so glad I didn't let Dad get rid of you, little girl."

"What do you mean, get rid of her?"

"He hated everything my mother loved. As fast as he legally could, he's dismantled all her good works. He's probably told Yancey to disappear Mitzi."

At her confused look Jericho explained. "Any employee of my father would know that meant, 'Kill the cat.'"

She gasped. "Your father would have that precious animal killed?"

"He never thought of Mitzi as *precious*. He hates her and the feeling is mutual."

Jericho's father is a fragger. A murdering fragger.

"Did you have breakfast before your meeting?"

"No." She was still stuck on how someone could order an animal killed. Like Reagan threatened Solo.

"Good. You can tell me about it while we have our sumptuous meal."

Instead of running on the red triangle after downing her protein drink and supplements, she stood in the gym's dressing room trying to pull on a *neurosuit* that Jericho said would help her melee skills. The white jumpsuit was thin. And sizes too small. Earth girls must be tiny.

Since it had no fastenings she stretched it over her feet, up her legs and over her shoulders. The sleeves ended in gauntlets. The suit encased her body like another layer of skin. She pulled the tight hood over her head, snugging her hair to her scalp. A glance in the mirror showed she couldn't step outside and maintain an ounce of dignity.

A knock sounded on the panel. "Everything okay?"

"This suit is microscopic. I'm not."

"It has to be tight to receive and transfer input." Jericho sounded worried. "Open the door and let me check it."

"No, it's too tight."

"I know you like loose-fitting clothes, O, but it's like a full-body bathing suit."

She considered his words, imagining him standing there talking to the closed door. She opened it a crack. "Do you have a larger size?"

"It's perfect." He took her gloved hand and pulled her out of the closet. "You're perfect."

His smile held appreciation. And invitation. "Heck, you could wear that suit into your melee and turn the men into slobbering fools. Then you could just beat them into the ground with your stick." He grinned. "But, if you don't want to try what I've got, you can change back into your jumpsuit and hit the treadmill."

Her cheeks heated. Oh, she wanted to try more of what Jericho had. "This will help me with the melee?" Her weakest event. If wearing this outfit to train could raise her score, she'd wear it. *But only in this room.* "Okay."

He led her to a large yellow square away from the red rectangle. "Stand in the middle. I'll bring you the stick."

She positioned herself in the middle of the square.

"Here you go." Jericho tossed her a staff.

It was shaped like a staff, but it was made out of a lightweight, semi-flexible ceramic instead of a crystal.

"Yellow square. Kendo sim. One opponent. Impact active. Level One. Begin."

An opponent materialized in front of her. She took a step back. She'd never seen a hologram bigger than her hand. A life-sized three-D hologram dressed in an ancient suit of war bowed. She looked at Jericho, and at his nod, returned the bow. The hologram swung its staff at her legs and she jumped. She raised her weapon and brought it down across the figure's shoulder, but instead of slicing through air, the vibration of the solid hit ran up her arm. She glanced at Jericho.

"Newest technology. If he hits you, you're going to feel it, but there will be no residual effects," Jericho said. He crouched beside the mat.

She returned her attention to the hologram in time to parry a sideswipe. Again she felt her staff absorb the hit and heard the crack of the weapons colliding. Her attacker moved closer and to the side, ramming the end of his stick into her stomach.

"Ouch!" She stepped off the yellow square and the warrior evaporated.

"You okay?" Jericho rose and placed a foot on the yellow mat. Her opponent re-appeared. "Pause program." The figure froze in mid-strike. Jericho crossed the yellow square to stand beside her. "Are you okay?"

She rubbed her stomach, but felt nothing. She pushed her skin harder. Still nothing. There would be no bruise tomorrow. "I'm fine." Stunned but fine. If only she'd known about this room

earlier. She stepped back on the mat, determined to take this opportunity to improve her skill. "Resume."

"That's it," Jericho called when she blocked the staff arcing
toward her head.

He yelled, "Duck!" when she reacted too slowly to her opponent's next move.

She tried difficult moves and felt the pain of a strike, but she
improved, advancing through the levels. So engrossed in the sim,
she fought as if the figure before her were real and no one else was
around.

———

AFTER A WHILE, Jericho moved away from the mat and leaned
against the bulkhead, watching, shouting less frequently. He knew
why winning the Battle was so important to her, and he wished he
could do more to assure her success. O looked so good in that
skintight outfit, she could star in an action vid without any pre-
filming body sculpting.

He pushed off from the wall, right after a staff whacked her
skull. She attacked the warrior who'd landed the blow, then she
leapt over the other opponent's staff. He smiled. She'd improved
quite a bit in her short time on the mat. Too bad they hadn't started
working together earlier. He could have trained beside her with the
holograms.

Last night, after finding the sim, he'd practiced with it. While
he'd worked out, he'd thought about staying on Prism with the
scientific team. That plan needed more work.

O paused the sim. "Did you see my footwork?"

He nodded. "Better. Keep at it."

It cost him nothing to use the holo program, but her smile was
worth a string of diamonds. Large diamonds. He wanted to twirl
her around in his arms and congratulate her on how fast she was
improving. Then give her a long, bone-melting kiss. He gave her a
smile of encouragement instead. She needed this practice.

"Level three," she called. After a few swipes of her staff she paused the program. "Would you be willing to fight beside me? Sometimes people work as a team at the beginning of the melee. It would help if I know how to do that."

She didn't have to explain. He kept himself from skipping to the changing room where he'd put his suit. "Be right back." He heard the clack of the bout behind him.

He pulled on the suit, cursing under his breath at the time it took to stretch the neuro-fabric up his legs and body. By the time he returned to the sim square, she'd worked up a sweat.

"Ready when you are."

She paused the program, and turned to him. Her gaze flicked down his body. Her chin jerked up and she blushed. Score one for working out.

He knew the suit displayed his body as faithfully as it did hers. *Hope you like what you see.* He grabbed a pole and stepped on the yellow square. "Want to see what we can do against four of them?"

She nodded. "Resume. Four opponents against two."

They fought back to back against warriors with better skills. By the time they could hold their own, Jericho could have started wheezing. "Let's see what we can do with six."

Six bodies filled the yellow mat, allowing little footwork besides a lunge. They hacked away with their staffs at the non-relenting, non-tiring holograms for twenty minutes. After receiving a particularly nasty hit across her back, O paused the program.

She bent at the waist, breathing hard. When she straightened, Jericho clapped. "Well, done."

He pushed back his hood, took her staff and tossed them both into the container on the edge of the mat. "That cap was tight enough to squeeze my brain out my eye sockets."

"I've suspected that Earther brains are tiny." She sidestepped him off the mat. "I'm going to change."

"Put on your swimsuit and we'll do a few laps," he called after her. "I'll meet you in the water."

After changing into her swimsuit, she joined him in the pool, straining against the strong current generated by the wave jets. Concentration on her form, using what Jericho showed her yesterday, she kept herself from being pushed back by the fast-flowing water. She didn't complain when, after forty minutes, he called a halt.

"Hot tub?"

The offer made her stiff, over-worked muscles start melting, but she needed to talk with Miguel about the skimmer readiness for the Battle and run through last minute course changes. Tomorrow was her final day before the competition. She didn't want to leave any details to the last minute. Ready and rested, she had a real shot at winning. "Tempting, but I need to head back to the Citadel."

He nodded. "Mattie's packed your dinner and supplements. They're waiting at the hatch." He laced his fingers with hers and they walked to Mitzi's room.

"Ready to go home, big guy?" Solo gently head-butted the little cat then walked to the door.

At the hatch, O gave Jericho a goodbye kiss. "Thanks for everything, today."

"Are you coming back tomorrow?"

How could she not? "If that's okay."

The sun shining over Prism's Great Plain couldn't have warmed her more that his smile. "More than okay." He handed her the container with her dinner and slapped the entry pad.

The hatch opened, and Solo started down the ramp. She almost called the tiger back.

"Go on. It's all right. I'll be waiting right here for you in the morning." Jericho put his hand on her hip, right below her waist and squeezed. Then he lifted her hair and brushed his lips across her neck. "Sleep well."

Her brain short circuited, because, though she told her legs to move, it seemed like hours before she took that first step to follow Solo. She glanced over her shoulder, expecting to see the closed hatch. But Jericho stood there, watching her. She snapped him a two-finger salute and followed Solo to her dad's skimmer.

24

J ournal of General Liam Neill, Prism, Day 3 after the Cryo-ship Landing (25 Years ago)
The landing site was a bloodbath. By my count almost one hundred crazies, along with another hundred civilians, were shuttled down first. By the time the politicos landed, half the first group were dead or injured. When the politicos tried to offer first aid, they were attacked and chased off with twenty-five percent casualties. Our shuttle arrived and the fighting became fierce and bloody. The first group (I call them the crazies because they seem to have reverted to primitive ways) had claimed the two mountains of supplies and had dragged off several politico women, whose screams continued throughout the day and night, although without their original vigor.

AT HOME, after landing the skimmer, O'Neill repelled off the side of the building then ran laps around the base of the Citadel. Quinn was on watch. He shouted encouragement while timing her; then he threw the rope over the side and she climbed up the sheer wall. Even though she was sweaty, he clapped her on the back. "You've got a real shot at winning. Jocko would be proud." He started pulling up the rope.

Maybe it was her success with the warden, maybe it was his comment about her dad, but she decided to see how he felt about the First Law. "If I wanted to keep living here, would you support me, Quinn?"

His smile was easy. "Of course. I have no problem with Cal moving in with you. He'll have to learn how to live in a soldier compound and share on duty rotations along with you, but I'd support you."

"Not what I meant. What if I refuse to marry Cal and I refuse to move in with my mother and her husband?"

Quinn stopped coiling the rope. "You can't break the First Law, O."

"It's out of date. Prism isn't like it was in the earlier years."

"Women still need to be protected."

"So do men. My father saw to it that I could protect myself. There are plenty of girls in the soldier compound who can fight better than their brothers, and they don't want to be forced into declaring for a protector either."

Quinn looked like a man who'd been handed a grenade without the pin. "The law's there for a reason. I'm sorry Jocko's gone. I know how hard it's been on you and how much you miss him. But he'd want you to be protected. You're going to have to make a decision."

He was wrong. Her father had seen to it that she could protect herself. He'd encouraged her independence. He knew how to bend the rules. Now it was time for her to learn that skill. "Good evening, Quinn."

She opened the trapdoor and followed Solo down the stairs. She fed him then drank Mattie's dinner. She'd been playing *Save the Princess* at night before falling asleep, but tonight she had more time. Maybe her dad would "visit" while she played. He had before.

Retrieving the game reader and lying across her father's bed, she activated the device. The usual figures materialized on the little holo platform, but the machine beeped and a new figure, a knight in chain mail, appeared. "Mind if I join you?"

When she played a game with her father, his character was introduced this way. Could he have been playing on his own when she wasn't here?

"Dad?"

"No. Just another player."

This wasn't part of the game. Her father had told her that on Earth, people from many different countries could play holographic games with each other. In fact, over a dinner at the soldier compound, a few of his first gen friends had talked about the old days, before the war, when they'd battled together, from their own continents, against electronic villains.

But no one else on Prism had the tech to connect with her holo player. A chill ran up her back and out her arms.

"I'm surprised to find you here. Mind if I join you?"

The hologram had the voice of the game character, not the person playing, so she couldn't identify the player's age or gender. Who could it be? "How long have you been playing?"

"Since it came out. Eight months. If you're new to the game, I may be able to help you advance more quickly."

"Who are you?"

"Knight in Shining Armor, my Princess."

She powered the player down, snapped open the unit and pulled out the chip. Heart beating a cadence faster than she could run, she tucked the chip under the insole of one of her father's boots and hid the device in his closet. Someone had found out about her clandestine Earth vice. Worse, someone else had illegal Earth tech that might lead to her.

She bit a fingernail, wishing that she'd talked to her grandfather about those bubble chips, even though he'd forbidden her to. Did those chips have something to do with the new game player? She had no idea who *Knight in Shining Armor* was. Friend or foe? Did he—or she—know O's identity?

She prayed there would be no knock on her door during the night.

———

O'NEILL WOKE EARLY. *One day until the Battle.*

After all her training, winning the right for one year of independence hinged on her performance. On her skill. During that year she'd work to convince her community, then the politicos that the First Law was outdated. Those who talked of colony status for Prism would be won over by the warden's argument. She could convince a majority of the Soldier Compound to drop the First Law. Frag. If somehow she ended up at her mother's, Solo's life would hinge on her performance. She'd pushed herself, but had she pushed hard enough? What would she do if she didn't win?

She had the mental and physical toughness, and she had piloting skills that were envied by most. But what about her strategy in each event? Could she plot the most efficient course for the flying the Fields? Would her stomach allow her to fly it?

Jericho's invitation to train on board his ship was the perfect solution to her last morning to prepare for the most important day of her life. Her thoughts circled back to Jericho. *Her Earther.* She wouldn't have thought affection could ever tinge those two words.

It had been easy to get used to spending time with Jericho. As much as she'd been irritated by his questions, she would miss his thought-filled quest for answers, his joy of exploring the beauty of Prism, his easy manner. She was going to miss her Earther. Way too much.

She laced her boots, worried that she was more nervous about the Battle than she realized. But the truth was that she was worried about what her life would be like without Jericho. She looked forward to seeing him every day, to planning new experiences for him, to sharing her thoughts with him. To the new experiences she had with him. To his touch and kisses. Oh, how she needed his kisses.

Her father had been wrong about the dangers of fraternization with Earthers. It wouldn't be Earth *food* she would crave in a week. It would be Jericho.

Did that mean she loved him?

Everything stilled while she pondered the idea of loving Jericho Montgomery. But she knew fragging nothing about love. Wasn't sure she wanted to find out. At least not now. Not the day before the Battle when she had to remain focused on only one thing: winning her independence.

She was having breakfast with him this morning. Maybe her last breakfast with him. And didn't that feel like a boot kick to her gut? "Let's go, Solo. Up to the roof. We're flying today. Miguel's going to work on the skimmer at the spaceport while I train."

Less than thirty minutes later, O stood in front of *Freedom's* closed hatch. Unusual, since the door usually opened when she stepped on the ramp. And if it didn't, Jericho's voice greeted her through the external com. Impatient to board, Solo padded in front of her and rubbed against the smooth alloy. She thought about rapping on the metal panel.

"Good morning, Lieutenant O'Neill. May I help you?" Yancey was monitoring the security screens.

Where is Jericho?

She stood on the ramp, aware that the early morning dock-workers took note she hadn't been allowed entry. "Good morning, Yancey. Jericho invited me for breakfast and a morning training session."

"I'll let him know you're here."

Embarrassed, she looked at her boots. *Has Jericho changed his mind?* After waiting a week of eternity, she patted Solo. What she really wanted to do was hide her face in his fur.

"O, I'm sorry. Yancey is on his way to open the hatch. I'll join you shortly." Jericho's voice boomed from the com. He sounded rushed. And tired.

The hatch slid open. Solo almost knocked Yancey down, bounding inside.

"Solo!" She called, but he'd already slid around the corner heading for Mitzi's cabin. "Sorry about that. I'll get him."

She strode down the corridor. Solo sat outside Mitzi's door. She bent on one knee and rubbed under his chin.

What had Jericho been doing? Didn't he care enough to remember he'd invited her? She remembered how he'd asked her to breakfast and train this morning.

Yancey, looking uncomfortable, led her to the dining room. Head down, Solo padded behind them. He looked exactly the way she felt.

The table was set for two. "Mattie will be here shortly."

She took the chair closest to the door and sipped the chilled water at her place. Solo paced. "Easy, boy. Don't you run to that door again." But that was what she wanted to do. Stand outside Jericho's cabin and pace. *Pathetic.*

Mattie entered carrying a pitcher of blue liquid. "I'm sorry, your breakfast isn't ready yet. Here is a special juice blend." She set the container before O.

"I appreciate the extra work you've done for me. Thank you."

"No bother. It's as easy to cook for two as for one." Mattie smiled and left.

She looked at the pitcher, waiting for Jericho.

How had she allowed herself to become so attached to him? Where had her good sense disappeared to?

Jericho entered the room, carrying his mother's cat. "Good morning." He bent and placed Mitzi on the deck then seated himself across from O. "I'm sorry you had to wait. I overslept."

I couldn't wait to see you either. Her cheeks heated. Had she misjudged his feelings for her? "I hope I didn't tire you out yesterday."

Jericho stared at her while she watched Solo nudge Mitzi's side. In return the cat's tiny claws swiped at his nose.

I know how you feel, Solo.

He smiled and poured a small glass for each of them. "It's not your fault I overslept."

Her fingers trembled around the delicate glass. *Nerves.* Nerves about the bubble chips. Nerves about the holo game. Nerves about the Battle. Nerves about Jericho.

He reached across the table and touched her hand. "I'm sorry I wasn't at the hatch to meet you. I didn't get to bed until a couple of hours ago."

She wanted to ask what he was doing, but that felt invasive. He didn't have to account for his time to her.

Mattie returned. She set identical tall mugs filled with green liquid in front of them before setting a large and a small bowl piled with bits of raw meat on the deck for the cats. They nudged each other and began gulping the food. "Who on Earth will believe Mitzi has a tiger for a friend?"

"Thank you, Mattie. It looks delicious."

"Yes, thank you, Mattie." O's breath caught. "I'll miss your meals when you go home."

"It's nice to cook for someone as appreciative as you, Miss." She shot a look at Jericho, took her tray, and left them alone.

"Will Mattie's meals be the only thing you miss when I leave?" Jericho's intent face waited for her answer.

"No." She wasn't going to lie to him, but she couldn't bear to tell him more than that single word. She nudged the mug. It was cool. The liquid was thick.

He inhaled a long breath. "It's made with a special sea protein grown for stamina and fast muscle response. Beet leaves and kale provide slow-release energy and pineapple makes it palatable." He raised his glass in a toast and swigged down a good portion.

Between tossing supplements into her mouth, she sipped.

He took another long draw. "Healthiest thing I do for myself when I'm in training."

She upended her mug and, in a series of slow gulps, finished the concoction with a shudder. *Earth food.* "I bet you and your father spend many happy hours over your mealtimes."

He shook his head. "We rarely eat together. An occasional breakfast or a business dinner. That's all."

She didn't think he could be so tight-lipped. *All at the mention of his father.* She wondered why. This wasn't the open, willing-to-share-information Jericho she knew.

What would her mornings be like knowing she wouldn't see Jericho during the day? What would her nights be like without planning what they would do, what she would show him? Something twisted in her gut. Something that felt suspiciously like loneliness, only with a new, sharp wrinkle.

A pensive look clouded his features. "What's your favorite color?"

Do I have a favorite color? Almost all of her clothes were army khaki. Not that she had a choice. She did have a favorite shirt, though. "Green. Emerald green."

Jericho looked pleased at her answer. Why would he care? Cal had known her for years and never asked her favorite color.

"Next time I'll bring you some Irish shamrocks."

Why would he bring her fake rocks? There were plenty of rocks on Prism already.

But there wouldn't be a next time. Earthers never returned to Prism. Why would Jericho be different? She concentrated on looking at the mugs to keep from crying.

This is what it feels like to have your heart break.

25

Official Montgomery Corporate Earth News, Present Day

We're hearing rumors that the shipment from Prism may not contain the full number of translithium crystals. There is no need to panic at this time. You are advised to conserve and be prepared for rationing if the prisoners have not met their quota.

Journal of Gatfield Montgomery/RETINAL SCAN REQUIRED:

I don't care that the PanAsian Conglomerate is cashing in on my news release. People across the globe are rushing to buy up the remaining translithium. They're paying top dollar for the privilege, and grumbling. It won't be long before Neill and his gang of thugs are despised by the majority of Earth's population. Then I'll be able to do whatever I want to them.

HAND-IN-HAND, Jericho walked her to Mitzi's room to leave the cats. She helped him set out water for them.

She'd taken his absence from meeting her at the hatch the

wrong way, and he wanted to make it up to her. "Let's go to the garden so you can pick out some plants to take home."

She exhaled a long breath. "They're too expensive."

No woman had ever told him anything was too expensive for him to give her. He couldn't suppress a chuckle. "That's your best argument?"

She blushed. God, she was gorgeous. He had to kiss her, had to see if, despite her distance when he finally got to the dining room, she felt for him what he felt for her. Resting his hands on her shoulders, he lowered his mouth to hers, watching her for a sign.

Her eyes widened, but she remained still. Very still.

Her lids slid down. His did, too, when their lips met.

Her palms skimmed up his chest, stopping at his collarbone. Even though he'd kissed more girls than he could remember, he couldn't help himself. He slid his arms around her back and pulled her against him, pressing his lips more firmly against hers. Her arms circled his neck. He hung on, clinging to her like a sailor clung to a lone oar after his ship sank. How would he survive the next six months without her?

At some point he realized she was scattering feathery kisses along his lips. He opened his eyes. She smiled, giving him one last firm kiss before pulling free of his arms.

"How will I survive for six long months without seeing you every day?" he whispered. He didn't know. Couldn't fathom a life without her.

Had she been wondering the same thing? She didn't answer him. But he knew her. Knew how she showed everything she felt on her face and in her body language. And he knew when she closed it down, she was knotted tight inside.

He wanted her to want something from him. No, *need* something from him. Something that would make her remember him every day.

They walked hand-in-hand to the gym. Hers wasn't soft like the women he dated, but it wasn't calloused. She held his with firm pressure. It felt good. *Better than good.*

As tired as he'd been when he finished the kendo sim lessons two hours ago, he'd still placed fresh sensor suits and shoes in their changing rooms. After pulling on his gear, he retrieved two poles that better resembled her staff, then leaned against the wall waiting for her.

She opened the changing room door. While she walked toward him he tried not to gape. He'd seen her in a suit yesterday, but fry-him-to-hell damn. Maybe it was the kiss, but he'd been at photo shoots with famous, beautiful models. O wasn't famous, but she had one laser burst of a body. And after that last kiss, he was very aware of how perfect that body felt against his.

Her gaze flicked down his body. Her chin jerked up and she blushed.

She accepted the staff, hefting it for balance. "Ah, this is more like what we use. Narrower, a bit flexible. Lighter." She slashed, cutting an arc in the air.

He stepped onto the yellow square. "Begin Kendo sim. Two opponents, Level Five."

Two holograms materialized in front of him. Their simultaneous attack would have been difficult to counter if he'd stopped the sim lessons at midnight when he was in the middle of level four. But he'd stayed with the program until he completed instruction through Level Seven. Just two hours before O showed up at the hatch. A combination of footwork, turns and six well-placed swings and jabs had both opponents laying on the mat at his feet. "Pause sim."

Jaw hanging open, she looked as if she expected him to shimmer away like the holograms. "You've learned how to melee."

He smiled at her reverent tone. "Last night. And this morning. The tutorial is quite good. I fell into bed a couple of hours ago. Slept like the dead and missed my wake-up alarm."

"Oh." The tension around her eyes melted away. "When you didn't meet me, I thought maybe you'd changed your mind."

That's what had made her standoffish. "There is nothing that's going to make me change my mind about wanting to be with you. Not today. Not tomorrow. Not ever."

"Okay." She cocked her head.

She wasn't convinced, but he wasn't going to tell her the other reason he'd been up all night working out the details of his return to Prism. That was a surprise that needed the right timing for her to accept and believe.

He wrapped his empty hand around the back of her head and gave her a long, thorough kiss. A kiss that would imprint him on her lips, in her heart. When she opened her eyes, it took a moment for her to focus on his face. "Are we good?"

She nodded. "Better than good."

He pulled his hand away, brushing a knuckle against her neck, and was rewarded with a little shudder from her. Nice, since his insides were a fragging earthquake. Maybe a new type of FTL drive had been invented while he was here so he could return to her faster.

All business now, she stepped onto the mat, got into position and twirled her staff once. "How about we warm up with Level Four?"

———

TWO HOURS later in the bathroom of Jericho's mother's cabin, O'Neill stripped off the sweaty sensor suit and stepped into the shower. Depending on which buttons she pushed, hot water sprinkled her from above, pummeled her from the sides or sprayed up from the floor.

She'd dialed the temperature setting to hot and stood beneath the rainfall of steamy drops for much longer than her usual two-minute shower. At home, she'd be lucky if the water in the roof tank was warm for a simple cleansing.

At least today, the children of the Citadel wouldn't have to work the pump in the building's basement to move water from the cellar well to the roof tank on her account. Everyone worked on

Prism, though as a child she'd enjoyed her chores around the building, particularly riding the bicycle with no wheels in the basement.
What an indulgent luxury this ship was—a specialness that Jericho
could not comprehend, living with such wonders. And servants to
clean his clothes and cook fresh food brought all the way
from Earth.

Relaxed, she stepped onto the drying grid. Warm air rose from
the floor, bathing her in a gentle breeze while she toweled her hair
with a piece of material that sucked the moisture from her curls.
The mirrored wall reflected her happy grin.

She pulled clean underwear and a jumpsuit from her pack.
She'd have to retrieve her other clothes from the changing closet in
the exercise room.

She heard a snort, but a visual check said she was still alone, so
the noise must have been Solo.

Jericho said he'd knock on the door when he was presentable.

How could Jericho think he wasn't presentable, ever? Sure,
he'd been sweatier than her after fighting off hundreds of holograms. But he'd fought beside her and they'd made it through
Level Seven of the sim lessons. She would never have guessed he
was so talented with a staff. Good thing that lucky upswing of a
hologram warrior in Level Six couldn't do permanent damage to
Jericho's tender spots. He'd dropped to his knees and inhaled
deeply for ten seconds before stumbling to his feet and declaring
that he was, "Good to go." For the next lesson, his more aggressive
protection of his crotch almost made her laugh.

Solo and Mitzi curled together, asleep at the foot of the bed.
She leaned on the edge of the mattress, watching them twitch in
their feline dreams. On the small metal chest next to the bed rested
a well-worn, old-fashioned paper book, bound in what was probably the skin of an Earth animal. Scooting closer she picked it up
and ran her fingertips over the smooth cover. Small gold embossed
letters in the lower right corner proclaimed the owner: *Jericho
Montgomery*.

Had he written a book? Or was this book written about him?

She opened it, expecting words. What she saw was a rough pencil sketch of the dock. On the next page, a more detailed sketch of Administrator Schultz. He had talent.

The next pages showed more than decent renditions of Convict Town, her grandfather, the melee practice, her standing in her swimsuit. Of all the times they'd been together, why had he chosen to draw her in a swimsuit? The artistic details of her body, its curves under the suit, the play of color and shadow, would have impressed her if it hadn't been so personal. Like he *knew* her body. Her checks heated. Somehow, with a minimum of strokes, he'd managed to make her look attractive. She turned the pages.

There was one of Solo, her mother, the crystal forest, and each of her friends. There were empty pages, but the final page stole her breath.

Different thicknesses of pencil strokes indicated that the last picture had been reworked many times. She could tell from the smudge marks around the edge that the page had been touched often. It was the only sketch in color. Was she that special to him?

A softness settled around her, like a warm, new blanket. The picture took her back to that day, back to the first time she'd realized she genuinely liked Jericho, back to when he'd almost kissed her. What a fool she'd been for stopping him.

He'd drawn a strikingly accurate representation of her pushing out of the underground lake. She could feel the wet droplets of water dripping from her hair to her shoulders. She saw the surge of joy on her face. The picture showed her feelings. He'd known what she felt then. She closed her eyes, smiling as she remembered how many times he'd shown he knew what was in her mind, and maybe, even what was in her heart. Did he know how special he was to her?

A staccato rap made her jump. She dropped the book.

"You dressed?"

"Uh huh." She bent to retrieve his sketchbook.

Jericho opened the door. "I thought we'd–" His brows creased.

She didn't want him to know she'd snooped. She replaced the book and met his gaze.

"You looked at my sketches?"

"Yes. They're … amazing."

"I forgot I left it in here." He looked like he wanted to say more.

"I'm sorry. I didn't mean to pry. I couldn't help myself."

"Sketching is a necessity for the design division." He tapped the cover. "My mother taught me to draw. She said every stroke of the pencil reveals a piece of the artist's heart."

Her throat tightened. If his mother was right, what did that last picture show? Could you draw love on a page? "I'm sorry for snooping. I didn't mean to dig up sad memories." Hers words sounded raspy.

"I'm glad you found it. I wanted to share it with you, but…" He exhaled a long breath. "My father thinks my sketches are a waste of time."

Gatfield Montgomery was a jerk. Jericho didn't judge her, didn't try to change her mind. He'd been lucky to have a mother who wouldn't let his father destroy the good in Jericho.

"Your sketches are not a waste of time. I love them." *I think I love you.* In an attempt to lighten the mood, she pointed to his sketchbook. "You like Novy. I could tell from his picture."

Jericho didn't have to be nice to her or her friends. He cared about her, and because she cared about her friends, he cared about them, too.

He nodded. "I like all of your friends, but yes, Novy is my favorite."

"Why?"

His head tilted and his lips pursed. "He's honest about his feelings. He loves Earth food and he's not ashamed of it. And he really cares about you. I think he'd protect you even if it meant he could die."

Would you? Do you care that much about me?

There was no one else on Prism for her.

Except now. Except Jericho.

"All of my friends protect me." She thought of the fight in Convict Town the night she met him. "Cal would die before he let anything happen to me."

With the heel of his hand, he rubbed a rib and nodded. "I got that message fast and hard at your mother's."

She knew something had happened when she was out of the room. She pointed to the sketchbook in Jericho's hand. "Of all the places we've been, why did you draw me at the underground lake?"

His eyes softened. "Yancey wasn't with us to take holographs. I wanted to remember you there. That was the first time you relaxed and were yourself with me. It was the first time you treated me like something other than an Earther."

She leaned on the edge of the bed, stunned. She'd never paid attention to any Earther's thoughts or feelings, and he'd been no exception. Until that day, when she'd started to like him. And he'd known.

She could tell from that picture he'd paid attention to her. Paid close attention to her thoughts. Her feelings. The force of that realization hit the tiny soft spot of her heart. The spot she kept shielded from everyone, except the only person she'd trusted absolutely–her father. Something *had* happened that day. Something she'd tried to push to the back of her brain. *Or her heart.* She could not, would not, allow him to take that piece of her with him.

Her throat tightened. She fisted her fingers to stave off the moisture gathering in her eyes. Jericho would return to Earth as soon as the Joint Committee awarded the shipping contract. Lips pressed together, she looked at the deck.

His arms came around her and she leaned into him, soaking up the comfort he offered. She wrapped her arms around his muscled back and pulled him closer, laying her head against his chest, listening to the steadying beat of his heart.

His hand came up to cradle her head and he murmured. "Everything will be fine. It's okay."

But everything wouldn't be fine. She'd gotten used to spending her days with him. She looked forward to seeing him every morning. Imagining her old routine held no joy.

She gulped. "I'm going to miss you."

His arms tightened. "I'm going to miss you, too. But I'll be back in six months. And I won't be going back when the supply ship leaves. I'm going to stay to coordinate the research of the scientific team."

He wasn't going back on the supply ship? He was going to stay for six months on Prism?

"You're talking like you already have the contract. Why would you want to live here?"

She felt his response rumble deep in his chest.

"*Act as if.* My mother's mantra. Act as if what you want is already here. I believe my proposal will be the best offer. Even if it's not, I'm coming back because of you, O." When she started to protest, he rested a finger against her lips. "And I'll stay because of you."

He kissed her. Without warning.

His lips pressed hard against hers at first, then she kissed him back. Her hands locked behind his neck and she held him tight. As if she could keep him forever.

"As soon as I can, I'll be back. I promise. Three months home, a few days to touch bases with the conglomerate execs and legal, then I'll be on *Freedom* for the three-month journey back to you."

Her heart beat in her ears. Her breaths grew shallow and rapid. Every cell in her body wanted this, wanted him. Wanted to plan their days together, go exploring together. Together, every day for the rest of their lives. How had she not known before this moment? *I'll stay because of you.* "Stay? As in forever? Stay with me on Prism?"

Before he could answer, her brain engaged. Her racing

thoughts froze. It would never work. They could have no forever. He would grow tired of life on Prism, or her, and he would return to Earth and its pleasures. She couldn't survive someone she loved leaving her again.

She clenched her teeth to keep from getting maudlin. She needed more time to think. "I wish I had a sketch of you."

He brushed a kiss across her lips. "I've got my portfolio on a reader somewhere. Press kit images from college sports, photo ops for promotions and ad campaigns. The holos Yancey has taken here. You can have whatever you want."

Her tongue refused to shape the words she had to say. "Jericho." She couldn't go on.

Head cocked to the side, his eyes narrowed. He knew what she couldn't tell him. "What is it?"

She took a big breath. "I love spending time with you. I love how you treat me—"

"But ..." His voice deepened and he drew out the word.

She stepped away from him and walked to the foot of the bed. She had to do this. "You can't live on Prism, any more than Mitzi can."

"Why not? I'm Jericho Montgomery, only heir to Gatfield Montgomery. I can live wherever I want to."

She shook her head. "You might move here, but some people still hate the conglomerates. You would always be in danger of kidnapping or worse. Even with a dozen Yanceys. What kind of a life would that be? And you're used to luxuries I can't even imagine. Food we can't store. Freedom to do whatever you want."

"I could care less about fancy food." His chin dipped. "Don't tell me you don't love me. I see it when you look at me. I feel it when we touch. When we kiss."

And she did, too. Her heart was full, not achy or bursting. Full of love. She wanted to spend as much time as she could with him before he left for Earth. No matter what he said, there was no guarantee he would return to Prism.

"My mother said she fell in love with my father the day she met him." He crossed his arms. "I think I started falling for you that night in the Burnt Engine."

Dad had said he fell in love with her mother when he first heard her voice. Could she pinpoint the exact moment she fell for Jericho? Was that important?

"You're comfortable with Cal. You've known him all your life. That's not love." He closed the distance between them. "But you do love me." Hands on hips, he stood there like he was daring her to deny it.

And she couldn't. If she were one of those politico girls who cried, she'd have a river running down her face. She looked at Solo's water bowl.

He tipped her chin up and gave her a tight-lipped smile. "How about this? You don't have to make a decision now. You can take as much time as you need to be sure. But I *will* return in six months, and I am going to convince you that you love me. Then I'm going to ask you to marry me." He hugged her. "We'll figure it out from there."

Ask me to marry him? Holy frag. He would leave Earth for her? He loved her that much?

She wouldn't leave Prism for him, so maybe she didn't love him, at least not as much as he loved her. Where would they live? How would he work on his Conglomerate business? Would Yancey still be his bodyguard? Would he be allowed to move here? Too many questions, crowding together to make room for more.

He planned to convince her that he wanted to marry her? She could live with that. Maybe he wouldn't have to convince her. Wanting, waiting for him one-hundred-eighty days to return was beyond her comprehension. Private communication between Earth and Prism wasn't allowed, so he couldn't send her messages. What if something happened on Earth so he couldn't return? What if he decided not to return? A lot could happen in six months. Look what had happened in ten days.

She shuddered. As long as she won the Battle she'd have the time to wait for him. But if she failed, and had to have a protector, she'd be married and pregnant by the time Jericho returned.

She needed to check in with Miguel about his work on the skimmer and the last update on the placement of the location beacons for the flight. His magic with a translithium engine and her piloting skills were going to make her dream possible.

———

HE'D LIED. Jericho wasn't going to wait until he returned in six months. He was going to ask O'Neill to marry him before he left Prism.

Despite what Wash's mother said, he knew, in the marrow of his bones, that he and O had a future together. All he had to do was put together another proposal, of a very different kind. This time he'd be using his heart instead of his brain, but he was confident he'd glimpsed enough of O's heart that he could capture it. Because this proposal was as important as the shipping contract. And he was a very good negotiator.

He'd have to convince his father that Jericho living on Prism would be better for the conglomerate's bottom line. His *story* could be used for marketing new products from Prism and releasing the scientific team's discoveries, which might prove helpful for Earth.

If his father refused to let him move to Prism, Jericho already had enough of his own credits to support starting a business and a family. He could find a way to earn credits on Prism, and he could use his connections to make trade deals with other Earth colonies. His uncle would manage Jericho's mother's trust to maintain her charities for a few years, until Jericho had starting amassing his fortune.

Daily life on Prism wouldn't be easy. The conditions weren't close to the luxury he took for granted. No one would prepare his meals, clean his clothes, or handle his mundane business details.

And two protein bars a day? Well, some of his credits could go for fresh food.

He'd have to contact the World Board about his plan to stay on Prism. Maybe he could offer them his services in some capacity. He knew better than to tell the WB or his father that he planned to spend the rest of his life on the exile world. They'd come up with a rule that denied him that opportunity. But Cornelia had spent most of her life on Prism, and she wasn't talking about moving back to Earth.

Yancey called the stateroom to give him a message from Aunt Cornelia, asking him to come to her office. O was leaving to check on her skimmer, so the timing was perfect. He left with Yancey, planning how to broach the subject of marrying O and living on Prism. He smiled at the field day the press would have with him being the first immigrant to the prison world.

Yancey waited on a bench outside her office door. Inside, Aunt Cornelia hugged him. "Thank you for coming to see me. We won't be long."

Did his mother's best friend want to talk to him about the shipping contract? Something chewed his gut. This wasn't going to be good news. Did it involve O? He wondered if he should begin the conversation. "I want to ask you if there would be any problems with me moving to Prism. Permanently."

Her jaw fell.

"I plan to return with the supply ship. If Montgomery Conglomerates gets the shipping contract, I'll stay here when it returns to Earth."

She tried to act like the administrator she was. "And if you don't get the contract?"

"I'll still come back. I'm going to marry O'Neill."

Her head shook like a museum bobble-head doll. "You've asked her? What about her grandfather?"

"I told her that I plan to ask her. I haven't mentioned it to her grandfather." He was a coward. He wanted to survive that encounter. O would have to be with him for that declaration.

Cornelia dropped to the couch. "Are you sure about this? Life isn't easy here."

"I am." He sat beside her. "I've never met anyone like O. I'm quite certain there is no one like her on Earth. I've fallen for her. Hard."

"Oh, dear." She clasped her hands. "What will Gatfield have to say?"

"If I can spin this so that it means an increase in his profits, he'll buy in. It's not like he schedules quality time for us. What I'm concerned about are any laws that may be a problem."

"I don't know of any, but I'll make some discreet inquiries." She sighed. "I've heard good things about you here on Prism." She glanced around her office, almost as if she expected someone to pop up from behind the furniture. "I've been waiting for a chance to speak with you privately about something."

Jericho lowered his voice to match hers. "I would have come to your office anytime."

"No. I don't want anyone to have any suspicions. Suspicions about us meeting privately. Suspicions about what I am going to give you. In fact, no one can know I've given you anything. Especially your bodyguard."

"This is about the shipping contract." He'd been so careful with his research and fact collecting on Prism. Could he have screwed it up so badly?

"No. Before your mother died, she sent me a holographic recording to give you if you ever came to Prism."

"Why didn't you give it to me when I first arrived?" If his mother had made a recording telling him her favorite places on Prism, the people she met, he would have made sure to visit those places and people. He'd been on the planet for more than a week. Now it was almost too late.

"She told me not to give it to you unless I knew, without a doubt, that you loved Prism as much as she did. And that you wanted to help Prismers have a chance for a better life. Your contract proposal, the way you've treated O'Neill, your generosity, all show that you are a young man with character and compassion. And now that you've told me you want to start a family here, well, you've more than met her stipulations."

She'd read his proposal? What stipulations? "I didn't do any of those things to try to get anything." He smiled. "Well, I did put together a contract proposal that I hope can't be rejected. I'll make a mountain of money from it."

"I got reports on what you were doing. Don't look shocked. As Warden, I need to have plenty of sources of information to know what's going on."

"I hope those sources didn't see me at my worst."

She tried to hold back a laugh. It came out as a snicker. "Well, General Neill gave you the thumbs up. That's as good a recommendation as you can get."

O's grandfather vouched for him? After kicking him out of his house? He wouldn't have bet on that.

"Do not let anyone see or hear the recording. Don't tell anyone that you've received anything from me. It could be dangerous for you as well as for me."

"I'll be very careful."

"You'll be able to view it just once because it will erase itself as the hologram is projected, so you'll want to have something to write down any information you need to remember." Her look was serious, just short of stern.

His body vibrated with tension. "Okay. Thank you for letting me know."

"Here's the container. Put it in your pocket. Don't take it out until you're alone behind locked doors on your ship. It's voice-locked. Only you can speak your full name to access the file."

"Yes, ma'am." How could he wait to look at what she was going to give him, let alone view the recording? O'Neill would probably beat him back to *Freedom*, so he wouldn't have a moment alone until after she left tonight. *If* she left tonight, which he'd hoped she wouldn't.

Cornelia faced him. "As far as anyone is concerned, I invited you here to discuss details about tomorrow's Battle. I'm sending that information through your personal link on *Freedom*." She pulled her hand out of her pocket and extended it to him. "It's been a pleasure seeing you again, Jericho. I hope you get that contract."

His arms shook, from the shoulder sockets to his fingertips. How could he possibly hang on to what she was sliding into his palm? He took a deep breath and grasped her hand. Something sharp bit into his fleshy thumb pad. "Thank you for your hospitality. I look forward to seeing you again in six months when the supply ship returns, if I'm awarded the contract." He closed his fist, trying for a casual look, and put his hand in his pocket while turning toward the door.

He flicked the foil from his palm into the lining of the pocket before opening the panel, then put his model smile on to turn around and wave. There was not a chance in hell Yancey would suspect he'd been given anything. And he wouldn't be telling his bodyguard about the plaz-tech.

What the hell is going on?

————

BY THE TIME he and Yancey returned to *Freedom*, Jericho's nerves were so raw he could have gnawed his own arm off for a distraction. O sat at the dining room table waiting for him. He breezed in and dropped a kiss on her cheek.

Even though he wasn't hungry and didn't think he could eat without throwing up, he thanked Mattie when she brought in the liquid lunches and O's supplements.

Excited, O talked about adjustments someone named Miguel had made to her skimmer. She opened a piece of paper, smoothing it on the table, to show him where she'd have to fly tomorrow. Looking embarrassed, she pointed to the part of the route they'd flown together. *Lab-enhanced rabbit.* He'd remember that feeling for the rest of his life.

With all the conversation, lunch drew out, giving him time to finish his drink in small sips, before they adjourned to the gym for a last swim in the lap pool. While O finished putting on the wetsuit he'd left in her changing room, he adjusted the settings on the wave jet for a faster current with more strength. As an afterthought, he added the randomizer, to make the experience more like swimming in the ocean.

Her voice surprised him. "Last one in has to…" She stopped, pursed her lips and tilted her head. "What's wrong? I noticed you didn't drink your lunch with your usual, uh, gusto." She strode across the deck to where he stood by the pool controls.

"Nothing." He closed the panel. "Ready for a good workout?"

She put a restraining hand on his wrist. "You were fine this morning. Better than fine before you left for the Warden's office. Now you can't eat. Did she tell you that you didn't get the contract?"

"No. She doesn't know who's getting the contract."

"So what happened with her?" Hands on hips, she looked like she was willing to wait out his silence. "And don't try that *nothing* with me again."

"She invited me to watch the Battle with her, and she told me how the security will work with the crowds." He couldn't look at her and continue the lie, so he grabbed a couple of towels.

She released the breath he hadn't noticed she was holding. "Is that it? Of course the Warden had to tell you not to bet on me. I'm the youngest competitor. And I'm a girl. Not the best odds in a soldier-saturated competition."

He nodded. Gave her his melt-off-your-panties model smile. "*Of course* I have faith in you. I've seen what you've done in our training sessions."

She shook her head. "Not buying what you're selling, Jericho. But you don't want to talk about it now, so I'll let you sit on it while I bust your balls in the pool." She walked down the steps into the water. "If you don't feel up to it, you can take a nap on your recliner."

His chin thrust out at her challenge. He tossed the towels on the seat and did a shallow dive into the pool. When he surfaced, he brushed the water off his face and took his place in his lane. "Ready?"

She scooted forward, but before she could answer, the wave jet finished its warm-up cycle and engaged. He dug his arms into the current and kicked like a water monster was nipping at his feet. She was about to learn the meaning of *a run for her money.*

————

AT LEAST THE grueling swim had burned off Jericho's mood. As soon as the jet turned off, he picked her up, threw her, screaming and kicking, over his shoulder and walked into the hot tub. He set her down at the far end on a long bench seat with the warning not to move while he set the controls. The bubbles hadn't gotten started before he squeezed in next to her, put his arm around her waist and pulled her to him.

His eyes sparkled in amusement. "Never question a guy's manhood."

Manhood? She hadn't questioned his *manhood.* She rolled her eyes. "Copy that."

He tugged her closer. "Are we good?"

"Better than before the swim. We'll be even better when you spill whatever is gnawing at you." At his long inhale she added, "No rush. When you've worked it out. Or if you decide you need help working it out."

He exhaled. "Thanks. I appreciate it." He settled his neck into the groove in the edge of the pool and sighed. "This feels good." His fingers gripped her waist. "Really good."

"Yep. Thanks for training me, feeding me, and, uh, everything else the last three days."

He snored his response.

She rested her check on his shoulder and turned sideways on the narrow benc, sliding her hand across his stomach to his waist to anchor herself. He was right. It did feel good. No, better. Every place her body touched Jericho, her cells pulsed with warmth. The steady rise and fall of his chest made her feel safe. Secure. It felt fantastic. She felt fantastic.

She couldn't imagine anything better than falling asleep listening to Jericho's heartbeat. Yes, she was in love.

26

From the Journal of General Liam Neill (Twenty-two Years Ago)

I need to do something to motivate my troops to stay fit and practice their fighting skills. I may pull a page from medieval history. Instead of a jousting tournament, we could have an annual competition with events like running, swimming, an obstacle course, and a big hand-to-hand fight. The winner would receive extra rations, building materials, and other boons. Since we will be negotiating with Earth every year for our translithium, we can demand additional supplies to improve our standard of living. I'm going to run my idea past Patrick tomorrow.

JERICHO WOKE when the hot tub jets shut down. He didn't move because O had wrapped herself around him and was hanging onto his trunks to keep from falling off the little ledge of a seat. Amazing that she could clutch the fabric while she slept.

He kissed her hair. This would be the last time he'd hold her like this for six months. He wanted to enjoy their contact.

Once awake, she'd want to return home to get ready for her big day tomorrow. He understood, since he'd followed a similar routine on game days. But the outcome of the Battle meant a lot more to her, and her future happiness, than a game ever meant to him. He would have loved to hold her tonight, calm her fears about the outcome of the competition. A muscle in the arm holding her to him twitched. His shoulder sent a message to his back about torque. He wouldn't be able to stay still much longer.

She nuzzled his chest and moved her hand to his stomach. His abdominal muscles clenched. When her fingertips trailed south something else clenched. He had to move. Now. "Sweetheart, it's time to wake up." He blew lightly across her hair.

Her nose moved back and forth on a small square on his chest. Either she had an itch or she was telling him no.

He relaxed his arm, the one that was securing her across his lap, and she slipped an inch lower into the water. She didn't wake up, but that lazy hand was traveling again, up his stomach toward his... Her fingers latched on to his nipple.

This was damned uncomfortable. "O'Neill, wake up, Sweetheart." He rested his chin in the top of her head and groaned. That hand was traveling south again. When it toyed with the band of his swimsuit every muscle in his body went on alert status.

Was she shaking? Just a little bit, in her torso. Was she... She wasn't asleep. She was laughing.

Two could play this game. His hand roamed between them, searching for the neckline of her suit while his other slid down her back to cup her butt.

She sputtered and slipped off his lap. When she stood, she looked like an avenging sea goddess. "What do you think you were doing?"

He wore his most innocent look and blinked like he'd just woken up. "What do you mean? I just woke up."

"You did not. You've been awake for a little while."

"How do you know? Were you watching me sleep?"

She blushed in the prettiest pattern. "No. I was asleep."

"Okay. Now that we're both awake, are you ready to get out of the water?"

"Yes." She led them out of the pool and tossed him a towel. "You weren't asleep. You were talking to me."

He shrugged. "Maybe I was talking in my sleep. Maybe you were dreaming."

She eyed him while she dried off. He could almost see her brain working to solve the question of whether or not he was asleep. She turned and ran her tongue across her lips. She'd never done that before. He wanted to kiss her, but he'd wait. Make her wait.

When she stepped out of the changing room, he was waiting. "Your dinner and a jar of honey are waiting for you at the hatch."

Her eyebrows snapped together. "Are you trying to get rid of me?"

"Not at all. I thought you'd want to get home early." He leaned toward her. "But if you'd like to spend the night, in my mother's cabin of course, you're welcome to stay here."

She tapped her foot. Another first. She didn't do well when she didn't get her way. Good to know.

She must have realized her foot that was tapping and, after a quick glance at it, she kept it on the floor. "In your mother's cabin."

I didn't say you'd be alone. He leaned back, hoping his smile wasn't too wolfish. "Or whichever cabin you'd like. There are many."

She strode past him, walked to Mitzi's cabin, and waited for him to palm the entry pad, which he did. Stepping through the door ahead of him she sighed and raised her fingers to her lips, whispering "How sweet."

Their cats were facing each other, napping. Mitzi's paw rested across Solo's neck. His massive paw snugged across her tail.

They watched the cats in silence until Solo opened one eye. "It's time to go home, big guy." O kneeled down to rub Solo's chin.

While she was distracted, Jericho pulled open a drawer, snagged a small box, and dropped it into his pocket.

When O stood, Solo did, too. Mitzi mewed in protest. Normally he would have picked her up, but holding her wouldn't work with what he had planned for O before she left.

He followed O and Solo down the corridor to the hatch, where a container sat on the deck. He picked it up and handed it to her. "Have a nice dinner, sleepyhead."

She looked confused.

"In the hot tub. You weren't asleep, but you pretended to be when I tried to wake you up."

"How do you know?"

He backed her into the closed hatch, caging her between his arms. "I felt you laughing."

After a sharp intake of air, she poked his chest. "If you weren't asleep, how do you explain your traveling hands?"

"The same way you explain yours." He leaned in close and got nose-to-nose with her. "Any time you want to go exploring with those hands, let me know." He winked. "If you need a roadmap, I'll supply one."

She looked beautiful with bright red skin. "Thanks for the offer." She tried to turn toward the exit.

"There's more." Did he really want to do this?

"Well, frag. I can hardly wait."

He dropped to one knee. "Marry me, O. Whenever you want. But, for now, say you will." He fished for the box in his pocket, pulled it out and flipped the lid open. "This was my mother's. If you don't like it, tell me what you want and I'll bring it with me next time."

She put the food container on the floor and kneeled beside him. Another first, tears streamed down her face.

Her mouth was contorted and her eyelids scrunched close. Crap. He'd made her cry. He couldn't tell if that was a good sign or a bad sign, so he started talking. "I didn't want to wait until after the Battle, in case you thought whether or not you won determined if I..."

Her lips interrupted his speech. She hung on to him like he was a big tree in a hurricane. And she kept kissing him. He sat, pulled her into his lap, then set about the business of kissing her back.

Sometime later, she pushed on his chest. "Yes."

His lust-filled brain hiccupped. "What?"

Her smile could have powered *Freedom* all the way back to Earth. "I. Will. Marry. You."

More kissing. Kissing O had become his favorite activity.

She ran her thumb along his jaw. "And I love your mother's ring. Will you put it on my finger?"

They had to search for the box. He removed his mother's emerald and slipped it on O's finger. After sealing her acceptance with another kiss, she smoothed her hand over his hair. "This is why you smiled when I told you my favorite color is emerald green."

"There are a couple of other rings of hers onboard, but this is the one she loved the best." He stood and helped O to her feet.

She looked at him with eyes that offered her soul. "I'm honored you trust me with this."

"I gave you the ring, but I'm trusting you with my heart. And my love."

The tears that had stopped while they were kissing started again. And he kissed them away.

———

WALKING across the dock to her dad's skimmer, O'Neill wasn't sure her boots touched the plazsteel deck. Saying yes to Jericho's proposal was the first impulsive thing she'd done in her entire life. All the details that had to come together to allow their marriage would make a holo game that would take years to solve. Starting with the issue of a protector. Now she had even more incentive to win the Battle. If she lost, could she declare Jericho as her protector if they got married before he left?

Her body was lighter than air, pumped full of joy and love. Kisses wrapped around her skin. No one would have been able to see anything different about her. Well, maybe if they noticed Jericho's mother's ring. Her ring now.

The dockworkers were gone for the day, and no one else was around. She pushed back the canopy of her father's skimmer and tapped the hull step. Solo jumped into the cockpit, and she followed him. She flipped the engine warm-up switch and started humming. The melody was off-key, but she didn't care. Jericho loved her. She loved him. He was returning to Prism. For her.

The short hop to the Citadel was uneventful, until she landed next to Cal's skimmer. He leaned against its hull until she cut the engine. She climbed out before Solo, who positioned himself in front of her. "What are you doing here?"

Cal strode to her. "Hi, O. I've been trying to find you for two days so we could talk."

"I haven't been hiding. I've been training with Jericho on his ship."

He took a step nearer. "He doesn't know how to win the Battle. How can he help?"

"Turns out he's won swimming competitions and..."

"You've been to Soldier Beach alone with him?" He moved to grab her arm, but she sidestepped away.

"No. He has a lap pool onboard *Freedom*. We've been working on my form."

He gave her a bet-the-jerk-would-like-to-put-his-hands-all-over-your-form look. "What about the melee? I've gone to the soldier compound every night for melee practice and you haven't shown up." Accusation screamed from the set of his jaw.

"He's got a holo program with a tutorial sim. I've improved much more than if I'd just gone to practice every night." Her gaze hardened. "What are you doing here, Cal?"

Hands at his sides, he looked down for a few moments before

meeting her gaze. "I've missed you, O. Hoshi talked to me and I understand better about your fear of having a protector. But you know me. I love you. I'd never do anything that would compromise your safety."

"But you would tell me I couldn't do something I wanted to."

"Only if it put you in danger and I couldn't protect you."

"And you'd take me to the Fertile Field right away?"

His stance relaxed and he grinned. "You bet. I want to start our family together."

"What if I didn't want that?"

"But we've talked about it."

"No. You talked about it. When I tried to tell you I wasn't ready for babies, you cut me off by laughing and waggling your eyebrows like Novy."

His back straightened and he nodded at the sentry on duty. "We can talk about that later. Privately. I came over to review your Battle strategy."

"Not necessary. My strategy is to go all out and win."

"Let's go inside and talk about it."

No. Her home was the one place she'd never had to be strong for anyone else. Where she could shed her cloak of confidence, curl up and cry if she needed to, especially now that Dad didn't live with her. She didn't want to share that space alone with Cal. "I never invited you inside when Dad wasn't here. What's different now?"

"I don't understand. We've eaten at your table, played on the floor in the kitchen when we were kids, and washed vegetables from this garden in the kitchen sink. Got in trouble with your mother that time for a water fight." He gestured toward the plant containers then put his hands in his pockets. "You don't want to be alone in your own home with me?" He shook his head, grimacing like he was in physical pain. "You meant it, didn't you? You really meant it when you said you don't want me for your protector."

She felt like he'd slapped her. He hadn't tried to understand anything she'd told him. Maybe if he had, they wouldn't be in this position. He wouldn't be acting like she'd done something wrong. "I did. I still do."

He took a determined step toward her then turned around and strode to his skimmer. He climbed in, but before he sat, he glared at her long enough that his eyes, had they been lasers, would have bored a hole through her. "When the Earther's gone, and you're desperate for a protector, I'll still be here. It won't be as good as it could have been, but I'll live up to my responsibility to you. I keep my promises." He dropped into the cockpit, closed the canopy, slapped the engine switch, and pulled away from the roof without a backward glance.

She watched his skimmer until it disappeared in the glare of the setting sun. Prism's glorious sunsets had lost their appeal.

She nodded to Brode, tonight's sentry, and pulled up the trap-door to home. Solo squeezed past her to do his inspection while she pulled the door closed. Cal had stripped off her warm glow from Jericho's proposal.

By some lucky chance, she'd clung to her dinner container. She tossed it on the counter, where it thunked and slid to a stop.

I'm proud of you. You held on to your guns up there.

Her father was here. She was happy to hear his voice in her head, but she felt like a limp rag. She still wasn't a hundred percent certain that her imagination had conjured her father tonight—and in the past. Her emotions couldn't take another hit. She sighed. *Hi, Dad. I'm not doing well. I wish Cal wasn't so hard-headed.*

He's good-hearted. He's smart. If you want him to, he'll figure it out and, with time, everything will be fine.

A hard cage of treason crowded her heart. How could she tell her father she didn't want to marry his best friend's son, like they'd planned all her life? *I can't marry Cal. I'm engaged to Jericho.* She hadn't meant to think that. Could she take it back? She squeezed her eyes shut.

Whoa. Say again.

Jericho proposed tonight before I came home. I said yes.

Two very real arms wrapped around her shoulders. Her breath

started hitching; her chest starting shaking. The arms hugged tighter.

Let it out, sweetheart. I've got you.

How she needed this release. Needed her father. *Are you angry with me?*

Have you done something stupid? Unsafe?

I don't think so.

Then why would I be angry with you?

You thought I'd marry Cal.

And I thought I'd live with your mother until my dying day. Circumstances change. Life isn't ruled by our expectations. He paused. *Are you in love with Jericho?*

Absolutely.

Is he in love with you?

Yes.

Then I hope the two of you can figure out a way to be together.

How long can you stay?

I came to help you plan your flight path for tomorrow. Thought we could strategize, then play a little Save the Princess.

The last time I played, someone else, Knight in Shining Armor, wanted to join the game. Was that you? She thought she saw a shimmery frown floating in the air when she looked up.

Negative. What did you do?

Slammed the unit shut and powered it down. I haven't used it since.

She felt the warmth of his smile. *Smart girl. Someone has the tech, program and power to connect with other players. That capability goes way beyond our games. My reader should be fine here at the Citadel, but make sure it's well hidden.* The pressure from his arms disappeared. *You can eat that dinner while we talk about tomorrow.*

They discussed her flight path, the swim course at Soldier Beach, and the melee. Her father was very interested in her description of Jericho's holo program. She didn't want to go to bed, but he made the case that she needed a full night of sleep. When he insisted on tucking her in, her worries faded away.

I'll see you in the morning. She felt his kiss on her forehead. *You should probably know that I've talked to your grandfather.*

Did that mean she could talk to Granddad about their talks? Could she ask Dad about the bubble chips? She could have sworn a finger rested on her lips to keep her from asking questions.

I talked to your mother, too. If you see her tomorrow, you may want to try to calm her down. He chuckled, then she thought the mattress shifted. *Goodnight, Sweetheart. I love you.*

I love you, too, Dad. She didn't bother to ask if he was there. She knew he'd heard her.

———

AFTER O LEFT, Jericho ate his dinner then went to Mitzi's room, following his usual routine, even though he was dying of curiosity about his mother's message. After locking the door to his suite, he fished the holo chip out of his pocket, walked through the connecting door to his father's office, and sat at his father's desk. Activating the holo projector, he inserted the chip into the projector's data reader, then pulled out his sketchbook.

His finger shook as he pressed the play button. A red light blinked on the data recorder while a mechanical voice said, "Thumbprint and full name required to access this file." Thumb pressed to the lighted indentation he said, "Jericho Thorsøngud Montgomery." The red light blinked while the chip's security protocol checked his voice pattern and thumbprint.

What could his mother have to tell him that was so secret it had to be sent to Prism and only given to him under specific conditions? And why had she included high-level security and an auto-destruct order? Didn't she know he would want to replay her final message?

The hologram projector shimmered to life, coalescing the form of his mother years ago, when he was around sixteen. Without thinking, he reached toward her. His lung seized with grief and he sat back, recognizing his uncle's library in the background.

She looked to the side of the camera and nodded. "Thank you, Ric."

In the pause he heard a door close. His mother looked right at him. "My dearest Jericho. I have no idea what my future, what your future, holds. But I cannot go to my grave without telling you information you have a right to know. Times are difficult with Gatfield." She sighed. "If you had never gone to Prism you would not need to know the truth. But I suspected he would send you one day, and now that you're on the planet, I know you feel what I felt when I went there on my archaeological dig before you were born."

He reached again for the image. He wanted to touch her, smell her perfume. *Mom.*

She lifted her chin. "When I left Earth, Gatfield and I had the understanding that upon my return, he would divorce me. We'd been married for three years and he desperately wanted an heir. Nature nor science gave him what he needed, and we had a contract. I wanted to be free of him as well.

"The official press story painted a romantic tale about him missing me so that he flew out to awaken me on the cryo-ship, where you were supposedly conceived. That story was a lie. When I climbed into the cryo unit on Prism for the return flight to Earth, I didn't know I was pregnant. Your real father is not Gatfield Montgomery. And for that, I thank all the gods."

"Pause." Jericho couldn't get the word out fast enough. He wasn't sure he wanted to hear any more. How could Gatfield Montgomery not be his real father? And his mother thanked the gods he wasn't? What the fuck? That meant his entire life was a lie. No wonder she didn't want anyone else to know. Did Aunt Cornelia know? His dinner churned, threatening a revolt. "Resume."

"On Earth, when I found out I was pregnant, Gatfield was ecstatic, even though he knew the baby wasn't his. He'd despaired about being able to father a child. Now he could publicly claim an heir. The cryo had slowed the pregnancy, so I was only a month along. His lawyers drew up papers giving me endowments and allowances beyond my wildest dreams, but only if I would stay with Gatfield and raise you as his heir. The good that I did with that money.

"But I could never reveal he wasn't your real father or I would lose you forever. And to guarantee my silence, if I revealed this truth to you, the Conglomerate would take control of my half of Thorsøngud Ships, leaving you with nothing. Only my brother knows the truth. Visit him when you return to Earth. He is your one true ally.

"I feared, and still fear, that Gatfield would send an assassin to murder your real father on Prism. I will take that name, and the wonderful memories of the only man I ever loved, to my grave. But as you stand on the planet of your conception, I want you to know how much your real father would have loved you had he known of your existence."

"Pause."

Jericho swallowed, but his throat closed tighter. *My real father is a Prismer?*

His mother had fallen in love during the two months she'd been on the archaeological dig. *Hell.*

But he'd fallen in love with a Prismer in less than two weeks. How could he point a finger at her? Who was his real father? He pushed back an uncomfortable possibility. "Resume."

The holo image of his mother sat back in the upholstered chair, looking exhausted. "I know that the only way you've received this message is that I've died. I am sorry I can't be there to hold you and answer your questions. I beg you not to try to locate your real father. Although I did abide by the agreement I had with Gatfield, he cannot let the truth of your real parentage become public. It would make him a global laughingstock. I have no doubt he would have your father, if he is still alive, killed in revenge. He might even harm you."

"Pause!"

Motherfucking sonofabitch bastard asshole. Gatfield Montgomery would send an assassin all the way to Prism to murder Jericho's real father? His gut twisted. According to Liam Neill, Gatfield's father had sent *fraggers* to kill him. The man had access and certainly had the funds to contract a hit on Prism. But would Gatfield pay an assassin to kill Jericho? Would he be watching Jericho to see if his attitude toward his *father* and the corporation had changed? Thank fuck Jericho hadn't told his Captain, Mattie or Yancey about his proposal to O. His heart thundered in his chest. *I've put O in danger.* It was probably worse than that.

He spread his hands across the finely polished grain of the desktop. With the speed of an FTL drive, his brain sorted through options. First, he needed to discover who his real father was, without anyone on Prism suspecting what he was trying to find out. Next he had to develop a strategy to convince his father—no, Gatfield—that Jericho was the best son he could ever have—just in case the man found out Jericho knew this secret.

He needed a plan to protect O during the six months he was away. His fist connected with the desktop. O's father had been his mother's pilot and protector. He would have known who she spent time with. Jocko Neill had spent even more time with his mother than Jericho had spent with O. A sour taste rolled up his throat. "Resume."

"You may hate me right now, but I have only love for you. You have filled my life with joy. And hope. Please, do not fight Gatfield on this. Remember the lesson you learned yesterday from your Uncle Ric out in the barn. *Brawl with a pig and you go away with his stink.* I will love you forever, my dearest Jericho."

He stared at the holographic platform. The image of his mother blurred. Then she disappeared.

He remembered that day at his uncle's farm. He'd wanted to wrestle one of the pigs. His uncle tried to talk him out of it, but Jericho was used to getting what he wanted. He'd tried to pull down the slippery pig, but ended up covered in mud and pig shit, bruised by the pig's hooves stamping his leg and an arm. His uncle had hosed him off behind the barn, but Jericho smelled that stink on his skin for days. His mother was right to remind him. Gatfield Montgomery was covered in far worse than pig shit.

He couldn't move. He stared at the empty space that no longer contained the image of his mother. His brain pulsed.

My whole life is a lie.

———

HE HAD no idea how long he'd been staring at the empty holo platform when the com rang. "Mr. Montgomery, your father on burst laser connection."

He's not my father. How could he talk to the man right now? *No wonder he's never said he loved me.* "Give me a minute, then put it through."

He interlaced his fingers and brought his clasped hands to his lips. For the first time in his life he needed a drink to steady his nerves. He rose and crossed to his father's, *no, not his father's*, bar and poured two fingers of ancient bourbon. Standing with one hand on the counter, he threw back half the contents of the glass. It scoured a path down his throat. He pulled back his shoulders and returned to the desk chair. He set the glass within view of the camera and waited.

The man he'd called father all his life materialized in miniature on the holographic platform, sitting at his desk with a tall drink in his hand, an odd expression on his face. "Well?"

Jericho lifted his glass and pasted on a confident smile. "I'm sure I got the contract."

"Wonderful. Are you on your way home?"

"Not yet. They should announce who they're awarding the contract to in a couple of days. And I need a few days to tie up some loose ends."

His father shifted and moved a hand below the massive wooden desk. "Yes, like that, honey." He sighed then refocused on the camera. "I need *Freedom* for a trip to our colony. You don't need to wait on Prism for the decision. You need to get home. I have a new project for you."

The connection went dark.

The bourbon bubbled up his throat. Jericho ran to the head and puked. Puked until his gut threatened to crawl out his throat. He wobbled back into his father's, no *Gatfield's*, office.

Strident mewing reminded him to open the door for Mitzi. She bounced in, rubbed against his shin and looked at him before reaching her paws up his legs and flexing her claws.

"Okay, girl." He bent and lifted her into the cradle of his arms. "You don't care that I'm a bastard, do you?" *The bastard son of an exiled prisoner.* What would all his Ivy League corporation-heir *friends* think?

Mitzi purred and rubbed her cheek against his hand. Her problems revolved around food and attention. Maybe in his next life he'd come back as a cat.

He wasn't leaving Prism before finding out who his father was. He'd be discreet, but his mother knew him. She couldn't have believed he'd walk away from that bombshell.

Gatfield wouldn't react well to being defied, but Jericho needed time to talk to Cornelia 'and to convince O to hand over her father's logs from the time of the dig. Maybe Jocko Neill knew who had been her mother's lover and wrote something, somewhere in them. If only Jericho had another week on Prism to make circuitous inquiries. Gatfield would have already contacted the Captain of *Freedom* and told him to head for Earth. Or be fired. Jericho would have to make a few extra days on Prism worth Jamie's while.

Another possibility, the one he'd been trying to ignore, hit him like Thor's hammer battering his chest. What if Jocko Neill and his mother…? His hand went to his heart. Rubbed the pain in his sternum. *Oh, God, no.* O might be his sister. His half-sister.

Had there been anything remaining in his stomach, he wouldn't have had time to make it to the bathroom, so fast and violent was the pain in his gut.

If only his mother's message had remained buried in Cornelia's files.

What had he done? At least he'd kept his dick in his pants. But he loved O, and not like a brother loves a sister. His jaw clenched. The idea of her with another man made his teeth ache. But the truth was, he'd played a role in convincing her to throw over Cal, and Cal might be her only choice for a protector if she had to pick one after the Battle tomorrow.

He'd asked her to wait for him. To marry him. And she'd said yes. How could he fix that now?

Damn it to hell.

27

From the Journal of General Liam Neill (Twenty-one Years Ago)

Jocko's Earth squad has volunteered to build a watch-tower on the mountain above Convict Town. He and I used a bit of subterfuge, staged a loud argument ending with him vowing to move away from the Soldier Compound. One of his buddies won the first Battle and requested building materials that they'll used to begin their new home. I'll feel a lot more comfortable with constant surveillance on Convict Town and on the spaceport that the World Board is constructing to store the translithium and our supplies.

It was the morning of the Battle and O'Neill had no idea where Miguel and her father's skimmer were. She wanted to scream.

Except for the sentry, the rooftop had been empty this morning. She'd awakened at dawn, rested and ready, then gone to the roof to run through pre-flight checks. No skimmer, no Miguel. The sentry on duty told her the late-night guard said Miguel had taken the skimmer for a *final run*. Over six hours ago. What had happened to him? Had someone ambushed him and stolen her skimmer? She couldn't compete, couldn't win without flying.

Without that boon, her engagement to Jericho meant less than squat.

After a shower and a special breakfast bar Jericho had given her, she went back up to the roof to nothing. She packed her ready kit with supplies, her swimsuit and Jericho's wetsuit, and the special clothes and shoes Jericho gave her for the melee. She spared extra time with her morning exercises and meditation before dressing in her best uniform and boots. All the time, listening for the shriek of a skimmer's breaking baffold. A few minutes past the time she should have been on her way to Soldier Beach, she heard a distant engine. She bolted up the stairs to the roof and waited.

The vehicle landing couldn't be her skimmer. Newly painted, its white fuselage glittered with designs of translucent prisms. But from behind the wing to the tail, in tall bright green letters, *O'Neill* proclaimed it was.

Miguel pushed back the canopy. "Like her?"

"Oh." Circling the craft, the single syllable was all she could repeat. She met Miguel at the nose. "It's beautiful. Thank you."

"I had lots of help. Including your mother. She mixed the paints."

She bit her lip. Her mother had helped? What had that cost her with her husband? She hadn't had time to talk to her mother since the dinner with Jericho. Her mother's confession had rattled her. Now that her mother knew Jocko was still alive, O needed to talk about her mother's *options*. And her own.

"I stripped out the backseat to lighten the old girl, but she's big to start with and if you insist on taking Solo we should remove the canopy, too."

She wasn't leaving Solo unprotected, making him a target for Reagan. "Solo's flying with me. Let's do it."

The guard insisted on helping with the heavy lifting so she took over scanning Convict Town.

It didn't take long for the men to remove the canopy and prop it against the water tank. She climbed into the cockpit and ran her hand across the front panel, across the instruments and gauges. Her father had taught her to fly this skimmer when she was eleven years old.

Her throat tightened and her stomach twisted. Would her father really fly in the cockpit with her today, like he'd promised? Could she win?

Miguel levered himself onto the foot ledge outside the cockpit. "The altimeter is better, but it may stick if you get into a maneuver with lots of torque." He raised an eyebrow. "Throttle and joystick are smooth like…" Cheeks coloring, he paused. "Well, they're real smooth."

"With about the translithium array?"

"New conducting fluid. Quick release and easy insert traps. Know where you'll swap out?"

"I have a couple of options. Depends on how I'm feeling when I clear the fields."

"I can't believe how deep the marker is into the Retching Field. I put three shubs in your side pocket. Extra water canteens on the hook."

She felt for the shubs and adjusted the straps of the canteens so they wouldn't tangle. "Thank you for all your hard work, Miguel. If I can fly half as well as you maintain this rocket, we'll be taking a nap when the rest of the pilots cross the finish line."

"You're the best pilot on Prism now. Show them how a Neill flies."

She gulped and nodded. "Copy that." She hugged him. "I need to grab a few things inside before I go."

He helped her down. She patted the hull. "Be right back, girl."

Down the stairs, Solo lapped from his water bowl. "Good idea." She filled a mug with water and downed it before walking into her father's room to sit on his bed for a last-minute review.

Jericho's swimsuit and a towel for the swim after the flight. Protein bars. Extra water pack. She tapped the pocket that held his talisman.

Helmet! She'd need a helmet with the canopy removed.

Take my spare.

She couldn't help looking around the room, even though she knew she wouldn't see him. "Hi Dad." She said the words out loud. Her gaze landed on his spare helmet resting in its place of honor on a crate in the corner of the room. The helmet he brought from Earth. The helmet he'd worn fighting the Corporation War in service of the governments.

Go ahead, wear it. It will look good on you.

She laughed. She could give a burned-out bright crystal about what she looked like, but she grabbed his helmet, her pack, and whistled for Solo to mount the stairs. She followed him to the roof.

Miguel handed her up, then followed Solo into the rear, strapping the big cat into his safety harness before snapping his own. "Thanks for giving me a ride. We better blast if we're going to get there in time."

She checked her watch. Frag. Even pushing it, she'd have less than two minutes to spare before the start of the race.

———

SITTING in a makeshift grandstand next to Cornelia, flanked by Yancey and guards in World Board uniforms, Jericho checked over his shoulder for O's skimmer. Even if he'd been trying to follow the conversation in the box, the flapping canopy obscured every third word.

Eleven skimmers of varying sizes and colors were arrayed in the field before the spectators. A brass horn played a series of strident notes and the pilots strode to their planes.

He touched Cornelia's wrist, interrupting her conversation with the Dockmaster. "Will they start without O'Neill?"

Zendee leaned forward. "If she's not here on time, she'll start when she arrives and will have to make up the time." He twisted toward the spaceport. "Something must have happened to make her this late."

Streaking toward them, sunlight reflecting from the fuselage, a skimmer's straining engine noise preceded its arrival. The crowd's attention focused in the direction of the sound, arms in the air, fingers pointing. But the vehicle wasn't O's. It wasn't the right color and it had no canopy. Jericho stood, shielding his eyes from the sun.

Landing away from the cluster of parked skimmers to avoid showering everyone with dust, the engine shut off. The emerald green letters above artfully painted clumps of prisms proclaimed the pilot to anyone in doubt. The helmeted pilot stood, and the Prismers roared in approval. O pulled off her helmet and pumped it above her head.

Cornelia leaned close. "That's her father's helmet from the war. It's a folk symbol that reminds them all what they fought for. That girl sure has her father's flare for an entrance." She joined in the clapping.

The crowd had started chanting. "O. Neill. O. Neill. O. Neill."

She climbed to the ground, followed by Solo and an older man with only one leg. The man hugged her, then limped aside.

Cal sprinted to the craft. He said something that made her raise her chin and give the barest shake of her head. Grabbing her wrist, Cal raised O's hand in the air. Another round of stamping feet and shouting filled the air.

Aunt Cornelia shouted, "Everyone loves those two. It's going to be a big party when they get married."

Jericho waved both arms in the air to get her attention, wishing he were down on the field with her. Wishing he was the one holding her. No. Cancel that thought. She might be his sister. He'd stayed up late last night comparing Earth file photos of her father, O'Neill, and himself, looking for family resemblances. There were plenty between O and Jocko Neill, but between Jericho and her dad, not many more than two random strangers. Still, everyone on Earth said he looked like his mother. Even Cal's father had said so.

Seeing her stand next to Cal, while the guy amped up the crowd as if she were his, set the beast in his gut to ratchet up from gnawing to full out chomping. Falling in love on Prism hadn't been on his agenda. But no amount of rational logic had deterred his heart. How did she feel right now with Cal's fingers wrapped around her wrist? If she won the Battle, did she trust Jericho enough to wait for his return?

He was going to have to stay on Prism longer to discover who his father was. Risk to reward ratios skimmed the surface of his thoughts. He couldn't leave her thinking she had a fiancée if what she really had was a half-brother. Worse, what if he *was* her brother and he'd screwed her chances for happiness with Cal? What if she didn't win the Battle? How could he guarantee her freedom?

A piercing whistle got the pilots climbing into their respective cockpits. Solo leaped behind O. She secured him before settling at her controls.

Cal helped the one-legged man to the sidelines amid the dust of revving engines, then hustled away like he had somewhere more important to be.

Jericho missed whatever signal started the race, but eleven skimmers rose and veered to the left. Hovering above the ground, O waited, then roared straight over the crowd.

"Good grief." Cornelia's jaw hung open.

The crowd shouted.

All Jericho knew was that everybody flew one way, and O wasn't following them.

"What's she doing?"

Cornelia shook her head. "Going for the red marker first."

"Why is no one else?"

"Not a good strategic move." Zendee looked at him. "Everyone flies that leg last."

"It can mess you up for the rest of the race."

They didn't tell him, but he knew. She was going to the Retching Field first, but he wasn't going to get her in trouble by letting them know he knew about the fields. Seeing her grandfather approach, he stood and extended his hand. "General Neill."

"Montgomery. I'm surprised you're not headed back to Earth." The man shook his hand.

"I wanted to root for O." At the wrong end of a steely look, he added, "I'll leave after you announce the winner of the shipping contract."

———

THE SKIMMER RACED toward O'Neill's first beacon.

Hold your line.

O's father's voice didn't come through her earpiece. It hovered inside her head.

You look good in my warrior's helmet, by the way.

Was that a chuckle?

It was good to hear her father's voice. Particularly in the pilot's seat today. *Hi, Dad. Glad you could make it.*

Wouldn't miss it for the world. Definitely a chuckle. *The old girl looks good.*

She checked her heading and increased her speed. *Miguel got a crew together to paint her. Mom mixed the paints.*

Did she now? I wander how Reagan reacted to that.

Can't you just, I don't know, pop in at her place like you do with me?

I could, but I'm not going to invade her privacy, if I can help it.

The skimmer dipped. *Did you talk to her?*

Hold your line.

The stern admonishment hung between them. Of course she'd remember the three words he used most often during her flying lessons. *What did she say?*

Need to know basis.

Do I need to know why I'm going to the Retching beacon first?

Two reasons, like I told you last night. You won't have to dodge other pilots or worry about moves designed to slow you down. If you pulled out your maps and drew the chart...

I did.

That's my girl. Then you know that you'll be flying the shortest route possible.

But what if I'm too sick to get to the Healing Field fast enough?

You won't be. Because I'll get you through this first leg. He laughed, right inside her head. *Now, check your heading and see what Miguel's engine can do.*

She made a minor adjustment and opened the throttle. Several minutes later, the tallest spires of the Retching Field crept into view. She'd never piloted the skimmer without its canopy, but she remembered the few times her father had taken her flying with the top off. How her hair flew in the wind. The helmet constrained her curls and protected her face from the bite of the screaming air.

Course in a straight line toward the beacon's signal, she wet her lips. *Dad?*

Right beside you, Sweetheart.

You haven't said anything. I thought maybe you'd disappeared.

I'm right here. Will be as long as you need me. I wanted you to have a chance to think.

Four minutes until she'd feel the first effects of the crystals. She twisted to glance at Solo. Well-protected inside the skimmer's hull, he rested with his eyes at half-mast as if he were in silent meditation. "Get ready, Big Guy."

Turning back to the windshield, she pulled in a deep breath. The skimmer was still too far away for the energy of the field to reach her, but her stomach began to knot. She plucked a shub from its side pocket and put it between her knees. A quick look over the side of the hull provided another choice to empty her stomach, if she needed it.

Her father chuckled. *Shame to ruin that pretty new paint job. One minute to event horizon.*

Roger that. You going to fly this bucket while my head's over the side?

Your head's not going over the side if I can help it.

She felt pressure on her hand. She looked and saw his shimmering hand covering hers. "Dad?" She'd spoken the word.

Fly this thing like hell is chasing you. I'll modulate the planetary energy so it won't affect you, for as long as I can.

How long will that be?

No idea. His fingers squeezed hers and disappeared. *Are you feeling anything yet?*

Only the warmth of his love. And his hand, before. God, how she'd missed him. She concentrated on her stomach. Nothing. Looking down, she'd already crossed the boundary of the field. *No. I'm fine.*

Hold that thought.

She plunged deeper into the field.

When you planning to swap your translith?

Her father was trying to distract her through the middle of the field. They'd crossed the beacon and rather than turn around, she continued on a route that kept her in the field longer but shortened her overall route.

After the second beacon. She glanced at her hand. His hand shimmered above hers. Her stomach lurched then righted itself.

I'm having trouble holding it all off, Sweetheart. His unspoken words brushed across her senses.

I know.

I'll get you through the worst of it.

You have. Though she was sweating, a chill rippled through her body. *I'm fine.*

That's my girl. I'm going to step out so you can use your shub in privacy.

And he was gone.

She grabbed the shub, hoping it was deep enough.

———

BITS OF CONVERSATION whipped around Jericho.

"A week's worth of rations on Stillwell to win the flying."

"I'll take that, since Fortuna's the favorite."

"What about Jocko's daughter?"

"She's got a shot at placing. Don't know why she went to the puke grounds first."

"Hope it don't hurt her chances none. I bet on her to win."

"Benji the Book is giving ten-to-one odds on her winning the whole thing."

Jericho heard the announcement that the frontrunners had cleared the first beacon, but O's name wasn't mentioned since the Retching Field was farther away.

A whistle pierced the air. The spectators quieted.

"Red beacon crossed by O'Neill. She's out of the Retching Field and heading for her second beacon."

Excitement rippled across the crowd along with shouts and hoots.

"Thank God." Jericho hadn't grown up with prayers, but he was willing to offer whatever he could. "Help her recover quickly."

———

SHE'D FILLED TWO SHUBS, but now that she was outside the effects of the field, O's stomach settled quickly.

Heading for the Healing Field from this direction, she wouldn't cross paths with any of the other pilots, so she could keep the throttle open. She had no idea where she placed so far, but no one could best her time in the Retching Field. They'd have to slow down to deal with its unsettling effects and the line they'd take out of the field was longer than she had to fly.

The translithium register showed less than fifty percent. As soon as she cleared the Healing Field beacon she'd angle to the swap point.

Only an idiot would run out of power on this race. The crystals were good for four hours of flight time, but the route took five. Crystals could break, swapping snafus could happen. Low-powered crystals could mess with the guidance system. She'd evaluated the straight-line flight paths to and from each beacon with her father.

Dad?

Here, Sweetheart.

Still think I should swap the crystals after the Healing Field?

That station is the closet to your route. Are you having a problem with power?

No. Just worrying.

Pretend this is any normal run. Don't second guess yourself.

Thanks, Dad. She checked her course and held steady for the Healing Field and the white beacon.

Solo stirred and she reached back to touch him. His presence always had a calming effect on her. Today was no different.

Kilometers racing under the hull, her worry had nothing to do with any field. Even if she won this race, so many outcomes needed to align for her to win the Battle.

Her stomach settled and her chest muscles loosened. She'd crossed into the Healing Field. Opening the toggle of her water tube, she sipped a bit, rinsing it around her mouth before she swallowed and took another drink. She pulled up her jumpsuit's sleeve to check the heading she'd written on her arm. A slight course correction had her on target to cross the beacon soon. By the time she swapped out her fuel crystals, she'd be almost three-fourths of the way to the finish line. Her competition should be on course to the Retching Field now.

She checked the crystal charge and refrained from pushing the throttle all the way forward. On her own, in a race against Novy, she would have pushed her equipment. But she wasn't willing to take a chance that her guidance system would fritz. The white beacon registered her call sign, and she banked hard to starboard toward the Fertile Field and the last beacon.

Dad?

Still your co-pilot.

It was going to be nice to have him there during the translithium swap-out, if something went wrong.

If, if, if. Her life had devolved into a series of iffy ifs. Her breaths reverberated inside her father's helmet.

The anger about needing a protector boiled in her chest, spilled into her torso and down her arms and legs. It bubbled up her throat. When it began to cloud her vision with its bloody fire she punched the autopilot and closed her eyes, envisioning Solo stretched out in the sun, purring. Too bad she wasn't headed back to the Healing Field.

She couldn't tell how long it took until her breathing evened out. The autopilot beeped. Opening her eyes, she reengaged manual control and checked her heading.

Feeling better?

Yes, thanks.

Two clicks to the swap station. Five more to the Fertile Field. Then the race to the finish line.

28

J ournal of Gatfield Montgomery (Present Day)/RETINAL SCAN REQUIRED:

Fucking doctors don't know crap. I have a dozen holes in my skin and they still can't tell me why I hurt all the damn day. No word from Jericho if he's gotten the shipping contract. I may have to go with my backup plan and marry Jericho off to the South American Conglomerate's daughter when he lands. She's climbed my tree a few times and, with the right incentive, will be willing to warm my bed as well as Jericho's. It's time for him to get an heir so I know Montgomery Conglomerates will continue. Who knows, maybe their baby will be mine.

O HAD REPLACED ALL but the last crystal in what she was sure was record time.

No way am I losing because of this swap. The last crystal stuck halfway into its slot. She couldn't get it to slide down and she couldn't pull it up. Too much force would crack the delicate structure. "Come on." O'Neill never had trouble during fuel transfer.

"Fragging translithium cutter."

Her father's hand appeared on her wrist. She felt his pressure. *Relax. Don't force it.*

Okay. She rotated the prism a couple of degrees and it slipped into place. She slammed the hull panel shut and bolted it. Grabbing the handhold, she swung into the cockpit and jammed the helmet on. "Let's blow this dump, Solo!" She heard her father chuckle.

Vertical lift engaged, the skimmer rose, hovered a split second before she pushed the throttle all the way forward, then took off, engines screaming, toward the Fertile Field. "Bat outta hell!" Her father's war cry seemed appropriate to start the final leg of the race.

You're on your own now. Hold your line. He squeezed her shoulder, and she could have sworn he kissed her cheek.

Thank you, Dad.

I love you.

Within four minutes she crossed the boundary of the Fertile Field. Less than thirty seconds later her body made its wants known.

She wet her lips and rocked in her seat. It wasn't enough. She wriggled. Her hand went to her breast. It wanted to move lower. Her skin ignited. At least it felt that way. A low moan echoed in her helmet as she raced toward the blue beacon. *I can't take this much longer.*

Her eyelids threatened to slide shut, but she couldn't switch to autopilot and win. She squirmed, changing position in the tight seat. If she could just get pressure in *that* spot. She imagined being held, kissed, held tighter. It was Jericho holding her.

Bad idea. She sat straighter. The back of her seat reminded her of her back pressed against him, him pulling her closer when they'd argued on the dock. She'd tucked her engagement ring into a pocket. Grabbing the outside of that pocket her fingertips worried the outline of the ring with its stone. "I love you, Jericho."

Her body didn't care. Her body wanted Jericho's body pressed against hers. And maybe tonight, it would get what it wanted. If she spent the night with him. Frag that. If he were here, she'd climb all over him.

She remembered Jericho's arm around her when she walked. *Freedom* would lift as soon as her grandfather announced the shipping contract winner. *Jericho has stayed on Prism with me.* To support her in training for the Battle. *And he's returning for me.* The immensity of the idea of marrying Jericho would probably shake her teeth loose once she had time to think about all the difficulties they'd have to overcome.

The beacon pulsed below her. She took a three-g turn to starboard. The faster she cleared this field, the sooner her brain could be back in control.

———

THE PEOPLE around Jericho faced the opposite direction. They expected the first plane to come from the Retching Field.

He would have given his annual salary for her to win. He had to settle for staring in the direction Cal and Wash faced. Watching them for a reaction.

A man next to him had field glasses trained toward the Retching Field. "I think I've got one. Yes!" He pointed in the distance. "Got the winner in my sights."

Jericho twisted around, but couldn't spot anything. Not even a speck. Then, in the opposite direction, closing fast, a skimmer raced toward him. A big skimmer. O'Neill. "There she is!"

Wash stood on a rock, waving his arms.

Jericho looked over his shoulder. The speck grew. Fast.

The wind carried the screech of baffled air. O was reversing the engine. Hard.

The other pilot started braking. Jericho couldn't make out the difference between the shrieks of straining machinery and the screaming crowd. He pushed his way to the rope, standing just outside the boundary of the landing rectangle.

Gritty dust rose around him, forcing him to close his eyes. He cupped his hands and raised them to shield his face. O'Neill's glittering skimmer hovered above, but a few meters away, another skimmer was coming in to land.

O must have cut her engine's power, because her craft dropped to the ground like a bomb. It bounced twice before coming to rest near him.

He smiled at the roughest landing he'd ever seen her make. She'd won! By the way she jumped up in the cockpit and pulled off her helmet, she knew it. He got to her skimmer ahead of the crowd. She had one foot on the hull step, balancing to release Solo's safety harness.

She slipped and he reached for her. But he overbalanced and they went down into the dirt together. He'd landed on his back and cushioned her fall, but she stayed on top of him, seeming uninterested in standing. Her arms went around him and she rained kisses across his face before locking onto his lips. He pulled her tight against him and returned the favor.

A kick on his shin distracted him. And jogged his memory. *Half sister.* Maybe.

Novy grabbed his shoulder, pulling him away from O. "Cal comes." The Russian put both hands around her waist and pulled her to her feet.

She frowned, looking dazed and kissed Novy. On the lips.

Novy waited a fraction of a second longer than necessary to disengage himself.

Jericho was becoming seriously pissed until a man behind chuckled, "That girl definitely just flew over the Fertile Field."

The crowd around them joined in the laughter.

Jericho remembered the brief time they'd spent flying over the Fertile Field, and explaining enhanced lab rabbits to her later. The muscles in his clenched jaw relaxed. He hoped she wouldn't be too embarrassed when she heard people talking about what she'd done.

If his teammates on Earth saw her, they'd give him the same advice his father had. Take her to bed, pay her off, and walk away. They'd say that personal courage, integrity, and sense of duty were useful—in others. Those in your employ. But if he were looking for a mate, they'd say connections, business savvy, and ruthlessness were the goal. And love? Love had become an elusive myth on Earth, replaced by the drive for connections that provided more wealth and power.

Thank God he'd come to Prism and found O'Neill. Even if she turned out to be his half-sister.

Cal elbowed his way to the skimmer. "You did it, O!" He grabbed her arm and raised it over her head. "The winner of the race! O'Neill!"

The crowd chanted, "O. Neill. O. Neill."

Cal kissed her.

Jericho didn't like it. His muscles bunched. He wanted to pull him off her.

But she kissed him back before pushing him away. She whispered to him and he stepped aside, put his arm around her waist and together, they waved to the crowd in the grandstand.

The pilot of the second-place skimmer ducked under the hull and clapped O on the back. She turned and hugged the first-gen. He said something to her and she shook her head. He moved closer to her ear and shouted.

She nodded and kissed his cheek.

The man removed his glove and brushed something out of her eye before turning and accepting his own accolades.

Other skimmers began landing and everyone moved away from the dust storm. Jericho hauled himself over the railing of the grandstand to join Cornelia.

"I can't remember a closer race." She clapped her hands. "What do you think of your pilot now?"

"You said she was the best. You were right."

———

CAL WALKED beside her to the beach, hailing the politico spectators and being, well, Cal.

"Are you okay?" When her head bobbed, he said, "Good," and turned to talk to someone else.

But she wasn't good. She rubbed her palms together. Her palms never sweated, but they were cold and wet now.

Dad?

She felt the warmth of his smile.

Who else? You flew a great race. You'll do fine in the water, too.

Better than fine, now that you're here.

We brought you here when you were what...four?

Yep. I know this beach. And the ocean.

That's my girl. You don't need me in the water; I'm going to go talk to your mother.

She'd be fine without him. She had Jericho's voice from the underground lake and the lap pool workouts. His words and encouragement would sustain her in the cold water during the grueling kilometers ahead. His wetsuit would help, too. *I've got this, Dad.*

Invisible fingertips smoothed her cheek. *I love you, Sweetheart.*

Then, it was as if a cloth had fallen over a bright crystal. His spirit no longer illuminated the space around her like it had for that brief time.

Cal didn't notice. The sun still shone, warm air sluiced across her body.

An arm across her back pulled her into a real body. Cal. "Let's position you for the start." Without waiting for her consent, he led her to an empty spot in the middle of the line of competitors. "Your winning flight gives you a little cushion, but you still need to swim fast as you can so you don't lose ground."

She nodded. "Okay. I'm good."

"I know you're good." He touched his forehead to hers. "We're good together."

They had been good together, for all of her life. In less than four weeks that had changed. How? No wonder Cal looked bereft. She'd stripped away his future.

Jericho pushed through the crowd. "Congratulations!"

Cal turned, saw Jericho, looked at O. "Good luck, O." He walked into the crowd, urging them to move back as a group of politico volunteers roped off a walkway for contestants and judges.

She hugged Jericho. "I did it. I won the flight!"

His arms held her, steadied her, calmed her racing heart. "You are the best pilot on Prism." He kissed her cheek. "And you're my pilot."

Not worried who might see them, she kissed him on the lips. She'd take that warmth with her into the cold water. Remember it at the far away turning point. When he gently set her back, she frowned.

He squeezed her hand. "Not the time, O."

But they were engaged. "We can tell everyone we're getting married."

"I don't think it's the right time for that." His frown said more, but she couldn't decode its message. "You need to focus on the Battle, not on well-wishers and detractors." He glanced at her ring finger. "Where's your ring?"

"In a safe place." She tapped her pocket.

He took her hand. "Leave it there. At least until you come to my ship."

She couldn't help a sly smile. "Tonight?"

"Still feeling the effects of the Fertile Field, eh?"

He knew it by name. Probably heard comments about all three of the fields during the flight. "Maybe."

He took both her hands. "You need to concentrate on swimming the best race of your life out there. Remember your form, your breathing, your legs."

She nodded. He was a good coach.

"And you remember one more thing. I love you." He pulled her fingertips to his lips and kissed them before turning her toward the water. "Go show 'em what you've got."

She looked over her shoulder, smiled, and walked to the shoreline, Solo at her side. She held onto his neck fur and knelt beside him. "You have to wait for me here, big guy. If I need you, someone will let you know." When she rose, she saw one of her father's aides nearby and motioned him over. "Can you stay with Solo until I get back?"

His head bobbed once. "Yes, ma'am, Lieutenant Neill."

At least Reagan wouldn't be able to grab-and-run with her tiger. "If I need help, send him into the water."

"Won't need to do that, ma'am." At her frown, he added, "But if it's necessary, I will."

"Thank you." She walked toward the water, pulled up the top half of the wetsuit, put her arms in the long sleeves and zipped it. She pulled up the head cover and put on the gloves and special shoes Jericho had insisted were part of the *outfit*. He'd called the suit *better than a second skin*, saying it would insulate her from the extreme cold of the water. She'd be happy if it just protected her from stray crystal spikes.

The competitors lined up on the sand. The whistle pierced the air and they all splashed into the water.

JERICHO REFUSED another offer of food, keeping his field glasses trained on O. Wondering if her visible tremors were from exhaustion, pain or fear. Wash, Novy and Hoshi had joined him under the hillside tent, taking advantage of the view of the entire ocean course. Cal stayed on the beach with the other coaches.

Jericho would have been willing to pay swimmers to drop out for her. His father—no, Gatfield— would have figured out a way, probably illegal as well as immoral, to guarantee O the win. He'd held the field glasses to his eyes for almost two hours. His biceps cramped in protest. But that was nothing compared to what O had to be feeling.

He stretched one arm, then the other, never losing sight of her.

AS LEAST SHE'D managed to keep up with the frontrunners. She wasn't too far behind the third-place swimmer. She was tired. Exhausted. At least the cold hadn't made it to her bones yet. Jericho's thermal suit had blocked the almost freezing water temperature.

She checked her form. It had gotten ragged, so she counted, paid attention to the scooped shape of her hands, and used the large muscles of her legs in her kicks. She counted her breaths to her strokes and paced herself for the speed Jericho had recommended for the last half of the race while the first three swimmers rounded the halfway buoy.

That's when the leg cramp hit. She screamed and saltwater filled her mouth. Grabbing her angry muscle, she spit the ocean out. The swimmer behind her closed the gap. She stroked toward the marker, but when she kicked, the pain in her leg bit deeper.

She couldn't let fifth place pass her; sixth and seventh were close behind him. Horizontal again, she stroked deep and fast, without kicking. At least she was moving. After she rounded the buoy, she tried a tentative kick. It hurt, but she could stand it. She added what Jericho called a *flutter kick* and increased the pace of her strokes, hoping she could maintain that speed for half the race.

The first gen soldier ahead of her drifted back, while fifth place gained on her. Soon the three of them were swimming together. They saved all their energy for the contest, wasting no words on each other. When they were almost halfway back to the beach, the fifth-place man pulled ahead as if he hadn't just swum three miles.

If she could keep up with the soldier beside her, maybe she could sprint ahead of him at the end. She tested a stronger kick to no cramping and adjusted her breathing. The first gen kept up with her. They were tied for fourth place. And she was a machine.

Jericho told her that somewhere in the second half of the race she should *become a machine*. She'd laughed at him. But he'd explained that her muscle memory would take over and she wouldn't have to think about what she was doing anymore, and he'd been right. Of course, he'd swum many more kilometers than she had. And he'd been *professionally* trained.

She could see the beach in the distance. She dug her fingertips into the water harder and kicked faster. Her leg muscles complained, but she was almost to the finish line and if she didn't get at least fourth place she had no chance of winning the Battle. She sucked in her pain, counted her tempo and headed for the beach. The first gen couldn't match her drive.

She swam past the finish marker and headed for the beach. When she tried to stand, her cramping leg couldn't hold her and she fell to her knees. A wave washed over her. She struggled to stand, but couldn't. When the wave receded, she opened her mouth and filled her lungs, crawling forward. Another wave crashed across her back. Her lungs burned. She kept crawling and inhaled, catching water up her nose. Coughing kept her from getting a good breath before the next wave hit.

Strong arms lifted her from the sand, carried her what could only have been ten steps, and set her gently on the beach. Still coughing and gasping for air, she didn't have the strength to open her eyes. A rough tongue licked across her cheek.

———

JERICHO HANDED the glasses to Yancey, who stood behind him. "I'm going down there."

"Not a good idea, sir."

"Cornelia, would I break any rules by meeting O'Neill at the finish?"

She shook her head. "No. Take Yancey. There will be a crush of people on that course after the last whistle."

"Then we'd better get going." Jericho vaulted over the container of drinks in front of him and sprinted toward the roped-off area. Ten feet ahead of him, O's grandfather was pushing his way through the crowd.

After crossing the finish line, O continued to the shore, but when she'd tried to stand, she'd crumpled into the surf. And she hadn't been able to get up on her own. Chest heaving, Jericho sprinted through and over people to get to her, while he willed her to stand and continue walking out of the water. He willed her his strength.

She'd just been buried by another wave when he reached the water's edge. He kept going, and when he found her lying in the sand under three feet of water, he scooped her up and carried her the few steps out of the ocean. He laid her on the sand, stripped off his shirt, rolled it into a pillow, and put it under her head. He'd watched her chest rise and fall when she'd been in his arms, so he knew she was breathing.

She'd stopped coughing, but looked like she'd accepted defeat. Tears ran down her cheeks. Could she be contemplating quitting?

"Make a hole. Make it wide." General Neill's words worked. The crowd parted as if he had the authority to give them orders. "You're beginning to be more trouble than you're worth, Montgomery." Motioning his medics to care for O, the older man gave him a sidelong glance.

"Given my credit balance, particularly after I secure the shipping contract, that would be a tremendous amount of trouble, sir."

"Impertinent, too."

"Yes, sir."

"I believe I've already told you once not to *sir* me. I'm not your CO."

"Merely paying deference to your age, General."

Her grandfather turned to Jericho. "Best to stay out of what doesn't concern you. You'll be leaving to go back to Earth soon, won't you?"

Good Lord, if Jocko Neill is my dad, the general is my grandfather. If he'd been walking, he would have tripped. He fought to control his heart, to keep it from hammering out of his chest. "Not for a few more days. And I'll be back in six months."

"Leave her alone. You're confusing the hell out of the poor girl."

Jericho's chest warmed. He didn't try to hide his smile. "When I come back, I intend to spend more time with her to unconfuse her." After lobbing that grenade, he leaned over O.

A man with an official's armband was talking to her. "You did well. By the way, this is the best suit of body armor I've ever seen. Did your father get it for you before he, uh, …?" He stood, shaking out his leg like he had a cramp.

"No. I borrowed it from," she smiled, "him. Hi, Jericho." She gave him a pathetic wave.

"You looked great out there. Are you okay?"

O clasped her fingers together and rested her hands on the top of her head. Her eyes closed. She looked tired. He wasn't sure if she were trying to figure out an answer to his question or if she'd fallen asleep.

Jericho didn't need the shadows of her friends to recognize they'd arrived.

Novy, Wash and Hoshi chattered about the race.

"Move off." The general had returned.

Her three friends moved away, gazes swinging among Cal, O, Jericho, and General Neill.

O lowered her arms. The official who'd talked to her shook her grandfather's hand and walked away. Her grandfather leaned in, said something, and she shook her head. Vigorously. He helped her to a wobbly stand.

Cal moved his finger in a stirring motion.

She stuck her arms out to the side and did a slow pirouette.

"You look good," he said, putting his arms around her waist to steady her.

Cal released her, and Hoshi moved in for a closer look. "Be still." He pulled a piece of crystal out of the upper sleeve of the suit.

"Ouch. Stop." O's weary voice held the sting that crystal probably had.

"Let's go, O." The set of her grandfather's jaw said he didn't expect a discussion. A muscle worked along the general's jawline.

The man looked like he wanted to throw her over his shoulder and carry her off. Or hit something. "My medics will take care of you." He glanced at her friends. "The rest of you are dismissed."

"Da. Yes, sir." Novy saluted. He left with Hoshi and Wash.

Cal didn't salute. "Yes, sir. Thank you, sir." He whispered something to O, she smiled, and he walked away, stopping to talk and shake hands with the people reaching over the rope.

Her grandfather's spine softened and he looked at the sky. "You are your father's daughter. He'd be proud of what you've accomplished today." He nodded to his men. "Let's get her to the medics."

Jericho watched as the men convinced O to sit, then lay, on a stretcher. When they carried her away, she gave him a sorry-about-my-grandfather look and a tired smile.

29

F rom the Journal of Liam Neill (Fourteen days after landing on Prism)

We've camped far enough away from the crazies to avoid constant battle, but I assigned twenty-four-hour sentries to watch for an attack. We raided one of their encampments two days ago and rescued six women who had been serially raped and beaten. My medics say two of the women probably won't make it. We had a meeting tonight of politicos, soldiers, and what's turned out to be convicts. We agreed that no woman can go anywhere without an escort. Every female must choose at least one male protector who is responsible for her safety. We can't survive as a community if our women are abducted and die. The women were more than happy to agree with what we're calling the First Law of Prism.

O AND CAL watched the other competitors in the middle of the roped-off melee field. "Everyone's tired and sore, but they're all going to participate in the melee."

"No matter what you think, I love you." Cal put her staff in her hand. "Win this one. If you can't manage that, at least come in third and you'll have enough points to win the Battle."

She wanted things to be the same easy way between them, but they weren't. Couldn't be, with Jericho in the mix. And that made her pause. What would have happened if Jericho hadn't arrived on Prism? Would Cal have been more reasonable if he hadn't been faced with someone he perceived as a rival? She was torn with guilt and self-accusations. Cal had always had what he thought were O's best interests in mind.

Jericho seemed different today. Had he changed his mind? He was so reserved. Aloof. Until he'd kept her from drowning at the water's edge.

The first whistle sounded for the competitors to take their places around the giant circle marked off in the dirt. Her grandfather had coached her on the best opening moves. She would defend herself until only six people remained. Then she'd go on the offense.

Foot stomping, shouts and the general uproar didn't drown the calls from the crowd. "O. Neill. O. Neill." Of course, other names filled the air, too.

She leaned into her staff. "I'm going to win this." She bounced on the balls of her feet, holding the staff in a tight-knuckled death grip. The rules said you could battle as long as you held your staff. If she dropped it, her chance of winning would crash to the ground with the length of crystal.

The whistle blew twice and the fighting began. The first-gen soldier nearest her chuckled. "Easy pickin's." He turned to his left to meet the man advancing on him.

I hope so.

Staffs clanked as combatants beat against each other. The men on either side of her were busy fighting against those on their other sides, so O had a moment to watch the action. A second-gen girl on her knees raised her staff above her head to ward off the blows of her opponent. She threw her staff to the ground and raised her hands in surrender. The victor pulled her to her feet and she loped to safety beyond the rope. The man assessed the fighting around them then charged toward O.

"Steady." She repeated the word until her opponent's staff crashed against hers.

———

JERICHO COULDN'T HELP WINCING every time a staff collided with O's body. He knew the crack of contact. She fought two opponents and blocked most of the moves, but too many rained against her.

Movement at the edge of his vision drew Jericho's attention. A shabbily dressed man ducked under the rope at O's end of the fighting and kept to the edge of the field, just inside the rope.

Jericho glanced at the spectators in the grandstand. Concentrated on the fighting, no one seemed to notice the extra man on the field.

A glint from something in the man's hand brought Jericho to his feet. The man had a dagger. And he was sprinting toward O.

Jericho vaulted the rope separating the grandstand from the melee field, thankful that he didn't have to push his way through the spectators pressing against the other barriers ringing the field. Shouting O's name, he ran across the field to intercept the man. She was so busy defending herself she couldn't hear him.

His vision narrowed to his quarry. The sounds of the melee faded, replaced by the relentless pounding of his heart. He had to get to her in time.

O's unprotected back offered the perfect target for the knife.

Closing the gap, the assassin raised his weapon overhead.

O spun and rammed the end of her staff into the man's stomach. He crumpled and she turned back to defend herself from a melee attacker.

The man was struggling to stand, gripping his knife. Fury propelled Jericho forward. He lowered his shoulder and rammed the man's side just like he'd done hundreds of times on the football field.

They tumbled into the dirt, stopping with Jericho underneath. The knife bit into Jericho's side. He slammed his fist into the man's jaw. A knee rammed his inner thigh. He threw a roundhouse punch to the guy's head but missed.

Face to face, the man's dank breath assaulted Jericho's nostrils. The man grinned.

Jericho's side burned.

A staff cracked against the side of the man's skull. The grin slid from his mouth and his body went limp. Solo, trailing a trio of long ropes hooked together into a harness, skidded to a stop between the fallen attacker and O.

Jericho struggled to his knees. The silence was eerie. Either the melee was over or it had been stopped.

Someone rushed past him, pulled out a long knife and slit the throat of the unconscious attacker.

"You didn't have to do that!" Jericho yelled.

"I'm going to be O's protector, and I'm not letting a convict bastard hurt her." Reagan held the knife high, grandstanding to the crowd.

A few feet away, O stood, holding her staff, frozen in stunned shock.

Jericho tried to stand, but couldn't. Yancey materialized from somewhere and helped him up.

"I'm probably disqualified because you fought someone for me." Her wail sounded like she was in pain. "Why did you interfere?"

"The bastard had a knife." He sank to the ground at her feet. He was having trouble thinking, but he was pretty sure that his tackling the would-be assassin didn't count as if he'd fought one of her melee competitors. "I'm not the one who killed him." His argument sounded weak.

"I had a staff. I've fought off convicts before."

Cal strode up and stood, looking down at him. "You fragging Earther." He hefted a staff like he wanted to pummel Jericho. "If you lost the Battle for her…"

Tears tracked through the dirt on O's face. "Cal, have the officials made a decision? Are they restarting the melee?"

I need to make her understand. Jericho tried to stand and fell.

"Frag! He's bleeding." O sounded panicked.

Jericho's hand went to his aching side. Sticky. Warm.

Crap.

His eyelids slid shut, the ground tilted away, and darkness engulfed him.

———

O'NEILL WATCHED the medics work to stop Jericho's bleeding. He couldn't die. He was too strong. Too healthy. Too good to her. And his mother's ring was in her pocket.

The chief medic stood. He looked worried. "We need to treat him in the tent. Now." Two soldiers ran up with a stretcher. They loaded Jericho onto the crystal plank and carried him away. Yancey and two medics followed, pressing bandages against Jericho's side.

"I'm coming with you."

Battle participants and officials milled around her. One of them stretched his arm in front of her. "You have to stay here."

She leaned against her staff, trying to hide the shaking that threatened to swamp her. As soon as they let her leave the field, she'd go to Jericho. "Why would a convict attack me?"

Cal rested his hand on her waist. "Probably crazy. We know they get contraband drugs from the supply shuttles. *Mind blowers*, they call it."

"Maybe. But why would your uncle kill an unconscious man? That convict couldn't have hurt me once I hit him."

"Maybe Uncle Ray saw him move."

"The guy crumpled like a skimmer that lost power. Trust me, he was out." She nodded in the direction of the med tent. "I need to check on Jericho."

Cal's eyes narrowed. "My uncle was probably trying to prove

to your mother that he could protect you." He looked around. "Where did he go?"

O followed his gaze. Cal's father, her mother and Reagan, and her grandfather strode toward them, followed by a grim Warden Schultz.

They circled her.

"Are you hurt?" Her mother's face was as pale as Prism sand, without its sheen.

"The convict didn't touch me. Really, Mom."

"Lieutenant Neill." Warden Schultz cleared her throat. "Your stepfather has demanded your formal declaration of a permanent protector to replace your father."

"But I'm supposed to have more time. Until after the Battle winner is announced."

Reagan widened his stance and puffed out his chest. "You don't have a chance of winning now."

O met the man's triumphant leer. She wanted to kill him, choke the air from his throat. Her vision blurred but her mind was sharp. No matter what happened to her, she had to hide Solo to keep him safe. She wanted to run from them all. Rubbing her clammy palms together, she tried to catch a breath. Her heart beat harder than it had anytime during the Battle.

Her jaw locked on words she couldn't utter. The ground slanted and her knees seemed to melt.

Cal's arm tightened around her waist. Mouth by her ear, he whispered, "Tell her you choose me."

She struggled to open her mouth. "I–"

"As her mother's husband, I will be the girl's protector." Reagan's chin raised, defying anyone to disagree with him.

Cal's father bristled. "Cal and I planned to discuss options with her. With you."

Her grandfather stepped forward. "This is *not* the time or place to do this." Feet wide, he looked like a large immovable boulder. A large *angry* immovable boulder.

Reagan glanced at the warden. "Her mother is next of kin. As her husband, I am O'Neill's rightful protector, under the First Law. She's not eighteen yet."

A sizeable crowd had gathered, pressing close to hear the discussion.

O squeezed her lips together. *I'll run away. I'll take Solo and run into the hills.* She fisted her hands.

No, you won't.

Her mouth opened. Her eyes opened wider. She strained to take in the view around her. Her heart pounded a path up her throat. "Dad?"

Ray Reagan chuckled, a sound laced with evil and greed. "He's dead."

"Wrong, Reagan." Her dad—in his body—stood behind her mother, then circled around to stand behind O.

He looked fine. Alive. She wanted to hug him. Even if he couldn't stay for long, he was here for her. The love between them shimmered in the air. How had she never seen that before?

Patrick Reagan's shock showed in his furrowed brow. "Jocko, you're alive." The inflection made it sound like a question.

Her stepfather's face purpled; his eyes looked ready to pop from their sockets. He reached toward her father, as if he wanted tactile verification of what his eyes saw. "You couldn't have survived out there."

The warden was no less surprised. "Jocko? Where have you been?"

"Healing, in the tunnels under the Great Plain."

A collective gasp rose from the onlookers. More spectators had joined the crowd. Sentiments of disbelief rippled to the outer circle of newcomers. Everyone jockeyed for position, craning to catch a glimpse of the suddenly-resurrected Jocko Neill. Soldier guards kept people from pushing forward. A few shouted welcomes or questions to Jocko.

Her father coughed and smiled. "I raised my daughter to take care of herself. She can do that better than many of her peers in soldier compound."

A line creased the Warden's forehead. "I don't understand where you're going with this, Jocko."

"She's taken care of herself since I went missing." He held up a hand to keep the three Reagans from interrupting. "The Citadel agreed to be her temporary protectors, but they never had to advise or save O from anything." He smiled at her. His pride beamed warmth into her heart. "She fought off attackers in Convict Town. Yes, she was with her friends. And Solo. My daughter was smart enough to be with her friends. They fought as a unit. And they won that fight."

Cal nodded. "O'Neill faced down their leader and his body-guard. By herself. Then she disabled them. On her own. I wouldn't want to fight her." He gave her an embarrassed grin that played well with the crowd, judging from the chuckles and comments it received.

Schultz sighed and signaled for the spectators to be quiet. "We know all this. That doesn't change the First Law."

"Then you know that she doesn't need a protector. She makes her own decisions. She's smart enough to know when she needs a group of friends around her."

"The First Law…" Ray Reagan sputtered.

Her father stepped beside her. "Lieutenant O'Neill pilots a mining shuttle. Last week, she had no co-pilot. She had no protector while piloting over a hundred miners." His finger pointed around the circle. "Were any of you concerned enough to ride with her? To be her protector then?" He looked at the far-reaching circle of onlookers. "Were any of you miners afraid to ride in her shuttle?"

"Hell, no. Girl's as good a pilot as you, Jocko."

"I never even thought about her being alone in the cockpit."

Similar responses were shouted. All were positive in their assessment of her skill, and her ability to take care of herself and those for whom she was responsible.

Her father rested his hand on her shoulder. "My daughter is a competent adult who is capable of defending herself. I'm not her protector. The truth is, I never have been a very good one." He looked at her mother before squeezing O's shoulder. "Sweetheart, if they make you choose a protector, don't pick me. I am your father, but I refuse to be your lord and master." He turned and walked down the path behind the med tent.

They all looked at each other. Ray Reagan broke the silence. "Nothing has changed. The girl still needs a protector. And if her own father doesn't want the job, I will pledge to be her protector."

Before they could start arguing, O stood tall and faced the Warden. She didn't know if her father was back in his body permanently, if he'd ever live in the Citadel again, or if he'd agree to be her protector just to get Reagan off her back. Right now, those things didn't matter.

"I choose to be my own protector." Her voice rang out. Clear. Strong. Determined. "If I'm not disqualified, and I win the Battle, I will choose a boon. That boon will be to remain in my home with my father and to continue living my life as my own protector. I will defend myself. I will take responsibility for my own safety. And during my boon year, I will work with the females of Prism and press the Joint Committee to rescind the First Law. All females deserve the right to live their lives as they see fit. There are other girls who can take care of themselves. One person having absolute rule over another—for life—cannot be justified."

Fear slid across her mother's features.

"Mom, don't worry." O walked across the circle, held her mother's sad face in her hands, and reflected back strength, resolve, and the will to stand up to her husband.

Reagan glared. "The girl can't declare that she's her own protector. Frag it all, Francine, tell them O has to come home with us now. That you want me to protect her."

Her mother stepped back and shook off his hand. "Be quiet, Raymond."

Administrator Schultz cleared her throat. "Mrs. Reagan?"

Francine stared at O like she'd never seen her before. A tear ran down her cheek. "Her father spoke for both of us." Her voice was steady and calm.

"What?" Reagan grabbed her mother's wrist and jerked her to him. He turned to Schultz. "She'd like to state her decision for the record now. I am her husband."

Her mother glared at him.

"How dare you?" The man wailed. "I've done everything for you, but you give your loyalty to your freakish daughter. This is our chance to get rid of her, marry her off so we won't have to see her anymore. She isn't your family. You have me and the twins." He jerked her mother's arm, pulling her off balance.

Granddad stepped beside him and touched the man's forearm at a pressure point. "Let her go, Reagan." His soft words carried restrained power, with a promise to unleash that power if the man didn't follow the command.

"I don't answer to you, old man. I'm her protector. I can do whatever I..." Before he'd inhaled another breath, his inflated chest caved and he fell to his knees, cradling his arm.

Wry smile on his lips, her grandfather nodded. "Francine, it may be best for you to stay in the soldier compound tonight. Your boys are welcome as well. My aide will corral them for you."

Ray Reagan struggled to his feet. "You can't tell my wife what to do. And you sure as fuck aren't taking my boys. She's going with me. Tell them Patrick. You're the leader of the politicos." A vein throbbed visibly in his forehead. He crossed his arms and sneered before pointing at O. "And, you. You conniving little bitch. You won't last a week without me as your protector. You're hellbound."

Her grandfather motioned to his executive officer. "Take him." He looked at Cal's father and raised his eyebrow, daring him to interfere. "You heard him threaten O. He'll be my guest in the brig for a week."

Cal and his father watched as four soldiers moved forward and restrained the struggling politico before hauling him away.

Her grandfather smiled at the Warden. He knew his power and

influence on Prism. "You heard his threat. This man's a menace to his family right now. We'll see if some time in the brig helps."

"You'd better be sure nothing happens to him," Cal's father said. "The politico community is going to take a dim view of you hijacking one of their own, particularly their supply manager."

"What about you?"

Cal's father shrugged. "I let you do it, didn't I?" He eyed O. "We still need to figure out what to do about a protector for her."

They looked at the warden.

"This is Joint Committee business, gentlemen. In my opinion, O'Neill has proven that she is a *person* who is fully capable of making decisions related to her safety, including travel, meetings, and choosing the company she keeps. If the men of the Citadel are willing to continue as her protectors for the week, that should be enough time to work out a solution." The Warden walked past O'Neill and gave her a private, lopsided smile.

O looked at the remaining adults. "If you'll excuse me, I'm going to the med tent."

———

JERICHO WOKE SLOWLY, aware of soft voices and movements close by. He was flat on his back on a not-very-comfortable narrow bed. Like the cots he'd seen in the med tent at the Battle. He opened his eyes, and sure enough, he looked straight up at poles and ropes and plaz-canvas.

A medic's face entered his field of vision. "Ah, you're finally awake, Mr. Montgomery. We were worried about you. You lost a significant amount of blood." He motioned to someone.

Jericho swiped his tongue across his dry bottom lip. Memory trickled back. Jumping the rope barrier, fighting a poorly-dressed man, a very-angry O, his bloody hand. "What happened?" The words didn't sound right, so he tried again.

"You were injured. But someone is here to see you. I'll let her answer your questions."

O shook the man's hand. "Thank you, corpsman."

He gave her a brief nod and walked away.

O settled her hand on top of Jericho's. Not soft, but warm. "I was so frightened when they told me you were here."

"In the med tent?" His gaze wandered to the medics checking patients on the cots along the next aisle. He couldn't come up with a rational thought.

"In the soldier specialty med tent."

Where? Somewhere no one had talked about.

She nodded at the confusion that had to show in his eyes. "The medics were afraid you might not survive. Granddad gave the okay to transport you here. They stopped the bleeding and stitched you up on the flight here. You slept all night." She didn't look demoralized, so maybe, somehow, she'd won the Battle. He hoped so. She deserved to be happy. She deserved the independence that was so important to her.

He'd been *transported* here? Where was *here*? Jericho had no idea what had happened. He pushed up to one elbow, and searched for answers in her eyes. The events of the past twenty-four hours came flooding back. The proposal. The hologram. The Battle. Cal. O.

Too much data. He closed his eyes.

He knew he needed to back off until he found out the identity of his real father. Hell, if he were her half-brother, he'd deal with his feelings for her, even though it would be easier to cut off his own arm. He loved her. More than he should. But he wanted her to be happy. And safe. Cal could protect her on Prism. He couldn't. "Where's Yancey?" His voice sounded like a hundred-year-old frog.

"On *Freedom*, probably seething because he wasn't allowed to come with you."

"My father will flay the skin off his back if anything happens to me." Jericho rolled his head to the side, opened his eyes halfway and locked onto O's concerned gaze. "Relax. Nothing more is going to happen to me." With all the ears in the tent, he wasn't going to tell her about his mother's hologram message. He wasn't looking forward to breaking both of their hearts and reneging on his promise of a shared future with her. But being surrounded by General Neill's medical staff would table that discussion for later.

O propped pillows behind Jericho's back so he could sit up. She didn't wait for his questions. "You're not going to believe what happened." She settled on the little stool next to his field cot, placing his hand in hers. "Ray Reagan brought the Warden and my mother onto the melee field and demanded he be named my protector. Cal and his father were there, too."

"I thought you had more time."

"I did, too. So I proclaimed that I would be my own protector. My dad showed up, and my mother finally stood up to Reagan and said she agreed with Dad. Reagan argued and hurt Mom. Then he threatened me. Granddad had him taken to the soldier compound, so he could *talk* to him, and Cal's dad didn't do anything. Nothing is settled yet." She bounced on the stool.

"Wait. Your dad showed up?" And where is he now? If he could only talk to Jocko Neill about his mother. And her … *lover*.

"Another. Time." Her look followed the medical corpsmen making their rounds, then she cleared her throat and tapped her heels on the canvas floor of the tent. She didn't want anyone to overhear what she would tell him. "Next question?"

"When can I meet him?" How soon?

She shook her head. "It's not that easy. Next question."

"I have to see him, O. It's important."

"I don't know when I'll see him again." She glanced at the medics checking other patients.

"What about Cal?"

"Well, he wasn't happy. He was waiting for me at the Citadel last night. He didn't argue with me then, but that won't last for long."

"Why don't you pick Cal for your protector?"

She stopped tapping her heels. "How can you say that? What… Are you saying you don't want to marry me?"

He shook his head. "No. But he can keep you safe...until I come back. I would pay him."

His words couldn't have hurt more if he'd cut his heart out with a dull blade and fed it to Solo.

"You know Cal wants me to marry him. As my protector, he could insist on it." Her cheeks reddened. She leaned close. "Have you changed your mind? You know I don't want to give up my independence..." Her jaw snapped shut, but her eyes kept talking. "You and I are engaged. I can't have another protector."

She raised her chin. Frost could have formed in the space between them. "You're having a reaction to something the medics gave you, because you can't be saying you think I need a protector."

She was his half-sister. Most likely. He may have messed up her future so much that she'd hate him if Jocko Neill were his father, too.

Her bewildered expression preceded a short laugh. "You really don't know, do you?"

He shook his head. "Know what?" He pushed back into the pillows to put more space between them. "What don't I know?"

The confusion in her eyes was replaced by determination and fire. "I'm not marrying Cal because I love you. Just like you put together a proposal that benefits both Prism and you, my actions will benefit all females, not just me. As long as men prey on women, they must be punished. Women shouldn't be punished by having our rights taken away for our entire lives."

He agreed with everything she said. How could he tell her that without sounding condescending? "My credits are on you."

The medic returned. "Good news, Mr. Montgomery. You've been cleared to return to your ship. A medical shuttle is waiting to transport you to the spaceport. Two corpsmen will accompany you." He pursed his lips, looked at the plaz-canvas floor of the tent, and raised his gaze to O'Neill. "Sorry, but there's not room for you, Lieutenant Neill."

Her smile fell.

O's grandfather entered the tent and strode toward them. Jericho swung his legs over the side of the cot and tried to stand. Tried being the operative word. His legs were not ready to support his wounded body. He sank back, butt smacking hard against the latticed rope that passed for a mattress.

The medic stepped aside and the general filled his space. "The Joint Committee has made its decision on the shipping contract."

A little gasp parted O's lips.

"General Neill." Jericho balanced on the edge of the cot and straightened his back. "Before you tell me the decision, I need to speak with you. Privately."

Her grandfather raised an eyebrow.

"Not to try to change your mind, but to tell you some things I think you need to know."

The general looked at the medic. "Can he walk?"

"For a short distance. With assistance."

"Get him to my field office."

"Granddad…"

When the general looked at him, Jericho gave a slight shake of his head.

"O, why don't you check on your mother? I'll send a runner when Montgomery is ready to return to the spaceport."

She opened her mouth to argue, then closed it. "Jericho?"

The unsure way she voiced his name almost cracked his resolve. "It's fine, O. It's just business." He glanced at her grandfather. "You'll send for her before you tell me the Joint Committee's decision?"

"If that's what she wants." He couldn't miss O's vigorous nod. "Wait for my order. Now, move it." He gave her a shooing motion.

Hands on hips, O pursed her lips and exhaled a snort before turning to leave.

"My tent. On the double," the general ordered the medic before striding away.

Jericho stood, and leaning heavily on the arms of the corpsmen who flanked him, he shuffled slowly outside and down the path to a much smaller tent. Two guards stood in front of the closed flap. They stepped aside; one opened the flap while the other announced, "Montgomery has arrived, sir."

O's grandfather looked up from behind a small desk and nodded. The corpsmen settled Jericho in a canvas chair in front of the desk, saluted, executed a sharp about-face and left. The flap slapped shut.

"What do you need to talk to me about?"

"I believe Gatfield Montgomery plans to send a mercenary force to Prism within a year."

That got his attention. Squinting, as if he were in bright sunlight, the general leaned forward. "And you're telling me this about your father because…"

He'd thought all night about whom he could ask for help in finding his real father. O would have been the obvious choice, but he didn't want to endanger her with the knowledge. "Gatfield Montgomery is not my father. My real father is a Prismer."

"What makes you think that?

"Last night I watched an encoded hologram from my mother. She, uh, met someone when she was on the archaeological dig here."

Neill's cold stare said he wasn't buying it. "This could be a nice story to gain my support for the shipping contract or to give you the go ahead with O." Eyes wide, palms pressing into the desktop, his throat growled. "Who is he?"

"I don't know. But I must find him."

"Does O know?"

"No. Telling her would have put her in even greater danger."

Her grandfather nodded and sat back in his chair. "Maybe someone here does know. Perhaps that's why the kidnappers were sent. Do you have any ideas about who your mother, uh, who your father is?"

Jericho readied himself for the full force of Liam Neill's fury. "Well, there's a good chance it could be your son."

"No." The general stood. "No." Anger vibrated off him. He

rounded the desk, walked to the side of Jericho's chair and studied his face long enough to memorize every pore. "You don't take after the Neills. But then, after you left the Joint Committee, Patrick mentioned in passing that you look a lot like your mother." He paced around the inside perimeter of the small tent several times, appearing lost in thought. His lips moved, but Jericho couldn't distinguish any words other than an occasional *Jocko* peppering his inaudible rant.

O's grandfather returned to the seat behind his desk. "If you're telling me the truth, this changes everything. The kidnapping. The grab-and-run attempt two weeks ago. They could have been ways to get back at Jocko." Outrage lit his eyes. "Fragging whore fuckers." His fist balled and he looked like he wanted to hit something. Hard. "I knew my son wouldn't crash his skimmer on a simple run across the Great Plain."

Had someone sabotaged Jocko's skimmer? Shit. O suffered, thinking her father was dead because somebody on Prism knew his secret? "General Neill? It can't get back to Gatfield that I'm looking for my real father. He can't find out who it is, or he *will* send a fragger."

"And he'll come after you as well. Does he know you aren't his own?"

"Yes. He made my mother sign contracts, contracts that would give him her inheritance if she ever revealed I wasn't his son. I'm his major publicity asset. He uses my image, my activities to build goodwill with the public. He ran a whole ad campaign before I left about my willingness to travel here at great personal risk for the greater good of the people of the North America Union."

The older man rested his chin on his steepled fingers. "This is a real cluster fuck. You know, you are at risk, too. Do you trust your Earther bodyguard? Your Earther pilot?"

Although the general's posture was relaxed, the keen gaze he fixed on Jericho made Jericho feel like a live frog pinned to the platform of a dissecting microscope. He was being tested. "Yancey has put himself at risk enough times on Earth that I never considered him anything but a very dedicated bodyguard. However, on this trip, he's been a bit lax. I thought it was because I trusted O. But he spent a lot of time in the kitchen with O's stepfather. More than two strangers would need to bring out some dishes."

Jericho thought about Matilda and her husband, *Freedom's* pilot. "I don't have a sense about my pilot and his wife. They are pleasant and perform their jobs efficiently. But they are Gatfield's employees." He shook his head. "I haven't gotten to know them well. This trip is the first I've been on *Freedom* without my father. I focused my outbound time on the shipping proposal and maintaining my business responsibilities at home." If only he'd taken the time to get to know his crew. He couldn't guess how invested they were in Montgomery Conglomerates.

Liam Neill nodded. "Gatfield could use your death to fire up the population for vengeance. Make them willing to pay more taxes to send a mercenary expedition here for revenge for their *golden boy*."

Golden boy? Had his father built up Jericho's popularity to use it for his own purpose? His stomach clenched. Of course, he had. Last night he'd learned his life was a lie. Now he contemplated that his father might have him killed to obtain a business goal. He grabbed his midsection and looked for a wastebasket or other container. He was going to heave up his guts.

"Medic!" The general's voice sounded a lot calmer than it should.

Two men wearing the medic patch on their shoulders rushed in. They took one look at him and one of them pulled out a shub, shook it open, and held it in front of Jericho.

He was shaking, but he wasn't going to have someone hold his shub. He took it and, holding on with both hands, held it to his mouth, then dry heaved. After a couple more attempts, one of the men handed him a small glass of water. "You're too dehydrated to puke. Small sips of water for the next twenty-four hours, or you may vomit from the after-effects of the...uh," he looked at the general, "treatment."

He took a swallow and watched the men depart. He kept the shub on the theory that if he had one, he wouldn't need to use it.

O's grandfather pursed his lips. "We were talking about Gatfield."

Jericho collected his thoughts, trying to compartmentalize them into an emotion-free zone. "He's told me several times, 'We're going to reclaim that planet.' I think he's already got a plan in motion. How could I not have seen this before?" He scrubbed his hair in frustration. "There's something else. He secretly funds a radical propaganda group called LTS—for Let Them Starve. Their goal is to stop all shipments to Prism."

"Montgomery always covered his ass."

Would the man who'd raised him have him killed? Maybe. If it was good for business. His death would solve a number of possible problems. But it would also leave Gatfield without an heir. And the man wanted an heir more than anything else. He had to have someone to carry on his legacy, his name. Jericho would use that knowledge as his insurance policy.

Neill stood, walked to the tent opening, whispered to a guard, and closed the flap. He returned to his desk and poured a glass of water from a pitcher on a stand, before offering to refill Jericho's cup. O's grandfather finished his water and set the glass on his desk. "Are you willing to do something that could get you killed if you're found out? A Trojan horse that will tell us exactly what Gatfield Montgomery is planning?"

Jericho's stomach went into freefall. With no parachute. An invasion. A Trojan horse. Another possibility for his death. Fuck. He'd just graduated from Harvard with his MBA. He'd taken no classes to deal with this shit.

What would happen if his actions brought down Montgomery Conglomerates? What would happen to the man who'd acted as his father? If he sided with the exiles, he would become an exile. Well, he was already half-Prismer. The World Board would use that to fry his ass. O's safety was his prime interest, and a shipload of mercenaries would be her end. "What do I need to do?"

Liam Neill leaned forward, a gleam in his eye. "I've got chips with a computer game that I guarantee will go viral once people start playing it. The code embeds in the host and spreads through the network, collecting the data we're looking for."

"How...Never mind." His brain felt like it was going to implode. Too much information. "What do I have to do?"

"Just give the chip to the right people. Your friends, the sons and daughters of corporation owners. Their parents." The general *winked*. "Your *father*." He called for his aide. "Wrap up the chips, Trace, and give them to my shuttle pilot. Double time."

Jericho had just agreed to be a traitor to his corporation and the North America Union. The name Jericho Montgomery would become synonymous with Benedict Arnold. "This will be my last trip *home*. The few days I have on Earth will be my last on the planet." The enormity of what he'd agreed to do settled like a stone in his gut. "Why do you trust me to do this?"

Neill cocked his head. "I didn't say I trust you. I've given you a task to complete. Consider it a test." He breathed out what passed for a sigh. "O trusts you. If you care about her, you'll do this and you'll return."

"I'll do it."

"Don't come back to Prism unless you do. I can't control the actions of every soldier in my command." He raised his chin. "Perkins, send for my granddaughter," Neill called to the guard outside.

The man poked his head inside the tent. "Yes, sir." He ducked outside.

General Neill relaxed into his chair. "When O returns, we'll talk about the shipping contract; then my pilot will return you to the spaceport and you'll leave for Earth immediately. I suggest you act like you took advantage of us when you return home. Ensure that your father knows we're the scum he's always believed we are. Insist that you want nothing to do with us other than to make your fortune. Watch your back. Trust no one."

He stared at Jericho with laser-like intensity. "I'm taking a risk trusting you. You may very well be the son of Gatfield Mont-gomery and be telling me a lie. You could have seduced O with lies because you thought it would help you win the contract." He heaved a sigh. "But I haven't survived all these years without listening to my gut, and my gut says you're not like Perseus or Gatfield. Don't screw with my gut, Jericho."

"Yes, sir." Jericho nodded. "May I speak privately with O?"

"No can do. She can't know anything. She wouldn't let anything slip, but her demeanor would be different. We may need you to stay on Earth rather than return on the supply ship. If there is another supply ship."

No. He'd promised O he'd return. "I promised her I'd come back in six months."

"Would you rather keep that promise or keep her alive?"

He hadn't had nearly enough time with her. Things were moving too fast. Half-sister or fiancée, it didn't matter. Choosing between seeing O again or her safety? "No contest." O needed to remain safe. That would take priority at every single decision point.

The general looked at Jericho. "Correct answer. You might be able to manage both. I hope so, for your sake."

The flap opened and O hurried in, following by Solo. "Mom left. I've been waiting forever."

Jericho smiled. O didn't play games; you knew exactly where you stood with her. Except when she didn't know. She looked tired and had a bruise under one eye, but he'd never seen a more beau-tiful sight. When she spared him a glance, he winked and was rewarded by the prettiest blush.

Her grandfather chuckled. "I've been alive forever. You're one-fourth my age. Not forever by a long shot."

"Okay. Tell us about the shipping contract."

"Montgomery, the real possibility of producing our own food won you the deal. We believe the agronomist, medical biologist and entomologist will provide the testing and research capabilities to help us become self-sufficient within the next few years."

General Neill stuck out his hand. "Congratulations. You've got yourself a three-year shipping agreement."

Jericho was stunned. He'd been such a slack-jawed fool in this past hour, if he'd been on Earth he would have ingested a meal of insects. Now he had a reason to return, and he could make sure the supply ship brought enough food for six more months. He'd put together a good proposal. The winning proposal. He smiled.

The general shook his hand. O squealed and clapped her hands, then wrapped her arms around Jericho. He hugged her back, looking over the top of her head at her unsmiling grandfather, who raised a brow at O. "And you, young lady, have an appointment with the Joint Committee tomorrow morning. You are no easier to raise than your father was."

Her grandfather's head jerked to the right, his face painted with surprise. The man completed a deliberate scan of the medical tent while he frowned. "You may want to come with me for the announcement of the winner of the Battle, O."

———

O AND JERICHO had flown with her grandfather in his shuttle from the Healing Field to Soldier Beach. O walked with Jericho, flanked by two corpsmen and Granddad, who had tried to tell her that Jericho had to return to his ship. Jericho had insisted he had the energy to go with her, so she'd argued her grandfather into submission.

They stood away from the crowd, a ring of soldiers circling them. Her friends stood outside the ring, but Cal nodded a polite greeting and said something to one of the soldiers, who let him pass. Cal stood on her left. To her right, Jericho's fingers threaded with hers.

Not used to being nervous, she chewed her bottom lip.

I don't care about the points. You're my winner.

Hi, Dad. Nice trick showing up in your body.

Glad you liked that. I'm working on staying in physical form longer and longer.

She felt a hand on her shoulder, but when she gave it a sidelong glance, there was nothing there except a shimmer. She tilted her head back and let the warmth of the morning sun bathe her face as she concentrated on soaking in her father's touch. *Thanks for your support. It was so good to have you there. And to see you.*

I love you, O.

I love you. You talked to Granddad in the med tent, didn't you?

He needed to be reminded that you are much better behaved than I ever was. Heck, you're almost eighteen and you've only broken one nose.

I've broken Novy's nose twice.

He laughed.

The Joint Committee went up the steps to the platform that now stood in the melee area. The pressure on her shoulder disappeared. The crowd quieted.

Cal's father stepped forward. "Let's give all the Battle participants a round of applause. They trained hard and gave us a good show." Claps, foot stomping, and whistling reverberated across Soldier Beach.

The politico leader raised his hands for silence. It took a while before he got it. "We've assessed point values for each competitor's time and finish in the events. As is our custom, I will announce only the winner of each event before I announce the name of the winner of the Battle. Further details and standings will be posted by your Joint Committee representative."

Cal reached around her waist. O intercepted his hand and pulled it between them. She shifted her stance. When had Patrick Reagan become so long-winded?

Jericho's thumb rubbed her palm. How long had he been doing that? She looked at him and he smiled reassurance.

Cal's father nodded. "We all know the flight winner."

"O. Neill. O. Neill. O. Neill." The cadence of the crowd's refrain sounded like a lumbering cart filled with supplies.

When the shouts fell off, Cal's father continued. "The winner of the swim was Marsh Trainor."

There were hoots and clapping for the politico.

"And the winner of the melee was Oz Burn."

Another soldier. A first gen.

Patrick Reagan raised his hands for silence. "This year, the winner of the Battle did not win one of the individual events."

The ground tilted then fell away. She wasn't the winner.

Patrick Reagan's voice droned on. "The winner took second place in each of the three events, earning the most points. I give you this year's Battle winner, Mario Paul."

If Jericho hadn't been holding her hand, she would have fallen to her knees. Swallowing against the pain in her chest, Jericho's arm went around her waist, pulling her against him, giving her support. But his support wouldn't keep her from being required to declare a protector. And it couldn't be her father. He'd seen to that.

Disappointment and fear fought a personal melee battle across her skin. Now she couldn't ask for a boon. Couldn't be guaranteed her independence.

"I'm so sorry, O." Jericho's words floated past her ear.

A very unladylike snort escaped her lips.

One of the soldiers coughed. "Are you ready to depart for the spaceport, sir?"

Jericho gave the man an irritated look. "You'll know when I'm ready." He pulled her aside. "I wish I had more time. There is so much I want to say to you, tell you." He held her like he wouldn't allow her to be pried away from him.

"Me, too." Her voice sounded like a squeaky hull plate hinge. She couldn't be another man's wife, her belly huge with someone else's child when he returned. "I'll fly to the spaceport as soon as I can get away from here. I, I want to…"

He shook his head before she could tell him she wanted to spend the night with him. "*Freedom* has to leave for Earth as soon as I return." His arms encircled her.

The tears started and she sobbed into his shoulder. How would she survive six months without him, even if she managed to stay free of a protector?

"It's going to be a long six months, but I want you to remember two things: I will be back. No matter what happens, I love you." His hands on either side of her cheeks, he kissed her forehead, pressing his lips to her skin long enough to imprint their touch in her memory.

She wasn't going to give him a watery good-bye or all the reasons why she wouldn't be able to marry him if she had a protector, especially in front of the soldiers. There was nothing he could do. But she couldn't stop her tears.

She'd lost the Battle. She'd lost the chance to ask for a boon. She'd lost everything she wanted. How could she achieve her goal? What could one second gen girl do to fight the First Law of Prism? "I'll be on the dock when you return." Would he still want her, like her father had wanted her mother after Ray Reagan took her to the Fertile Field?

His arms wrapped around her. He held her tight for not nearly long enough before releasing her and turning to his escort. "I'm ready to return to my ship." He walked past them, leading the way.

Had it been only three weeks since she'd declared that all she wanted was to find her father alive? Well, soon everyone would know that Jocko Neill was alive. She would talk to him, feel his arms around her. She'd gotten exactly what she' asked for. The trouble was, now she wanted more. Now she wanted Jericho Montgomery, too.

He was coming back to her.

He loved her.

And she loved him.

"Earthers go home, Solo." She dug her fingers into his ruff. "But *my* Earther is coming back to me. Jericho is coming back for *me*."

The End

THANK YOU FOR READING **_P.R.I.S.M. Book One_**. For news on **_P.R.I.S.M. Book Two_**, sign up for my newsletter at my website www.faerowen.com. You can also sign up for *The Hangar Deck*, a private area of my website to read character blogs and sporadically released deleted scenes. Want to read about Jocko Neill's crash? It's posted on The Hangar Deck.

DID you enjoy reading this book? If so, please consider helping others to enjoy it by *recommending* it to friends, readers' groups, and discussion boards. You can also *review* it at the retailer site you purchased it from or on other sites like Goodreads. You are the key to this book's success. If you write a review and you'd like to share it with me, please send me an e-mail at fae@faerowen.com so I can thank you personally. I'm also available at my website http://www.faerowen.com .

TO TIDE YOU OVER, here's a snippet of **_P.R.I.S.M Book Two_**.

SIX MONTHS *after leaving PRISM*

IN THE SPACEPORT ON PRISM, Jericho Montgomery stood in the hatch of the supply shuttle, watching the flurry of activity around him.

Dock workers, convicts, soldiers and politicos hurried to unload the supplies that would sustain them for the next six months. Every container, whether it held protein powder or more valuable Earth products, was checked by an Earther crewman, then checked again by a Prismer. The third and final sign-off was by a representative from Administrator Cornelia Schultz's office.

Jericho listened to the voices, the shouted comments, hoping to hear the only voice that mattered. He'd endured hours of meetings with his not-father, Gatfield Montgomery, agreeing to whatever the head of Montgomery Conglomerates dictated, including a marriage with a piranha-like daughter of the owner of the South American conglomerate. But Jericho had departed on the supply ship to P.R.I.S.M. and avoided that entanglement. Because he was in love with O'Neill, his pilot and security officer during his first trip to this exile world.

There was only one small problem: She might be his half-sister, and she didn't know that.

Finding his real father was the first agenda item on his long to-do list.

His gaze darted between jump-suited bodies, looking for her tiger, Solo. He saw a change in the pattern of movement and glimpsed the animal. O'Neill was close behind, engrossed in conversation with Cal, Novy, Wash, and Hoshi. A chill ran up his arms. Had O married Cal in the past six months? Personal contact with Prismers was forbidden by the Earth's World Board, so he hadn't communicated with her.

As they drew closer, he watched O's animated interaction with her friends. Her hands pointed and she used her whole body to convey her responses. She turned around and walked backward on the dock, facing what had been his Prism security detail. Given the containers and stacks of Earth goods that looked like they'd been spewed hap-hazard from the cargo shuttles, his gaze checked her path for dangerous obstacles. But her friends were watching, judging from her course corrections and occasional glances over her shoulder.

Hoping he'd meet her without her friends, he'd practiced at least a thousand versions of what he would say to her on this dock. Not one word from any of those speeches formed in his tightened throat. His brain couldn't even make his tongue run over his dry lips. A knot deep in his gut threatened to bring him to his knees.

Two empty berths separated them now. O started laughing and jabbed Cal's shoulder.

One berth between them. Cal saw Jericho and stopped walking.

Novy followed Cal's not-so-friendly stare, then his boots stayed unmoving on the plazsteel dock. Hoshi and Wash caught Jericho's gaze before they, too, froze. O kept walking backward. She was nearly at his ramp before she said, "What? You guys are not fooling me again with that, 'Oh, there's a scary bad thing behind you' act. That's really gotten old." She let go of Solo's fur and turned.

Tiger's have good memories. At least Solo does. He ran up the shuttle ramp and pushed his nose into the interior, probably looking for Mitzi. Jericho dropped to one knee and petted the only animal on Prism. "Sorry, big fellow, she's not in there."

He looked up to O's open-mouthed stare and stood, rubbing his palms against his pants.

She looked from Jericho to Solo to the shuttle. Cal stepped beside her.

Jericho wanted to hug her. Lift her up and twirl her around, feet swinging in a circle. He settled for, "Hello, O."

Carefree actions gone, she looked dazed. After a shaky, deep breath she whispered, "Jericho. You came back."

ABOUT THE AUTHOR

Fae Rowen discovered the romance genre after years as a science fiction freak. Writing futuristics and medieval paranormals, she jokes that she can live anywhere but the present. As a mathematician, she knows life's a lot more fun when you get to define your world and its rules then watch what happens.

Punished, oh-no, that's published as a co-author of a math textbook, she yearns to hear personal stories about finding love from those who read her books, rather than horrors of calculus lessons gone wrong. She is grateful for good friends who remind her to do the practical things in life like grocery shop, show up at the airport for a flight and pay bills.

Fae Rowen began writing after reading her favorite author's entire backlist in three weeks and couldn't bear the thought of waiting nine months for the next book. A "hard" scientist who avoided writing classes like the plague, she now enjoys sharing her brain with characters who demand that their stories be told. Amazing, gifted critique partners keep her on the straight and narrow. Feedback from readers keep her fingers on the keyboard.

Connect with Fae at: www.faerowen.com or fae@faerowen.com